CATCH HER WHEN SHE FALLS

CATCH HER WHEN SHE FALLS

a novel

ALLISON BUCCOLA

RANDOM HOUSE · NEW YORK

Published in the United States by Random House, an imprint and division of Penguin Random House LLC, New York.

RANDOM HOUSE and the HOUSE colophon are registered trademarks of Penguin Random House LLC.

LIBRARY OF CONGRESS CATALOGING-IN-PUBLICATION DATA
Names: Buccola, Allison, author.
Title: Catch her when she falls : a novel / by Allison Buccola.
Description: First edition. | New York : Random House, [2022]
Identifiers: LCCN 2021019141 (print) | LCCN 2021019142 (ebook) |
ISBN 9780593231296 (hardcover ; acid-free paper) | ISBN 9780593231302 (ebook)
Subjects: GSAFD: Suspense fiction.
Classification: LCC PS3602.U226 C38 2022 (print) |
LCC PS3602.U226 (ebook) | DDC 813/.6—dc23
LC record available at https://lccn.loc.gov/2021019141
LC ebook record available at https://lccn.loc.gov/2021019142

Printed in Canada on acid-free paper

randomhousebooks.com

9 8 7 6 5 4 3 2 1

First Edition

Book design by Jo Anne Metsch

FOR RHODES AND ADA

CATCH HER WHEN SHE FALLS

1

Ten years ago, my boyfriend killed my best friend.

For a long time, that's all anyone thought about when they looked at me. Christ, for a long time that's all *I* thought about when I'd catch my reflection in the mirror: sand-brown eyes, so plain compared to Emily's vivid green, with dark shadows forming in the creases underneath. *I am Micah Wilkes,* I'd say to myself, *former girlfriend of Alex Swift, former friend of Emily Winters.* Or: *I am Micah Wilkes, and I make bad decisions.* Or, in my darker moments, *I am Micah Wilkes, and the one thing I've learned, the one thing I know for sure, is you can't trust anyone but yourself.*

Those old mantras come back to me now, and I try to put them out of my head, to focus instead on the rhythmic sweep of the windshield wipers, the sharp pings of sleet against the glass. I glance up toward the rearview mirror, study the ice-slicked road behind me. A white sedan approaches, moving fast; I hold the steering wheel tight as though my grip could provide some protection against what's about to happen. But the sedan jolts to the left at the last minute, speeding past me, continuing on its way, and then I'm alone again: just woods and road and snow.

I shouldn't have let my guard down, shouldn't have let myself forget. These past few years have been good—even better than good, at times. They've been normal. I'd find myself at Stomping Grounds, laughing at a customer's corny joke, or burrowing into Ryan on the couch, his yellow and black fleece pulled up over us, my cold toes warmed under his feet, and I'd think: *Maybe this is what other people have been doing all this time. Maybe this isn't so bad.*

I reach out across the passenger seat for my messenger bag and pull it toward me, across a bed of crumpled-up papers and loose wrappers. My car isn't usually disheveled like this, but I've had things other than cleaning on my mind. I fish around in my bag until my fingers touch my phone. I pull it out, take a breath, and check the screen.

Five missed calls. None of them from you.

I need to talk to you, Joshua. You need to talk to me. It wasn't him. I got it wrong. I'm trying to fix things. I just want to make things right.

That's why I'm coming to find you.

2

've been trying to think of what to say when I see you, how to make you understand. I should start a few weeks ago, I think; that's when everything began to shift out of focus. In fact, I can pinpoint the day: the first Sunday in November, the first day it really felt like winter was approaching, when the temperature dropped twenty degrees and the clouds threatened snow, and Mrs. Klein nearly died right on the floor in the middle of Stomping Grounds, with everyone twisting around in their seats to get a better view. That's what took me back to the campsite for the first time in almost ten years. That's what set this all in motion.

I'm sure you remember how seriously everyone takes the holiday season in Calvary, and I think things have only escalated since you've been gone. The entire downtown was plastered in competing decorations, with dancing skeletons or turkeys in pilgrim hats displayed prominently in most of the shop windows. Hotel Calvary—always ahead of the curve—already had garland wrapped around the poles supporting its awning, and someone had recently tied big red bows around all of the streetlights in preparation for the holidays. I set up my chalkboard easel on the sidewalk, which featured a large pumpkin sketched out in orange chalk, and scribbled GOBBLE GOBBLE! next to the block of text advertising our apple cider.

I unlatched the doors at my normal time. The high schooler who helped me out part-time on weekends, Anna McCarron, arrived twenty minutes late, which was also her normal time. We were busy, but not overly so: the Sunday crowd is more steady than the typical weekday crowd, but without the rush of people around seven-thirty trying to get coffees on their way to work. It wasn't busy enough for Anna, apparently, who rested on her elbows in between customers, swiping listlessly on her phone, blond hair brushing the countertop. Her hair was always down, no matter how many times I asked her to tie it back. I bussed tables and cleaned coffee mugs and—maybe just to make a point to Anna that there was always more work to be done—wiped down the windows overlooking Main Street.

I opened Stomping Grounds when I came back from Chicago, using the money I got from selling my mother's place. We're right in the spot where Mr. Hunt's ice cream shop used to be, the place you, me, and Emily used to walk to on Saturdays when we couldn't come up with anything better to do. Sometimes we'd take Culver Street down from your house, shuffling along in single file, diving off the street onto the narrow dirt ridge lining the road when an unexpected car hurtled around a bend. Other times, we'd cut through the woods—the better way, the more direct way—but then we had to pass through some of Mr. Reeves's property, and he used to get so mad that he posted signs promising to shoot the next kid who came through.

"I think he'd really do it," you used to insist after the sign went up, turning red and angry and sullen if one of us suggested the shortcut. Emily would laugh at you, tell you that was stupid, but, if I'm being honest, we were all a little scared to find out what would happen if we tested him.

I was thinking about Mr. Hunt's ice cream shop that morning, those huge cardboard cylinders of mint chocolate chip and rocky road ice cream lined up behind that glass pane, fitting snugly beside each other in the refrigerated counter that I ripped out two years ago to put in the coffee bar. I could almost see us, slouched down in those white plastic chairs, bored and sticky and trying to figure out what to do next. That's when the door jangled and four teenagers tumbled in, shouting and howling at each other, two boys and two girls.

The blond boy strutted across the coffee shop, his hair meticulously waxed, a self-important smirk on his face. His camo sweatshirt, distressed to look old and fitted to look expensive, probably cost more than everything I was wearing combined. His beefy friend swaggered next to him, hands in the pockets of his sweatpants, and the girls followed close behind, giggling, in matching black puffy coats and high ponytails. They bypassed the counter entirely and settled in at a table in the back, purses, coats, and scarves scattered everywhere.

"Friends of yours?" I asked Anna, and her raised eyebrow let me know I had asked a stupid question, that any one of a hundred different cues—the shimmering eye shadow, the fluffy boots—should have clued me in on the fact that they ran in different social circles.

"An-na!" the blond boy shouted in an exaggerated baritone, emphasizing the last syllable. This sent the girls into another fit of high-pitched laughter. Anna rolled her eyes, flipped her hair over her shoulder, and returned her attention to her phone, and in that moment I actually felt a surge of affection for her.

I ignored the teens, or tried to, for about fifteen minutes. But the heavy stench of the boys' cologne hit me as I walked past them with a tray of two lattes and a tea kettle. I turned to see the bigger boy crouched over and snorting a line of Sweet'N Low, to the delight of the other three. Ripped-up pieces of sugar packets and a thin layer of granulated sugar covered the table. The boy slammed his hands down in victory and pushed his chair back suddenly, almost crashing into me.

"Out," I ordered, pointing toward the door. All four mouths dropped in mock surprise and offense.

"Fuck you, lady," said the blond boy, sneaking a glance at the girls to see if they were impressed. They elbowed each other, watching to see what I would do next. "You can't kick us out. This is public property."

"No, it's not," I said. "It's my property. Customers only."

"Fine. I'll take a small coffee, then." His smirk grew bigger, and the girls stifled giggles. The beefy boy stared off vacantly, with a lazy, stupid grin, a few grains of sweetener still clinging to his upper lip.

"Nope. Out."

The boys dumped more sugar on the table before leaving, and the blond one slammed the door on his way out for good measure, the bells I put up to announce new customers rattling behind him. But they didn't go far, instead loitering on the sidewalk in front of the Main Street windows, right where I couldn't help but see them. The boys roughhoused and the girls squeezed together for warmth, and all four of them looked back into the shop every few minutes and then broke out into peals of laughter all over again, as if to say: *You can kick us out, but you can't get rid of us that easily. We're not going anywhere.* One especially aggressive shove sent the blond boy careening into the windowpane, and when I raised my phone in the air and mimed calling the police, they regrouped and quieted down. The blond boy wrapped his arms around the waist of one of the girls, leaning back against the window, and the other girl looked on with poorly concealed jealousy.

That's when Mrs. Klein came in, carrying a bag with her from Charlene's Closet, which, miraculously, is still in business after all this time. I think our moms may have single-handedly kept that shop going during the nineties, and I'm not sure that any of the styles on offer have changed since then. Mrs. Klein, with her short gray hair that shot out in all directions and her wide-eyed, confused expression, looked a little as though she had wandered in by mistake, but she looked that way every Sunday morning. She glanced around the shop as if to figure out where she was, then finally made her way over to the counter with slow, deliberate steps.

"Oh, hello, Micah!" she said. She always sounded pleasantly surprised to see me, although I'm not sure why. I was always there.

"Hi, Mrs. Klein," I said. "What can I get for you?"

She examined the pastries on display carefully, as though she were deciding which ones to get, even though she always ordered the same thing: a blueberry scone and a small coffee, with room for cream. I looked over at Anna, still draped over the counter, while half-empty mugs and crumb-covered plates piled up on the tables in front of us. The warmth I had felt just a moment before evaporated.

"What are these like?" Mrs. Klein asked, pointing with her knobby index finger at a ham and cheese croissant.

"They're good if you're in the mood for something savory."

She made a small, disappointed noise and looked back to the pastry display.

"And what's this one?" A tap on the glass.

"Pumpkin spice muffin."

"Ah."

The door chimed and a couple walked in, taking their place in line. Anna glanced up briefly, then returned to her phone.

"Let's do a blueberry scone and a small coffee," Mrs. Klein said. "Room for cream."

"Got it." I already had the scone bagged up and waiting.

She waited for me to tell her the total before scrounging through her wallet for cash, and then took her normal seat by the Church Street windows, where she could watch people pass in their coats and scarves, out doing early Christmas shopping or admiring the decorations. I greeted the couple that had just entered and took their order, then steeled myself for another conversation with Anna about work expectations.

"Anna—" I started, in the voice I use when trying to be authoritative, a voice that Anna clearly recognized because she looked up sharply, a flash of irritation spreading across her face. But, before I could launch into my speech about cellphone usage in front of customers, the look of irritation morphed into something else, eyes widening and jaw dropped, and then she started screaming.

I spun around and saw Mrs. Klein, one hand on her throat and the other clutching her table, her skin taking on a bluish hue. She let go of the table and dropped to her knees, eyes panicked and confused. And everyone around her just watched, turning their heads and craning their necks, trying to see what was happening. I swear to God one of the customers—whom I immediately pegged, based on his age, Joy Division T-shirt, and long, unkempt hair, as an Easton student who had found his way off campus—had his phone out recording the whole thing. It makes me sick, now, thinking about it. But at the time, I wasn't thinking about anything. I darted around the counter and across the shop, wrapping my arms around Mrs. Klein and doing my best approximation of the Heimlich maneuver. It was close enough. The chunk of scone dislodged itself, shooting out onto the floor in front of us, and I got a polite round of applause from the patrons, who all seemed very happy that someone had decided to do something. It wasn't until that applause started that my knees almost gave out beneath me and my heart started racing and I realized what had nearly happened.

Mrs. Klein sat down at her table again, looking frail and confused. She took some time to collect herself, rifled through her purse and pulled out a handful of tissues, dabbed at her eyes and underneath her nose. Then she pushed herself back up again, took a few deliberate steps to where I was standing speechless, watching her, unsure of what to do. She squeezed my arm with an unsteady hand, gave me a small "thanks," and left slowly, eyes fixed on the door, not making contact with any of the other customers. She seemed embarrassed, and that was almost the worst part of it; she looked so ashamed.

Once she left, Stomping Grounds slowly returned to its normal volume, chairs scraping the wood floor and coats rustling as patrons shifted in their seats and turned toward each other to discuss what had just happened. I took in slow, steady breaths, trying to pull myself back together. The college student with the phone crossed the shop and started comforting Anna, who had worked herself into tears behind the counter.

"She's in high school," I said once I finally made my way back to the front counter. The boy tensed and Anna bit her lip but didn't say anything. I tried to straighten myself out, brushing a hand down my sweater, tugging my hair down and pulling it back again into a short ponytail, reminding myself to breathe. *It's fine,* I told myself. *Everything is fine.* I grabbed a washcloth and wiped down the counter over and over again, putting my full weight into it. Anything to keep my hands busy, to stop the shaking.

"Miss," said a tan and heavily made-up woman I didn't know, "we're still waiting on two lattes. We ordered them just before . . ." Her voice trailed off and she stretched her mouth into an exaggerated grimace.

"Oh, of course," I said, shaking my head and turning toward the espresso machine. I slid the cups into place beneath the spigots and tipped the steam arm right below the surface of the milk in the metal pitcher. My mind slipped, and I pictured Mrs. Klein, her lips blue and getting bluer, waving her hand helplessly in the air. I imagined what might have happened: Mrs. Klein falling, writhing around on the floor helpless, like a fish, back arched and eyes bulging, looking for help.

The milk bubbled up out of the pitcher, scalding my fingers, and I cursed quietly, shook out my hand, looked around to see if anyone had noticed, started again. I brought the lattes out to the table, the porcelain cups rattling violently on their little plates, liquid splashing up over the sides.

"Sorry about the wait," I said, setting the cups down on the table. "And the mess." I grabbed a napkin and wiped up the droplets.

The tan woman shook her head and smiled at me, a big, sympathizing smile, as though she were graciously forgiving me. "That was some quick thinking you did back there," she said, raising her thin eyebrows knowingly. The friend sitting next to her nodded along but examined her cup with a frown, dabbing at a spot I had missed.

"You should be very proud of yourself," said a man in his sixties sitting at the table behind me. "You saved a life today."

I turned to face him, a jolt of anger shooting through me. He sat there nodding at me, approving, just one table away from where Mrs. Klein had been sitting, from where it had all happened.

"She was right there," I said, quietly at first, pointing toward the now empty table. The man nodded at me again, not comprehending.

"Why didn't *you* do something?" I asked, my voice wobbling. A flash of understanding crossed the man's face, which contorted into a frown. I turned back toward the tan woman, whose smile had disappeared as well.

"You just *sat* there." I kept going, unable to stop myself. "Why didn't you *do* something?"

The good-natured chatter that had picked up again once Mrs. Klein left stopped, replaced by a sour unease. Only Anna seemed unperturbed, watching intently to see what would happen next.

I grabbed the empty mug out from in front of the man, marched back up to the front counter, and thrust it into Anna's hands. She looked down at it, uncertain, like she didn't quite know what to do with it.

"Think you can handle things here by yourself for a few hours?" I asked. Anna lifted one shoulder in response.

"I'll be back to close up." I left before she could say anything. I walked quickly, skeletons jeering at me as I tried to shake the image of Mrs. Klein. I couldn't do it, though. It stuck with me, and even now, when I close my eyes, I see her desperate look, that hand to her throat, signaling helplessly, and then blood on the white-brushed wood, seeping into the cracks. But I'm getting ahead of myself: those streaks of blood, they weren't from Mrs. Klein. The blood came later.

I held it together until I reached my car. I pulled the door shut, pushed down the lock, and the tears started. I tried to compose myself. Deep breath in. *C-A-L-M*. Deep breath out. *D-O-W-N*. But I couldn't focus, couldn't keep my mind from drifting. I wiped the tears from my cheeks and looked outside. I couldn't hear the people passing by, but I could see them, carrying about their day like everything was fine, like nothing had just happened. A young couple strolled down the sidewalk together, the girl nudging the boy with her shoulder playfully, the boy grabbing for her hand. A mother walked in the opposite direction, fussing with a knit blanket hanging down from her stroller and stopping to rustle through her diaper bag.

Nothing did *happen,* I reminded myself. *Everything* is *fine.* Even so, I couldn't steady myself, couldn't get my heart to stop racing. I could almost hear it, pounding against my chest, the pulse of blood through my temples. I rolled down the window and lit a cigarette.

The owner of Calvary Art Studio—Liz Grogan, who was three years ahead of Emily and me in school, but always seemed much older, much more sophisticated—stepped out of her gallery, a dramatic shawl wrapped loosely around her neck. She squinted in my direction for just a moment too long but then had the decency to pretend she hadn't seen me. I threw the cigarette butt out the window and angled the rearview mirror toward myself: face pale and grim, with eyes red and swollen from crying. It really rattled me, the sight of Mrs. Klein so helpless like that, and the patrons just *watching,* and then Anna with her crocodile tears and that college student who went to comfort *her* but never said two words to Mrs. Klein, didn't even ask if she was feeling better.

A girl with dark, curly hair piled on top of her head skipped by, four steps ahead of her mother, a pair of ballet slippers in hand. She had just come from the Lionels' studio, probably, up that rusted stairway above Merlock's Collectibles. Emily and I used to race up those stairs when we were ten and thought we were both going to be dancers when we grew up, leading extravagant lives in the city. Through the heavy black door and down a narrow, tiled hallway, past scuffed walls and a long line of lockers and into the studio.

The Lionels had divorced, last I heard. Mr. Lionel left and Mrs. Lionel stayed, although I hadn't seen her since my return to Calvary. I'm sure she never touched caffeine, and so had no use for a new downtown coffee shop. I could still picture them both clearly, though: Mr. Lionel, always in colorful drawstring pants, chain-smoking on the stairway landing. ("Setting a good example for impressionable minds, I see," my mother used to shout up from the sidewalk while I cringed with embarrassment.) The too-bright streak of blush in the hollows of Mrs. Lionel's cheeks, the sleeveless turtlenecks she used to wear, her thin, muscular arms always held out, just a little, at her sides. Her sharp bark: "Shoulders open, Emily!" "Pull up, Emily, pull up!"

It's funny, but for a brief period of time I took all those orders directed at Emily as a sign I was doing better: that my shoulders were straight enough, my pliés deep enough, my feet angled correctly. Then Emily got her pointe shoes and I didn't, and I realized the Lionels saw potential in Emily that they never saw in me. I quit ballet soon after.

I threw my head back against the headrest, then straightened up in my seat. I turned the key, shifted my car into gear, and started driving.

I've found that things are easiest when I don't think of Emily, when I push her back into the corners of my mind. Maybe you'll think that's wrong of me—or maybe, if you're being honest with yourself, Joshua, you'll admit that you've done the same. You're the one who left for good, after all, the one who stayed away. I came back, but I made sure to avoid places with special significance. I'd always turn off Main Street earlier than I otherwise would have to avoid the Northridge Roller Rink, where Emily and I became friends over a skinned knee (mine) and a shared granola bar (hers). I'd drive past your neighborhood but wouldn't drive through it. And I never went back to the campsite. I hadn't been back, not once, in the ten years since Emily died.

That day, though, I wasn't thinking right. I wasn't really thinking at all. I don't remember making a specific decision; all of a sudden, I was winding up Culver Street's sharp incline, up out of downtown Calvary, back into the woods. It's more developed now than it was when you were here, with new, hastily built subdivisions popping up along the edges of the road where thick forest used to be. But the developments become less and less frequent as Culver becomes steeper and steeper, and soon I found myself back in the same empty forest I recognized from when we were young. The forest where Emily, Alex, Ryan, and I would go, back before everything changed.

I eased off the side of the road and came to a stop. The stone pillars marking the entrance to the campsite were visible from the street for someone who knew where to look, moss-covered and misshapen, but still standing. I used to enjoy imagining how they would have looked when new: grand and imposing, welcoming guests to a nineteenth-century resort (*"sanatorium,"* Ryan always corrected, "resort was just a euphemism for sanatorium back then") and warning others to keep their distance. The resort stopped existing sometime in the early 1900s ("burned down,"

Emily always said, although who knows if that's true), and the space became a camp for city boys, bussed in from Philadelphia. Years later it was just abandoned, cabins locked up but beds and shelves left in their places, desks in the offices and pews in the chapel still intact.

I stepped out of my car, slammed the door behind me, and made my way up to the pillars. I rubbed my index finger along the cold, gritty stone. A series of foot trails jutted out into the forest, the same ones I had stumbled down dozens of times. I knew those paths well. One led straight back to what people in my class called the "lodge"—that large concrete slab ringed with stones that marked what must have once been a reception area for vacationers or campers. To the left was the "theater," the old wooden stage circled by an arch of bleachers, now mostly caved in and rotted through. Only a few stubborn beams had managed to stay upright over the years. The path to the right wound its way to the "altar," the four large stone slabs piled up on top of one another, maybe four feet high, and beyond that, narrow hidden trails led to old cabins and administrative offices and an algae-covered pond.

I stopped at the pillars. The wind breathed through the forest, rust-colored leaves shivering on the trees, and I wrapped my arms around myself for warmth. Quiet and empty, the forest looked so different from the last night I had been there. Then, a mass of people swarmed through the trees, and everything smelled like cheap beer and Abercrombie and Fitch—sharp and sweet and chemical. Loud laughter and shrieking giggles, dozens of conversations competing for dominance. Me, sick off of too much vodka and hunched over by the altar, twigs digging into my palms. Ryan sat with me, holding back my hair. Emily and Alex, gone, vanished into the forest. At the cinder block house, I know that now. I didn't know it then.

Beneath my feet, the root of an old tree snaked out of the ground, tangled and exposed. I traced it with the tip of my sneaker, slipping my foot underneath and pulling back to see how strongly it resisted. I was always the one who fell when Emily and I used to come back here. She was always so sure-footed.

It was wrong to go back. I should have stayed away. As I stood there by those pillars, all I could think of was the picture of Emily they used at Alex's trial, blown up on poster board and displayed on an easel in the middle of the wood-paneled courtroom. Emily's body, broken and sprawled out on the forest floor. Dark curls spiraled around her face, wet with blood. Her eyes, open and bulging, judging, asking: *Why didn't you help me?*

3

My phone lights up and I glance down at the screen. A picture of Ryan, smiling up at me from our blue velvet couch, the one we found at Calvary Basement a week after moving in together. His hair, dark auburn, sticking out at the sides, a hand just run through it. His eyes, so focused and intent, locked on mine, almost as if he were looking back at me.

I feel a sob catch in my throat and bite down on my lip hard. I'm starting a new life now. I can do this. I can begin again.

Ryan was always so nice to you, wasn't he? Not in Alex's big-smile-and-pound-you-on-the-back kind of way, but more gentle, more likely to look you in the eye and listen when you told him how your day was going.

One day in particular stands out to me, the summer before Emily died. Emily had finally returned from a ballet summer intensive in upstate New York. We were at your house, so it must have been a Monday. The Lionels' studio was closed on Mondays.

The overhead fan and two floor fans were working at full blast, but they couldn't keep the heat at bay. I had come straight from marching band practice and was sticky with sweat, my freckles more pronounced than usual after weeks of practice, marching from yard line to yard line for hours in the sun. I had settled onto the patchwork couch next to Alex, his arm draped behind me. Emily sat on the braided rug that covered the dark wood floor, kneading her calves, while Ryan perched on the stone hearth of your fireplace.

I always loved your house: the grass that grew an inch higher than the trim lawns that bordered yours. The uneven stones that led up to bamboo wind chimes, clinking hollowly together by your front door. The vines that crept up the siding, like something out of a fairy tale; the deep-red poppies and bright yellow snapdragons that had claimed the backyard, circling the raised garden bed full of snap peas and cherry tomatoes. The Victorian upright that your mother played, music filling the whole house.

"Yeah," Emily said when I expressed that sentiment to her, "but there's something to be said for central air."

Your mother wasn't home that day, so the TV was on: a crudely drawn cartoon, each scene intended to repulse its viewers: close-up on a scalp with one hair slowly emerging from a follicle, close-up on an eyeball with red bulging veins, a meaty finger inching toward it. Alex repeated his favorite lines, doing a bad imitation of the voices.

"Let's go somewhere," Emily said. She twisted at the hip, a hand tented at her side. "I don't want to waste my day off on this garbage."

"Oh, come on, Em. It's not garbage," Alex protested. "It's art! Just because you don't get it . . ."

"I get it just fine." A twist in the other direction. "We could go to the rope swing?"

"Cut down," Ryan said. "Some genius decided to try a double back flip but didn't jump far enough out. Broke both legs."

"Fuck," Emily said.

That's when you bounded down the stairs and rounded the wooden banister, eyes wild, in that dragon T-shirt you wore too often. The shirt was black with a golden, scaly tail wrapping up and over your right shoulder, three fake claw marks slashed down your left side. It carried with it a sour, musky odor that hung in the air, announced your presence in any room, and lingered long after you had left.

"Flee, doomed men, to the ends of the earth!" you shouted, throwing your fist into the air. Emily breathed in sharply and pretended not to see you.

"How's it going, Josh?" Alex asked. He slid his arm down from the couch to around my shoulder.

"Good!" You took a seat on the piano bench and pulled one knee in toward yourself, the other leg swinging rhythmically. "Ryan, have you read Herodotus?"

"Bits and pieces," Ryan said. Ryan had read bits and pieces of everything.

The office door creaked open, and your father wandered out. "Built like a string bean," my mother once said of him. He walked stooped over, as if to avoid bumping his head on a phantom doorframe or hanging light. He waved his hand in our general direction, without looking at us, and peered into the kitchen.

"She's not home, Dad," Emily called out. "Rehearsal. There's a casserole in the fridge."

Your father scrunched his face and blinked, hard, without saying anything, then made his way back into the office.

"The dumbest smart person I've ever met," my mother also used to say about him, then she'd throw her hands up in the air like someone had called her out on it. "I'm just being honest."

"What's the rehearsal for?" I asked Emily.

"Some community theater travesty," she said, stretching out both legs.

"Harsh." I nudged her gently with my foot.

Emily rolled her eyes and reached up, then bent down at the waist. "It's just the truth. She's forty-five and accompanying a half-rate Dorothy at the Easton Playhouse three nights a week. That's why I won't be having kids."

"Emily: the great mistake," Ryan said, and Emily lifted one shoulder.

"I mean, hey, selfishly I'm glad she made the decisions she did." She straightened her back, then bent down again. I could see the knobs of her spine through the thin fabric of her shirt.

"You'll change your mind," Alex said. He drummed his fingers on the couch behind me, an irregular *pat pat pat,* some song I couldn't quite place. "Women always do."

"How would you have any idea what women do or don't do?" Emily said, spinning back toward him.

"You know, people think overpopulation is a new concern, but it's really not," you said, trilling two high notes on the piano. "It was actually one of the main reasons for Greek colonization."

Emily stiffened and finally turned to look at you. "Don't you think it might be time for a haircut?" she asked. I watched you freeze, then tuck a stray lock behind your ear.

"Leave him alone, Em," Ryan said. He started using the nickname after Alex did, although it never sounded as natural rolling off his tongue. Then, more pedantically: "The Spartans wore their hair long, you know. Said it made a handsome man more handsome, and an ugly man more fierce."

"That's right!" you said, nodding your head enthusiastically.

"Last I checked, we're in Pennsylvania, not Ancient Greece."

"I just read the section on the Battle of Thermopylae," you said to Ryan, ignoring your sister. A dramatic hand in the air as you quoted a passage: " 'They resisted to the last, with their swords, if they had them, and, if not, with their hands and teeth.' "

"Don't you have something else to be doing right now?" Emily asked, cutting you off.

" 'If the Persians hide the sun,' " Ryan quoted back, " 'we shall have our battle in the shade.' "

"Yes!"

Emily rose, one hand on her hip. "I don't want to sit around here all day," she said. "Let's go to the quarry. We don't need the rope swing."

"You guys go ahead," Ryan said, waving us off. "I'll catch up later." He turned back to you and listened intently as you started rambling about oracles and mountain passes and arrows blotting out the sun. You looked so happy, so at ease. A little like you used to when we were in fourth grade and you were in second and Emily let you tag along on our trips down to Mr. Hunt's ice cream shop.

Ryan and I moved in together a little over a year ago—eight months after I moved back to Calvary and six months after we started dating. He gave up his place and moved into my apartment in the Calvary Lofts, which you might remember better as the Calvary Apartments. Or maybe the tail end of our bus route, which is how I used to think of it. Appalachia, is what Matt Penna and Brian Wasserman used to call it, and then they'd start imitating that banjo song from *Deliverance,* a movie I'd never actually seen but didn't have to in order to know what they meant. Ryan and his mom used to live out there, you know, starting around the time we were in middle school, when Ryan's dad left them.

The apartment complex has changed a lot since we were in high school, and it's pretty nice now. It was all renovated about eight years back, turned into housing mostly for graduate students at Easton. They've painted the outside of the complex, so it looks a lot less ratty than it used to, and all of the second-floor units, like mine, now have a small balcony off of them with just enough space that the students can try their hand at raising herbs or small, potted plants if they feel so inclined. They also ripped up those old, tannish-brown carpets that always used to look discolored and dirty, pockmarked by cigarette burns, so now we have fake wooden floors that are easy enough to keep clean.

I wonder if Ryan ever thought it was strange, being back in the same place but having it look so different. It strikes me, now, that I never asked him.

Maybe you'll be surprised I ended up with Ryan. I know I would have been if someone had suggested it to me back in high school. Ryan was always small—only about an inch taller than me—and, while he eventually filled out to something more akin to "lean," at seventeen he could only really be described as skinny. Back then, I liked Alex's broad shoulders, the way he towered over me, the way I felt like I was being engulfed when he wrapped his arms around me. Back then, I didn't notice Ryan's sweet, lopsided smiles, the intensity of his slate-gray eyes, set off by thick lashes.

Still: Ryan, after all this time. Why not someone new, someone different? Why not start over? I dabbled with online dating while I was in Chicago but was never very good at it. My last date was with a high school teacher who worked with kids with learning disabilities at a low-income school. I didn't ask, but I bet he volunteered at homeless shelters in his free time, too. I walked through the doors of the River North restaurant he had chosen, five minutes late and skeptical. I assumed he'd be one of those holier-than-thou types who gets off on being a better person than everyone else. I scanned the room—loud and trendy, tables made of refurbished wood with industrial-looking lights hanging down from the ceiling—and confirmed for myself that he was image-obsessed, completely superficial. But then he turned out to be really nice, good-natured and polite, not at all what I had been expecting.

"I've been talking too much," he said after the entrées came out to the table. "Tell me something about yourself."

I froze up, couldn't think of anything to say. I blinked at him a few times, then looked down. "I—uh . . ." I poked at my chicken with my fork, moved some brussels sprouts around on the plate. How do people ever answer that question? *I'm a waitress at an overpriced restaurant in Wicker Park who watches reruns of* Friends *during the day.*

He smiled at me, kindly, waiting. *Sometimes* The Voice. *You never realize how much time there is in a day until you start trying to fill it with TV shows.*

"Do you like waitressing?" he asked, and I smirked back at him but then caught myself and tried to turn it into a smile.

"It pays the bills," I said. "Well, sometimes."

I wanted a cigarette.

"So what's your dream job?" He leaned forward on his elbows, playfully, intimately.

When I stammered again, he pulled back, and asked: "What did you major in in college?"

All I could think about was how stupid the conversation was, as though a half-hearted decision at eighteen and thirty-six credits somehow said something meaningful about who I was. Who was I? *My name is Micah Wilkes, and in high school my boyfriend fucked my best friend and then killed her. Grabbed her by the arms and sent her flying out of a second-story window.*

"I was a psychology major," I said, and he smiled back encouragingly, asked a few more questions. What drew me into that? Had I thought about grad school? Other jobs in the area?

"Maybe someday," I said, smiling weakly and sinking back into my chair, pulling the sleeves of my jacket up over my hands. We ended the date, and he walked me back to my apartment, and he said that he'd call me but he didn't, and I didn't really mind.

It wasn't long after that when I moved back to Calvary and Ryan and I met for coffee at the Northridge Diner to catch up. We sat across from each other on those same red-leather seats the Northridge Diner has always had, a rip down the center of mine revealing tightly packed yellow foam. Ryan rested his hands on the cold metallic table and told me he had missed me.

"It hasn't been the same here without you," he said. He looked at me, not breaking eye contact, and I found myself thinking that there was something charming about the way he smiled.

"Yeah, well." I smiled back, in spite of myself, and grabbed a cheese fry from the center of the table. The same cheese fries that Northridge Diner has always served, yellow cheese melted on top and then cooled to a semisolid mass. They were still good.

"I always thought I'd get out of Calvary. Live somewhere new. Exciting." I shrugged and shifted in my seat. "When I moved to Chicago, I thought: This is it. This is the start of my new life. But . . ." I threw up my hands and gave Ryan a self-deprecating smile. "Here I am. Back."

"Calvary's not such a bad place to be," he said. I raised my eyebrows, but he didn't waver.

"It's not," he insisted. Not defensive, just earnest. "Everyone always wants to get away from their hometown, do big things, and I guess that's normal. But Calvary . . ." A waitress refilled our water glasses from a plastic pitcher, and Ryan looked up and thanked her, then continued what he was saying. "Calvary is objectively a nice town. We've got Easton, which is a great college, lots of forests and trails for hiking, the downtown has been growing—"

"Good public schools," I added, and Ryan grinned back. He knew I was teasing, but he didn't care.

"We *do* have good public schools!" he said. "I'm just saying. There are worse places to be stuck."

I bobbed my head noncommittally and took another fry, pinching off a chunk of cheese to go along with it.

"Well," I said, "I think I might need you to show me what's so good about it. I'm still not convinced."

"I can do that."

We stayed in that booth talking for two hours. Ryan had become a librarian at Easton and loved it. Days spent surrounded by books, digging up data and old sources. The other librarians were characters, he said—Howard, who had an encyclopedic knowledge of Calvary fauna, and Martina, who barely ever spoke above a whisper but always wore bright pinks and greens. "They're good people," he told me, fondly. I told him about being a waitress.

"Hate it," I said.

"That doesn't surprise me."

"Why?" I asked. "Because I'm antisocial?"

"No," he said. "Because you're independent. I always saw you being your own boss."

He asked me how I was feeling about my mother, and told me how sorry he had been to hear the news.

"She always had such good snacks for us," Ryan said.

"Snacks?" I laughed, surprised.

"She was always feeding us! We'd come over and there would be chips and salsa out on the table, waiting. We'd be watching a movie and she'd bring in individual bowls of popcorn for each one of us. And there was candy in every room, all the time."

My mother had kept tiny ceramic bowls of candy stocked throughout the house: Andes mints or fun-sized chocolate bars or jelly beans. I had never thought much about them—they had always just been there in the background—but once Ryan brought them up I could see them clearly, my mother's bowls decorated with rings of flowers and blue paisley prints.

"That's a funny thing to remember," I said, but my eyes were tearing up, and it took me a moment to compose myself.

I asked him about his own mother, and he answered me frankly. She hadn't been doing well these past few years. He spent a lot of time visiting her, making sure she was taking care of herself.

It wasn't until well into the second hour that the subject of Emily and Alex came around, as it always did, eventually.

"Do you miss them?" he asked, really looking at me, really listening, waiting to see how I would respond.

"Miss them?" I scoffed. "How could I miss them? I've never even managed to get *away* from them." That serious expression never left his face. He just nodded, holding my gaze, and reached across the table to squeeze my hand.

.   .   .

When I left the campsite, that day Mrs. Klein nearly choked to death, I was shaken, more troubled than before. I drove back to my apartment thinking I'd be able to spend a few minutes alone. I wanted to collect myself before facing Stomping Grounds again. I turned the knob to our front door, which swung in easily—it always felt too light, cheap and hollow, like a fake door for a movie set. All the lights were on and the smell of microwaved Thai food hung in the air. Ryan was stretched out on the couch, one leg crossed over the other, halfway through an eight-hundred-page tome on the Napoleonic wars.

"What are you doing here?" I asked as I slipped off my army jacket and wiped my mud-caked sneakers on the welcome mat.

Ryan grabbed his bookmark off the coffee table and delicately placed it between the pages of his book. He always cringed when he saw me dog-ear something I was reading.

"Nice to see you, too."

"That's not what I—I thought you'd be at your mom's place."

"I was. I came back." Ryan set down his book and pushed himself up a little straighter. "What are you doing home so early?"

I could feel my jaw trembling, my forehead creasing. Ryan jumped off the couch and walked over to me, pulled me in toward him.

"Mrs. Klein started choking today," I said. "Like, *really* choking, almost passed out, or . . ." I rubbed at my eyes. "It all ended up fine. She was fine. I helped her; I got to her in time. But it was just—a lot, you know?"

He rubbed a hand along my lower back.

"I can't stay for long," I said. "I left Anna there alone."

Ryan pulled back and studied my face. "Can't she handle closing up?"

"Anna?" I snorted through my tears.

Ryan smiled and pulled me in again. He never liked to speak poorly of people, but Anna McCarron is difficult to defend.

"She could have died," I said. "What if no one had helped her?"

"You helped her," he said.

I closed my eyes, rested my chin on his shoulder. He must have seen the mud on my sneakers, the brown leaf that still clung to my sweater, but he didn't say anything. No hero comments or gruesome speculation or commentary on how I should be feeling. No probing questions.

That was the thing about Ryan. Ryan never asked me to "tell him about myself." Everything worth knowing, he already knew.

4

grope around in my bag again, pull out a pack of Parliaments. Ryan didn't like it when I smoked. He wouldn't say anything about it, usually. Instead, he'd rub his hand along his beard, watching me, sometimes giving a disappointed sigh. He drew the line at the car, though.

"That's trashy," he told me five months into our relationship, as I rolled down the passenger-seat window, lit up, and let my forearm dangle out of the car.

"You don't say anything when your mom does it." I threw the cigarette out onto the street and cranked the window back up again.

"She's too old to change. You're not."

I roll down my window now and the winter air bursts in, a sudden jolt of cold. It stings my bare hands, my face, but there's something cleansing about it, too, wet and fresh and sharp. I light a cigarette.

Chestnut oaks and birch trees climb the rocky incline to my left, a tangle of bare bushes beneath them. The Delaware River sweeps in on my right and then drifts away again, leaving behind marshy forest, trees suspended in ice. An approaching billboard promises that adventure awaits, just five miles ahead on the left.

It's a nine-hour drive from Calvary to Stonesport if you stick to back roads, but maybe you know that already. Maybe you've driven down these same roads, past the same Dollar Generals and old red barns and go-kart tracks. Maybe you've come home, and I just didn't know it.

I understand now why you left. You wanted to start over and do it right. Stonesport, Massachusetts: Why not? It's a beach town, I think. I looked it up online. Small and historic, with a Latin town motto: *Post tot Naufragia Portus*. "After so many shipwrecks, a safe harbor." I picture little houses with sandy yards, everything pastel-colored and salty, seashells hanging up tastefully as decorations. Old-fashioned wooden signs displayed on posts in front of historic houses and shops, rickety wooden boardwalks leading down to the sea. A new life, a new beginning, hundreds of miles from Calvary.

I thought I had put the past behind me, too. I should never have gone back to the campsite. That's what started all of this, what set it all in motion. The reminders started the next day. I promise: I never thought they were from you. I know you better than that.

When the initial text came through, I was driving to work down Mechanic Street, the rusted pipes and scaffolding of the old steel plant towering over me in the twilight. I had the street mostly to myself. Every once in a while, I'd pass a lone car, someone getting an early start on the day, or the occasional school bus, transporting bleary-eyed teenagers to school. When that silence was interrupted by the rattle of my phone in the cup holder beside me, I assumed that it was Ryan, texting to say that I had forgotten something at home or could I pick up this-or-that-thing if I had time today. I balanced my thermos of coffee on my lap—which, I know, is always a bad idea—and fumbled for my phone. And then, there it was, no name attached and the number blocked, just that line of text:

It should have been you, not Emily.

All of a sudden, there were headlights and the blare of a horn and the bulk of another car coming toward me. I swerved the other way, the coffee splashing up onto me, the hot liquid soaking through my jeans, scalding my legs. My phone fell from my hands, slipping between my seat and the car door. I jammed my hand down into the gap as far as it would go, trying to find the phone, fingers just brushing on the plastic edge of its case.

I realized I had been holding my breath, and exhaled a long, shaky sigh. I eased my car off onto the gravel by the side of the road, alongside the old railroad tracks, now overgrown with weeds and brush, and tried to steady myself. Deep breaths, in and out. I cracked open the door and reached down under my seat, pulling out my phone. I tossed it into the bag next to me quickly, without looking at it again.

It's nothing, I told myself, still gripping the steering wheel to steady my hands. *There's got to be an obvious explanation.*

It seems silly now, in retrospect, but my first thought was that it was probably a prank. Those teens from the coffee shop, the ones I had kicked out the day before. *They must have gotten my number from somewhere,* I reasoned. *That has to be it; it all fits.*

I started the car again and drove the rest of the way to Stomping Grounds slowly and cautiously, five miles under the speed limit. I parked in my normal spot on Church Street, just like always, and reassured myself that everything was fine. Nothing out of the ordinary.

Even so, I took an extra moment in my car, doors locked, to study the sidewalk sloping down to Stomping Grounds. I braced myself, got out, eyeing each gap between the storefronts and the small alleyway that ran behind the shops on Main Street, each blind corner seeming to pose a new and unfamiliar threat.

This is silly, I chided myself. The sidewalks and alleys were the same as they always are in the mornings: still and empty. *What was I expecting? A shadowy figure, armed with a knife and phone? It was those kids. Kids are assholes.* Still, I walked briskly to the front door, holding my keys defensively in my fist.

I did a quick once-over of the shop. Everything was how I had left it: the chairs flipped over and set on the tables, a note to myself—ORDER GREEN TEA—on the counter. I worked up the courage to flip on the lights in the storage room behind the counter and take a cursory look around, just long enough to confirm there was no one lurking behind any of the boxes. A bare bulb illuminated stacks of napkins and paper cups piled up on chrome wire shelving. Boxes of sweetener, coffee stirrers, and cleaning supplies were lined up next to the antique coffee grinder that Ryan bought for me as an opening-day present, its rectangular cast-iron top embellished with a web of vines. Large cardboard boxes full of unpacked supplies took up most of the floor space, leaving only a thin path back to a plywood desk and an eight-year-old computer. Everything in its place; everything exactly as I had expected.

I stripped off my damp, coffee-stained pants and grabbed my pair of black jeans off the shelves. I began keeping a spare outfit around after opening week, when I forgot about the step dividing Stomping Grounds into two levels and drenched myself in iced tea. *Those kids must have been sitting in the back of the bus together this morning, snickering over all the different texts they might send me,* I thought as I slid on one pant leg. *Then one of them must have thrown out my dead friend, and they realized they couldn't do any better than that.*

Dry and reassured that everything was as it was supposed to be, I took down the chairs from the tables, all mismatched, found at thrift stores and antiques shops in the surrounding area. One with a teal blue seat, specked with tiny pink flowers; two with orange and red stripes and padded armrests; another with faded mint-green silk upholstery and wooden legs carved into claw feet.

"This one's my favorite," Ryan had said of the "lion chair," as we loaded it into the back of the car. "Very regal."

I slid the chairs into place, then turned on a radio station playing inoffensive hits from the nineties and started the coffee brewing. *They must have heard about Emily from an older sibling, a cousin. A parent, maybe.* "Torn" faded out, replaced by the opening chords of "Wonderwall." I unlocked the door, took my place behind the counter.

And my phone number . . .

My heart began pounding; my chest tightened. I had the sudden urge to rush over to the door and bolt it up again. *I'm getting worked up over nothing,* I told myself. *Just some stupid kids. A prank.*

The jingle of the front door made me jump, and my cheeks burned with embarrassment. A middle-aged man in a button-down shirt came in and gave me a polite smile and head nod. I didn't know his name but, as was the case with most of my morning customers, I at least recognized his face. Brunette-with-tight-ponytail followed. She was part of the normal morning crowd, too, but she had always seemed familiar to me, even before she became a regular. Maybe we had overlapped in high school. The first time she came in, though, she gave me one of those pitying looks, like she was well aware of who *I* was, so I had never pushed the subject.

Then came a steady stream of faces—the rest of the rush-hour crowd—and I lost myself in the routine. There was something calming about making latte after latte, cranking the portafilter into the machine, hearing the hiss and chirp of the steam arm. When Stomping Grounds really got going, I could clear my head almost completely, just focusing on the orders to be filled and what needed to be done next. I took orders, made friendly chitchat with customers who looked like they wanted to talk to someone, and got the coffees ready.

As the rush-hour crowd began to calm down, the door chimed and Natalie Smith—now Natalie Smith-Linden—pushed the door open with her back, holding the handle of her six-month-old's car seat in both hands. Her two-year-old weaved through her legs, pulling at her fleece vest.

"Straight ahead, Ashton, keep moving. No, not—not *there,* Ashton, not there. This way." Natalie's voice rang through the coffee shop. She's never learned to modulate her volume.

"How's your morning been?" I asked, pouring a cup of coffee for her.

Natalie rolled her eyes dramatically and pretended to slam her head down on the counter. "Don't ask."

Natalie hasn't changed much from high school, with the notable exception that she's a mother now. She went to Easton for college, where she met Jack, then a doughy-faced business major, now a doughy-faced manager at Jenkins Plastics.

"This one," she said, lifting the car seat, "was up every two hours and that one . . ." A head nod toward Ashton, who was on his toes, his tiny fingers just scraping against the tin holding the coffee stirrers. "No touching, Ashton, leave that alone. Here, sit down here. I'll sit next to you."

I know you never liked Natalie. You thought she was brash and inconsiderate, and it's true; she certainly could be those things. But she was also there for me when Emily died in a way that others weren't, and when I came back to Calvary she welcomed me back like no time had passed at all. She filled me in on everything I had missed when I was away: who had stayed in town this whole time, who came back on holidays and got too drunk at the Tavern, who became a substitute teacher and got in trouble for ogling the fourteen-year-old girls. And she could talk, filling up silences with friendly chatter, putting me at ease.

"You'd think Jack could help, but he just sleeps right through it, like there's nothing going on at all," Natalie continued from her table, twisting around toward the counter. "Sometimes I think he's faking, I really do. Last night I just *stared* at him for a few minutes, to see if there were any changes in his breathing. And I think he must have known I was watching, because——"

"Something strange happened this morning," I interrupted in a low voice. I grabbed my phone off the counter and sat down at her table.

Natalie leaned in toward me. I pulled up the text and slid the phone across the table.

"Shit," she said, loudly, then looked over at Ashton and held up her index finger as a warning. "I didn't say that." She turned back toward me and lowered her voice to something resembling a stage whisper. "Who is that from?"

I took the phone back, shrugged, trying to look unconcerned. "I think it might be some kids I kicked out of the shop yesterday."

Natalie frowned and shook her head. She never made any effort to hide what she was thinking. "How would they know about Emily?"

I bristled and pushed myself up from the table, began bussing the tables nearby. "One of them must have an older brother or sister. Or——"

"And your phone number? They just happen to have your phone number?"

"I'm sure it's available somewhere," I said, returning to my spot behind the counter. Natalie leaned over the back of her chair again, raising an eyebrow at me. I shrugged, waved one hand in the air. "There's probably some kind of search you can do."

"Sit down," Natalie instructed, nodding at the empty chair next to her. "There's no one here."

I did as ordered. She leaned in again, her eyes big and serious.

"Do you think there's any chance it's from Joshua?" she asked, lowering her voice when she said your name.

"No," I said.

She leaned back in her chair again, pursed her lips.

"Absolutely not." I defended you, just like I always have. I was adamant that it wasn't you, but you can't really blame her for thinking what she did. She didn't know you as well as I did, back then. All she saw was that dirty-blond hair grown out to your shoulders, small tendrils curling into greasy waves and hanging down into your eyes. The Joshua who shook with rage and shouted Ancient Greek incantations at Matt Penna and Brian Wasserman on the bus, sending them into fits of giggles.

Natalie leaned back in her chair like she was about to relent, ran her hand through her highlighted hair. Then she sighed, scrunched up her face, and leaned back toward me.

"It's just—this is how it started before, right?"

She wasn't wrong, you know. You remember the email you sent from Emily's Hotmail account three months after she died. It lay in wait in my inbox, sandwiched between a slew of chain emails and fifth-period updates from Natalie. Sender: ~*~*eMiLy*~*~; subject line: *Have you forgotten about me already?*

But I know you had reasons for acting the way you did. Your sister *dies,* for Chrissake, and then instead of sympathy you're welcomed back to school with whispers and rumors, stares when people think you're not looking, averted eyes when they know you are. Conversations stop suddenly when you round a corner; girls raise eyebrows at one another and stifle giggles when you pass by; *that was almost so awkward, wasn't it?*

The speculation about you started almost immediately after Emily's death. I would overhear it in the halls before people realized that I was nearby, that I was tainted, too. *It has to be her brother,* they'd say. *It was only a matter of time.*

"I called it," a snub-nosed girl in your grade announced in

third-period study hall a week after Emily died. "I always said if there were going to be a school shooter . . ." She looked so pleased with herself, like she had just won some kind of bet.

I stood up from my chair forcefully, its legs scraping against the floor. Then I pushed it, hard, sending it toppling over, the attached wooden desk hitting the ground with a crack. There was silence, and then, when I left the room, an eruption of uncomfortable laughter.

That same girl tried, unsuccessfully, to divert a poorly conceived petition away from my desk a week later. I felt the poke of a sheet of paper against my back, twisted around to reach for it, and saw her maneuvering around the desks through the room, reaching out to snatch it away, but not in time. I grabbed it, unfolded it before she could reclaim it, and managed to read the first few lines. PETITION TO REMOVE JOSHUA WINTERS FROM CALVARY HIGH SCHOOL, it began. "Joshua Winters has proven himself to be a threat to the student body, and his continued presence on campus creates a hostile environment not conducive to learning."

Alex's arrest slowed down the rumors but didn't stop them entirely. They just took on new form. *Maybe he didn't do* that, everyone reasoned. *But he must have done* something.

I can only imagine how alone you must have felt. It doesn't help much now, but I've thought a lot about the things I could have done differently, things that might have let you know I still cared. One I always come back to is Emily's funeral: I should have gone.

I had been planning on going. I had even spent that morning getting ready. I showered for the first time in a week, the first time since the day I found out what had happened. I took the time to dry my hair and spent at least half an hour in front of the mirror, dabbing at the dark gray rings under my eyes with different colors of concealer, hoping that one might work. Yellow, green, beige; it didn't matter. They wouldn't go away.

Three calls from Alex. I refused to talk to him. I could hear my mother downstairs, her voice firm. *Please stop calling. Please stop calling. Please stop calling.*

I brushed my teeth slowly, deliberately. Rinsed. Examined my face in the mirror. Washed off the makeup I had applied, started again. My mother called for me from downstairs, breaking my concentration. "Sweetie?" she said, with strained patience. "It's just about time to go." She was being nice. It had been time to go for fifteen minutes.

I slunk down the stairs and sat sideways on a kitchen chair, one with a loose spindle. I spun it absently as my mother lowered the piece of toast she had been eating and looked me over.

"You're not wearing that." Her eyes traveled from my black jeans, frayed at the cuffs from the heel of my boots, up to my black hoodie.

"What? It's the right color."

Strain spread across my mother's face. She pursed her lips, deciding, I assumed, how strict she should be with me, given the circumstances.

"Micah," she said, in her calm voice, "that's not appropriate. Go get changed."

I shrugged, spun the spindle more forcefully, wood squeaking against wood. I kept her eye, daring her to push further. Her jaw tightened, and she leaned in close toward me.

"People are watching," she said, whispering forcefully, as though someone else might be listening in. "This is not appropriate."

I stomped back up the stairs, each step loud and emphatic. I went to my closet, pulled out a gray knit dress and slid it off the hanger, then crumpled it into a ball and threw it on the floor. Then the next dress, and the next. Once my closet was empty, I threw myself down on my bed and pulled the sheets over my head.

After a few minutes, there was a soft knock at my door.

"Micah, it's time to go."

The door creaked softly as it swung open. My mother caught her breath and composed herself, visibly choosing to ignore the pile of clothes on the floor.

"I understand that you're upset, but you need to come out here. If you miss this, you're going to regret it."

She was right, in a way, although not for the reasons she thought. My mother always believed funerals had this magical quality, an ability to give closure and peace to "those of us left behind." But I was mad at Emily. Am I allowed to say that? You'll understand; you must have felt it, too, for your own reasons. I was mad at her, and I had every right to be. She slept with Alex over and over again. Each time a secret, a betrayal. Some hymns and a few nice words weren't going to change how I felt.

But what I didn't think about at the time was you and your family. Your mother, grief-stricken and pale; your father, eyes fixed on the crucifix at the front of the church but not really looking, retreating back into his own mind. You, between them, nervously tapping the wooden pew, unsure of what to do with your feet, your hands. Unsure of what to do with your mother sobbing beside you, unsure of what to do with the family friends who came over to express their condolences but also to pry—*Do the police have any leads? Do they know what happened?* Usually, Emily would have given you instructions, bordering on micromanagement—*stop fidgeting, stand up straight, tell Aunt Lynn that's none of her goddamned business*—but Emily was gone now. You were all alone.

Maybe it wouldn't have made any difference if I had gone. But at least you would have seen me there paying my respects to your sister and your family. Then, maybe, you wouldn't have thought that I had forgotten about Emily so quickly, that I had just moved on.

I hadn't forgotten. I never have. I've never been able to get away. Maybe you've figured out how. I picture you waking up early, making your way into town before the vacationers take over, before the sidewalks become a sea of flip-flops and red, peeling shoulders and globs of sunscreen. You exchange a few words with shopkeepers and friendly waves with the other locals milling around.

Do they know your real name, Joshua? Do they know who you really are?

5

turn up the volume on the car radio and scroll through the stations, looking for news. Two talk show hosts jab at one another, their laughs loud and mean. Severe winter storms expected in the next two hours, continuing late into the night. Big sales at Midway Car Dealership, significant delays on the Parkway, important game for the Eagles next weekend.

It wasn't easy to find you, you know. A Google search for Joshua Winters turns up a lawyer with "vast experience" handling "high-stakes litigation and complex business disputes," a well-groomed man with a rectangular face and professional smile against a hazy blue background. An actor/bodybuilder with muscles ballooning up around his neck, hawking a strict dietary regime that he'll share for forty dollars. A Unitarian minister—no picture, but I had a hard time imagining your life going that route.

"Joshua Winters Calvary" yields a smattering of results. An article from 2003 about a gaming night at Merlock's Collectibles. There you are, your slim arm extended, throwing dice onto a gaming table. Results from cross-country matches your freshman and sophomore years. Emily's obituary. Articles about Emily's death, gossip and speculation. But after Calvary, you disappear. It's like you vanish off the face of the earth.

I tried different combinations in an attempt to track you down. "Joshua Winters cross-country." No luck. "Joshua Winters Minnesota"—your grandparents' home, the last place I knew you to be. Nothing. You didn't lead the Minneapolis Bulldogs through an undefeated season, and you weren't running a start-up focused on connectivity and collaboration. "Joshua Winters Ancient Greece." "Joshua Winters Ancient Rome." "Joshua Winters Classics." I thought maybe you'd be a professor somewhere, teaching some ancient language with fiery enthusiasm, but that was a dead end, too. Joshua Winters had disappeared, a slate wiped clean.

I tried to get away from Calvary after high school, too, you know. Four lackluster years at college, another four in Chicago, but I was only ever treading water. I never figured out how to do it right.

My last night at the Oat & Barley, the last in a slew of restaurants I waitressed at, was a Friday night, busy, and the hostess had seated a bachelorette party in my section. There were five bridesmaids, squeezed into black dresses with their hair straightened and their faces looking unnaturally tan for December in Chicago. The bride wore white, to stand out from the group, and I was ready to hate them immediately. I thought I could see how the evening was going to go: the girly, ridiculous cocktails, the long lists of substitutions for each order. Voices rising as the drinks settled in, dirty looks from the patrons nearby (who, feeling grumpy about a night out ruined, would also tip less), a long discussion about how to split the bill, made more complicated by the fact that the bride, of course, would not be paying. Phone calculators out. A taxi to a Boystown club after.

A heavily freckled bridesmaid waved me down as I passed by

carrying a tray full of "upscale home cooking"—cornbread muffins drenched in local honey, plates weighed down by ribs.

"Um," she said. "This table is a little dirty?" She wrinkled her nose and gave me a tight smile, and I could feel my tip vanishing.

"Sorry about that," I said, adjusting the tray on my shoulder. "Give me one second, and I'll get you moved." Calm and professional. I was good at my job; I had, after all, been doing it for years. The restaurant sometimes changed, and the waitstaff turned over—a friend suddenly gone, a new face replacing her at the next shift—but the work was the same thing, night after night. My work friend, at the time, was Alice, a pixielike twenty-three-year-old who had recently graduated with a degree in fine arts. She passed me as I made my way to the hostess station, glanced over at my bachelorette table, and mimed a blow job. In the deep pocket of my server apron, I could feel my phone vibrating.

"Excuse me, miss." The couple in my booth, splitting a twelve-dollar s'more, ready for the check.

"I'll be right back," I promised. One thing I always liked about waiting tables: you have to keep moving.

The hostess found a new spot for my bachelorette party on the other side of my section, and they settled in, slinging their massive coats and small, impractical pocket bags over the backs of their new chairs. I dropped the check at table 34 before returning to take their order.

"Something to drink?" I eyed the table for any overlooked detail that might knock my tip down further: a stray crumb, a smudged menu.

"Do you have a wine list?" the bride asked. She looked around the table at her friends for affirmation, and they bobbed their heads in agreement. In my pocket, my phone vibrated again: another call. No one ever called me multiple times.

"Right here," I said, grabbing the clipboard between two jars of mustard at the center of the table and handing it to the bride. "I'll be right back if you have any questions."

"Um." The freckled brunette again, leaning in her chair to share the menu with the bride. "What's this cab like?"

"Bold," I said.

She looked around the table, waiting for reactions, and I shifted my weight and tried to maintain a pleasant, neutral expression.

"You can try it if you'd like," I said.

My phone stopped, then buzzed one final, definitive time: a voicemail.

"Are we doing a bottle?" asked the slim brunette to the bride's right. "Does everyone like reds?"

My call log at the time: a few outgoing calls earlier in the week to my landlord, who was supposed to send a repairman to fix my dishwasher but kept forgetting. Between those calls, a six-minute conversation with a potential date from Bumble, awkward and uncomfortable. An incoming call from a telemarketer that I had accidentally picked up. My mother never called; she always waited for me. ("I just don't want to disturb you," she'd always say, after commenting on how long it had been since we had spoken. "I know you're so busy.") No one depending on me, or interested in when I'd be home, or curious about my whereabouts. No one who would call twice and leave a voicemail.

"Amanda, what do you think?" asked another bridesmaid, this one blond and fully midwestern.

The bride looked nervous, stressed by the pressure of making a decision.

"How about one white, one red?" suggested the slim brunette. She glanced down at her phone, impatient.

"Great idea." The bride's eyes shifted to another column on the menu.

"I'll give you—" I started.

"We can order." The slim brunette. "The cab and the—?"

"I like chardonnay," a second blonde with a squeaky voice offered.

"I think Amanda prefers sauvs."

"Oh, I like everything."

"The cab and the sauv blanc," the slim brunette said, turning her attention toward me. "Please."

I nodded and turned away from the table before they could ask for anything else. A new couple had been seated at table 34, and they were starting to glance up from their menus impatiently. I pretended not to see. I pushed through the swinging doors into the kitchen and pulled out my phone. Two missed calls from my mom's best friend, Cindy, an ever-present figure in our house growing up. I had talked to her a few times since moving to Chicago, but we weren't regularly in touch. I put my phone to my ear and tried to hear her voicemail over the shouts and clanging dishes in the kitchen. *News . . . call . . .*

"No phones." Jo, my manager, stern behind me. I held up my index finger and turned to face the wall.

"Micah," Jo barked again. I let my phone drop back into my apron and swung back out to the restaurant's main floor, then tapped in the wine orders at the server station monitor. *Cindy.* My stomach tightened. I told myself it was fine, tried to think of benign reasons why she might be calling: her son, a freshman in college now, coming out to Chicago to visit and in need of a tour guide/babysitter. *Two calls.* I'd handle it later. I went to greet the new couple at table 34, dutifully took their order, and ignored their irritated tone.

Wyatt, the bartender, set the bottles out onto the bar mat.

"We going out tonight?" Wyatt asked. He was maybe the most reliable presence in my life at the time. He had been bartending at the Oat & Barley since I started working there, almost six months before, and probably long before that. We had slept together twice, when I first started, but now just drank together. I knew he was from Iowa, or maybe Indiana, and that was about it.

"I think I'm still recovering from last night," I said, grabbing the bottles and whisking them out to the bachelorette party.

"And Brandon—" the bride was saying as I approached the

table. I presented the labels to her, and she nodded without really looking.

"Brandon!" said the freckled bridesmaid. "Brandon is coming? I haven't seen him in—God, eight years?" She turned toward the squeaky blonde. "Is that right?"

The squeaky blonde nodded enthusiastically in response. "Do you remember," she said, squeezing the freckled bridesmaid's arm in a familiar, affectionate way, "the brand?"

The freckled bridesmaid grimaced, and the bride burst out into peals of laughter.

"I still get nauseous thinking about it," the freckled bridesmaid said, placing a palm over her wineglass—*no*—without looking up. "That infection he got afterward—"

"Sam knows Brandon," the bride said, shooting the thin brunette a meaningful look.

"No!" said the freckled bridesmaid.

"Youthful indiscretion," the thin brunette said, holding up her hands in front of her in protest and leaning slightly to the left to make space for me to fill her glass. "A Sigma Nu mixer. Amanda didn't warn me—"

"I did!" the bride insisted. "I absolutely did! I woke up the next morning, and—"

This was obviously a story they had told before. I could see, in their meaningful glances, the pauses they left for the other to fill in the details, that they were falling back into a comfortable groove.

"Brandon," said the freckled bridesmaid, shaking her head. "You know he drank his own urine back in high school. It was, like, his party trick."

"I didn't know that *then*."

"I'll be back when you've had a moment to look over the menu," I said, annoyed by the chatter but aware I was being a little unreasonable. I hated it, the small gossip and silly, exaggerated stories that bound groups together. "Grow up," I always wanted to tell them. "You're not in high school anymore." I dropped my server pad back into my apron, where it hit against my phone.

A surprise party for my mom's fiftieth, I told myself. *An offer to go in together on some kind of present.*

"Miss," called the man at table 34. "What IPAs do you have on tap?"

It was fine. The call could wait.

I made my way back to the bar. Alice leaned against it, deep in conversation with Wyatt about how Pilsners are underrated.

"It's harder to hide their imperfections," Wyatt was saying. That was a second thing I knew about him: he brewed his own beer, and he liked to talk about it.

"Yeah, but there's nothing *to* them, though." This was a debate they had had before. Alice stepped aside to let me through, then leaned back with both elbows on the bar. "I need that bitter edge, you know?"

In my pocket, my phone buzzed again.

"Shit," I said, checking my screen, but knowing, before I did, that it would be Cindy's name again.

"Need me to cover?" Alice asked.

"Please."

I swung through the kitchen doors again, grabbed my coat, and slipped out the back door into the alley that ran behind the restaurant. Cindy had gotten into a fight with my mother, maybe, was calling to ask me to help patch things up. It was certainly possible: my mother was strong-willed and stubborn and knew how to hold a grudge. I zipped up my coat—which was insulated and down to my ankles but still couldn't keep out the cold—and grabbed the box of Parliaments from my pocket. She had seen a movie that was set in Chicago, thought of me, wanted to say hi. *Three calls.* I lit my cigarette and called Cindy's number, my fingers stinging as the phone rang and rang.

Her son was engaged and did I know his fiancée.

Her son had knocked someone up and did I know the mom-to-be.

Her son had come to Chicago and she *hadn't* told me, but he had been picked up for disorderly conduct at a Wrigleyville bar and could I please go to the police station to—

Cindy picked up on the last ring. "Oh, Micah," she said. "Oh, honey."

Could I get to Calvary by that weekend, she asked, and I said *maybe, maybe* like I'd have to check my schedule first, find out if I was working a shift, and then caught myself. *No, of course. Of course.* That weekend. Jo peered outside and gave me a pointed look and I thought about leaving right then, without a word to anyone, but then realized: Where would I go? Back to my apartment, with its bare walls and stack of crusted dishes waiting for me? I dropped my cigarette onto the ground and stubbed it out with my toe and went back inside.

Two plates waited for me under the heater, the ticket on the screen above them red. I grabbed them, took them out to the table, told the couple sitting there to enjoy, to let me know if they needed anything else. My head buzzed. The last time I had talked to my mother had been a week before, a short call. After her standard guilt trip about how long it had been, she had asked me about work, if I was *looking*.

"I have a job," I had said.

"Well."

"Well what?"

"I just think maybe you should think about moving back. It's been—"

I cut her off—"I can't do this right now"—and that was it.

The freckled bridesmaid was craning her neck to get my attention, her eyes wide and pointed.

"Um," she started again when I reached their table, and I wanted to smack her, tell her that wasn't how you begin a sentence, wasn't how you address a person, but I pushed that down and smiled and said instead: "Are you ready to order?"

"The pear and blue cheese risotto?" said the bride.

"Oh, that one looks good," said the freckled bridesmaid. "That's what I was thinking about, too."

I hadn't been back to Calvary in two years. Two years. Not for any good reason. I just hadn't gone.

"Pork chops for me," said the blond bridesmaid. She tapped her empty glass. "And could we get some more water?"

No, I had good reason. There were too many memories in Calvary. The last time I had gone back, my mother had picked me up at the airport. I sat in the passenger seat, one leg pulled up to my chest, and realized the direction we were going: up Culver Street, the dirt ridge still there, your neighborhood quickly approaching on my left.

"Not this way," I had said, and my mother hadn't reacted, except to say: "This is the way to the house." I could feel my chest tightening, my breath growing faster. "Turn around," I insisted. "Turn *around*."

"I've been listening to this great book about facing your fears—"

"This bullshit," I snapped, "is exactly why I don't come home."

"—without walnuts?" the slim brunette was saying. A flick of her wrist as she handed the menu back to me. "Please."

I took the menu and retreated to the kitchen. I braced myself on the steel prep table, closed my eyes, tried to get a grip. I hadn't meant to let so much time go by. It had just happened, the months running into each other, and my mother asking when I was coming home, and me giving the same response each time: *Soon. Soon.* Behind me, the line cooks were shouting something in Spanish at Alice, who laughed, a piercing, awful noise, and another server leaned around me to grab a garnish, placing his sweaty hand on my back, and Jo swung through the kitchen doors, eyes fixed on me.

"Micah!" Jo said. "Table 34 is looking for you. Let's go!"

.   .   .

The bachelorette party lingered at the end of my shift, ignoring the check resting on the corner of the table. Back in the kitchen, I scraped old Caesar dressing into the sink with a plastic spatula and stretched plastic wrap over the remaining metal tubs of salad dressing. The kitchen smelled like the kitchen of every restaurant I had ever worked at: sour milk and grease, a smell that stuck to my skin after every shift. The floors slick and splattered with a thick red sauce. Behind me, Alice ran a wet rag over the inside of the dessert refrigerator, her movements quick and assured.

"I've got a show Saturday," Alice said. "If you want to come." She did photography, I think, or maybe mixed media. I forget now. Maybe I never knew, exactly.

"I can't," I said. "My mom died."

Alice laughed, high pitched and grating, before registering my expression. "Wait, you're serious?"

"Yeah," I said, trying it on, waiting for some kind of emotion to take hold. "I'm going back home this weekend."

"Shit, man." She threw the rag down on the counter, wiped the side of her face with her hand. "That sucks. I'm sorry." When I didn't respond, she shifted, grappled for the right thing to say. "Are you okay?"

Of course not, I wanted to tell her, but what good would that do?

"I don't want to think about it," I said, sliding the metallic lid of the salad station shut. "Let's go out tonight."

"For sure, man," Alice said. "For sure. That we can do."

The next morning, I woke up alone in my apartment, the taste of bile in the back of my throat. I peeled myself off the bed, damp with sweat. The water glass on my nightstand had been knocked over at some point in the night, water beading on the surface, pooling on the floor beneath. Cindy's call hit me again: *your mother.*

I grabbed my computer, pulled up a website for cheap flights, and started thinking about return dates. A week? Jo wouldn't be thrilled if I pushed for too much longer, but fuck Jo. There were plenty of restaurants in Wicker Park if it came down to it.

I looked over the small boxes on the calendar, two weeks out. Three. My head throbbed; the act of making a decision seemed impossible. I closed the lid of my laptop and grabbed my phone— a little damp, but still functional—off the nightstand. No new notifications, no texts from Alice checking in. Maybe she was still sleeping, but I wasn't really expecting anything. She wasn't that type of friend. And the thought hit me, along with a sudden and overwhelming wave of self-pity: *I don't have that kind of friend.* I didn't have a single person in Chicago who really cared what I was going through.

Another thought: *Why come back at all?* I studied my sparsely furnished apartment. Pushed against the wall was my IKEA bed, the frame split open since the day I had unloaded it from its box. Next to the door, a bare-bones dresser that could be left on the curb out front with a cardboard sign: FREE. The rest of it—the television, the coffee maker, the small stack of plates in the chipped plywood cabinets—could all be loaded into the back of the car, taken with me. I could just *go home.*

It only took a few hours to pack up my car. By that evening, I was on the road to Calvary. I left a message for my landlord, told him I didn't need the dishwasher fixed after all, and let him know he should find a new tenant. I didn't tell work anything. I got a few texts from Alice: *when u coming back?* and then silence, and that was fine. I was starting over, I told myself. I would do it right this time. I'd give Calvary—and myself—a second chance.

I thought it was working, for a time. But then that text came through. *It should have been you, not Emily.* And after, I couldn't stop thinking about Emily. Emily at ten with her wild hair hanging

down over the back of one of Mr. Hunt's chairs, you with chocolate ice cream smeared across your face. Emily and me, climbing
those steep stairs to the Lionels' dance studio, ballet bags slung over
our shoulders, clutching the railings tightly in our right hands, you
disappearing into Merlock's Collectibles below us. Emily, sprawled
out alone beside the cinder block house.

Natalie was tending to her children while I swept the floor,
finishing one spot and then beginning again, from the Church
Street windows to the counter, and then working my way back. I
was on my third loop toward the Church Street windows when I
saw Julia Reynolds—whom I had successfully avoided since my
return to Calvary—standing almost completely still on the sidewalk outside, looking in. Her pale white cheeks were splotched
with red and she sniffled repeatedly, twitching her nose like a rabbit. She wore her straight, straw-colored hair just like she always
has, tied back in a long braid that swung down to her waist. And
there, hanging on her shoulders, engulfing her small frame, was
Alex's letterman jacket, frayed at the cuffs and the waistband from
a decade of use.

"What is she doing here?" I said, letting go of the broom and
letting it fall with a clatter onto the floor. Ashton startled and then
scampered down off his seat, grabbing the broom for himself. Natalie barely seemed to notice. She had leaned to the side of her chair
to get a better view.

"What a nut job," she said, shaking her head disapprovingly.

Lots of murderers get girlfriends in prison: strange, lonely
women who search out dangerous men on websites and start writing them letters. Alex didn't go quite that route. Instead, he got
Julia.

When her obsession with Alex began exactly, I can't say. But I
do remember her lingering nearby in high school, eyes fixed on
Alex, studiously avoiding me. She'd blush deeply whenever Alex
acknowledged her, her pale, almost translucent skin taking on a
purple tone, but she wouldn't start giggling, like some of the other

underclassmen who found Alex attractive. To the contrary, she took all of her brief interactions with Alex very seriously. When he spoke to her—which didn't happen very often—she stared back at him like she was trying to make sure she got every word right, nodding along carefully at whatever he said. If he cracked a joke, she'd stare solemnly back at him, her thick eyebrows pinched, nodding her head intently. When she responded, she spoke carefully and meticulously, as though she had planned out each word in advance. I always thought she was odd but never realized the full extent of it.

Outside the window, Julia wrinkled her nose again, then reached into the tote bag slung over her shoulder and pulled out a sheet of paper and roll of tape. She pushed the paper up against the window and began fixing it in place.

"Hey!" I shouted, shaking my head as I marched across the shop. "Hey! You can't do that!" I slammed my hand on the glass pane, causing her to jump back. But she regained her composure and ripped off another stretch of tape.

"Unbelievable," I said to Natalie, who watched the whole thing with barely concealed enthusiasm.

"I mean, she's out of her *mind*," she said, almost gleefully.

You were gone by the time Alex's trial came around, but Julia was a regular in the courtroom. She'd be there every morning, right on time, sliding down the wooden bench at the very back of the room at eight o'clock. She wasn't the only one from school who came to watch—there were a lot of people who were feigning some kind of close relationship with Emily, girls who would appear in groups of three or four and get all teary-eyed whenever a new picture was unveiled or a new piece of evidence introduced—but Julia stood out. She sat alone, that sad, serious expression plastered across her face, her eyes perpetually watery and her pockets overflowing with tissues, a worn spiral notebook on her lap. Once the bailiff announced that court was in session and we all sat down again, she'd begin scribbling notes, stopping only occasionally to look up toward Alex and give a small, disbelieving shake of her head.

I grabbed my coat from the storage room and then marched out the door, the chimes clanging behind me. Julia stood defiantly next to her sign, a grainy printout of Alex at seventeen. I knew that picture. I took that picture. At the top of the page, Julia had scrawled out in permanent marker: I'M INNOCENT.

"What is this?" I said, tearing the paper off the window and crumpling it into a ball.

"I'm raising awareness." Those serious eyes, fixed firmly on me.

"You need to stay away from my shop," I said, pointing down Church Street with a forceful gesture. Maybe too forceful. A man walking toward us stopped, assessed the situation, and then crossed to the other sidewalk. Across the street, Martin, the Hotel Calvary front desk clerk who seemed to spend more time out beneath the hotel's awning than actually at the front desk, lit a cigarette and positioned himself to get a better view.

"Ten years," she said, her voice wavering, climbing in pitch. "Ten years in jail. Ten years that we could have been *together*."

"This is harassment," I said, leaning in toward her and speaking quietly. "Do you understand? I'm going to call the police if I see you back here again."

"Call the police." She was shrill, hysterical. Her eyes widened and the red on her cheeks deepened. "Lie to them again. Just like you always have."

"You need to leave," I said.

"She's a *liar*," Julia shouted to the man who had crossed the street, who pretended not to hear her.

"I don't want to see you here again," I said, and then I turned and walked back into Stomping Grounds, left her alone on the street to fume and rage. That's important: I tried to be the bigger person. I tried to walk away.

Julia began calling herself Alex's girlfriend a few weeks after his arrest. I first heard it for myself on the bus to school. Julia was slouched down with her knees pushed up against the brown vinyl of the seat in front of her, scribbling out a long, handwritten note, eyes brimming with tears.

"Love letter?" Brian Wasserman had asked, meanly, hanging over the back of her seat to get a better look. His hair stood straight up in tiny spikes, held together with globs of gel, the white of his skull showing underneath.

"It's a letter to Alex Swift," she had responded, as if Brian had been asking a genuine question. "He's my boyfriend now."

She always responded that way—earnestly and graciously, like the questions were coming from a place of interest and concern. "He's very scared," she told Brian a few weeks later when he asked for an update. "But he's innocent. We have the truth on our side."

"We" and "our." The way she spoke about him was always so possessive, even from the beginning. "My Alex," she'd call him, with those sad, rounded eyes. It infuriated me, that possessiveness, even when I doubted there was any truth to their relationship.

"He needs me, now more than ever," she said. "He needs someone he can depend on." She spoke firmly, loud enough that I could hear over the rumble of the bus, the chatter around us. "Someone who won't betray him."

I didn't betray him. I didn't lie for him; there's a difference. When the police asked me to confirm that he was with us all night, on the tarp we had set up just past the altar, I told them he wasn't there. I told them the truth.

I just didn't mention seeing you.

6

see the red glow of brake lights in front of me. I slow reluctantly, coming to a stop in front of a gift shop hemmed in by a white picket fence, its front yard covered in large metal bobbles, aluminum roosters, and plastic flamingos. The sidewalk is ten feet away. I turn the knob on the radio again, bite down hard on my bottom lip. I glance up into the rearview mirror at the line of cars now forming behind me. I'm surrounded on all sides.

The problem with back roads is that they feed into towns, and towns have stoplights and then I'm just waiting, sitting and hoping that no one will recognize me or this car, which would have been nondescript two weeks ago but now has a taillight cover bashed in and BITCH scratched out in ugly jagged lettering on the passenger door, right there for everyone to see.

I tell myself to calm down, to breathe. No one will be looking for me yet.

I twist around, grab Ryan's faded navy baseball cap from the back seat, PECK HARDWARE embroidered on the front in white thread that's starting to come undone. Ryan's favorite hat. The

Easton students who loitered in his library probably thought it was ironic. They didn't understand anything.

I slip the hat on over my unwashed hair, run a hand down my face, my skin tight and grimy. I angle the rearview mirror toward myself. Tiny creases branch out from around my eyes, deepened from lack of sleep. I adjust the mirror back into place, focus on the brake lights of the car in front of me, and wait.

I wonder if you'll recognize me after all this time. I recognized you as soon as I saw your photo: ten years older, for sure, and you've finally cut your hair, but it was unmistakably you. You sell old maps and pictures, records of old shipping routes, sketches of battles. Of course. It all fits, all makes sense. Who we are—who we *really* are, our essential selves—that doesn't change, does it?

I bet you found a run-down place to fix up in Stonesport, a hundred-year-old structure that had been left to fend for itself against the storms and salty beach air. You probably studied each beam carefully, learning the history of the place—the type of wood used, the methods of construction—patching, polishing, rebuilding, until it felt like home. Painting the outside something cheerful, cerulean blue siding against sandy weeds and the gray ocean in the background. Does someone live there with you—a girlfriend, maybe? A wife?

It's hard to find a place for yourself, to make it work. My mother left me the house I grew up in when she died, and I tried living there when I first got back to Calvary. I slept in my old bedroom, the walls the same dark shade of maroon from my teenage years, the heavy dresser from my childhood still pushed into the corner. The top left drawer was stuffed so full of old postcards and carefully folded notes that it was difficult to open; the bottom drawer full of old dance uniforms, camp T-shirts, a ratty pastel pink sweatshirt from a trip to the shore. Emily had the same one in a pale shade of blue. I lived out of the two large suitcases I had brought with me, which sat on the floor of my closet.

I spent most of my time at home in that tiny bedroom, too

uncomfortable venturing out into the rest of the house, which felt cavernous and empty. I entertained the fantasy of changing things, improving them: a new couch for the family room, less wallpaper, and more modern shades of paint. But then there I was, wall scraper in hand, in tears on the kitchen tiles, unable to bring myself to scratch off the cats and chickens that lined the walls. I decided, after that, that the job of modernizing should be left to someone else, someone without any sentimental attachments to the checker-printed bathrooms and the sponge-painted study. I found the apartment in Calvary Lofts the next day, with its blank white walls and laminate wood floors. It felt empty, like a place that no one had ever lived in before. It was exactly what I needed.

The apartment stayed bare and minimal until three months later, when Ryan moved in. He brought with him his collection of miniature figurines, tiny soldiers that he painted with delicate care, first washing their tiny plastic bodies with a toothbrush and white vinegar, then brushing them with a layer of white paint, then dabbing on acrylic skin and carefully researched uniforms. Brick-red coats with white trousers for the soldiers, burnt umber for the miniature horses that some of them rode. The miniatures, and the boxes of supplies needed to make them, took over the second bedroom we designated as our office, a tiny space that barely fit our rarely used futon and Ryan's massive oak desk. Our velvet couch sat in the middle of our family room, topped with Ryan's mottled yellow and black throw blanket. Our kitchen cupboards, which once held two coffee mugs and three water glasses, filled up with pint glasses that Ryan won at the Tavern's trivia night, each glass advertising a different beer. It looked like a chaotic mess, but it also looked like a home. It was *our* space, a place where I was safe, where I was *Micah Wilkes, capable of a normal and healthy relationship.*

I should have known better. There are no safe spaces in Calvary.

.　　.　　.

That was why Julia came to Stomping Grounds, you know. She wanted to send that message; she wanted to make it clear. *You can't move on,* she was saying. *I won't let you.*

"Does *she* have your phone number?" Natalie asked when I marched back inside, nodding her head toward Julia, who still stood by the windows, watching, and it had all come together for me: the text—*it should have been you*—was from Julia. Anger shot through me, but it was charged, directed, and, in some ways, a relief. Julia was the problem, and she could be managed.

I drove home that evening alongside the overgrown railroad tracks, the same route our bus used to take to drop off Ryan at the Calvary Apartments. I used to watch the rusted tracks pass by with my temple pressed up against the cold bus window, the bus's vibrations pulsing through my clenched jaw. Two seats ahead, Julia would field questions from Matt Penna and Brian Wasserman, enjoying the attention, not even realizing she was being mocked.

"Does it feel dangerous?" Matt asked, in a low, serious tone, a trucker hat resting on the top of his head, its brim angled to the side. "Dating a murderer?" The bus careened over a deep rut that was never filled, and Matt lunged forward, steadying himself on the back of the seat.

"My Alex would never hurt anyone," Julia said. I couldn't see her, but she spoke loudly enough for me to hear: each word slow and enunciated.

"Do you get conjugal visits?" Brian asked next, and Matt squeaked beside him, stifling a giggle.

"He'll be out soon," Julia responded. "He's innocent."

An empty warehouse with crumbled brick and dusty, opaque windows sat idly beside the railroad track, roughly marking the halfway point between town and the Apartments, now the Lofts. Beyond that, an expanse of brown fields. I squeezed the steering wheel and pictured Julia, with her red, sniffling nose and those watery eyes, Alex's self-appointed advocate. What right did she have to confront *me,* after all this time? To dredge up old, painful memories, when I had only ever done what I was *supposed* to do, when I was the one who had lost my best friend?

On my left, the police station, a large concrete block with small windows, a sprawling parking lot. Inside it, a sparse waiting room with blue plastic chairs, a smooth metal desk, a small table set out with flyers for apple picking at Golden Acres Orchard next to pamphlets about domestic abuse. A disembodied black eye, the words DON'T LOOK AWAY printed beneath it.

Julia didn't know what it was like to sit in that tiny interrogation room full of artificial heat, dry and crackling with static. She wasn't there. I was. I had sat in that room at seventeen years old with my shirt sticking to my body and hair clinging to my neck. The tables had recently been wiped down and sterilized and still smelled like bleach, a smell that, when the door was closed, made my eyes water and head spin.

"He wasn't with you on the tarp that night, was he?" Detective Heller had urged, like she already knew, making me feel as if, by answering, I would only be confirming a foregone conclusion.

I had tried to smooth out my hair, which only clung to my dry hand. I looked down at the items on the metal table: a stack of official-looking papers in a manila folder, a chain-link heart necklace in a clear plastic bag. "No," I responded. "He wasn't with us."

"Now before you said—"

"I know what I said. He asked me to lie for him. He wasn't there."

I did the right thing. I told the truth.

I dropped my foot down on the gas pedal, and the engine strained. I couldn't shake the image of Julia wrapped in Alex's jacket, self-righteously affixing her homemade flyer to my window. The first time I caught sight of her in that jacket, she had been climbing aboard the bus, aware of the eyes on her, wearing a small, proud smile. I had slouched down in my seat, pretended not to notice. I told myself that Alex wouldn't be interested in someone like her, that she must have stolen the jacket somehow or convinced Alex's mother that she was someone she wasn't. She had rung the doorbell, and Mrs. Swift had answered, and as soon as Julia had identified herself as Alex's *friend,* Mrs. Swift had burst into tears, ushered her in, invited her to take any memento that she wanted. A fantasy, I reassured myself. The whole relationship was just an elaborate fantasy.

As I pulled into Calvary Lofts, I imagined Julia curled up alone on her bed, wearing that jacket, pictures of Alex that she had found online decorating her nightstand, cropped to cut me out. Sniffling self-righteously as she pulled out her phone and typed out a message to me.

I climbed up the dimly lit stairwell, thinking of Julia in high school, lingering five feet away from Alex as I spoke to him, staring as if I couldn't see her. I slid my key into the lock and swung open the door. No sign of Ryan in the kitchen or the living room, and no light shining through beneath the bedroom door. The hook that normally held his jacket was empty. I slipped off my shoes and removed my coat.

Ryan usually would have been home by then on a normal day. He didn't go out with friends after work. His visits to his mother were always earlier in the day, before she started drinking.

"Ryan?" I called out, but I knew he wasn't there. My stomach sank, and the self-righteous anger that I had been nursing found a new subject.

He had gone out to SCI Frackville. He had gone to visit Alex.

When Ryan first told me he still visited Alex, we had been walking along Church Street, carrying supplies from his car to Stomping Grounds, or what was to become Stomping Grounds in a few weeks' time. I asked an innocent question about what he had going on that week, and he swung around to face me, hands clasped awkwardly around an oversized cardboard box, and said, with a searching, sincere look: "I'm going to see Alex." Then he waited to see how I would react.

In addition to paper cups and napkins, the trunk of Ryan's car contained three boxes of books, a laundry basket filled with chargers and electrical cords and CDs, and a garbage bag of clothes he had pulled out of his closet. This was to be the third of many trips between Ryan's old walk-up above the Tavern and my apartment, or what was to become our apartment, at Calvary Lofts. I held a bucket of cleaning supplies in one hand and a bag of framed pictures in the other, and as the wire handle of the bucket dug into the crook of my fingers, all I could think was: *Who is this person who is this person who is this person?*

"At Frackville," Ryan continued when I didn't say anything, as if to clear up any potential confusion—some other Alex, some other meeting place.

I didn't respond. I delivered my supplies to Stomping Grounds in silence, returned to the car in silence, and didn't speak for the first five minutes of the drive. I took in Ryan out of the corner of my eye. He thrummed his fingers on the steering wheel, then rubbed his palm up his cheek and down along his jaw, that same pattern every time he was angry or frustrated or concerned, up the cheek, down the cheek, along the jaw.

"I don't understand," I said. *I thought you hated him. I thought we both hated him.*

"I have to go," he said. "It's something I have to do."

"You don't think he did it?"

"It doesn't matter," Ryan said. "I'm not just going to abandon him."

I pulled my legs in toward me, turned toward the window. The crumbling warehouse rushed by to my right. "I didn't—"

"That's not what I mean," he said. "You don't owe him anything. I do. I have to go."

.   .   .

I stood in the empty kitchen of my empty apartment, heated a pot of water on the stove, and dumped in a package of tortellini, just enough for me. *Ryan could be somewhere else,* I told myself, although I didn't believe it. *And if he is at the prison, that's fine. It's something he has to do.*

I poured the tortellini into one chipped porcelain bowl and sat down alone at our drop-leaf table. I chewed the pasta, the gummy dough sticking to the roof of my mouth and sitting heavily in my stomach. Every few minutes, I looked up at the door, still closed, and imagined Ryan sitting in a yellow-lit visiting room with Alex, chatting about old times, laughing over old jokes like they were back in high school together and nothing had ever happened.

Visiting a murderer doesn't make him good, I thought to myself, tossing my bowl into the sink and throwing myself onto the couch, pulling Ryan's throw blanket up over my head. To Ryan, no one was ever *bad,* really. Everyone was potentially misunderstood, or having a bad day, or a product of a painful upbringing. *It just makes him naïve.*

The memory I always tried to focus on when I thought about Ryan still talking to Alex, after all this time: Alex helping Ryan up off the waxy floor of the middle school gymnasium. Ryan had a rough few years before high school started. It wasn't only that he was smaller and more timid than the other kids, although that certainly didn't help. It was also where he lived, and the way his khakis fell just at his ankle, even when he was standing, and the worn necklines of his T-shirts. Everyone gave him a hard time. I even remember Alex joining in once or twice, although he always denied it later when I brought it up.

But Alex came to Ryan's aid in eighth-grade gym class when

one of the boys, Daniel Myers, went too far. Emily and I had been sitting next to each other on the bleachers in our baggy white T-shirts and gym shorts, using a marker that Emily had snuck in to draw fake henna tattoos on our hands.

"Like this," Emily instructed, drawing a curving vine that looped up the side of my hand and around my pinky. I could barely hear her over the thud of thirty basketballs bouncing off the hardwood floor, the rattle of backboards, the sneakers scuffing against the ground.

Then suddenly the gym went silent, one basketball dribbling quietly to a stop, and we looked up to see Ryan on the ground, Daniel standing over him, chest puffed out and shifting his weight from foot to foot menacingly, like he might attack if Ryan tried to push himself back up. Ryan's hand cradled his shoulder. He looked frozen, like he didn't know what to do. He had no good options. He stayed on the ground.

"I didn't hit you!" Daniel was shouting, in a way that was not at all convincing, that seemed to say *I'll hit you again if you say otherwise.* "I didn't hit you. You were in my way."

Coach Dodd noticed the commotion at this point and started making his way across the gym toward them, whistle in hand, track pants swishing. Ryan's face turned a dark shade of red, and I know now what he must have been thinking: *This is going to be so much worse.*

But before Coach Dodd could work his way around the mass of students who had stopped what they were doing to watch, Alex approached Daniel, placed a friendly hand on his back, and leaned in toward him, saying something to him that made him back down. Alex held out his hand to Ryan, who took it gratefully, then gave him a few quick pats on the back and tossed a basketball to him.

A misplaced sense of duty. That's how I tried to understand Ryan's visits to Frackville. Loyalty. Alex looked out for Ryan when they were younger, and now it was Ryan's turn to repay that debt.

But then there's the memory I always came back to, that always sent those bad feelings flooding back. This was another Daniel Myers incident, one that took place two years later. Daniel was the only sophomore with a driver's license and a car, by virtue of having been held back a year. His parents had gotten him a gold Mustang, which he sped conspicuously through Calvary and eventually wrapped around a tree. He was fine; he staggered away drunk and unscratched. But before he totaled that car, he almost ran me over with it in the Calvary High parking lot. I was crossing toward the school's side entrance, a Styrofoam cup of Diet Coke in one hand and an empty paper carton in the other, when I heard him gun around the corner and screech to a halt. The Mustang stopped close enough to me that I could touch it. I smelled the burnt rubber from its skid marks. I spun to face the car, saw Daniel smirking back at me, and pitched the remains of my Diet Coke at his windshield.

"You stupid bitch!" he shouted at me.

"Watch where you're going!" I shouted back, kicking the front bumper. I marched back inside the school to find Emily and Alex sitting next to each other, backs against the faded red lockers, Emily picking the cheese off a slice of pizza from the cafeteria. Ryan sat across from them, eating a sandwich he had brought for lunch.

"What's wrong?" Alex asked, pushing himself up to standing when he saw the expression on my face.

"Daniel's a prick," I said. "He came this close to running me over."

"Jesus." Emily tucked a lock of hair behind her ear, then stretched out her legs and crossed them at the ankles. "He's going to kill someone someday."

"You want me to take him out for you?" Alex asked, jokingly, wrapping his arms around my waist.

"Please," I said. "You'd be doing the world a favor."

Ryan was quiet, eyes focused on his sandwich, and that bothered me. I wanted him to agree.

"Ryan knows," I said, maybe too loudly. "Remember that time he almost beat you up in gym class?"

"I wouldn't put it that way," Ryan said, his voice barely audible.

"Emily and I saw the whole thing, and I'm not sure how else you would describe it," I continued at the same volume. "If Alex hadn't been there . . ." At that point, Ryan cringed, and I realized I had gone too far. "He's just an asshole, is all I'm saying."

"I get it," Ryan said, and, for a second, I felt vindicated. But then he continued: "We don't know what else he has going on, though."

"No one likes a martyr, Ryan," I snipped. That's when the bell marking the end of lunch rang, and I went to class feeling irritated and angry and guilty, all at the same time.

I lay there under his fleece blanket waiting for Ryan, trying not to think about waiting for him, trying not to picture Alex, ten years older, just an hour-and-a-half drive away, still reachable when Emily was not. *He's loyal,* I reminded myself, but it only made me angrier, as if I wasn't allowed to be upset because Ryan was *doing the right thing.*

It was an hour later when he finally came home. He nodded at me, then looked down toward the ground, scratching his head guiltily, as if waiting for me to say something. I waited a few seconds before asking him how his day was.

"Fine," he said, not volunteering any additional information. "Have you eaten?"

"Yes."

Ryan nodded, then made his way to the fridge, studying its contents while rubbing his beard: up the cheek, down the cheek, along the jaw. His clothes fit him now. He wore an Easton shirt under green flannel, jeans that were the right length. He turned away from me when he closed the refrigerator door again, focusing his attention on the microwave, the numbers ticking down.

"Anything interesting happen at work today?" I asked, and Ryan's shoulders relaxed and his weight shifted to one side. I could tell, even without seeing his face, that he was thankful for the mundane question.

"Library training for the seniors working on a thesis." He turned back toward me with an expression that was halfway between a grin and a grimace. "Everyone's favorite day."

I frowned at him sympathetically, told him I was sorry, and really meant it. I never understood how Ryan spent so much time around the Easton students, with their lazy self-importance and loud, chaotic way of barreling through life, as if there were no other people in the world. Stomping Grounds isn't that far from the campus—probably not even a mile—but the river that divides downtown from campus acts as a natural barrier. It would have required just enough initiative to cross over that they usually stayed away.

Ryan sat down at the table with a bowl of leftovers I didn't recognize. I wondered how long they had been hiding in the fridge. "I had an idea for the coffee shop," he said, poking at a noodle with his fork.

"Oh yeah?" *On your drive?* I stopped myself.

"We should put up some flyers on campus!" He grinned at me and waited, as though that deserved a big reaction.

I turned away from him, folded the throw blanket, and placed it neatly over the back of the couch. "Flyers? That's the idea?"

"On campus!" Ryan shook his hands for emphasis. "Break into a new market! It might help with the afternoon slog. Students drink coffee at all hours of the day."

"Students sit in coffee shops at all hours of the day. They don't buy anything."

Ryan bit into a cob of baby corn and shook his head in playful disagreement, now completely at ease, like this was just a normal evening. Like he hadn't done anything wrong. *He didn't do anything wrong,* I reminded myself. "It could help," he continued. "I read that—"

"I'm doing fine," I said. "I don't need your help." My voice must have been sharper than I intended, because Ryan tensed and stopped talking. I sat down across from him, rubbed at the corners of my eyes. I adjusted the orange silk flowers poking out of the glass vase on our table, moving one of the flowers up to the front and back again. Ryan watched, waiting. I pushed the vase back toward the wall.

"Julia Reynolds came by the shop today."

"Julia?" Ryan's head tilted in confusion. "What was she doing there?"

"Raising awareness," I said, using air quotes. "Harassing me. She came by to give me a picture of Alex, to remind me of how innocent he is."

Ryan shook his head. "She's not trying to harass you," he said. "She's just misguided. She's had a tough—"

"*She* opted into this," I said, my voice raised. I had suspected that Ryan would push back—he always had a soft spot for the underdog—but it still stung. "I know she plays the grieving, put-upon girlfriend, but she *chose* this. She had no relationship with Alex or Emily. For all I know, she still doesn't have any relationship with Alex. All we have is her word, and—"

"She does have a relationship with Alex," Ryan said, softly, and I grabbed the fake flowers again, took one out, stabbed it back in, like it was important to get them just so, the right angle, like they could make the tiny table that took up too much space in our kitchen look homey, not just small.

"I know you haven't always gotten along in the past—" Ryan began.

I pulled up the text on my phone, pushed it toward him.

"She sent me that."

He looked down at the text, his eyes widening.

"What is this?"

"Just a friendly message from your poor, misguided Julia."

Ryan shook his head again. "There's no number on this."

It's her, I wanted to shout. *I'm telling you, it's her.* I tried to stay calm.

"I got this text this morning, and then Julia shows up outside my door ranting and raving about how I'm responsible for getting *her* Alex into trouble." It seemed so obvious. "She's unhinged. And she hates me."

Ryan's forehead creased with concern. He rubbed the side of his face. "Micah, that's disturbing," he said. "Whoever sent that—"

"*Julia* sent it. I don't know why you're defending her." I stood up from the table, intending to walk away, but then thought better of it.

"I mean, I get it," I said. "She had a hard time in high school. Is that it?"

Ryan clenched his jaw and didn't respond.

"That doesn't make her nice. Not everyone who had a hard time is *nice*. She might just be pathetic."

Dark patches of red grew on Ryan's cheeks.

"She's obsessive and vindictive. She's trying to *hurt* me."

"You don't know where this came from." Ryan enunciated each word carefully, his eyes rising up again to meet mine. "There's no number on it. And this seems out of character for Julia."

"Because you're such a good judge of character."

"No worse than you." Ryan held my gaze for a second longer, then looked down and resumed eating, his cheeks still burning red.

"How's Alex?" I couldn't hold it back any longer.

"Jesus, Micah."

"What? That's where you were."

He put down his fork and stood up without looking me in the eye. The half-eaten leftovers hit the bottom of the trash can with a thud. He disappeared into the office, closing the door behind him. He didn't slam it, like I would have, but shut it gently, the latch of the door clicking softly into place.

.   .   .

Ryan apologized the next day, or offered what I chose to view as an apology at the time. I woke up to find him already in the kitchen, hunched over a mug of coffee, eyelids heavy and eyes glassy like he hadn't slept well. I hadn't slept, either. When I shuffled out of the bedroom in a ratty T-shirt and sweatpants, hair matted down to the side of my head, I saw him sitting there and averted my eyes. I didn't know if we were talking. But he stood up, came toward me, and wrapped his arms around me. I burrowed my face into his neck.

"I love you," he said, and I heard *I'll stop going*.

"He took her away," I said, and he said, "I know, I know."

7

Alex and I were lab partners our sophomore year of high school. We entered the classroom that first day seconds before the late bell rang and took seats that happened to be next to each other. I leaned across the aisle toward Natalie and passed her a note I had carefully folded into a pull-tab envelope, the corners shaded in like a checkerboard. Alex twisted in his seat to talk to Matt and Brian behind us. It must have been a game day because all three of them were wearing their navy spandex soccer jerseys, and Brian was sporting an American flag–print sweatband.

I had a knee-jerk skepticism of athletes back then—a holdover from middle school, probably, when the height of comedy was tricking someone less popular than you into thinking you actually wanted to have a conversation with them. But I had noticed Alex eating lunch with Ryan at one of the picnic tables in the school courtyard, and so my guard was a little lower than it might otherwise have been. Mr. Polis cleared his throat and handed Chelsea Keene a blank seating chart to pass around.

"These will be your seats for the rest of the year," he said. "No switching, no drama. I don't care if you're not currently sitting next to your best friend. That's not my problem. Understood?"

I glanced over at Alex, who twisted around again to face the front of the classroom and leaned back in his plastic chair.

"Looks like we're stuck together," I said. Maybe still a little on guard. I wanted to let him know this wasn't my first-choice arrangement, either.

He leaned over, so close that our shoulders were almost touching.

"I'll do my best not to blow us up," he said, giving me a conspiratorial smile. "But no promises."

Mr. Polis looked in our direction, a warning, and then turned his back and chalked out a diagram on the board: mixtures, pure substances, elements, compounds. Alex bumped my shoulder with his, then leaned back in his seat, his legs spread out wide.

"So," Mr. Polis said. "What is *matter*?"

I stood next to Alex at our lab station two weeks later, my head barely up to his shoulder. He squeezed our metal striker, his forehead creased with concentration.

"I think it's the same stuff they use to make WarHeads," he said.

"I don't think they'd trust us with explosives."

"No, the candy." He set down the striker and stuck his finger in the small dish of white powder on the table.

"You're not supposed to touch it." I winced. Mr. Polis had given us a long list of instructions on how to handle experiment materials: no touching, no direct inhaling, the emergency shower and eyewash station were in the corner.

Alex pulled his hand back, examined the crystals on his finger. He opened his mouth.

"Don't!" I said, grabbing his wrist. He grinned, and I tried to hold in a laugh. I snorted instead.

"Ms. Wilkes. Mr. Swift," Mr. Polis said, bored, from the front of the room. At the table next to us, Natalie met my eyes, raised an eyebrow. Michelle Peterson, beside her, focused intently on lighting their Bunsen burner.

Alex relaxed his arm, and I pulled the lab sheet closer to me, studied the instructions. "It looks like we're supposed to—"

Alex opened his mouth and lifted his hand again, and I grabbed it, pressed it down onto the table, stifling another laugh. "Don't *do* that!" I said, and he grinned back down at me, our faces close. He pulled his hand out from my grasp, stuck his finger in his mouth. I gasped, and he made a small, choking sound, then laughed and wiped his hand on his jeans.

"It's the WarHead stuff," he said. "Sour."

I swatted his arm.

"Holy shit," I whispered at him. "That was dumb."

"It's not bad," he insisted, pushing the bowl toward me. "You should try some."

"I would have thought this went without saying, Mr. Swift," Mr. Polis said, suddenly behind us. "But no *eating* the lab materials."

"Ah, sorry," Alex said. Both of us tried to keep a straight face. "My bad."

Mr. Polis shook his head and returned to the front of the classroom, and I snorted again, and across the table I could see Natalie watching, a knowing, amused smirk across her face.

"Oh, *Alex,*" Natalie crooned at me by my locker after class, fluttering her eyes and pawing at my arm. "Oh, Alex, *don't.*"

"That's not what I did." I laughed, pushing her off of me.

"Sure," Natalie said, unconvinced. "The two of you—"

"What's this about?" Emily, behind us. She opened her locker, right beside mine. Winters and Wilkes: always together.

I smiled bashfully, feeling a little like I had been caught.

"Micah's new boyfriend," Natalie said, elbowing me. I elbowed her back.

"He's not—"

"Alex Swift," Natalie continued. "He—"

"It was nothing," I explained, talking over her. "We were doing an experiment—"

"If that's what they're calling it now," Natalie said. She turned back to Emily. "They basically can't keep their hands off each other."

"That's not—"

"Oh, *Alex,*" Natalie said again, leaning in toward me.

"He was trying to eat the acid," I said, and Natalie and I both started giggling again, and Emily gave me a thin smile.

"Sounds like maybe you had to be there," she said, the locker clicking shut behind her.

I felt a twist of guilt, like I had been rebuked. When I didn't see her again between our afternoon classes, I left her a note on the inside of her locker. I still have her combination memorized, after all this time: combination 18-36-14, locker number 235. Sitting on the shelf of her locker was a shoebox for the notes we passed each other, folded carefully into hearts and pull-tab envelopes and triangular paper footballs that could be flicked across a desk or easily concealed and passed from palm to palm. Hanging on the door, a mirror with a blue plastic frame at eye level, her name written down the side in Wite-Out, a small white board, and a strip of photo booth pictures from the shore, Emily tanned and me freckled.

I grabbed the dry erase marker from the white board and wrote out a message—*you okay?*—along with two bubbly hearts. She answered later that day on my own white board: *Fine. I'm just fucking exhausted.* I erased my last message and replaced it with a new one: *I MISS YOU!!!*

My chest tightens. I've spent so much time trying not to think of them. Even after Julia's visit to Stomping Grounds, I tried to put all of them out of my head the best way I knew how: I gave myself tasks to keep occupied. I made a new sign for the outside of the shop, large planks of wood stained dark and STOMPING GROUNDS stenciled on using the "Cold White" acrylic paint that I nabbed from Ryan's workstation. I booked a musician to play on Thursday evenings, to give the shop a more "urban" feel. His name was Tony Swanson and he played mostly kids' birthday parties, but the customers didn't know that. Acoustic guitar is acoustic guitar. And I gave in to Ryan's suggestion and put together a flyer for bulletin boards on the Easton campus, spending a whole afternoon trying to find the right font and the right clip art coffee, one with tiny lines of steam rising out of a classic mug.

"It has to look just right," I told Ryan as he leaned over my shoulder to see the semifinished product.

"It has to have the name and address on it," Ryan said. "And maybe some incentive to get them to cross the river, like free coffee. That's about it."

Whether it was the new sign or the flyers or the musical genius of Tony Swanson, something seemed to be working, as things got markedly busier. We still had the regular morning crowd, of course—the commuters who stopped in on their way to work and got a cup of coffee to go—but new faces started showing up. College kids entered in groups of twos and threes, books and papers and highlighters spread out across their tables, the cords of their laptop chargers stretched into low-hanging trip wires. Most of the books went unopened. They chatted with each other or stared at their computer screens. But they did buy just enough that I couldn't complain.

It made me forget, for a little while. "You have to have goals," is what the therapist I saw after Emily died, Dr. Sanders, used to tell me. "They give you something to focus on." She was my mother's idea. That is to say, my mother made me see her; the sessions were "nonnegotiable" as long as I was living in her house. Every Tuesday after school, my mother would drop me off on the curb outside Dr. Sanders's office, which was housed in a strip mall that seemed vaguely medical in purpose, between an orthodontist's office and a wellness center. She'd watch me go through the frosted-glass front door like I was seven years old again and had to be monitored to make sure I made it inside safely. Whenever anyone asked me what I was up to on a Tuesday, I told them I had to visit my grandmother at the nursing home. I must have seemed like a very devoted granddaughter.

The waiting room in Dr. Sanders's office was just like the waiting room of any doctor's office, except with better reading material: *Vogue* instead of *Reader's Digest* and *Highlights*. The walls were beige and decorated with drab geometric prints, all sharp lines with browns and dark greens and purples. A row of chairs faced the receptionist's desk, each with a plastic frame. A stack of pamphlets like the ones at the police station, but nicer, less blunt. *Relationship Health,* these said, a picture of two hands clasped together on the front. I'd sit in that waiting room, slouched down and hunched over, reading through back issues until my name was called.

Once the receptionist let me know it was my turn to enter, I'd pass through the doorway into Dr. Sanders's office, where everything was brighter and more welcoming. I assumed that it was designed that way, a trick that Dr. Sanders had picked up somewhere. She always seemed like that kind of person—the kind who listens carefully for tips and tricks at therapist conferences and implements them faithfully, the kind who uses modules and strategies rather than listening to what her patients actually have to say. She had painted the walls a creamy white and hung pictures that were impressionistic and soft, made up of light blue and pink dabs of paint.

The couch I sat on, across from Dr. Sanders's chair, was big with brightly colored throw pillows, comfy-looking and welcoming.

Only, the couch wasn't really comfortable at all, despite all appearances, and I could never figure out why. The cushions were too soft, maybe, or the couch was just deep enough, the seat just far enough off the ground, that I couldn't lean back and keep my feet on the floor at the same time. I assume Dr. Sanders planned that out, too: an interrogation technique, designed to keep her patients disoriented and off-balance, to make them talk.

She was adamant that routines and goals were a cure-all, capable of smoothing over any psychological problem. "It might be tempting to just curl up in bed and pull the sheets over your head and never come out," she told me with a small, knowing smile, blond hair smoothed into a sharp bob, "but that won't make you feel any better. What will help is giving yourself tasks to complete, things to get done, and then accomplishing those things. Let's work on setting some manageable goals today. College applications?"

Maybe that's what I've been doing all this time, after all. I've been giving myself goals, focusing on tasks. *How much coffee do we need to order from the roaster this week?* It worked for short bursts. Days or weeks would go by when I wouldn't think of Emily. But it never took much to send it all rushing back: a teenage boy wearing too much cologne, a sip of vodka masked with powdered Kool-Aid, the crunch of leaves beneath a boot.

Or, in this case, a photograph from Emily's locker that I hadn't seen in ten years, small white patches along the top edge where some of the glossy finish had been pulled off by tape.

The morning the photograph reappeared, Stomping Grounds was unusually quiet. The few customers that we did have trickled in, shuffling to the counter with dripping umbrellas and soggy boots that left small rings of water on the floor. Natalie, who had her baby strapped onto her, swayed gently from side to side next to the counter, talking inappropriately loudly as usual about how Jack had seen Michelle Peterson at the Tavern that weekend "sloppy as ever." "Now, what *Jack* was doing at the Tavern while I was stuck at home with these two monsters—"

The door chimed and my head turned. The long-haired Easton student—the one who had just watched while Mrs. Klein struggled—ambled in, his black sweatshirt nearly soaked through. He sat down at the same table where Mrs. Klein had been sitting, a puddle beginning to form beneath him. He pulled out a laptop and then scanned the room, looking from Ashton, who was snapping crayons into small pieces, to Natalie, to the closed door of the storage room.

"She's not here," I said, figuring he had come back to flirt with Anna. "She's got school."

He smirked back at me, like he was just shrugging it off, no big deal. But his eyes—small and a little too far apart—flashed with irritation. He stood up again, his jeans peeling wetly off the seat, and walked toward me.

"I'll take a small coffee," he said, placing a few dollar bills down on the counter. "Thanks."

He took his seat and I turned to Natalie, who had watched the exchange with amused interest.

"Who is that?" she stage-whispered to me.

"No one."

Natalie raised her eyebrows long enough to make it clear she didn't believe me but let it drop. She pulled her phone out of her diaper bag and glanced down at it.

"Did you see this?" she asked. "From Chelsea Keene?"

"I've been ignoring those," I said. Chelsea Keene had planned our class reunion for Thanksgiving weekend, when a substantial portion of our class would be back in town visiting family. She had announced the date six months earlier, and we had been receiving monthly reminders ever since.

"Hi gang!" Natalie read, opening her eyes wide and stretching her mouth into Chelsea's permanent grin, her teeth never quite touching. "I can't believe reunion time is almost here! I feel so old! Crying laughing emoji crying laughing emoji!"

"Ugh. Chelsea." I poured a coffee for the Easton student and set it down on the counter. He could come and get it himself.

"Looks like we're renting out the back room at Rosalina's," Natalie continued as she read through the rest of the message, dropping Chelsea's smile. "God, I love their bread sticks."

"I'm not going to that."

"What?" The baby started squawking, short high-pitched shrieks, and Natalie's bounces became more enthusiastic as she patted him with her empty hand. The Easton student shot a glance in our direction.

"I said, I'm not going. I have no interest in seeing any of those people." I ducked into the storage room and grabbed a mop.

"I'm definitely going," Natalie said. "I want to see who's gotten fat."

"Natalie."

"I'm just kidding. I already know who's gotten fat. That's what Facebook is for."

I glanced over at the long-haired boy and pointedly sopped up the wet footprints that covered the floor.

"Oh, come on, Micah," Natalie said, a few quick taps on her phone before she slipped it back into her pocket. "It'll be fun."

"No." I replaced the mop and grabbed my raincoat off the back of the storage room door. "I'm stepping outside for a few minutes. Can you text me if anyone new comes in?"

"That's a nasty habit," she scolded.

"Yeah, yeah," I said, already halfway out the front door. Natalie didn't really want me to quit. She liked bumming cigarettes off me after two glasses of wine.

I slipped around to the back alley, not hiding, exactly, but far enough in that I couldn't be easily spotted from the street. I slid a cigarette out of the pack, keeping an eye on Church Street the whole time in case a customer strolled by, or an old friend of my mom's who would have been disappointed to see me smoking. No one came past.

I noticed something affixed to one of the Main Street windows as I turned the corner to return to the shop, and I stepped closer to see what it was. There, dripping with beads of rain, was a photograph from Emily's locker, one that she added our junior year. Me, Emily, Ryan, and Alex at the Northridge Diner, four mugs and tiny piles of white plastic creamer cups in front of us. Emily sat straight-backed and poised, head turned toward the camera and tilted downward with a closemouthed smile, eyes angled up. Ryan peered around her in his scruffy sweatshirt, leaning in toward the table so that he could be seen. Alex stretched out in the corner of the booth, taking up space, his arm draped over the seat lazily. I leaned in toward him, giddy, smiling.

I sucked in my breath and pulled the picture down off the window. I slipped it into my pocket and turned around, looking for any sign of movement on Main Street. It was empty. I opened the door to Stomping Grounds slowly, half-expecting to see Julia Reynolds sitting with folded hands at one of the tables, waiting for me.

"Did she come back?" I asked Natalie.

"Who?" Natalie was cutting an apple into tiny bite-size pieces for Ashton, who picked each one up to examine it and then threw it down onto the floor. She seemed to barely register that I had come back inside.

"Julia," I said, my heart dropping. Natalie was supposed to have been keeping an eye out. "She was here again. She left this on the front window."

I pulled the picture out of my pocket and handed it to Natalie.

"Where did this come from?" She turned it over in her hand, studying the light-gray Kodak imprint on the back.

"She stuck it right there," I said, gesturing toward the street.

Natalie flipped the picture over again and squinted at it, trying to discern its significance. "You were all such babies." She handed the picture back to me and took a sip of her coffee. "Ryan looks like he's twelve."

"It was taped up in Emily's locker."

Natalie's eyebrows rose. She set the coffee down, sliding it toward the center of the table, where small hands couldn't reach it. "Why would Julia have that?"

I bristled and stuffed the photograph back into my pocket. "She must have gotten it from Alex."

"How would *Alex* have gotten it?" She lifted her eyebrows further, foundation caking in the creases of her forehead.

I shrugged, pulled off my raincoat, and hung it in the storage room. "We all knew her combination."

Natalie twisted around in her chair to face me, her lips pressed together skeptically. "You know who *would* have access to Emily's things?" She waited for me to respond, and when I didn't: "Joshua."

I shook my head, blasted the water in the dishwashing sink, felt its hard sting as I stuck my hands under.

"Oh come on, Micah," she said, rolling her eyes in frustration. "This is exactly what he did back in high school."

The pictures had been taken from the decorative frames that sat on top of Emily's dresser and the nightstand by her bed. You slipped the first picture through the slats in my locker, and it fluttered out as I was changing out my books between history and physics. Fourteen-year-old versions of me and Emily looked back at me, eye shadow and lip gloss carefully applied for freshman-year Homecoming, nervous grins showing braces. I sucked in air through my teeth. Heads turned and I stuffed the photo back into my locker, letting it fall into the pile of junk at the bottom, where it settled between the locker's steel back and my old health class binder.

"He hasn't been back to Calvary in a long time," I said.

"I mean, would he call you up if he were back in town?"

"It's not him. This is different." I shut off the water, dried my hands, ducked down to rearrange glasses on the shelves behind the counter.

"Yeah, what he did before was worse," Natalie said, raising her voice in response to my disappearance. "He left you death threats."

"He never left me death threats."

"He left you something."

I rubbed at my eyes with my palms. "Pages of Emily's diary."

"Right," Natalie said, holding up one hand and nodding her head slowly, as if that confirmed what she had been saying all along.

I went back to cleaning dishes, and Natalie shook her head in disbelief. "You need to be careful. He's not stable."

"*Julia Reynolds* isn't stable," I shot back, steaming water ricocheting off of a spoon and spraying up out of the sink. "And she's *here*, in Calvary. She was just here at Stomping Grounds. She hung up a picture of Alex in almost the *exact same spot*." I gestured at the window with the spoon. "She's the one who's doing this."

"Fine," Natalie said, raising her hands in a dramatic gesture of defeat. "O-*kay*. It's from *Ju*-lia."

The diary entries that you left me had been folded up into little paper footballs. You stuffed them into my backpack when I left it unattended in the hallway, so tightly that when I unzipped my bag a few of them tumbled out onto the gray-speckled floor. I unfolded one of them right there in the science wing, smoothing out the creases with my fingers, and immediately recognized the hasty handwriting, letters switching indiscriminately between cursive and print, small and tight on the page.

Alex was waiting for me at the studio today. He came straight from practice, his hair still damp with sweat. I stepped out onto the landing and saw him leaning against the brick wall beneath the stairwell. I felt that same tangle of emotion I feel before a performance—adrenaline, nerves and excitement, almost indistinguishable from one another.

There was a split second when he hadn't yet seen me when I thought I might turn and go back inside. Wait him out. The Lionels wouldn't mind if I hung around. The next day at school, he'd pretend he hadn't come to see me, and I'd pretend I didn't know. Everything back to normal. Order restored.

But then he looked up. He raised his hand, pretending to be sheepish, and grinned. I looked behind me to see if anyone noticed. Mrs. Lionel had already started ushering the Wiggle Worms into the studio, and Mr. Lionel was in his office at the end of the hallway, his door closed. I rushed down the stairwell and swatted Alex on his arm.

"Someone might see," I told him.

"So what?" He hooked a finger through my belt loop. "We're just two friends taking a walk."

The door to the studio opened again, and Mr. Lionel came out, resting his palms against the railing. I backed away from Alex and waved up at him. I'm not sure what he saw.

"They wouldn't approve," I told Alex.

"That's what you're worried about?" Alex laughed, sticking his hands back into his pockets.

"I worry about everything," I told him.

I froze, unsure of what to do. A part of me worried it was *wrong* to have them, that at any moment a teacher or police officer might swoop in, ask me what I was doing with those, and drag me off to God-knows-where.

Why do you have those, Micah? they'd ask. *Why do you have a dead girl's diary entries?*

She was my friend, I'd say—a weak defense—and they'd shake their heads at me, disappointed.

We thought you didn't even like her.

I looked around to see if anyone else had noticed, sure that there would be a cluster of girls peering out of a nearby alcove, watching, or a teacher rushing down the hall's slight incline. But all around me was movement: freshmen grabbing books out of their lockers and slamming them shut with a metallic click, bags being zipped shut and hoisted onto shoulders for class, jeans and khakis and legs moving past me, students flowing out of the science wing and into the main hallway that looped the school. I stuffed the notes back into my backpack as quickly as I could, pushed myself up, and inserted myself into the stream of movement, allowing myself to be carried toward the trash can at the end of the wing. I stopped, peering down into it. It was filled almost to the brim with leftover pieces of lunch—pizza crusts, grimy plastic bags, chocolate-stained wrappers—and I couldn't bring myself to leave Emily's diary entries there, mixed in with everyone's trash. I slid down the wall next to the garbage can and tears started rolling down my cheeks.

It was Ryan who finally came by and asked what was going on. I nodded at my backpack, which lay on the floor next to me. Ryan unzipped it, unfolded a note, and then stuffed it back into the bag with disgust. He sat with me beside that trash can for the whole next period, waving off the occasional wary administrator who started toward us like they were about to deliver a lecture before realizing who we were and doing a quick about-face, unsure of what to say to two grieving teens. When the bell rang again, Ryan helped me up and grabbed my backpack, taking it with him. The notes you left were gone when he gave it back the next day.

That was a long time ago, though, and on the same day the photograph was taped to Stomping Grounds' window, the Stonesport Maps & Prints Gallery hosted a lecture and small display on "the Cape's ocean graveyard." The display featured pictures of the reconstructed hull of the *Sparrow-Hawk,* wrecked at Potanumaquut in 1626, with a careful look at how it was pieced back together centuries later. Basic proportions gleaned from guidelines for ship-building documented in the sixteenth century; specifics shaded in using the report of nineteenth-century shipbuilders made when the wreck was uncovered. There was a write-up on the event, and others like it, in the local paper, which included a quote from you in the second-to-last paragraph.

"It's a fifty-mile stretch where more than a thousand ships have gone down," you told the reporter. No picture, but I could imagine how you might have looked when you said it. Eyes wide and shining, hands waving excitedly in front of you, long fingers outstretched. "We have such an incredible, tumultuous history here," you said, "and pieces of it are still out there, just off that shore. We're looking forward to bringing some of that history to life."

That's how I know it wasn't you this time. I never thought it was, not really, but you can't blame me for checking. You know what happened before.

8

The corpse of a deer sprawls across the shoulder, one hoof stretching out into my lane. Its neck has been snapped; its head twists back around toward me, watching me approach. Its eyes, bulging and glassy. I give it a wide berth, wonder how long it will be left out here in the cold before the Game Commission comes out to collect it.

I check my phone. Discomfort nags at me, but I try to set it aside. It's been a long time since we've spoken, Joshua, I know that. But we have a shared history: I've known you since you were a child. I still remember that animal collection you had at eight. Your bearded dragon, sunning himself on a plastic rock in a terrarium lit by a heat lamp. Your cockroaches clinging to the sides of a clear box with a red plastic cover, small vents in the side and a handle on top for transporting around the house. The snake you found in your mother's garden, scooped up from the dirt, and brought triumphantly inside.

The day you found the snake, Emily had set up her room to be a stage, seats for the audience demarcated by pale pink, beaded throw pillows scattered across the floor, and we were rehearsing an Emily and Micah original. The music was piped in from the Casio keyboard in the corner. Emily was practicing a series of spins and I was fiddling with the settings on the keyboard when you strode into the room, holding your new discovery out to us. It wound around your wrist, its head bobbing.

"It won't hurt you," you said. "It's an eastern milk snake. *Lampropeltis triangulum triangulum*. Sometimes people confuse them for copperheads, but you can tell it's not because of this marking here." You traced the U-shaped marking on its head with your index finger, and it arched its body in response. "The belly is different, too. It looks like a checkerboard. See?"

"Get that out of here," Emily said.

"It's an eastern milk snake," you said again. "It's not venomous. Here, I'll show you." And you ran back to your room to grab an illustrated encyclopedia of reptiles, the corners worn down and the binding split open, the front and back cover held together by masking tape.

"I don't *care* if it's venomous," Emily said. "I don't want it in here."

"Usually two to three feet in length, but sometimes they can grow to almost five feet," you said, reading the fact sheet next to a carefully inked drawing.

"*Out,* Joshua," Emily said, pointing toward her bedroom door. *"Get out."*

"It's not a—"

"Mom!"

You blinked, finally realizing you weren't welcome, and I remember the hurt that washed across your face, the disappointment.

"Can I see it?" I asked, and the hurt subsided, replaced by cautious optimism.

"Micah, stop encouraging him."

"You want to hold it?" you asked, holding it toward me.

"No," I said, stepping back a little. "I'll just look."

"They don't usually bite." You held your arm out toward me. The snake curled around your wrist, its movements slow and fluid. I reached out tentatively, ran a finger along its scales, pulled back when it swung its head toward me.

Your mother hovered in the doorway, amused.

"Mom," Emily huffed, her arms crossed over herself. "Joshua won't leave us alone."

Your mother ruffled your hair, then turned to me and winked. "I think somebody's got a little crush."

"Mom!" Emily said again.

"Okay, okay." But she lingered a moment longer. "I was just talking to Mr. Lionel about last weekend. He said you were fantastic. Really fantastic."

Emily glanced at me out of the corner of her eye.

"He gave me a list of things we're going to work on to be competitive. He said—"

"Can we talk about this later?" Emily interrupted.

"Of course," your mother said. "Of course. I'm just proud of you, that's all."

"Mom."

"I'm going, I'm going!" She turned her attention to you. "Come on, kiddo." She placed her hand on your back and guided you back out into the hallway as you continued to explain your find to her: the black-and-white scales on its belly, the rounded blotches along its back.

"All right," Emily said, clapping her hands together. "Let's take it from the top."

I take another glance down at my phone. Still just a blank screen.

After finding that photograph at Stomping Grounds, I left Natalie in charge of the shop and set off for Harris Law Offices, the personal injury firm where Julia worked. Julia answered the phone and managed calendars and, I assume, pressed the lawyers for legal insights into Alex's case. The devoted girlfriend, all aspects of her life dedicated to Alex's cause.

I pulled up the hood of my coat, but it did little to stop the rain, which soaked through the thin fabric and crept up the legs of my pants. I didn't mind it, though. It felt good to have a specific direction in mind. I marched along Main Street to the edge of downtown, where consignment shops and boutiques selling homemade jewelry start to give way to drab, reddish-gray office buildings with banks and convenience stores inside. *Julia is behind this,* I told myself with each slam of my boot against the sidewalk. *Julia is the one bringing all of this back.* Each time the image of Emily threatened to surface, her body broken and twisted at the wrong angle on the forest floor, I thought of Julia instead, sitting in a dark corner of her home, chewing absently on the cuff of Alex's letterman jacket. Writing him a letter: an innocent request for a photograph, something to remember him by. *Sure,* he'd say, unassuming. *Just ask my mom. Help yourself to whatever you want.*

I slowed when I reached her building, yellow brick with a decal of a large, tilted scale stuck to the storefront window. Blinds covered in a thin layer of dust blocked my view of inside. I straightened myself, reminded myself why I was there, and pushed open the frosted-glass door.

A television on the back wall, turned down with closed captioning, showed a man examining a fishing hook, then holding it up to the camera, turning it in his hand. A few chairs were pushed together in clumps. Only one was occupied, by a middle-aged man with his arm in a sling, tufts of hair sticking out around the side of his head, an old T-shirt hanging down over his swollen gut. To the side of the television was the front desk, and Julia behind it, wearing a crumpled gray sweater. Loose tendrils of hair had escaped from her braid and hung down around her face. Her nose twitched, and she rubbed at it with the back of her hand.

"You want—you'd like to come in Monday? We're not usually— well, let me check." Another sniffle. She turned to look at her computer screen and must have caught a glimpse of me as she did so, because she startled, then averted her eyes, focusing with exaggerated intensity on her monitor. She shifted in her seat as I moved closer, wrapping the loops of the telephone cord around her index finger. I leaned over the side of her desk.

"No, we can't do that. Maybe Tuesday? At nine?" She gnawed on her thumbnail, already short and ragged.

"Julia," I said, softly but firmly. Colored Post-it notes stuck off the sides of her monitor. Usernames and passwords. *All of our dreams can come true if we have the courage to pursue them.* She held up a finger without looking at me, then poked a few keys on her keyboard with an aggressive *tap tap tap.*

"Okay, we'll see you then. Okay. Thank you."

She placed the phone back into the receiver, then turned to face me. Her eyes were narrowed, her jaw clenched.

"What are you doing here?" she asked, the tone of her voice so different from the breathy, passive voice she had been using on the phone that it caught me off guard. I rolled my shoulders, pulled myself together.

"I came here to talk to you."

"If you don't have an appointment, I'm going to have to ask you to leave." She swung back around to her computer and grabbed the mouse, *click click click,* as if to make a point that she had more important things to do.

"Julia, I know we—"

To the right of her computer sat a white picture frame with tiny decorative flowers along the edges, dust settling into their petals. I leaned forward over her desk to try to make sense of the photograph inside. It showed Alex as an adult. His hair, once sandy blond, was cropped short, shaved down to look like a shadow. His shoulders had filled out; he clasped his arms, heavy and muscular, in front of him like he was posing for a prom picture. His brown eyes still had the same warmth, but with more pronounced lines at the edges. He stood in front of a colorfully painted backdrop that seemed to contain a little bit of everything: a bridge crossing over a serene-looking creek, snowcapped mountains in the background, a rose garden in the forefront. Painted by fellow prisoners, maybe; rolled out on special occasions so that prisoners could take photos as keepsakes for family or pen pals.

I thought of Alex, at fifteen, in gym class. Emily and I had shuffled next to each other at the perimeter of the gymnasium, on our third lap of four, our hands hanging loosely at our sides. A metal cage of rubber balls had been wheeled out of the storage closet for dodgeball day. In front of us, Alex and Matt and Brian jostled and elbowed at each other, until finally Brian went flying across the waxed floor, rolling dramatically onto his hands and knees and pulling the back of his shirt up over his head for no apparent reason.

"Man down!" Alex laced his hands behind his head, and the group of them laughed, Brian rolling onto his back and rocking from side to side.

"I mean," Emily said as we gained on them, "they're basically primates."

"Nice form, Wilkes!" Alex shouted, jogging backward, and I could feel my cheeks warming. I was trying to think of something to say back when Matt grabbed a loose dodgeball that had rolled across the gym floor and pegged Brian.

"Gentlemen!" the gym teacher called from across the room, as Brian mock-howled, then sprang to his feet.

"Barbarians." Emily rolled her eyes. Alex flashed me a grin—me, he had picked me out, smiled at me—and kept running.

I must have been staring at the photograph for too long, because Julia noticed and turned it facedown on her desk. I drew back.

"I know we haven't always gotten along," I started. A concession, a way of easing into the conversation. Julia sniffled again but still didn't look at me.

"Julia," I said, a little sharper, trying to get her attention. "I know you don't like me. I understand that. But you need to leave me alone."

"I don't know what you're talking about." She kept clicking and typing, clicking and typing, but I could see it was all just a ruse. Microsoft Outlook opened, closed, opened, closed. Behind her, an umbrella leaning up against the wall dripped water into a small puddle on the floor, confirming my suspicions. It seemed, to me, that the edges of her lips had begun to curl up into a barely contained smile, like she thought she was getting away with something.

"Oh, come on," I said. "Your visits to Stomping Grounds? The texts? It's fucking twisted."

Julia's eyes flashed toward me, just for an instant, but then she caught herself and focused her attention back toward the screen. She sucked in her bottom lip and clicked through the emails in her inbox.

"This might be fun for you," I said, moving to the front of her desk, right in front of her, where she had to see me. "But it's real for me. Do you understand? Emily was my best friend. And Alex—"

"Fun?" Julia said, finally meeting my eye, her hand still wrapped around the mouse. "My boyfriend has spent the last ten years in prison for a crime he didn't commit. I've had to wait for him—and I'll continue to wait, as long as it takes—but it has not been *fun* for me, Micah."

"Jesus Christ," I said, throwing my head back in disbelief. The man in the sling looked up from his phone to watch. "That's all make-believe. You do know that, right?" I walked to the other side of her desk, grabbed the overturned photograph. "This?" I said, holding it up. "This is not your boyfriend. This is a lonely prisoner who knows you're desperate."

Julia reached up for the photograph, but I held it back, out of reach. *She needs to hear it,* I told myself. *She needs to hear the truth.*

"You need to give that back," she said, straightening in her chair. She shot a nervous glance toward the man in the sling, who quickly looked down at his phone. He wasn't the type to help. I could tell that right away.

"What even is this?" Alex's uncomfortable pose, the stream cutting down the shot at a strange angle, the mountains flat in the background. "A souvenir for women who get off on dating murderers?"

"My Alex," she said in a low voice, "wouldn't hurt anyone."

"He's not *your* Alex."

Julia glanced at the wooden door that led back into the office, as though one of the lawyers might come out and rescue her. It stayed closed. "Alex didn't want anything to do with you back in high school. If he was *nice* to you, it's because he felt *bad* for you. And he's not going to have anything to do with you once he gets out of prison."

"Alex loves me," she said, her voice tight. "And I love him." She looked back to the monitor again. "I wouldn't expect you to understand." *I wouldn't betray him like you did,* her eyes said, full of righteous self-satisfaction.

"Alex is in prison," I said, leaning forward over the desk, "because he *murdered* Emily. Not because of anything I said or didn't say. He shoved her out a window and left her there to die." Suddenly, before I even knew what was happening, the picture flew across the room, hitting the wall behind Julia's desk with a dull thud, then falling back down to the ground, glass shattering. Julia twisted in her chair to look at the mess, then looked back toward me, her mouth hanging open.

The man in the sling had the back of his phone pointed toward us, no doubt recording. He fidgeted when I turned back toward him, put his phone down again, and pretended to be engrossed in some article.

"Fuck you," I told him, and he inhaled sharply but kept his head down.

"You need to leave," Julia said, reaching out for the phone beside her.

Too far. It had gone too far. But she was the one who had provoked me.

"You need to stop contacting me," I said, backing toward the door.

Julia started dialing.

"I'm going," I said, holding my hands up in front of me. "I'm going, okay? Just leave me alone."

I wonder if he'll go to the police station, that man in the sling. I can just see him, sitting in one of their plastic chairs and toying nervously with his phone, eyes flitting between the diploma on the wall and the stack of papers on the desk, anywhere but at Detective Curtis, who sits right in front of him. Detective Curtis leans back comfortably in his chair, hands laced behind his head, sizing up this man who probably does not have a sprained wrist. *I shouldn't have gotten involved,* the man thinks. *This was a big mistake.*

"Well," Detective Curtis says, pausing and leaning forward in his chair. "Let's take a look." He says it in a way that sounds friendly but lets the listener know they don't have a choice, not really. The man in the sling feels that pressure and hands the phone over, then tells himself that he's doing his civic duty, the right thing, that he's practically a Good Samaritan here. Detective Curtis taps the screen, squinting at the video and nodding his head thoughtfully.

"Unhinged is how I'd describe it," the man says, cautiously, scanning Detective Curtis's face for approval. "Definitely unhinged."

Detective Curtis sighs loudly, disappointed in the video or in me, the man can't tell which. "Thanks for this," Detective Curtis says in his professional voice, masking any reaction. "You did the right thing bringing this to our attention."

The man nods eagerly. Detective Curtis stands, and the man follows his lead, almost unaware that he's doing it.

"So—what's happening now?" the man asks as Detective Curtis starts toward the door. "In the investigation, I mean? Do you—"

"Thanks for coming in," Detective Curtis says, pleasant but clipped, the end of the conversation. "We'll be in touch if we need anything further."

9

Coming up on the right, a sign for NYSDOC Eastern Correctional Facility. I picture a sprawling institution, fenced in by barbed wire, and my chest tightens. I breathe in, try to focus instead on the yellow lines on the road in front of me.

Over the years, I've thought about who Emily would be today. Emily, no longer as tiny but still lean, gauzy sweaters and leggings, living with girls from her dance troupe in a cramped apartment in the city. She had an audition coming up for Juilliard our senior year, and we were all so sure the spot was as good as hers. We thought she was so talented back then—and she *was* talented, and committed, and hardworking, of course, but who knows how she would have compared to the hordes of other girls who had spent their childhoods working toward the same thing. Maybe she wouldn't have made the cut after all. Maybe she would have ended up a teacher at a dance studio, wrangling five-year-olds in leotards, or a yoga instructor. Meditation and sun salutations might have been good for her.

I've wondered, too, about Alex—what would have happened to him in an alternative world where Emily hadn't died, where he had gone on to Penn State with hopes of playing on their soccer team. He'd make the team, I've decided, but would have sat on the bench most of the time. He'd get a job in sales after graduation. A dad in a button-down shirt and gray slacks, big arms and the hint of a rounded belly, aging the way bulky teenagers age. Sometimes I imagine him balding, his hairline creeping up around the edges, a sparse blond triangle of hair left behind.

Late fall my sophomore year, Alex showed up at my front door. I opened it expecting to find a mailman with a package to sign for. Instead, it was him, hands stuffed into the pockets of his jacket.

"Hey," he said, and I looked over his shoulder at the empty street behind him, trying to figure out what was going on.

"What are you doing here?"

"Nice to see you, too," he said. He smiled, not really offended. Alex always assumed he was welcome everywhere. "Want to take a walk?"

"Now?" I asked. Stupid. What a stupid thing to say.

"I mean, if you're busy . . ." Alex peered over my shoulder into my empty house.

"No," I said. "I'm not busy, I mean. A walk sounds—let me get my jacket."

Cars were infrequent on my street, and the houses were set back on wooded lots, so it felt almost like we had the world to ourselves. We walked in the center of the road, beside each other, Alex taking slow, easy steps, in no rush to be anywhere.

"So you know where I live," I said.

"I asked around."

"Okay, stalker."

Alex grinned back at me. If he felt worried or self-conscious, he didn't show it.

"I live in Quail Run," he said as a car crested the hill in front of us. He put his hand lightly on my waist and guided me closer to the side of the road. It was like the ground had dropped out from under me. "Two-forty Eagle Drive. So now you know as much about me as I know about you."

"Fair enough." I brushed him with my shoulder, and he pushed back, lightly. "Where are Matt and Brian today?"

Alex shrugged. "I didn't want to see Matt and Brian. I wanted to see you."

A light, giddy feeling. I couldn't look at him directly. Instead, I focused on my Keds, their white bands inked in with blue pen. Not visible: the blue lilies that Emily had drawn on their tan soles at lunchtime, carefully holding my foot in her lap.

"Plus," Alex said, "I just needed to get out of my house."

"I get it," I said.

"Yeah, I thought you might."

The Dawsons' wolfhound ambled down their driveway toward us, sat obediently at the property line, and cocked his head toward us.

"Hey, boy," Alex said, grabbing a stick from the other side of the street and throwing it for the dog, who darted off to find it and then trotted back, stick in mouth. Alex scratched behind his ears.

"You're a dog person, I see."

"Oh yeah," Alex said, tossing the stick again. "Want to know an embarrassing secret?"

"Absolutely."

Alex leaned in, his face inches away from mine, and lowered his voice.

"I cry every time those rescue animal commercials come on. The ones with that sad song?" He pulled back, studied my face for a reaction, and raised his eyebrows. "Like, full-on tears rolling down my face."

"You do not."

"I do. I have to change the channel or leave the room when they start playing. Can't handle 'em."

"I would never have guessed."

"It's the truth," Alex said, grinning at me. "Someday I'm going to live out in the country and adopt all of the old, three-legged, one-eyed dogs from the animal shelter and give them a home."

"So what you're telling me," I said, "is that you're basically a cat lady in disguise."

Alex's jaw dropped in mock offense. "This is very different."

"Hmm."

"I'm baring my soul to you here, Miks."

Miks. We turned the corner, and our fingers brushed, and it was all I could do to contain the rush of excitement that shot through me. The same thought, over and over again in my head: *for some inexplicable reason, this person has chosen* me.

The last time I saw Alex was at his trial, squeezed behind a wooden table at the front of the courtroom. He was wearing a suit that fit him just fine, but he was uncomfortable in it and it showed. He fiddled with his jacket when he rose and sat, unsure of whether it should be buttoned or unbuttoned, one button or two. His hair was parted and combed neatly. He rested his hands on the desk in front of him, then brought them down to his side and then back up again, brushing back a piece of hair that wasn't out of place. He looked to the jury, then quickly averted his eyes, looking over at his lawyer for reassurance. His lawyer, a thin man in a brown jacket with sleeves wrinkled at the elbows, squared up the stack of papers in front of him and slipped them into a manila folder. Alex's leg jiggled beneath the wooden table.

I used to pretend, sometimes, that Alex stopped existing when the bailiff led him out of the courtroom's back door, just like Emily stopped existing when she slipped away from the rest of us at the campsite and passed through the heavy door to the cinder block house, the chain of an old padlock swinging clipped and useless from the door handle. *Gone,* I'd tell myself. They were both gone, no longer part of our world.

But Alex didn't stop existing. The bailiff led him down the back halls of the courtroom to a small holding cell where he waited until he could be transported. Then he was sent to Frackville and processed, given a cell and a job in the prison kitchen. Years later, he's standing in front of a painted creek in a blue button-down shirt with the sleeves rolled up to his elbows and dark blue pants. Meeting with Ryan. Taping photos of Julia to the walls of his cell. Calling her collect from prison, telling her about his day. Listening as she talked about what their life would be like when he was finally free, when they could finally be together.

I couldn't wrap my mind around Alex and Julia. But that picture of Alex—*adult* Alex, twenty-eight-year-old Alex—was right there on her desk, a memento from Frackville, proof of some kind of relationship. She did have access to some legal resources, and she had nothing but free time to advocate for him. And he must have liked the attention, her reassurance that he still mattered.

I was still puzzling it over as I returned home to my apartment after my confrontation with Julia. Ryan stood at the stove, garlic sputtering and popping in the frying pan. I came up behind him and leaned into his shoulder. His dark hair brushed against my cheek.

"Smells good," I said.

"How was the shop today?"

"Another visit from Julia." Which was true, I told myself, even if I hadn't actually seen her at Stomping Grounds myself. Who else could have left the photograph? "I told her she needs to leave me alone."

I could feel Ryan's shoulders stiffen, felt my own pulse rise. *This isn't fair,* I wanted to say. *Just listen.*

"Natalie—" I started.

"Oh, Natalie was there."

"What's that supposed to mean?" I stepped back and crossed my arms over myself.

"Nothing." Ryan raised an apologetic hand, without looking toward me. Minced onions hissed as he dumped them into the pan. I waited. He must have felt me watching him. He took a moment, collected himself, turned to face me.

"Natalie just brings out a—I don't know—your 'mean girl' side."

I stared at him, unsure of how to respond.

"Not—that's too harsh. But you know what I mean."

"No," I said. "I don't know."

Ryan's shoulders sagged. "Come on, Micah," he said. "This doesn't have to be a fight. I'm just saying that Natalie can be a little cruel sometimes."

"That's not what you said."

"I misspoke."

He was trying to catch my eye, a peace offering. I looked down at the small ridges that ran between the laminate wood beams.

"I just want her to leave me alone," I said. "I don't think that's too much to ask."

Ryan turned back to his frying pan, slid the onions around with his spatula. The nonresponse bothered me even more than disagreement would have. *No point in arguing,* he seemed to be saying. On the table, a loose stack of mail. I flipped through: credit card statements, bills for Stomping Grounds. A save the date from one of Ryan's college friends, a hall mate from freshman year and his longtime, very blond girlfriend.

"Did you see that email from Chelsea today?" Ryan asked. A subject change. "I RSVP'd."

"Why?" I asked, still on the defensive.

"It's our reunion." He balanced the spatula on the lip of the sink and leaned back against the counter. "It'll be good to see everyone. Find out what they've been up to."

"Who cares what they've been up to?" I set the mail down on the kitchen table, straightening the edges. "They're not our *friends*. We're not still in touch with these people."

"That's what reunions are for," Ryan said. "Reconnecting."

He sounded hopeful. He wanted to show people what he had become. A new Ryan, the kind of person who got save the dates with an engagement shot of a good-looking couple staring off into the sunset together. He didn't understand that our high school classmates wouldn't see him for who he was now. It wouldn't take five minutes for old dynamics to reemerge.

"I think it's a bad idea," I said. "I don't like any of those people."

"Micah."

"I don't," I said. "And they don't like me."

"That's not true."

"Even though I'm a 'mean girl'?" I mimed air quotes. Ryan rolled his eyes.

"Come on, Micah. You know as well as I do that Natalie can be a little much."

"She speaks her mind."

"Yeah, and a lot of what's on her mind is offensive."

That was true.

"I just bumped into Joy Brennan the other day, and she was asking about you. People like you."

I sank down into my chair at the kitchen table. "She's just mining for gossip," I said. "She wants to see how damaged I am."

"She seemed genuinely interested to me."

I picked up an envelope, ran my index finger under the seal, thought that over. "What am I supposed to say when they start asking about what I'm doing? 'Still in Calvary. Working at a coffee shop.'" *Dating Alex's best friend from high school.*

"You're not 'working at a coffee shop.' You *own* a coffee shop." Ryan left the stove and sat down across from me, leaning in. "You're running your own business. I think it's great."

My guard lowered. I shrugged.

"And what's wrong with Calvary?" Ryan pressed. He squeezed my hand. "We've got our life here. We've got each other. I'd say we have it pretty good."

I squeezed his hand back and he smiled, looking relieved—*all forgiven*—then returned to the stove to dump strips of beef into the mixture. I could tell that he was picturing our reunion: our old classmates at Rosalina's, standing around tables draped with creased white linens, cheap red wine and crostinis in hand, inviting him into their circles. He was going to be so disappointed.

"They're going to want to know about Alex," I said—gently this time, not aiming to wound. *He has to be prepared,* I thought to myself. *He has to face reality.* I could see him cringe again, his mood flattening. "You know he's the first thing people are going to think about when they see us."

Alex, who was sixty miles away, maybe walking through the prison halls right now, in transit from dinner to a religious service, nodding his head at prisoners passing in the other direction, like teammates in a school hallway.

"What are you going to tell them?"

Ryan turned to study my face, trying to determine what I was asking.

"How is he doing?" I asked. I wasn't trying to lure him into another argument. I wanted to know.

Ryan set the spatula down again, rubbed his hand along his face. "He's hanging in there," he said. *Hanging in there,* like enduring prison was an act of bravery, something noble, not mandatory.

"Does anyone else visit him?"

"His mother comes when she can. His father doesn't. Neither does his brother."

"And Julia?"

"She visits."

"What do you talk about?" I traced the hinged edge of the table with my index finger.

Ryan sucked in his lower lip.

"When you visit him," I said, emphasizing the "you." "What do the two of you talk about?"

"Normal things." Ryan scratched his head, his hair sticking out to the side when he dropped his hand back down to the counter. "Current events. What we've been doing."

That's enough, I told myself. I could feel my anxiety creeping back, the unease I always felt when I pictured Ryan and Alex sitting across from each other in the prison visiting room, surrounded by prisoners' mothers, wives, children. *Let this drop.*

"What does he do?" I asked, against my better judgment. "In prison. What is there to do?"

"Well," Ryan said, "he's gotten involved in this program that trains shelter dogs, puts inmates in charge of them to teach them to sit, stay, that sort of thing. And there's this reading group—"

"Oh, like a book club?" I interrupted. "For murderers? That sounds nice." I pictured Alex in a circle of prisoners, all with copies of some new Jonathan Franzen book in hand, talking about how it made them feel, his shelter dog sprawled out loyally at his side.

"They're rehabilitative programs designed to—"

"Does he talk about Julia?" I interrupted again, and Ryan rubbed his neck and rolled his head, clearly regretting the turn this conversation had taken.

"Some. Not much. I just know she visits sometimes."

I nodded, rested my head in my hands, and looked down at the table. I waited until Ryan's attention was fixed back on the stove before asking: "Do you talk about me?"

"No," Ryan said, not turning around. A lump formed in the back of my throat.

"That's probably for the best."

"Probably."

Ryan split the food onto two plates, and I grabbed a bottle of wine off the top of the fridge.

"You don't have to go to the reunion if you don't want to," Ryan said as we sat down. "I'm not going to pressure you."

"How kind."

"But I'm going," he continued, looking down at his plate. "It'll be nice to see everyone again, after all this time."

It's not going to be what you're expecting, I wanted to say. *I don't want you to get hurt.* But instead I nodded and swallowed, the food sticking in the back of my throat.

That night, Ryan breathed heavily beside me, a half-snore, sleeping easily. He never took more than ten minutes to drift off. I closed my eyes and my mind raced: Julia, armed with Scotch tape and photographs, covering the Stomping Grounds windows with high school mementos. Alex, alive and well at twenty-eight years old, crouching down to scratch behind the ears of a pit bull with a wagging tail, *hey, boy, good boy.*

Emily.

I thought about the last time I was in her room. Everything folded and pristine and kept neatly in its place; elegant and refined and adult, or what I thought adult looked like at seventeen. I had sat at the foot of her bed, fiddling with the loose brass knob on her bedpost. Emily tried on a yellow dress, which tied at her narrow waist and then ruffled out again, feminine and flattering. She placed her hand on her hip, bit her lip, then returned to her closet, organized neatly by color.

"Expecting your secret lover?" I had asked, half-jokingly, and Emily flushed in response.

"Wait—are you?"

Emily had become adamantly opposed to dating when we started high school. "A waste of time," she told me, more than once. Mr. Lionel had told her she had a shot at going professional, but only if she kept focused on the goal.

"Of course not," she responded. She slid back a pink blouse, the wire hanger scraping against the metal rod. I sat up straighter.

"Are you *interested* in someone?" I asked. "Who is it?"

She pulled a green tank top out of the closet, studied it, put it back. "It's no one."

I lay back on the bed, staring up at the ceiling fan.

"Well, it's someone who's going to be at the party tonight, so that narrows it down—"

"Micah."

"Is it Ryan?"

"You're being ridiculous."

"Oh, come on," I said, pushing myself back up. "I'm just teasing."

She settled on an outfit: a T-shirt that fit more tightly than mine, the hem not quite touching the loose waist of her low-rise jeans. A white-washed denim jacket and a chain-link necklace with a heart charm that fell right at the base of her neck. I told her she looked great and wondered how the whole ordeal had managed to take an hour.

"There are my special girls," your mother said as we came down the stairs. "Emily, I've been thinking about your Juilliard audition—"

"We're going to Micah's," Emily interrupted. Your mother eyed us, taking in the change of clothes, the makeup, heavier than normal.

"Be safe" was all she said.

I flipped now, to face Ryan, my legs tangling in the sheets. His shoulders rose and fell, rose and fell. I tried to mimic his breathing, clear my mind. Eyes closed, I saw you, forehead leaned up against the narrow window that framed my front door, a small circle of fog from your breath. *Micah, let me in.* I flopped over on my back and looked up at the ceiling fan, watched its small, almost imperceptible wobble. I turned back onto my side, pulled the covers over me, and stared at the light gray wall.

The wall was covered with pictures Ryan and I had found together on trips to scavenge items for Stomping Grounds or to furnish our home. They had little in common except that we both liked them. A lithograph with carefully detailed caterpillars and moths, each with tiny numbers printed beside them corresponding to their Latin names. A splatter of orange paint in a white frame. An oil painting of a seaside town in the fog, a cluster of houses leading down to the water, one house with bright blue siding standing out from all the browns and grays.

The closet, split evenly in two: my sweaters and sweatshirts clumped together, sleeves tangled; Ryan's shirts carefully spaced. The overflowing wicker hamper in the corner, the black arm of Ryan's hoodie and one leg of my jeans hanging over the side. On our dresser, Ryan's books commingled with mine: *The Art of Warfare in the Age of Napoleon* on top of *Business Model Generation* and *The Coffee Dictionary*.

I pushed the covers back off of me and pulled my laptop off of my nightstand, angling it away from Ryan. My fingers hovered over the keys. Ryan grunted and turned, his back now to me. I typed in "Alex Swift."

I was expecting archived news articles from around the time of the trial, then a ten-year silence. Other Alex Swifts, maybe, pushing the Alex I knew down in the results, relegated to history. But the first result that came up was new, and it was relevant. A blog: No Stone Unturned, a short description that read: *Alex Swift has spent a decade in jail for the murder of Emily Winters with virtually no forensic evidence linking him to the crime. . . .* The link brought me to a page that was black and white and sepia, with a faded photograph of smoothed stones as the background. It featured the picture of a man in his mid-thirties doing his best to look brooding: his brow furrowed, two fingers resting on his temple, his face angled to highlight sharp cheekbones. His wavy hair was slicked back and tucked behind his ears, giving him a distinctly faux-French appearance. *Through my work as a journalist, I've been shining light on injustice for the past fifteen years,* said the text under the photograph, identifying the man as Brent Williams. "But I can't do it alone."

Below, some featured cases that Brent Williams had taken an interest in. A picture of a clean-cut man posed with his family, his wife in a light-blue cardigan with carefully straightened hair, his daughters in matching ruffled dresses and big bows. The man had shot the wife and daughters in their beds a few months after the picture was taken, then called the police in a panicked state. *A burglar,* the man said. *It must have been a burglar.* A burglar who took nothing and left the man alive. A black man in his twenties, lanky and quiet-looking in his photo, serving twenty years for the death of a convenience store clerk in a robbery-gone-wrong. *It's him, I'm sure of it,* one of the other convenience store patrons had told the police and the jury. The other patron, it was pointed out, was a squat white woman in her late fifties.

And below that was Alex. The site used a picture I knew well. You'd recognize it, too, if you saw it; the first news reports used it over and over again, before the existence of a confession had leaked. Set in one of the soccer fields behind the field house, the photo showed Alex, flushed and youthful with a wide smile. He looked as though he had just run over to slap the backs of his team-mates, congratulate them on a game well played, and there was a camera, capturing the moment.

I clicked on the link to "Alex's Story," and there was Emily's picture. She was onstage, arms held out at her sides and back leg crossed behind her, visible through a long blue tulle skirt. Her hair was pulled into a crown braid, dotted with small white flowers. The same photograph had been blown up and used again my se-nior year as part of a two-page spread memorializing her, then blown up even larger and set next to a picture of her corpse at Alex's trial.

Below that picture was Brent Williams's analysis of the case, and, next to that, a list of links to what Brent Williams had labeled "key documents." I looked over to Ryan, back still rising and falling steadily, then turned back to my computer screen and began to read.

EMILY'S FALL

This case ticks off all my boxes for Wrongful Conviction. You've got a minor and a "confession"—if you can even call it that—word of which travels quickly around town. The confession is excluded from evidence—and rightfully so—but you can be sure that at least some of the jury members know about it, and that it played a key role in the jury deliberations. (See my earlier posts here and here about what an absolute mess our jury system is.) Next to no physical evidence was presented at trial, just a story about a lovers' quarrel and the fact that the accused doesn't have a good alibi. And, there you go, you have yourself a conviction. Two lives ruined for the price of one.

So, let's start at the beginning. Alex Swift, by all accounts, seemed to be mostly a good kid, with one major character flaw: he's got two girlfriends. The first is Micah Wilkes, a girl he's been seeing for two years. Pretty serious, by high school standards. The second is Emily Winters, an intensely focused dancer who also just happens to be Micah's best friend. Not the smartest move on Alex's part, but he's seventeen, so we shouldn't be surprised that he's a little stupid. By the time of the night in question, Alex and Emily have been carrying on in secret for a few months, and Emily—according to the official story—is tired of her role as the other woman. She wants to make things more official.

Alex and Emily, "carrying on" together. The whispers behind me when I returned to school: *Did she know?* Looking back, I could see it: Emily's comfort with Alex, a stray brush of his arm as she reached across him to grab her backpack after lunch, the flash of guilt across her face when he offered to drive her home from my house, when she accepted. We had been friends since we were eight. I thought I could trust her.

That night, Emily and Alex—along with half of the senior class—go to a party thrown in a spot in the woods Calvary high schoolers apparently liked to frequent. There was some obvious tension between the two of them. Several of their classmates report witnessing a fight. And then, around eleven o'clock or so, they're both gone. No one remembers seeing either of them after that point. That timeline, mind you, is a little fuzzy. You know how high school parties can get.

The prosecution's story: Emily and Alex sneak off to be alone together, to the second floor of a run-down structure deep in the woods that housed administrative offices for a long-defunct camp. They fight. Emily wants Alex to break things off with Micah, and Alex is reluctant. Emily tries to end things, and Alex gets angry. He grabs her by the arms and pushes her out the window. Her head hits a rock, and she loses consciousness. She dies a few hours later.

Alex and Emily's relationship was a secret but not a well-kept one, and the police were on to them right away. Alex is brought in and questioned for hours—*hours*—without a lawyer or a parent present. Eventually, and not surprisingly, Alex breaks down and starts apologizing, saying "I'm sorry. I'm sorry. This is all my fault." And that's it. That's the supposed confession. You can read the transcript for yourself here. Of course, "I feel bad that my girlfriend is dead" is not even CLOSE to the same thing as "I murdered her, and here's information that you can use to verify that statement."

"He's a seventeen-year-old boy facing an immense amount of pressure," said Dr. Lisa Nicoletti, the criminal psychologist I spoke with regarding Alex's interrogation. "And the police played on the guilt he would very naturally feel. He abandoned his partner, and something terrible happened. There are a lot of I-statements here, strong expressions of emotion, but that's what we'd expect to see from these circumstances. You have to keep in mind how vulnerable he was. We have this idea of who is likely to give a false confession—someone with a low IQ and little education, someone who is easily confused—but the truth of the matter is that false confessions may be more prevalent than we realize. Alex may just have been a boy who was in the wrong place at the wrong time."

But news of the confession spreads fast—with, I'm sure, some rhetorical flourishes added on with each retelling—and, soon enough, everyone is sure that he did it. Including, probably, Alex's defense attorney, a local guy whose prior criminal experience was mostly made up of DUIs, DVs, and possession charges.

Then we get to trial, and the confession is excluded because Alex's parents weren't around when Alex started waiving all of his rights. Good for Alex's lawyer; he did one thing right. What he didn't do, though, was get the case moved to a less prejudiced venue, or make sure that all of the jurors who had been following this case on the news were dismissed. We know at least some of the jurors had been following along before being chosen for jury duty. Here's the transcript from the voir dire examination. Sure, they promised to keep an open mind, but if you think any juror has the cognitive wherewithal to separate things they heard before and during the trial, you're fooling yourself. So, now we have some people on the jury who are going into this case thinking Alex confessed and who won't see that the purported "confession" is actually nothing of the sort.

Alex's lawyer does nothing with the forensic evidence in this case. We know from post-conviction proceedings that his lawyer didn't even consult an expert to review the autopsy report. And he doesn't introduce any alternative suspects. His theory is that we don't know there was a push. It could have just been a fall. A tough sell when there are hand-shaped bruises on the deceased's arms. The jury goes into deliberations, and it takes some time but they come back with a guilty verdict. Ten years and multiple appeals later, Alex is still in jail and maintaining his innocence.

"He's taking it day by day," according to Alex's current girlfriend, Julia Reynolds, who contacted me about Alex's case. "He's forgiven the people who are responsible for putting him here. But he's still fighting. He's innocent, and the truth will come out. We just need people who will listen."

Julia said more, but I stopped reading. I inhaled, my breath ragged. *They make Alex sound like a child,* I thought as I wiped away tears with the back of my hand and eased the lid of the laptop closed. *Like he couldn't have known what he was doing, like he couldn't be held responsible.* He hadn't been a child.

I slid my head back down onto my pillow and pictured Alex: the panic that crossed over his face when the jury read their verdict. His eyes had widened and then hardened as he realized what had been said. Julia had burst into loud, ugly tears, and Ryan, seated next to me, reached for my hand, unexpected but not unwelcome. I twisted myself around to get a better look at Julia, and my eyes accidentally landed on your mother instead, exhausted with grief, your father at her side, his face stoic and empty, but not you—*where is Joshua,* everyone wanted to know but wouldn't ask.

After Alex was escorted out of the courtroom, the rest of us were left in the wooden benches, free to go about the rest of our day. Alex's lawyer, grim-faced, placed a hand on Mrs. Swift's shoulder and stooped down to tell her something—*this isn't over, we can still file an appeal, there's still hope.* Your parents stood, your mother shaking her head, and made their way to the exit at the back of the courtroom. A part of me wanted to run over to them, to give your mother a hug, to tell her I was so sorry. But instead I sat next to Ryan, shuffling through the contents of my messenger bag, pretending to look for something. I thought I could feel Mrs. Swift's eyes boring into me, blaming me. I kept my eyes down. *Not my fault,* I told myself. *I told the police the truth. Alex only has himself to blame.*

10

The needle on my gas gauge hovers around E, bouncing up hopefully as my car eases down a hill and then falling again as the road slopes back up, my stomach sinking along with it. Its small red light glows. *Stop*, it says. *You need gas. You need to STOP.*

"Just a little farther," I say, like the car can hear me, like it can just push a little more if it knows the end is near. "We just need to go a little farther."

The needle quivers, bounces and sinks, bounces and sinks.

When I woke the morning after finding No Stone Unturned, I found Ryan's warm imprint on the mattress next to me, the sheets bunched to the side. I pushed myself up from the bed and padded down the hallway. A thin line of light glowed beneath the office door. I knocked softly and eased the door open.

A small army of miniatures covered the desk, some posed with rifles, others crouching behind tiny rocks made out of spray-painted cork. Ryan sat behind them, facing the door, his jaw set in concentration. He pinched a half-painted soldier between his left thumb and forefinger and held a tiny paintbrush in his other hand. A dash of black paint had dried onto his cheek, just above the line of his beard.

"Morning," I said softly, not wanting to startle him.

"Good morning," he said, his eyes focused on the soldier as he dabbed on a black leather boot.

I leaned my weight against the doorframe.

"Hey, have you—have you heard of No Stone Unturned?" I tried to keep my voice light. "I guess it's a true-crime blog."

Ryan set down the soldier carefully and swiveled in his chair. "Those things are garbage." He grabbed a paper towel from the side of his desk and wiped his hands carefully.

I nodded my head and crossed my arms over my chest.

"Some of the Easton students are into it," he said when I didn't leave the doorway, shaking his head in disapproval. "It's sensationalized gossipmongering. They dig into these traumatic events like they're just fodder for entertainment and pick apart people who are hurting, or recovering, or just trying to live their lives. It's disgusting."

"Mm," I said, looking away from Ryan to the bookshelf that overflowed with his books: *Dividing the Spoils: The War for Alexander the Great's Empire, The American Revolution: A History,* a collection of speeches given by Winston Churchill. Above that, the window, where the branches of a magnolia tree bent in the wind. The translucent white curtains hanging down were the only sign that this was a shared space. "So you haven't looked at it?"

"No," he said definitively. "Why?"

"Nothing important," I said as I slipped back into the hallway. "I just overheard someone talking about it." That seemed to satisfy Ryan. He lifted the little soldier gingerly, dipping his paintbrush into a small plastic cup of paint, and began dabbing again as I eased the door shut.

. . . .

"Of course I've heard of it," said Natalie, unzipping her fitted hoodie and pulling her hair up into a messy bun. "Brent Williams solved that case in Ohio."

"What case in Ohio?" I asked. Two college students pushed through the doors, their cheeks red and shiny from the cold. They rubbed their hands together and scanned the shop for their friends. A group of four waved them over. They grabbed two chairs and dragged them across the floor, wood scraping on wood.

"That girl who went missing outside of Cincinnati," Natalie said, searching my face for recognition. "You know."

Anna, who was leaning back against the counter, facing away from the busy crowd, seemed to perk up.

"I don't know," I said, lowering my voice. "I don't follow that stuff." The college students squeezed their chairs as close as they could to the table, then dropped two green canvas backpacks onto the ground. One of the overstuffed bags wobbled then tipped backward, blocking off the narrow walkway between tables. The owner of the bag righted it, pulled out a laptop, and let it fall again, half open.

"She was seven years old. Good family. Very sad story. Everyone thought it was the parents for, you know," Natalie waved her hands, "the obvious reasons." A sleepy-eyed boy in his early twenties pushed himself up from his seat by the window and rolled his head from shoulder to shoulder. I readied myself to return to the cash register, but he turned for the bathroom instead.

"The police had no real leads, and then Brent and his Truthseekers—"

"His Truthseekers?" I asked. Two girls at a two-top by the window glanced back at me then whispered something to each other. *She's the one I was telling you about,* maybe. *She's the one on that website.* Or possibly, I realized as I remembered the order they had placed ten minutes ago: *What's taking so long? Where are our mochas?*

"Anna," I said, exasperated, maybe too sharply, "could you get that table their drinks?"

Anna glared up at me like I had just slapped her across the face.

"Or—that's fine. Fine. I'll do it."

Part of me wondered if Anna's sour mood had anything to do with the long-haired Easton student, who was back again and had set himself up in the corner of the coffee shop but hadn't, as far as I could tell, shown more than a passing interest in Anna all morning. She seemed to have decided that the best course of action was to avoid not just his table but the two adjacent tables as well. I fixed the mochas and brought them out, apologizing for the delay.

"Truthseekers?" I asked as I returned to the counter.

"That's what his followers call themselves." Natalie held up both hands to distance herself from the moniker. "They're amateur detectives, basically. Some of the stuff they do is really impressive. Like in the Ohio case, the police couldn't come up with anything for years, and then the Truthseekers came along and solved it."

"They solved it," I repeated, and Natalie shrugged and mixed a packet of Sweet'N Low into her latte.

"They came up with a *very* plausible story, anyway. They realized there had been other disappearances in the area, girls around the same age. So they combed through all of the pictures of the girls they could find online. One of the girls had some photos from a recent zoo trip posted on her mom's Instagram page, and there was a photo of *another* one of the girl with a souvenir tote bag from the zoo in the background. It turned out all of the girls had been to the zoo in the months leading up to the disappearances, and that there had been a *pedophile*"—Natalie whispered this last word, mouthing it dramatically—"working there for over twenty years."

The door jingled, and a girl with thick-rimmed glasses entered. Messy hair and sweatpants: she had to be a student. She looked around, saw that there was nowhere to sit, and then approached the front counter. She hesitated before placing her order, and I wondered if she was thinking about asking a personal question. *What was she like? Emily?* But no, it wouldn't be that. *What was he like? Alex? Do you think he did it?* Or: *Did you really not know?* She asked for coffee, no room for cream.

"So it's a popular site," I said to Natalie as the girl shuffled away. I looked past Natalie out at the coffee shop patrons and did a silent headcount. When had the uptick in business actually started?

"Oh yeah," Natalie said. "I was obsessed with it when I was nursing Ashton."

The six college students jammed into one table all bent down over their laptops, looking up only to elbow each other and point to their screens. Behind them, two girls with heavy bangs poked at their phones. One looked in my direction and I startled, then flushed and turned my attention back to Natalie.

"They're covering Alex's case," I said in a low voice.

"What?" Natalie's eyes widened, and she leaned in closer. "We're on there?"

"*We're* not on there," I said, looking back toward the girls at the two-top, whose attention had returned to their phones. Could they hear what I was saying from here, over the hum of conversation, the raspy-voiced singer from Goo Goo Dolls crooning over the speakers? "Alex and Emily are."

"Crazy." Natalie drummed her fingers against the seam of her paper cup.

"I don't understand it." I swept back a stray hair. A laugh, too loud, from the long-haired boy's table. It came from a girl with short, spiky hair, her mouth stretched into an exaggerated, wide-open smile, showing teeth that seemed too big for her tiny face. EASTON was written down the side of her sweatpants in big, blocky white letters. "He confessed. He said he did it."

Natalie shook her head back and forth and pressed her lips together like she was suppressing a smile. "That makes sense," she said, resting her elbow on the countertop and wagging her finger at me. "Brent is *very* into false confessions, especially when they involve minors."

"It wasn't a false confession," I said. I thought about Detective Heller, her clean, white button-down and fitted slacks, the clack of her heeled shoes as she approached the interrogation room, crossed toward the table, eased down into the chair. Crossed one leg over the other, placed her clasped hands down on the table. *Let's go over this one more time,* she had said to me. *I just want to get this right.*

Natalie wasn't listening. I could tell her mind was spinning, flooded by all the exciting possibilities. *We're on there,* like it was something to be proud of. She looked from table to table, all filled with college students, and then leaned in toward me conspiratorially. "Do you think that's why they're here?"

I felt my pulse rising as I scanned the room again. Twenty students, at least. *The flyers,* I told myself. *It has to be the flyers.*

"No," I said. My chest tightened. Outside the Church Street windows, a couple slowed, their heads turning toward me. *They're thinking about getting a coffee. They just want to see how busy we are.*

"I bet it is," she continued. This time, she couldn't keep herself from smiling. "You're a big part of the story. Alex's girlfriend, Emily's best friend—"

I slammed my hands down on the counter, and Natalie drew back.

"Hey," I said, addressing the shop, and then louder: "Hey, everyone."

A few heads turned in acknowledgment. The chatter quieted to a hum.

"We're closing early today. Ten minutes."

The college students who had just entered the shop a few minutes before groaned and made a show of rubbing their hands together again, looking down at the workstations they had just set up and then back at me. Anna looked confused but then relieved, turning her attention to wiping down the counter.

"What are you doing?" Natalie asked, her forehead wrinkled.

"I can't do this today," I said, grabbing paper off the shelves in the storage room and scrawling out GOOD FOR ONE FREE COFFEE again and again.

"Do what?" Natalie asked, looking skeptically at the stack of papers.

"This," I said, waving my hand at the college students loitering in their seats, packing their bags slowly, one highlighter at a time. "I can't deal with them."

"It's probably nothing," Natalie said, backtracking. She studied my face, realizing for the first time how agitated I had become.

"I just need some time to myself," I said, then I shouted out a five-minute warning.

"Should I stick around?" Natalie asked.

"No," I said, too sharply, but I caught myself and gave her an apologetic half-smile. "I just want an afternoon to figure out what's going on. That's all."

I weaved through the shop, saying, "Sorry, family emergency," over and over again as I handed out the small peace offering to each table. I tried, as I did so, to peek at the screens. YouTube, Microsoft Word, online shopping. No sign of Brent Williams. But it doesn't take that long to close out a window. The students took the coupons begrudgingly. Textbooks were stacked and straightened and placed in backpacks one by one while the students chatted with each other, forgot what they were doing, began again. Cords unplugged and wound carefully, laptops gently worked into bags, then pulled out again when they didn't quite fit, textbooks rearranged. It was twenty minutes later when the last college student fished his hat and gloves out of his pockets and lumbered toward the door. Anna was already gone. I turned the latch as soon as the door closed behind the last student. Then I grabbed the lion chair and carried it into the storage room, pushing boxes aside with my legs to make space. I set down the chair in front of the old computer and settled in.

.   .   .

The storage room in the back of Stomping Grounds smelled like cardboard and dust. A handful of paper clips had spilled out across the desk, the ring of an old coffee stain beneath them. I waited for the computer to load, my right leg bouncing, swinging back and forth. Its hard drive strained, unaccustomed to use. My mouse hovered over the link to the Truthseekers forum, and then I changed my mind, my chair scraping on the hard concrete floor. I stumbled over a box jutting out from under the shelving unit, then righted myself. I reached for my bag on the top shelf and pulled out my Parliaments. A small voice in my head whispered *health code violation,* but I shut it out, slouched back into my seat, leaning onto its sloping armrest.

People can be so cruel without realizing it. The ones who watch without helping. The ones who enjoy the spectacle. The day the news of Alex's arrest rippled through the school, there had been a palpable excitement. Michelle Peterson had rushed up to me at my locker, her blond hair fried into submission, her eyes ringed with black eyeliner and clumped mascara.

"Oh Micah," she had said, throwing her thick arms around me, and suddenly I was breathing in the heavy scent of vanilla body spray, her blond hair brushing my face. "I'm so sorry." My muscles had tensed in response, my arms frozen at my side. She had pulled back, leaned on the locker next to mine.

"I just can't believe it," she had said. "What you must be going through—I just can't imagine." *I'd never find myself in your position,* she meant. *I'd never be so stupid.*

"Did Alex ever—" she had started, and I slammed the door to my locker shut so hard that I could hear the tiny plastic mirror inside, just like Emily's but red instead of blue, slide down and thump against the pile of books at the bottom. Michelle had re-coiled and shuffled back to her friends, who looked on from a few lockers down, eagerly anticipating any crumbs of new information.

I had thought that was behind me. I braced myself and clicked on the link. At the top of the forum were a few pinned threads that set out the outlines of Emily's case. One for media coverage. One for official documents: search warrants, court documents, transcripts from the trial and police interviews pulled from filings in Alex's appeals. Another thread for "verified locals," identifying Truthseekers who had access to inside information. Below those threads, a free-for-all, where users could comment on the case and post their theories. The most recent post: *Abuse in the family??* My stomach turned. I'd work up to that. I started with the thread for official documents and found a link to Alex's confession. Or his "confession," in scare quotes, as Brent Williams would say. "If you can even call it that." I opened the transcript of the police interview with Alex, which was double spaced with numbered lines, a neat border around the edge. Alex's name was printed in capital letters across the top, bare-bones and official. A date just under that: November 5, 2006. The officers present: Detectives Curtis and Heller. I leaned forward in my seat, ashing my cigarette in an old coffee mug. Here it was, finally: a neat, tidy record of what happened in the interrogation room next to mine.

That day, Alex had looked tired and ragged, his eyes puffy from crying. He had been wearing his white sweater with two navy stripes running parallel across it, the one he saved for special occasions, like his cousin's graduation dinner the spring before, or our anniversary date to Rosalina's, a big splurge at seventeen. He must have put it on that morning thinking it could help, that looking nice would make the difference. We were walked past each other in the station's narrow corridor—a lucky coincidence, I thought at the time; a handy trick, I realize now. He had looked at me and then looked away, his arms crossing over his chest, his hands rubbing those blue parallel lines on his sleeves, and that's when things started to solidify and I started to realize what was going on.

I wonder if they had you there, too, somewhere, tucked away in another tiny, stifling room. Holding a Styrofoam cup of water too tightly, looking from the officer to the clock on the wall, to the door. *I don't know what I can tell you. I wasn't even there.*

I scrolled through page after page, the detectives asking the same questions, Alex repeating the same thing over and over again. He and Emily were friends through me. That night at the campsite, he didn't know where she had gone. He was on the tarp with me and Ryan.

Then a break, eighty pages in, and the interrogation resumes:

CURTIS: Alex, I don't think you've been completely honest with us about where you were that night.

[PAUSE]

CURTIS: Do you think we can try this again?

SWIFT: I've told you everything. I'm not sure what else you want.

CURTIS: Let's just go over this one more time. The last time you saw Emily, she was—well, could you tell me again where you last saw her?

SWIFT: I think she was by the bleachers.

CURTIS: You think?

SWIFT: She was by the bleachers. Talking to Michelle Peterson.

CURTIS: About what?

SWIFT: I don't know. Patrick? Makeup? Nothing, probably. Michelle just rambles, especially when she's been drinking.

CURTIS: And that's the last time you saw Emily?

SWIFT: Yeah, I think so. I mean, I might have seen her once or twice after that. I don't know. It's—there was a lot going on, and it's not like I was paying all that much attention, you know?

CURTIS: Sure. Let's back up a little. Early in the evening, before the party gets going, you and your friends set up a tarp so that you can camp out in the woods. Is that right?

SWIFT: Yeah.

CURTIS: Who sets up this tarp?

SWIFT: Me, Ryan, Micah, and Emily.

CURTIS: And where was it?

SWIFT: A little ways away from the lodge. That's the—that's where the main party was. Close to a big pile of rocks. It's less—less noisy out there, not many people go that far into the woods.

CURTIS: Okay. And, as the night starts winding down, you go to the tarp you and your friends set up earlier.

SWIFT: Uh-huh.

CURTIS: What time was this?

SWIFT: I dunno. One o'clock maybe?

CURTIS: Were any of your other classmates nearby?

SWIFT: I don't know. I don't think so.

CURTIS: So you and Micah and Ryan went back to your tarp and went to sleep?

SWIFT: Uh-huh.

CURTIS: But Emily wasn't with you.

SWIFT: No.

CURTIS: Did you know where she was?

SWIFT: No, I already told you.

CURTIS: And none of you thought it was odd that she wasn't there with you?

SWIFT: No. I don't know. I thought maybe she was angry or something. Maybe she had gone home. I didn't think about it.

CURTIS: Why would she have been angry?

SWIFT: What? I don't know.

CURTIS: You said you thought she might have been angry. Why?

SWIFT: Emily just had these moods sometimes. It didn't take—it's hard to tell what's going to set her off. She'd get upset and stop talking to me, or stop talking to Micah, and then a few days later everything would be fine. That's how she was.

I leaned against the cushioned back of my chair and slipped another cigarette out of the pack. *She wasn't there with you? And you didn't think to look for her?* In my interrogation room, no bigger than the Stomping Grounds storage room, Detective Heller had rested her chin in her hand, then neatened the stack of papers in front of her, her mouth drawn in a straight line. When she looked back up at me, it was with gentle concern, like she wanted to understand but couldn't. *She was your friend, Micah,* she had said. *Why didn't you look for her? Why didn't you make sure she was okay?* She waited, forearms resting on the cold metal table, watching me. *I want to understand,* her expression said. *Help me understand. I would have looked for her. Why didn't you?*

CURTIS: Okay. So you go back to the tarp at one o'clock, and that's where you stayed for the rest of the night?

SWIFT: Uh-huh.

CURTIS: All three of you.

SWIFT: Yeah.

HELLER: See, we've been talking to Micah. And she says you never came back to the tarp.

My stomach turned. I could see that moment clearly. Detective Heller, leaning in toward Alex. *We're just trying to understand what really happened.* Alex, straightening in his chair, looking around at the bare walls of the interrogation room, the sole narrow window cut down the middle of the door, dark lines crosshatching the glass, and finally realizing where he was, what was happening here.

HELLER: She says it was just her and Ryan, that she doesn't have any memory of you there at all.

SWIFT: Micah said that?

CURTIS: So do you want to tell us where you really spent the night, Alex?

The shift would have been immediately visible to the officers, the wheels straining to turn in Alex's head. Alex wasn't used to being on the back foot, was unfamiliar with the need to defend himself. He would have licked his lips, dry from the heat, and looked to the window again, wishing that Ryan were there to come to his aid. He would have realized that he was all alone.

SWIFT: I was—okay, I spent the night in my car.

CURTIS: In your car? You left the party and went to your car?

SWIFT: Yeah.

CURTIS: Why did you do that?

SWIFT: I felt sick, and I just wanted—I just needed to be by myself. So I went and slept in my car.

CURTIS: Why didn't you say that before?

SWIFT: I didn't think you'd believe me.

CURTIS: Okay. So you left the party, alone, and went to your car? By yourself?

SWIFT: Yeah.

CURTIS: What time was that?

SWIFT: I don't know. One o'clock maybe? One-thirty?

CURTIS: And you left by yourself?

SWIFT: Yeah, I already told you.

Alex would have been starting to take comfort in this new lie. He would have been looking from Detective Curtis to Detective Heller, trying to suss out any hints in their expressions that he was saying the right thing. His pulse would have started to rise at the repetition of questions, but he wouldn't have realized why.

HELLER: Because we have witnesses who said you left the party with Emily, that the two of you went into the woods together.

SWIFT: That's not—who said that?

HELLER: They said you were going in the direction of the abandoned structure where we found her.

SWIFT: I don't—

CURTIS: Were you sleeping with Emily, Alex?

SWIFT: No, I—

HELLER: Let me save you the trouble of coming up with any more lies and rephrase that. We know you were sleeping with Emily.

SWIFT: I don't know what you're talking about. I'm telling you the truth. That's what happened that night.

This is when Alex would have started to shut down and crumble. Head spinning and fragments of what he had said before echoing in his mind. He would have realized, finally, that he was cornered; that, in truth, he had been cornered for a long time. He would have realized there was no way out.

SWIFT: It's not—I don't remember. I don't remember what happened.

CURTIS: You and Emily went to an abandoned structure in the woods.

SWIFT: [inaudible].

HELLER: Alex, we know the two of you went off together.

SWIFT: We did. We just—

CURTIS: And the two of you had a fight. She wanted you to stop seeing Micah, or she was going to end it.

SWIFT: Oh god.

CURTIS: You had been drinking, things got out of control.

SWIFT: I'm sorry. I'm sorry.

CURTIS: You grabbed her arms, pushed her up against the windowsill.

SWIFT: [inaudible].

CURTIS: And when she fell, you ran.

SWIFT: I left her there. I left her there. I don't—I'm sorry. I wasn't thinking. I just—I'm sorry. I'm sorry.

I closed out of the PDF, lit another cigarette. The smoke clung to my skin and hung in the windowless room. Ryan would smell it in my hair when I got home, would pull back in disappointment, disappear into his office. *This was a bad idea,* I told myself. I rubbed at my temples and closed my eyes and reminded myself of all the reasons I knew it was Alex. *He was the last one to see her. He was there. He lied.* I opened another transcript and kept reading.

I read through old court documents until five, my normal closing time. I locked up the shop and got into my car, thinking over what I'd say when Ryan asked how my day had been. *Fine. Lots of Easton kids hanging around without buying anything. Just like I said they would.* I squirted a glob of hand sanitizer on my hands, grabbed a breath mint, and started down Church Street. But instead of continuing straight, like I normally would, I turned onto Culver Street, then took a quick left turn into your neighborhood.

I felt a jolt at the sight of those familiar roads, still the same after all this time. Left after the white ranch house with pale blue shutters, right after the house where Caroline Liu used to live, the large oak tree in her front yard always the base for neighborhood games of kick-the-can. Left again into your cul-de-sac, the houses small but well-tended, some with blown-up versions of Santa Clauses and Snoopys, others with lights and fake icicles strung up on the porches.

I pulled to the curb a few houses before yours. Your yard was empty and overgrown with patches of weeds, the eaves of your house plain and unadorned. At the top of your sloping driveway, an open garage door. There was only one car inside, much smaller than the minivan your mother used to shuttle us around in. The garage door led into a mudroom and then your kitchen.

I could almost see us there, still, Emily and I perching on barstools at the kitchen island, while Alex rummaged through your pantry.

"Can't your mom buy Cheetos?" he asked. Small baggies of cloves and cinnamon sat in a basket by the stove, next to zucchini muffins arranged on a cake stand and a glass jar of homemade granola. Nothing with artificial coloring or flavoring or too much corn syrup. "If it's neon," your mother would tell us, "it's not good for you." (I repeated that to my mother one time, while she was refilling one of her candy bowls. "Good," she replied, popping a few Skittles into her mouth and then rolling the bag up again, sealing it shut with a clamp. "More for me, then.")

Emily rolled her eyes at Alex in mock disdain.

"I'll let her know you disapprove of the selection."

That afternoon, you had come downstairs to get a glass of water and lingered, finding small tasks to do in the kitchen: a letter that needed to be opened, dishes that needed to be put away, an orange that needed to be fished out of the bottom of your mother's fruit bowl and examined and washed and peeled in small deliberate pieces.

"Don't you have somewhere else to be?" Emily asked.

"Nope." You frowned in exaggerated concentration as you picked off the orange peel, placing each small orange chunk on a small plate behind you.

"You need to get some of your own friends."

"I live here, too."

"He's fine, Em." Alex dug his hand into a near-empty tub of peanut-butter pretzel logs and licked the salt off his fingers.

I watched as you stuck your tongue out at Emily. She sighed and slid down from her stool, rounding the island toward the kitchen sink.

"You are an actual child."

You scampered up into Emily's now-empty seat, beside me, and pulled one leg in toward your chest.

"Did you know it's not really possible to go anywhere?" The question was directed toward me. Your other leg hit against the chair's steel leg.

"What do you mean?"

"It's one of Zeno's paradoxes. The dichotomy."

"Don't engage," Emily warned.

"What's the dichotomy?" I asked.

"Before you can get to where you're going, you have to get halfway to where you're going, right?" You picked a blue M&M out of the bowl of trail mix on the island, then a yellow. "Like, say you wanted to go somewhere a mile away. You'd have to go half a mile first."

"Sure."

Emily threw her barely touched toast into the sink and ran the disposal.

"But before you could do the half-mile stretch, you'd have to do half of the half-mile stretch, right? You'd have to go a quarter mile?"

"I'm already lost." Alex gave you a good-natured smile before turning his attention to the refrigerator, pulling open the freezer drawer.

"*What* are you looking for?" Emily asked.

Alex shrugged. "Ice pops?"

"And before you could do a quarter mile, you'd have to do half of a quarter mile—an eighth of a mile." You were grinning now, your voice rising. You plucked another M&M out of the trail mix and popped it into your mouth.

"Stop picking out all the good stuff," Emily ordered, "and get to the point."

"So the point is," you said, ignoring Emily and directing your attention toward me, "the point is that you can keep dividing and dividing forever like that. There's an infinite number of finite distances that you have to cover before you can get anywhere. So, logically, you can never even get started!"

"Huh," I said.

"That doesn't make any sense," Emily said from the sink.

"It totally makes sense!" You twisted to face her, gleefully. "That's what's so crazy about it!"

"It's stupid. See? Now I'm at the sink . . ." Emily took big, exaggerated steps across the kitchen, pivoting on the balls of her feet when she reached the table. "And now I'm at the table. I have reached my destination." A small curtsy.

"Sorry, Josh," Alex said. He had found a tub of soy ice cream and was examining it with skepticism. "Gonna have to side with Em on this one."

"No, no, that's what makes it a paradox. Right, Micah? You get it."

"I'm going to have to think about that one," I said.

"Don't indulge him."

Ryan swung through the mudroom door then, not knocking. None of us ever knocked. He stepped on the backs of his shoes to slide them off.

"Oh, Ryan, you're gonna like this one," you said, picking out another M&M and turning back to me. "Ryan is definitely going to side with us."

Emily grabbed the bowl away and placed it out of reach. "Feeding time is over," she said. "We're going upstairs."

From the warmth of my car, I looked up to the window that used to be Emily's, the one above the garage, its curtains drawn. I wondered if your parents had kept that room the same: pale blue walls and ivory bedsheets. A simple brass mirror and picture frames that matched hanging on the walls.

Your front door swung open, interrupting my thoughts. Your mother stood behind it. Her graying hair was pulled back out of her face, her shoulders hunched inward. She shut the door behind her and paused for a moment on the front step, and I held my breath and froze. She reached into her purse and pulled out an envelope, then continued to the mailbox at the end of your driveway. She looked more tired than I remembered, her lips turned down at the corners. I wondered if it was inevitable that she would age that way, or if you and Emily did that to her. She made her way back to the car in the garage, and I waited, minutes ticking by, for her to leave. Finally, she backed down the driveway and drove past me. She pretended not to see me as I continued to look straight ahead.

It was later than normal when I finally got home, and I was sure that Ryan would notice.

Busy busy, I rehearsed in my mind as I walked down the plain hallway leading to our apartment, white walls and scuff marks. *Swarms of students. Lots of cleaning.*

But I swung open the apartment door to an empty family room. The office door was closed, a light shining through beneath the door. I rubbed at my eyes, puffy and bloodshot, and slid out of my jacket.

"I'm jumping in the shower!" I shouted.

"Okay!" Ryan shouted back, his voice muffled by the door.

I scrubbed at myself, trying to rub off the smoke that I knew was still clinging to my fingers, my face, my hair. I could see Alex in his striped sweater, blinking from police officer to police officer, trying to figure out where he had gone wrong. You, dressed in all black, pounding your fist against the narrow window by my front door. Emily, denim jacket stained with blood. I twisted the shower knob until the water stung and my skin turned red.

"How was your day?" Ryan asked when I finally emerged from the bathroom. He was coming back from the kitchen, a glass of water in his hand.

"Fine," I said, giving him a quick smile, a shrug. "You know. Lots of Easton students. Busy busy."

"That's great," Ryan said, sliding back into the office. "I told you. Flyers."

"You did," I said. "I guess you were right."

11

On my right, two rust-covered pumps and a dilapidated building come into view. The gas station would look abandoned if it weren't for the sign out front announcing prices. Only one other car sits in the parking lot: a beat-up sedan pulled around to the side of the building, with a thin layer of snow forming on its roof. I pull in and turn off the engine, and my car shudders to a stop. Next to me, a trash can overflows with paper bags and soda cans, frozen together in a layer of ice.

The gas station attendant emerges in a large red puffy coat, a black cap pulled down over his ears. He starts toward my car, his boots leaving a trail of footprints in the snow.

I roll down the passenger window, give him a small wave. "I'm okay," I say. "Just getting some gas."

He waves back at me and keeps moving forward. I grab my steering wheel, unsure of what to do. *If I turned the key,* I wonder, *will you start?* I think the answer is no.

The attendant rounds the back of my car, and I know he's looking at the side panel, although I continue facing forward. He approaches, crouches down, taps gently on the pane. I roll down my window.

"I'm okay," I say again. "I just need some gas. I can get it."

"In this weather?" he says. His stubbled smile grows wider, revealing crooked front teeth, one crossing over the other. "Don't you worry about it." His body blocks my door. I nod and pull out my wallet, reach for my credit card, change my mind.

"Forty dollars' worth," I say, pulling out two twenties instead. I flip through the remaining cash: eighty dollars, a few spare quarters.

"Awful weather out," he says. He takes my money and lingers in my window, gives me another smile. His red lips are chapped from the cold, split open on the left side. "I wouldn't want to be out driving in this."

I give him a tight smile in return and nod my head.

"Where are you off to?" He rests his hand on my car door, his tobacco-stained fingers curling in through the open window. I look down at his nails, gnawed down to the quick and blackened around the edges.

"Visiting a friend," I say.

"Ah." He taps twice on the vinyl interior of my door. He's looking past me at the crumpled cups and napkins strewn across the passenger seat, the pile of garbage on the floor. And then, to the back seat. A large black garbage bag overflows with sweatshirts and jeans, the tan leather arm of a jacket, its fraying banded wrist resting on the fabric seat. A handful of jewelry, some that had belonged to my mother, in case it's worth anything. I had to pack quickly. I had to leave most things behind.

"Must be a good friend," he said, his smile widening, stretching out his cracked lip. I can smell stale coffee on his breath. My pulse quickens. "For you to venture out in this, I mean."

"Oh." I try to return the smile, but I can feel the sides of my mouth quivering. I take small, measured breaths; I hope he can't tell.

A click, and the attendant straightens himself up again and turns to face the gas pump. I rub my fingers down my cheeks and up to my temples. The attendant rubs his hands on his coat, then stuffs them into his pocket.

"Be safe out there," he says, and the smile is gone now.

"Thank you," I say, or I try to, but the words catch in my throat. I nod and roll up my window and ease the car to the gas station exit. I glance up into the rearview window and see him watching as I leave. Blood pulses in my ears.

I glance down at my phone, think about calling you again. I decide against it. You'll call back when you're ready. You have to. I need to talk to you, Joshua. I need your help, and I'm worried you might need mine, too.

It's possible you already know about the new interest in Emily's case. But part of me doubts you've seen No Stone Unturned. You seem to stay offline, to the extent you can. No Facebook profile, under either name. An amateur website for Stonesport Maps & Prints Gallery, with a few pictures of antique maps and an outdated calendar. A Twitter account that you seem to have put together for the shop and used twice, three years ago; no sign that any of the accounts it follows have any connection to you.

Maybe your limited presence online is because you still don't trust other people. I can't say I blame you, given how cruel our classmates could be. I still remember passing by the courtyard on my way to the science wing for lunch, the straps from my backpack digging into my shoulders. I glanced over toward the picnic tables and saw the back of your head, the unbrushed swath of hair that you couldn't see and didn't care about. Matt and Brian sat across from you, looking amused. Matt leaned forward on his elbows, intent. Your hands were extended; you were telling a story. A lump formed in the pit of my stomach. I stepped off the walkway into the courtyard grass.

"So," I could hear Matt saying as I stepped closer. "He fucked his sister."

"His *half* sister," you corrected. "By Zeus."

"Yeah, Matt," Brian said. "*Half* sister. Keep up."

No, Joshua, I thought to myself. *No no no.*

"You know, it's actually interesting." As I came closer, I could see your face in profile. You looked so earnest, your eyes flitting back and forth between Matt and Brian. "Athenian law permitted marriage between half siblings from different mothers, and Spartan law permitted it between different fathers. So it might seem strange to us today—"

"*Fascinating,*" said Brian, too loud.

"Hey, hey, hey," Matt said, sitting up straight again. "Let's be fair. I'd be interested in this shit, too, if Emily were my sister."

Brian squeaked, and Matt pretended to suppress a laugh that came out like a snort, and then the two of them dissolved into laughter. I watched the shift in your expression as you realized you were being mocked, your jaw tensing as you clenched your teeth.

"I'm not—"

"No, no, no," Matt said, still laughing. "I totally get it. Emily is *hot,* right, Josh?"

You grumbled something unintelligible, your eyes flashing with anger.

"What was that?" Matt leaned forward again, toward you.

"*Koprophaga ta zoa,*" you shouted, louder this time. "*Hippobinus.*"

More peals of laughter.

"What did he just say?" Brian asked between gasps.

"Manure-eating animals," you spat, too forcefully. "Horse *fucker.*" The words were clunky and awkward.

"Joshua," I called, stepping quickly toward the table.

"Holy shit," Matt said, laughing louder. "Holy fucking shit."

"Joshua," I said again. "I've been looking for you."

I saw, then, that you were shaking with anger.

"Come have lunch with us," I said, nodding toward the heavy doors that led back into the school.

You sat there, fuming, staring too long and too hard at Brian, who was audibly catching his breath. I shot both Matt and Brian a warning look.

"Joshua."

You blinked, looked back toward me.

"Come eat with us," I said again. You pushed yourself up from the table, your face still bright red, and grabbed the stack of books in front of you.

"You shouldn't give them ammo," I said to you as we made our way toward the science wing together. "Just don't engage."

Your eyes were fixed on the hallway floor. I could tell you were replaying the scene in your mind, trying to figure out where it had taken a turn.

"I mean, you're not wrong," I said, nudging you with my shoulder. "Those two *are* horse fuckers."

A small smile crossed your face.

"You're better than them," I said. "You know that, right? Someday, you're going to get out of Calvary and forget all about them."

And that's what you did. You left, and you stayed away. You didn't pick at that scab by scrolling through pictures on social media. No late-night googling dredging up the past.

I probably should have done the same. But I couldn't resist the urge to see what people were saying. I waited until after Ryan fell asleep, then slipped into his office. *Our* office: it was my room, too, even if Ryan had commandeered it for his little men. The desk, facing out toward the door, created a small enclave in the back of the room. I entered the room slowly, feeling a little like I was invading Ryan's space. My feet brushed against a stack of rule books for the games that Ryan played, piled on the floor behind the desk. *It's* our *space,* I reminded myself, easing into the office chair and moving cups of paint, plastic bayonets, and a half-painted soldier to the side. I opened No Stone Unturned and went to the forum.

Dozens of comments on Alex, on the improbability of his guilt, on the flimsiness of his confession.

False confessions are far more prevalent than you might think, wrote Wellsinceyouasked, who obviously considered himself informed. A freshman majoring in criminal justice, I guessed. *It's estimated that twenty-five percent of wrongful convictions—that's one in four!—involve false confessions.* I bit down hard on my bottom lip and reminded myself that wrongful convictions had to be rare in the first place. Who would confess to something they didn't do?

Almost no forensic evidence introduced at trial, wrote TheMissingKing. *The entire case turned on the fact that he was the last one seen with her. That's not at least reasonable doubt?*

The mesh back of the office chair bounced under my weight as I leaned back. *What do you want?* I wanted to ask. "The last one seen with her," as if that were nothing. *He took her into the woods, to the place where she died. He lied, again and again and again.* I realized I was gripping the armrests so tightly that my fingers were beginning to ache. I loosened my grip.

I needed a cigarette. I crept back into the bedroom and opened the sliding glass door that led out to our balcony as softly as I could. Cold air blew in, rustling the beige linen curtains, and Ryan stirred but didn't wake. I slid the door shut behind me.

I lifted the ceramic dish covering one of the flowerpots that littered the balcony and pulled out a crumpled pack. I looked back toward the dark of our bedroom, Ryan sleeping soundly inside. He'd be furious if he knew what I was doing, the apples of his cheeks turning bright red.

It's not fair, I thought, rubbing my arms for warmth. All I was doing was looking at message boards online. I wasn't the one who drove sixty miles out to Frackville once a month.

He'd tell me it wasn't the same thing. He'd tell me that he didn't want to see me get hurt.

I leaned my elbows on the black metal railing that ringed our balcony and looked down at the parking lot that surrounded Calvary Lofts.

"Don't smoke out there," Ryan had admonished me one of our first weeks in the apartment, glancing at the empty neighboring balconies.

"What else is it for?" I had responded, ashing into an empty flowerpot. "The view?"

I tilted forward, staring down at the hard sidewalk beneath me. I thought about what it would be like to fall. Just one push, and then the crack of my head against the concrete, impact then nothing. I could taste iron in the back of my throat. The wind gusted and I straightened myself and backed away from the railing.

I thought of Alex roughhousing with his foster dog in a prison classroom. I squeezed my eyes shut and pictured Emily in a pool of blood, alone beside the cinder block house.

We had gone together the first time, the summer before Emily died. Ryan and Alex had stumbled across it by accident while out shooting each other with paintball guns, a new building in the campsite that we hadn't explored yet. The paths that must have led back to it at some point had grown over, the forest overtaking them.

"The old filing cabinets are still there," Ryan told us as we followed the dried-out creek bed back toward the cinder block house. "They're locked, but I bet we could break into them, see what's inside."

"Receipts?" Emily guessed, stepping easily from stone to stone. "Fifty cartons of ketchup: paid."

"You never know," Ryan said.

"I don't think anyone else knows about it," Alex said. "It's pretty hidden."

"Is that it?" I asked, an abandoned structure coming into view through the trees. Two cinder block stories built into a sloping incline. A heavy chain had been looped through its two rusted metal doors, presumably to keep out vagrants and teenagers. It had been cut in half so that it swung uselessly—so, I thought to myself, *someone* else knew about the place, although it was possible they hadn't been back in a long time.

"The cinder block house," Ryan said, pushing through a thorned branch. I lifted my arm to protect my face and followed.

"After you," Alex said to me and Emily, holding open the heavy door. I eyed the inside carefully, hesitated.

"Is this place about to come crashing down on us?"

"It's fine," Alex said. "We were in here yesterday."

Emily forged ahead, and I followed, breathing in its wet and earthy smell. I scuffed my feet along the concrete floor, covered in dust. Wet leaves piled up in the corner and water leaked down along the walls. Against the wall, a rusted metal filing cabinet. I tugged at one of its handles. It wouldn't give.

"See? I bet there's some way to open that up," Ryan said, behind me. I stepped aside so he could examine the lock, eyes squinted.

"You know how to pick locks?" I asked, ready to be surprised.

"No," he said. "But how hard could it be?"

Alex wasn't interested in the filing cabinet. He had turned his attention to the concrete stairs that wound up to the second floor. He rested one hand on the banister, each finger leaving its print.

"*That* might not be a good idea," Ryan said, glancing up toward the dark water spots on the ceiling. But Alex, already halfway up, wasn't listening, and Emily followed close behind him. I could hear their footsteps above me but couldn't make out what they were saying.

"Come on," I told Ryan. "The filing cabinet will wait. If they haven't fallen through yet, it's probably fine."

I climbed the stairs. Emily was examining the empty space where a windowpane used to be. Alex stood across the room—exaggerated distance for my benefit?—head tilted up at one of the gaping holes in the roof. A faint barnyard smell hung over the place, like grass and urine, with shredded papers and twigs amassed in the far corner.

"A nest?" Ryan suggested. "Raccoons, maybe?"

"Do raccoons drink Miller Lite?" Alex nodded toward shards of brown glass on the ground, then turned his attention to an old flashlight left behind. He picked it up and tried to switch it on. Nothing happened.

"Check out this view," Emily said, and Alex joined her at the window. He leaned his head and torso out the window.

"Uhhh-ah!" he said, tipping forward, pretending to lose his balance, and then landing, again, with his feet on the floor.

Emily smacked him on the shoulder.

"Don't be an idiot," she said.

A gust of wind shot through my balcony, bringing me back. I caught my breath, stubbed out my cigarette on the railing, and returned to the office.

Users had posted dozens of alternative theories on the forum—some similar to ones that floated around town in the days following Emily's death, others I had never heard before.

TheMissingKing: I've pulled some Google Maps images of the woods where Emily died. The location was an old camp run by the Catholic Church in the fifties, but it seems to have shut down suddenly and there's next to no information available about it online. Lots of young boys who would have been campers there. 😵 😵

Redhandman: A cover-up? Who knows what Emily might have found snooping around in there. Maybe she learned too much . . .

Wellsinceyouasked: There's a local news item from around the same time Emily died about strange activity in that area. Weird noises at night and animal remains showing up on property bordering the woods (pics here,

NSFW, obviously). Some of the animals were large (I think the biggest was a sheep), and the cuts are much cleaner than something you'd expect from a bear.

MissMaya: Are you thinking cult? Ritualistic sacrifices?

wildturkey: that looks like something a big cat would do. cougar, maybe?

Wellsinceyouasked: Do they have cougars in Pennsylvania?

wildturkey: not officially. but ya, they show up from time to time.

Wellsinceyouasked: I've been researching other murders in the area (5 year timespan, 100 mile radius). Came across Samuel Carpenter, an Easton student when Emily was in high school. He's in prison now for strangling a girlfriend with a telephone cord a few years after he graduated. I found a cached version of his old Facebook page, and, turns out, he worked at a sandwich shop *just two stores down* from Emily's ballet studio. They definitely would have crossed paths.

helenaa: My money is on Mr. Pruitt, our old history teacher. He used to stare at Emily *all* the *time*.

Swagmaggie: What if Emily staged her death to make it *look* like a murder to get back at Alex? How can we be sure those bruises weren't self-inflicted?

TheMissingKing: What do we know about Emily's parents? Any signs of abuse?

leezybird: her dad was out there. like he was on his own planet. weird guy.

Not a murderer, though, I thought to myself. Your father, a statistician at Easton, was always puzzling through probabilities and models. When I think of him, I think of Emily's eleventh birthday at the Northridge Roller Rink: lights mostly dim, with small bursts of color from the rotating disco balls hanging overhead. You had run off to play the arcade games that surrounded the rink, the beeping and clanging and clink of coins and digital gunshots punctuating family-friendly pop hits. Emily and I and five other girls had laced up our rental skates, brown with scuffed orange wheels and a plastic break beneath the toe. Your father sat with a gang of mothers in the café, where old hot dogs rotated on a roller grill, drumming his fingers on the plastic table and staring at the carpeted half-wall that separated the café from the rink.

"Are we going to see you out there?" my mom had asked your dad. A stupid joke, an attempt at being friendly. "I bet you could really cut up the rink."

"What?" His concentration broken, he turned to face her, like he was registering her presence for the first time.

"You know," my mom had said, ducking her head down and swinging her arms out to mime skating, and I cringed in embarrassment. "I strapped on some rollerblades myself a few years back and nearly broke my ankle. It's a young person's game." Your father's forehead creased, like he couldn't figure out why this person was talking to him, and my mother had turned to strike up a conversation with one of the other moms, who seemed more game to make small talk.

TheMissingKing: And her mom?

leezybird: she was a hippie. i think she was an artist?

A musician. A flutist, primarily, although she seemed to be able to pick up anything and play it, if she wanted to. She had a circle of creative friends who drifted in and out of your house, women in kaftans and chunky jewelry, men who would grab a guitar from the corner and start to play. They went to festivals together, and when she used to talk about them I always imagined an artist's colony in the woods: pottery wheels and poetry readings in dappled sunlight, impromptu musical collaborations and glassblowing, a celebration of the arts. ("They set up booths at Calvary's annual art fair at the rec center," Emily corrected. "It always smells like chlorine.")

mrdrfn: Uh, hello? The brother?

Wellsinceyouasked: Looks like Joshua spent some time in a psychiatric unit the year after Emily died. How did this not come up at trial?

Ambivalentaardvark: He had an alibi.

Wellsinceyouasked: His parents said that he was home that night. That's not an alibi. That's two folks who don't want to lose both their kids in one go. Classic JonBenet situation.

TheMissingKing: What was he hospitalized for?

leezybird: he used to make everyone really uncomfortable. always sitting a little too close, staring a little too long. and he smelled awful.

TheMissingKing: People don't get checked into mental institutions for not using deodorant.

leezybird: there was a rumor going around that he was fixated on emily. like REALLY fixated on her.

I thought back to a conversation with Michelle Peterson in the school hallway, right after Emily's death.

"I heard Joshua was secretly in love with her," she said, wide-eyed and incredulous, shaking her head in disbelief. She pulled out a tube of lip gloss and applied it generously. "How sick is that?"

"Did you hear that from Matt and Brian?" I asked. Michelle shrugged and examined herself in my locker mirror, smacking her lips together.

"It's not *true*," I said, slamming my locker door shut.

Michelle's face fell, her shiny lips contorting into a pout.

"Well, I believe it," she said, like it was some kind of brave act.

I closed the laptop and rocked back in my chair, rolling my head toward the line of little men on the bookshelf. The clock next to them glowed 3:00 A.M. So much for sleep.

helenaa: Joshua was definitely disturbed. Micah Wilkes had to take out a restraining order against him our senior year.

Wellsinceyouasked: I haven't seen a record of that anywhere.

mrdrfn: Yeah, of course not. He was a minor.

helenaa: Everyone knew about it. He basically attacked her. Totally unhinged.

The restraining order. You had just lost your sister. You were lashing out. But you have to understand how frightening it was at the time. I didn't know what to do.

I was home alone that night. My mother was out with a friend—a date, most likely, but she never called it that. She would be out "late." I didn't like entering a dark room when I was home alone, so all of the lights were on, the fluorescent glare almost creating the illusion that it was the middle of the day. But the windows were all pitch-black; with the lights on, it was impossible to see anything outside.

A Lifetime movie I had seen pieces of before played on the television in my family room. Teenaged Ben Savage in a muscle shirt berated a young Candace Cameron for the way she was dressed, then slammed her against the wall of the high school field house. "Great," he said to her as the coach ran over to check on them. "You happy now?" He got away with a warning. I remembered how the movie ended, Candace Cameron's friend cleaning out her locker in tears, and changed the channel, flipping through the stations to *Law & Order*. My dog, Ollie, nestled into the space behind my knees, his small tan-and-white muzzle resting on my legs. On the television, detectives showed up at a brownstone apartment, a nervous maid opening the door. As they pushed their way up a rounded ivory staircase, Ollie's head perked up, his ears pricked. My shoulders stiffened. I scratched Ollie behind the ears. An emaciated boy with sad brown eyes looked up at the detectives, and they exchanged world-weary glances. Ollie leaped down from the couch and skittered toward the bay windows. Focusing on a point I couldn't see, he started growling, a low, guttural sound, his teeth bared.

"Ollie, stop," I told him, but he didn't listen. *It's just an animal. A deer wandering across the yard.* I grabbed the phone from the kitchen and returned to the family room. I rapped against the windows, hoping the noise would scare the animal away. Ollie kept growling. He turned away from the windows and sprinted across the floor to the hallway, his attention focused on the front door. The doorbell rang.

I couldn't remember if the door was locked. I edged toward it, carefully, fastening the dead bolt before flipping on the light out front. The front steps illuminated, I could see you, looking back at me through the long narrow windows that framed the door, chewing the inside of your lip. You wore a black fleece that couldn't have been warm enough, your dirty blond hair swept back into a short ponytail at the nape of your neck. One bare hand rested on the windowpane, your long fingers red with cold. I stepped back as you leaned forward, your nose almost touching the glass. Suddenly, you looked older: an adult, almost, thin tufts of hair on your upper lip. Your shoulders, wiry but broader than mine, your hands large. Your cheeks, like your fingers, scarlet from the cold. It looked like you had been outside a long time.

"What are you doing here?" I shouted through the window. Ollie scratched at the door, his growls punctuated by agitated whines.

"I just want to talk," you said, your shoulders hunched up toward your ears. Your eyes hadn't changed: the same eyes that used to plead with Emily to come along to Mr. Hunt's ice cream shop, the same ones that flashed with excitement when you found that snake in your mother's garden.

I hesitated, saw the way that your left hand clenched and unclenched in a fist at your side. "I don't think that's a good idea." I backed away from the door, squeezing the phone in my hand.

"Come on, Micah. Let me in. It's cold out here."

With the outside lights on, I could see the tail end of your footprints in the snow. They weren't leading up from the walkway; you had come up from the side, from the family room window. You had been watching.

I lifted the phone so that you could see it, a warning. "I'm calling the police if you don't leave now."

"Jesus Christ, don't be so dramatic. Just let me in. I need to talk to you."

I made a show of dialing slowly, so you could see, so you knew I was serious. "I'm calling," I said, holding the phone to my ear.

"911, what's your emergency?" said the voice on the other end.

Instead of leaving, you began pounding on the window, the glass rattling.

"Someone is trying to break into my house."

"What the *fuck,* Micah. Let me *in,*" you shouted, over and over, eyes blazing with anger. Not the ones I knew. The glass rattled harder and I turned and ran, up the stairs to my bedroom, locking the door behind me. I looked around at the dark maroon walls that now held me in, the single window on the other side of my bed, and wondered if I had made a mistake. If you broke in, the only way out was my bedroom window, a fall made longer by the sloping incline in my backyard. The lock had to hold. I could hear the banging downstairs, followed by the sound of broken glass, the door swinging open, slamming against the wall, footsteps up the stairs. I slid down against my door, hoping my weight against it would be enough to keep you out. I wondered how much pressure the flimsy lock on my door would handle; how long it would take for the police to come. I could hear the vibration from your fists on the wood against my back.

"I just need to *talk* to you," you said, over and over again, until there were more footsteps, charging up the stairs, a scuffle as they pulled you away. You were gone by the time the police coaxed me out of my room, but your blood was still there, smeared against the white of the door at eye level.

My mother made me get the restraining order. We fought often, but she was never a yeller. Instead, she'd go silent, aggressively cleaning, giving me angry, pointed looks when I passed through the kitchen. This time, though, was different.

"I don't want to do it," I said, and she slammed down the phone she was holding, poised to call an attorney.

"*Enough,* Micah," she shouted, and I startled, froze in place. "That's *enough.* I don't want to hear it. My job is to keep you safe. I'm going to keep you safe."

The next morning, I went with her to an attorney's office and told a skinny woman who didn't blink enough what had happened. She wrote it all down on a yellow legal pad.

"Okay," she said, clicking her pen and placing it back down on her desk. She laced her hands together, looked back up at me, and smiled, too wide, like I was a child. "Okay. Don't you worry. We'll get this taken care of."

12

Still no response from you, not even an acknowledgment. I grab my phone and type out another text.

I know I might not be your favorite person. But you need to call me back. We're both in trouble.

I hope it was easier for you in Minnesota. No one would have known you there. No memories of the Joshua in eighth grade who went on a shower strike for weeks before Emily finally put her foot down. She hid the power cord for the computer and told you she wasn't giving it back until you bathed. No memories of the Joshua in sixth grade who talked too loudly on the bus about criminals in Ancient Greece being roasted alive in a giant bronze bull.

"You need to knock it off," Emily said. "I can hear you all the way from the back of the bus."

"But it's so crazy!" you said. "They created a system of tubes in the bull's head that converted screams into *bellows*."

"Just stop," Emily responded. "It's fucking weird."

Like hitting a reset button: you left, and left everything behind you. Except it never really goes away. It's still there for strangers to nitpick and analyze, to shape and distort, to use to support wild conclusions, baseless accusations, slander.

Once I started reading those posts, they were all I could think about. At Stomping Grounds, I found myself surrounded by Easton students, groups of them clustering around tables and slouched down in their seats. I waited for a lull and then slipped into the storage room, pushing the lock as I shut the door behind me. If someone needed something, they could wait.

I went back to the forum. Strangers spoke about you—about all of us—with familiarity. They knew I was still in town. They knew I had been in Chicago before. They knew about Stomping Grounds. One post linked to its Yelp page. They had googled me, scrolled through my Facebook page and public records. Collected facts about me, tried to piece them together into something significant. As if you could piece together my life, my identity, from an Internet search.

They weren't all strangers, of course. I recognized the names of a few old classmates, eager to insert themselves into the drama. An old teammate of Alex's who claimed he had a violent, competitive side not many people knew about. A former "friend" of Emily's who asserted that she never believed the whole relationship angle. Emily was far too dedicated to dancing, she said, to get tangled up in something messy like that. Like that's all there was to her, like she wasn't a full person capable of mistakes and contradictions. "Helenaa"—probably my old classmate Helena Abrams—who couldn't help but point out how hard the whole thing had been for her, as someone who had attended the party.

helenaa: We were all there, so close by, probably close enough to hear something if the party hadn't been so loud. That thought haunts me, you know? It's just not something you think will happen to you.

It didn't *happen to you,* I thought, uncoiling a paper clip, twisting it around and around itself until it snapped in two. But that didn't matter to Helena. My guess is that every time she fills out an application for a reality TV show—and I'm sure she's filled out plenty—she includes "friend in high school tragically murdered" as an interesting fact about herself.

One commenter had dug up old pictures of us online. One of you and Emily at a cousin's wedding, sitting next to each other but not close. Emily's head angled down so she was looking up at the photographer, you with your hair combed and pulled back. I could imagine the fight that must have taken place before the wedding, Emily insisting that you *do* something to make yourself look presentable. Another of me, Emily, Ryan, and Alex, huddled together by Emily's locker at the far end of the science wing. Beside us, two heavy gray doors that let in a blast of cold air when anyone entered or exited, which happened all the time. Alex leaned back against the lockers, and I leaned against him, his arms around my waist. Emily sat beside Ryan, wearing his slate-gray coat, its shoulders too large for her tiny frame.

"My coat's not warm enough," she would complain every day during the winter, rubbing the light fabric of her sleeve. And every day, without fail, Ryan would take off his coat and hand it over.

"I don't mind the cold," he would say, but I knew that wasn't true because, after a few weeks, he began wearing extra layers of clothes to school.

I wondered where these pictures had come from, what else was out there.

"He-llo?" A muffled voice, full of irritation, from the other side of the door. I made my way back out to the main room, my eyes readjusting to the light. A line of customers waited by the counter, thumbing their phones and shifting from foot to foot with impatience.

"What can I get for you?" I asked the first girl in line, stretching my mouth into a smile. My right eyelid twitched, and I hoped it wasn't noticeable. The girl looked to the chalkboard behind me as if she hadn't just had ten minutes to make her decision.

"A caramel macchiato," she said, finally. And then, insincerely, "Thanks."

I eased foamed milk into espresso and caramel and tried to think back to the night of the party. There had been so many people wandering across the lodge's concrete slab, sneaking off to the bleachers, weaving in and out of the trees. Faces blurred in my mind as I tried to pinpoint them, memories slipping in and out of reach.

There were, of course, some people I knew were there. Matt Penna had been making a big deal about the party during gym class and wouldn't stop talking about the keg once we got there. And I know Michelle Peterson was there, just as clearly as I know Patrick Sellers wasn't. Michelle had been going on and on about how this was going to be their night, she just knew it, and then when Patrick didn't show up, she fell into a sulk and went around with a sour look on her face, trying to get people to ask why she was so upset and refusing to answer when they finally did.

You, a black cap pulled down over your hair, a flashlight, turned off, in your hand.

"Soy latte?" said a girl I was beginning to recognize as a new regular, the short-haired girl with teeth that didn't quite fit into her mouth. She leaned in over the counter to get my attention, stretching her upper lip over her teeth impatiently.

"It's coming," I said.

I tried to conjure up a memory: Helena leaned against the altar stones, smirking, her hair piled into a messy bun on the top of her head. A middle-aged man who dressed as though he was still in his twenties gave an irritated cough in front of me.

"Americano," he said as soon as he managed to make eye contact. "Please."

Once the drinks were made and the customers had shuffled

back to their seats, I returned to the storage room. I scrolled through the threads again until I came across one that knocked the air out of me.

Give me your questions for Alex, the thread title said. *I'm his girl-friend.*

"Jesus Christ," I muttered, snapping another paper clip. Julia, so desperate for attention, for recognition that Alex had chosen *her.* I unwound a third paper clip and snaked it around my left index finger. *It's not worth it,* I told myself, trying to move on to another thread. *I can't let her get to me.* But I couldn't help myself. I needed to know what she was saying. What *Alex* was saying, after all this time.

jules: Alex has been in prison ten years for a crime he didn't commit. I have been by his side throughout this ordeal, and I am so grateful to the No Stone Unturned community that this case is finally getting the attention it deserves. I am happy to answer any questions about his case, prison conditions, or what it's like to be wrongfully convicted. If I don't know the answer, I'll ask Alex at our next visit.

Three impatient raps at the storage room door. "Excuse me?" I heard from the outside. "Anyone here?" I ignored it. This was more important.

The questions, at first, were directed at Julia, not Alex. *Do you have conjugal visits?* a few commenters wanted to know. No answer.

MissMaya: What made you decide to get involved with a convicted murderer? Aren't you worried he might be violent with you once he gets out of prison?

jules: I've known Alex for a long time. He's one of the gentlest, sweetest people I know. He'd never hurt anyone.

forwardslapped: yea, except that time he sent his old girlfriend flying out a window lol

jules: His record at Frackville speaks for itself. He's been a model prisoner. He teaches one of the prison G.E.D. classes and has helped other prisoners learn how to read and write.

Bethlovesdogs: I just don't understand how someone could stay with someone who murdered their best friend.

MissMaya: Wrong person. Julia didn't come onto the scene until after the conviction. You're thinking about Micah Wilkes.

The mention of my name made my skin crawl.

Annieb: You know, we often paint the incarcerated as these monsters, unfit for contact with the outside world. The truth, though, is that they're real human beings, like you and me. I've had multiple prison pen pals, and each correspondence has been a really rewarding relationship.

forwardslapped: your as crazy as she is

TheMissingKing: Stop piling up on her. This is a real opportunity to find out more about Alex. Julia, what does Alex think happened?

jules: All that Alex knows for sure is that when he left Emily, she was alive. He thinks that someone must have followed them into the woods and, when Alex left and they realized Emily was all alone in the house, they saw that as an opportunity.

mrdrfn: Does he think it was Joshua?

jules: Alex knows the dangers of jumping to conclusions. He wouldn't want to point fingers without definitive proof.

Alex, so wise and enlightened.

Wellsinceyouasked: What piece of evidence does Alex think is most likely to exonerate him? What does he wish the jury had gotten to hear?

jules: It's not so much what evidence there was, as what evidence there wasn't. The prosecution pinned their entire case on the fact that Alex was in the wrong place at the wrong time. We've asked over and over again for more DNA testing to find out who else might have been at the crime scene, and over and over again we've been denied. They say there's not a "reasonable probability that testing would produce exculpatory evidence." But how could more information be bad?

Ambivalentaardvark: But they did fight, and he was the last one seen with her. Alex's guilt is the simplest possible explanation. What makes you confident that he didn't do it?

jules: I know him. I know his heart. I know he isn't capable of something like that.

Not capable, Julia said, like that settled it. Like it's possible to look into someone's eyes and see all his potential there, good and bad. *Could he have done something like that?* Such a ridiculous question, but the question everyone seemed to ask. News coverage showed Alex's big, ruddy smile; classmates retold and reassessed old stories, trying to find clues that he had really been a monster all along. "I just can't believe it," my mother had said in hushed tones on the phone when she thought I wasn't listening. I'd catch her staring at the kitchen table, at the chair he used to sit in when he came over for dinner and made friendly small talk over plates of spaghetti. "This is great, Mrs. Wilkes." Always so polite; was he *capable*?

Yes, I always wanted to shout back. *Yes, of course he was.* The truth is we're all capable of monstrous things.

Bethlovesdogs: But how can you possibly trust him, given that he's *at least* a cheater?

jules: Different relationship, a long time ago. I'm not worried :)

I hadn't been worried, either. In fact, every time I saw them together, it made me *happy:* happy the two people I loved most in the world were getting along. Early on in my relationship with Alex, they both showed up together to a late-season high school football game. I wore white gloves with the fingers cut off and kept small heat packs in my pocket to warm my hands between songs. I had played clarinet since sixth grade, and I was fine, but just fine. Always first clarinet, but never first chair. The drum major flicked his wrist and we lifted our instruments and the bass line rumbled. I shouted out *Hey!* on cue with the rest of the band, fists punching in the air.

"Micah!" I heard, and there was Emily, making her way through the steel bleachers toward me, navigating over hats and around knees. She had on high boots over tight jeans and a hoodie, and I straightened myself, suddenly too aware of my thick-soled black sneakers and pleated pants. Behind her: Alex. I saw him catch Ryan's eye, three rows behind me with the other trumpet players, and gesture for him to come down. Then he turned his attention toward me. Our eyes met, and my stomach turned over on itself.

"Look who I found," Emily said, gesturing back toward Alex, and I remember being so surprised—and so happy—that they had hit it off.

"Welcome to the marching band ghetto," I said to the two of them, loud enough to be heard over the drums pounding in front of us. The band was in its own section of the bleachers, cordoned off from the rest of the school.

"We brought you something," Alex said, a dimple forming on his right cheek, and if my face hadn't already been windburned from the cold, it would have turned bright red. He handed me a Styrofoam cup of hot chocolate from the concession stand. It was gritty and still so hot it burned the roof of my mouth and the best thing I had ever tasted.

"So this is what everyone is always going on about," Emily said, squeezing into the bleachers beside me. "I guess this makes me a teen stereotype now."

That was a category of thing that Emily talked about with growing frequency: things that teen stereotypes did. Things like french fries and frosties on late-night Wendy's runs, Keystone Light at parties in basements when parents were out of town, full days spent loitering at the mall. Frivolous things, things that were less important than ballet.

"This is your first game?" Alex said, addressing Emily but settling in on the other side of me, draping his arm over my shoulder. "You've been missing out!" I leaned into the warmth of him, the spiced scent of his cologne, too heavy, but none of us knew that then.

"Micah, you're freezing," he said, and he slipped off his letterman jacket, placing it over my shoulders.

"Guess I'm the teen stereotype now," I said, aware of how ridiculous it was—a football game, a letterman jacket, like something out of the 1950s. I didn't want to show how much I was enjoying it.

"How do I look?" Emily grabbed my plumed hat and placed it, tilted, on her own head, pretending to play an imaginary flute. *A joke for my benefit,* I thought at the time. I wonder now if it was at my expense. Somehow, she still looked good—no ring of sweat where the hat met her forehead, no gold shoulder epaulettes and fringe.

"Maybe you should think about joining," I said, leaning my weight into Alex's side. It was a joke. Emily had briefly considered trying out for the cheerleading squad, but she decided against it at the Lionels' suggestion. It wasn't serious enough, and it would eat into her *real* dance practice too much.

"I think the color guard still has openings." Ryan had sat down in the row behind us, displacing the tuba player.

Emily rolled her eyes and glanced back out toward the field. On the red paved track, the cheerleaders hoisted flyers up into the air, stiff and poised until they folded back down into the bases' arms. Past them, the football shot into the air and the marching band trilled, a jumble of notes. Emily glanced back toward Ryan, who lowered his trumpet.

"Distraction," he explained.

"Ah," Emily said, taking a sip of her own hot chocolate.

"I still can't believe you've never been to a game," Alex said. "Not even homecoming?"

"Nope," Emily said.

"Huh." Alex seemed genuinely confused.

Our running back broke a tackle and darted down the field. Everyone jumped up and started shouting, and Emily stood, too, crossing her arms over herself.

"Are the soccer matches like this?" she asked.

"Nah," Alex said. "No one cares about the soccer team. We're not very good."

"*You're* good," I said, and Alex shrugged and nodded. No false modesty, no bravado: just a fact.

"Maybe we should go to a game," Emily said.

"Absolutely," Alex said, tightening his arm around my shoulder.

It was weeks before Emily finally made it to a soccer game with me, though. She had a competition she was rehearsing for, something in Mississippi, "a big deal," she told me. I had fallen into a new rhythm, too. Alex would walk over after school, and we would retreat down into the basement, my mother coming down every fifteen minutes to find a box of old clothes that she needed, or a wrench, or a tangled web of Christmas lights that had to be dealt with right away.

"I've missed you," I told Emily as we sat down beside each other on the bleachers behind the field house.

"No you haven't," Emily said matter-of-factly, and she nodded toward the field. "Not with this one around."

One of Alex's teammates kicked the ball back to him, and Alex took it down the field, fending off the other team's defenders.

"He's good," Emily said.

"He is."

"Look at how much control he has over his movements. His center of gravity is right where it should be so he can turn and respond. Right there—see how he pivots and boxes out the guy who's supposed to be on him?"

"Huh," I said. When I watched a soccer match, I clocked how fast the players were moving, how close the ball was to the goal at any given time, how concerned Lonnie Dunne, our team's goalkeeper, looked. Without the crowd's excitement, there wasn't that much to hold my attention. But I could see it once she pointed it out.

A sharp whistle sounded from behind us as Alex got the ball, again, and made his way down the field. I turned to see Julia and her friend, a slight girl with a pinched nose and frizzy hair, sitting three rows behind us. It was the friend, I gathered, who had whistled. Julia elbowed her in the side, embarrassed, her face turning a deep red. She reached into her bag and pulled out a crumpled tissue.

"Looks like we're not the only members of Alex's fan club," Emily said to me, raising an eyebrow.

Alex took aim and launched the ball into the goal, narrowing the gap between the two teams. The small crowd around us stood and applauded, and Emily and I stood to join them.

"We should do more of this," Emily said, not looking at me.

"School sports?" I joked.

"You know what I mean."

"Well, after your competition is over, you can start wasting all your time again like the rest of us," I said.

"Yeah, it doesn't really work that way."

Alex got the ball again, and he and Brian ran down the field in tandem, passing the ball back and forth. Emily watched, never taking her eyes off of Alex, and even then, I didn't see it. I only saw what I wanted to believe.

. . .

I pushed myself away from the computer, reemerged, and took my place behind the counter. The long-haired Easton student had joined the large-toothed girl. The two whispered to each other conspiratorially, then looked back in my direction. *They're just talking,* I told myself. *I'm imagining things.*

My phone buzzed, and I pulled it out of my pocket. A text from Ryan. *Home late tonight,* it said. *Tournament.* A gaming night. Ryan would be scooping up all of his miniatures and taking them to Merlock's to compete. Rolling dice to see if his tiny men advanced or retreated, measuring out their movements by ruler.

I slipped my phone back into my pocket as the door swung open. I readied myself for more college students but instead saw two faces I recognized. Chelsea Keene and Caroline Liu, ten years older than the last time I had seen them, Chelsea with her sweater carefully tucked into the front of her high-waisted jeans, Caroline in a Sherpa jacket and leggings. They were laughing at a shared joke but stopped when they saw me, collected themselves. Caroline glanced toward Chelsea, as if to say: *Did you know she'd be here?*

"Micah!" Chelsea said. Natalie had captured her smile perfectly: a stage smile, too exaggerated to be genuine. "Wow! How long has it been?"

"Chelsea," I said, not quite matching her enthusiasm. "How have you been?"

"Do you work here?" Caroline looked around, sizing up the shop.

"I'm the owner." It came out more defensive than I had hoped.

"You're still in town?" Chelsea asked, still smiling. "That's great." Just a little too upbeat. Chelsea had done Teach For America in New York and then stayed in the city to work at a nonprofit. She didn't think there was anything great about staying in Calvary.

"Yeah, well."

The large-toothed girl rose from her seat and took her place in line behind Chelsea and Caroline. She pulled out her phone and pretended to look down at it, but I knew she was listening. I shifted uncomfortably. Chelsea noticed her and stepped to the side.

"Oh, go ahead," she said. "We're just catching up."

I tried to relax, made the girl a coffee. There was no need to be on edge, I reminded myself. I had nothing to be ashamed of. I turned back to them, tried to smile. "Can I get you guys something, too?"

"Just a coffee," Chelsea said. Caroline nodded.

"Make that two."

She started to pull out her credit card, and I waved at her.

"Don't worry about it. On the house."

Caroline glanced at Chelsea again, and I could tell she wanted to sit down, or leave, or do anything other than stand at the counter making small talk with me. But Chelsea pushed on.

"So, who else are you in touch with?"

I shrugged. "Natalie Smith. And I'm living with Ryan now—Ryan Terrasen."

Their faces registered surprise. Chelsea's smile grew bigger.

"That's great," Chelsea said. "Really great. Hopefully the two of you can make it this weekend."

"Maybe," I said. I stepped back, trying to imply I had work that needed to be done.

"Wasn't he—" Caroline started to ask. I knew what was coming next. She was going to ask about Alex, but Chelsea cut her off before she could finish.

"Just let me know. I need to give the restaurant a final head-count tomorrow."

"Gotcha."

They left, passing through the crowd of Easton students, saying something to each other in low voices. At the back corner table, the large-toothed girl shoved the long-haired boy playfully, her head thrown back in a loud, artificial laugh. *It's not strange,* I thought defensively, *that Ryan and I ended up together after everything we've been through.*

"Excuse me," said a man with a hairline that was just beginning to recede, too old to be an Easton student. I stuffed my phone back into my pocket. "Black coffee, please."

I poured the coffee and willed myself to focus on work. I weaved around the backpacks and clusters of chairs, collecting the empty mugs that had begun to pile up in my absence. *Alex's best friend and Emily's best friend, ending up together, that's what they see. Is it strange?*

I wiped down tables littered with crumpled napkins and damp wooden coffee stirrers with large swooping circles. *No,* I thought to myself resolutely, so resolutely I worried, for a moment, that I might have spoken out loud. I glanced toward the students beside me to see if they noticed. They at least pretended to be absorbed in their laptops. *We both went through loss; we understand each other.*

Ryan, who was off fighting imaginary battles while I fielded daily reminders of Emily. Tromping his little army around cotton-ball bushes, over tinfoil rivers. *He doesn't know what's been happening,* I reminded myself. *He doesn't know about the site.*

"How could she not have known?" I overheard the large-toothed girl saying. My shoulders stiffened. "She *has* to have known."

The long-haired boy shrugged and jerked his head back, adjusting a lock of hair that had fallen in his face. *They could be talking about anything,* I reminded myself. I turned my back to them and ducked down to change out the garbage bag beneath the condiment bar.

"Oh come on," the girl said, louder this time. "There's no way you wouldn't *notice.*"

"Hey," the long-haired boy said, the low volume of his voice a message: *Keep it down.*

"What?"

"Just—" He didn't finish his sentence. I imagined him tilting his head toward me, raising his eyebrows. My hand gripped the garbage bag so tightly I could feel the muscles in my fingers starting to cramp. I tied a quick knot, shoved in a new bag.

"Who cares?" The girl's voice was still loud, full of false bravado.

I slammed the door on the condiment bar and marched toward the table where the two of them were sitting. The girl's eyes flashed nervously; she pulled down her front lip over her teeth.

"You need to leave," I said, quietly so that the other tables couldn't hear.

The long-haired boy puffed up in his seat, drawing back his shoulders. "What?" he said, twitching away a phantom lock of hair.

"Just what I said. You need to go."

The large-toothed girl scoffed, raising her chin defiantly. "We weren't doing anything."

"I don't care," I said. "You're not welcome here. And . . ." I rested my hands on their table, leaning in toward the girl. "You shouldn't judge people. You don't know what they've been through."

The girl scoffed again, rolling her eyes at the boy. He didn't return the look. Instead, he stuffed his laptop into his bag and began coiling his headphones and computer cord. The girl pushed her chair back so that the legs scraped against the floor.

"Crazy bitch," she said, jamming her arms into the sleeves of her jacket. I could feel the students at the other tables watching, trying to figure out what was going on. Trying to figure out if I was the unstable one. I didn't care. I needed to defend myself. If there's one thing I've learned, it's that. If I don't watch out for me, who will?

13

The Connecticut roads are quiet, hemmed in by trees and well-maintained homes. I drive past a farmers' market with an honor-system produce booth out front. A stately inn with a pitched roof sits just off the side of the road. Everything done just so; everything restored and maintained.

I put everything into building Stomping Grounds, Joshua. I had wanted a place of my own, a project I could throw myself into. I wanted to be *Micah Wilkes, owner of the coffee shop downtown*, not *Micah Wilkes, friend of that dead girl. Micah Wilkes, the girl who didn't realize her boyfriend was cheating on her. Micah Wilkes, the girl who didn't wait for her best friend, who didn't even look for her.* I had just sold my mother's house when I heard about the vacancy where Mr. Hunt's ice cream shop used to be. His two daughters had taken over the shop when his health started to decline, but it had been more work than they expected, and neither of them wanted to run the store full-time. It was an old-looking space—run down and shabby, with chipped walls and old tile floors, and I thought: *I can do something with that. I can make it something better.*

But it wasn't mine, not really. All those Easton students, coming in to gawk. The large-toothed girl and the long-haired boy. *Crazy bitch.* After I kicked them out, once they finally gathered their things and left, the other students eyed each other with barely suppressed smiles, ducking their heads to conceal laughter.

"What the fuck is her problem?" muttered a boy with glazed-over, barely focused eyes, his legs stretched out into the narrow aisle. The girl sitting next to him snorted in response, then coughed to mask it. They were both enjoying the show.

I spent the rest of the afternoon at Stomping Grounds on edge, eyeing each new face that entered with suspicion. *Are you just here to watch me, too?* I almost shouted at a tiny girl in an oversized sweatshirt who shuffled to the counter and handed me a bottle of water from the display cooler without making eye contact, shaking her head skittishly when I asked if she wanted anything else. *Do you think I'm here for your entertainment?*

I went home that evening exhausted. I had kicked off my shoes and collapsed on the couch before I realized something in the apartment was off. It was just a feeling, at first: the sense that something was out of place, not where I had left it. By the door, an empty hook where Ryan's coat normally would have hung, an empty space beneath it for his boots. *He's at Merlock's,* I reminded myself. *He's not supposed to be here.* The feeling didn't go away. I twisted myself around, saw the glow of recessed lights in the kitchen. *Ryan could have forgotten to turn them off before he left.* Could have. Usually didn't. Usually was fastidious about that kind of thing.

I leaned back and was about to pull out my phone when I noticed what had been a neat stack of mail that morning scattered across our coffee table and one of Ryan's books overturned on the floor between the table and the couch. I crouched down, picked it up, and set it back in its place. *Ryan wouldn't have left things this way.* I picked up a letter addressed to me, its edges jagged where it had been ripped open. I hadn't seen that letter before. *Ryan must have opened it,* I reasoned, but the unease stuck with me. Ryan might open a bill or a bank statement, but this letter looked more personal, my name and address handwritten in loopy lettering on the front. I pulled out the letter and examined it: just a request for a donation. I flipped through the mail underneath: all typed out and corporate-looking, all still sealed.

My laptop rested on the end table, where I had left it that morning, underneath a stack of papers for Stomping Grounds. *But was it* under *the papers this morning?* I had finally emerged from the office, bleary-eyed after spending too many hours staring at the screen. Tossed the laptop down on the end table, dragged myself to bed. *Did I move it after that?* I pulled the laptop onto my lap and shuffled through the papers like that might be able to tell me something. All Stomping Grounds–related: an invoice for coffee beans, an inventory, a few handwritten to-do lists. *Ryan wouldn't go through these.* I opened the lid to my laptop, which lit up to a password-protected screen.

I set the laptop down beside me and took soft, careful steps toward the kitchen. I pulled open the top drawer next to the stove and eyed its contents: scissors on top of Post-it notes, Scotch tape in the back left corner. Nothing unexpected. On the fridge: photographs of me and Ryan, held up by magnets from Peck Hardware, Dr. Andrews's dental practice, Andrea's Flowers & Gifts. A wedding invitation stuck to the freezer. A shot of us in our ski gear in the Poconos; a picture from the shore. I squinted at a picture from a wedding we had been to the summer before for one of Ryan's college friends. In it, Ryan stood uncomfortably in a recently purchased suit. *Was it in the same place this morning?* A stretch of white space down the left side of the fridge, like something had been there before.

I rounded the kitchen and entered the unlit hallway. The office door was closed, the bedroom door cracked open. A cold wetness soaked through the toe of my right sock. I stepped back and looked down to see a small puddle of water, melted snow from outside.

Droplets of water everywhere, arching from the front door toward the kitchen, a trail down the hallway. *Not from me.* I tried to retrace my steps when I first entered. I hadn't gone back to the hallway. *Did I?*

A creak, soft but indisputable, behind the closed office door. *An intruder shifting his weight, crouching into a better position.* I seized up, staring at the metal doorknob, half-expecting it to turn.

"Hello?" I called out, backing away from the office door. *It's nothing. The sound of the building settling.* Another shock of cold as my left heel landed in a puddle. "Is someone there?"

No response. I tried to think clearly, rationally. *The door was locked. We're on the second floor.*

Another creak, louder this time. Closer to the door.

Call the police. I should call the police. I took another step back, feeling for the couch behind me, working my way toward the front door. I reached into my pocket and wrapped my hand around my phone. The apartment was silent. *It's nothing,* I tried to convince myself. *I'm overreacting. What would I say? Something feels wrong. An envelope that's been opened. A soft creak. Water on the floor. Yes, I know it's been snowing.*

I imagined a recording of my call to the police being uploaded to No Stone Unturned along with some faux-sympathetic note about all the stress I was under. The "Truthseekers" listening carefully for clues, judging whether or not I did the right thing, analyzing my mental state. *What did she say? What words did she use? Doesn't she sound kind of unstable? Hysterical? Over-the-top?* Or: *She's really losing it, isn't she? Crazy bitch.* One or two might try to take credit: *I did it! It was me in there!*

"I know you're in there," I said, my voice full of uncertainty. *Stop shaking.* I grabbed my shoes and turned the knob to the front door. "I just want you to go. I'm leaving now." No acknowledgment, no new noise from the office. Everything was still. *I'm being ridiculous.*

"I'm leaving," I said again, a little louder this time. "Please." A tremor in my voice. "Please just go." I moved slowly across the doorframe, easing the door closed behind me. When it finally clicked shut, I ran. Down the hallway and the winding staircase, taking the stairs as quickly as I could, still clutching my shoes in my hand. Not stopping to put them on until I had pushed through the heavy side door to the apartment complex, out onto the cold black tar of the parking lot, puddles of melted slush soaking through my socks. I looked back at those doors, which closed behind me and stayed shut, no sign that anyone was following me, no movement at all. Beside the doors, a key code box, additional security, further proof that it was all in my head. *Unless they followed someone in.* I cut across the parking lot, heading toward my car. *Ryan wouldn't have left the door open.*

The parking lot sprawled out across the whole block, taking up much more space than it needed, with my neighbors' cars scattered throughout. I eyed each vehicle cautiously, looking for unusual shadows or a stranger sitting quietly in the driver's seat. *Just get to the car.* No footsteps behind me. No sound except the steady buzz of traffic rushing past the complex. *I'll get to my car and go.* I stuffed my hand into my pocket, reaching for my key, and realized I had left it hanging on the hook by the front door.

"Shit," I muttered, glancing back toward the side doors, still closed. "Shit shit shit." *Walk. Go somewhere.* I crossed back over the parking lot and turned onto the empty sidewalk that must have been put in as an afterthought. Behind me, the wrought-iron gate that encircled the Lofts; in front of me, a four-lane road with cars zipping past. This wasn't an area where people walked. *Help. Get help.* I pulled out my phone and looked at its blank screen, considered calling Ryan. But it sounded so ridiculous: "I'm scared. It's probably nothing. Water on the floor." *There's no one in the apartment,* I told myself again. Ryan would do a quick search, opening closets and bending down to peek under the bed, peering around the shower curtain. "There," he'd say, patient but disappointed to have been pulled away from his game early. "See? There's no one there."

The sidewalk came to a sudden end, turning into weedy overgrowth, as if workers had gotten this far and then asked themselves: "What's the point?" A gust of cold air shot down the street, cutting through my sweatshirt. *Just water. I probably tracked it in myself.* My feet prickled with cold, my toes turning numb. I'd count to one hundred, I decided, plenty of time for an imaginary prowler to leave. Then I'd go back.

I stood and counted the cars as they passed, their headlights illuminating the short stretch of sidewalk. I took some comfort in their presence, as though nothing could happen to me with all those people around. *Thirty-four. Thirty-five.* I couldn't make out the drivers well in the dark, but I imagined them: the old sedan a large middle-aged man driving home from the office; the SUV a frazzled mom with two kids strapped into the back seat, driving back from daycare. *Would they stop if something happened? Would anyone help?* I rubbed my hands together for warmth, tried to curl my toes, which ached with the effort, kept counting.

When the hundredth car reached me, I began taking small, slow steps back toward the apartment complex. *Just a little extra time. Just in case.* I punched in the code at the entrance and climbed the stairs to the second floor. I reached out for the doorknob to my apartment and turned it. Still open. I peered in, scanning the room, trying to sense whether anything felt different. I couldn't tell.

"I'm back," I said, feeling foolish as I said it. *Who am I talking to?* I edged toward the kitchen, keeping my eyes on the hallway at all times. I opened the silverware drawer as quietly as I could and pulled out a chef's knife. I turned it over in my hand, its blade dull from years of use without sharpening. *What would I do with this?* I asked myself, slipping it back into the drawer. *I'm just going to get myself stabbed.* I reached into the bottom drawer, pulled out a Maglite instead. It felt heavy, substantial.

I started with the bathroom. The door, already cracked open, swung inward; I peered around to make sure no one was hiding behind it. I held my breath as I pulled back the blue chevron shower curtain. The force knocked an almost-empty shampoo bottle into the bathtub. I jumped, almost shouting but catching myself, and took a quick peek in the cabinet beneath the sink, obviously too small to hide a person, before shutting the door behind me.

The office was next. I opened the door quickly, before I could second-guess myself, swinging it hard to make sure no one could be hiding behind it. I scanned the room for possible hiding spots: the narrow closet, the space between the side of the bookshelf and the back wall. Beneath the desk. The desk chair, rolled back toward the window, left plenty of space beneath.

I sidestepped to the right, keeping my back to the wall. It took just a few steps to reach the closet door. I reached out my arm to slide it open, looking over my shoulder to get a glimpse inside, without fully turning my attention away from the desk. A few plastic containers, long and shallow, were stacked on top of each other, full of papers and notebooks and odds and ends: Ryan's things. Small cardboard boxes sat on the white wire shelving, closed with masking tape, MISC written on the front in Ryan's careful handwriting.

I continued stepping cautiously to the side until I could see the space between the bookshelf and the wall: empty, except for a small trash can brimming with crumpled paper towels, spotted with red paint. Next was the desk. I cut across the room, rounding the desk from the side, my hand stiffening around the flashlight. Just empty space.

The only room left was the bedroom. I swung open the door, the doorknob making contact with the wall. I scanned the room for potential hiding spots. The closet. Behind the bed. Beneath the bed. Behind the floor-length curtains. I started, again, with the closet, running an arm through my thickly packed clothes, just to be sure. From my closet, I could see the space between the side of the bed and the back wall. I approached the foot of the bed, crouching down to lift the bed skirt obscuring my view, flashlight drawn back. Nothing but dust and two mismatched socks, crumpled on the ground. The curtains were next, half-shut, their beige folds billowing out. I pulled them back: no one. *Of course there's no one there.* I reached for the handle of the sliding glass door to the balcony and pulled. It slid open easily, its latch up. *A way in.* My stomach turned. *Did I lock the door when I came back in last night? Why wouldn't I have locked the door?* I stepped out onto the wooden planks, ignoring the small splinters that poked through my socks. I looked over the balcony railing, its thin metal rails suddenly looking like handles, the thick metal beam the rails grounded into a foothold.

I stepped back through to the bedroom, sliding down the latch behind me. *There's no one here now,* I tried to reassure myself. *That's what matters.* And nothing seemed to be missing, as far as I could tell. A wad of cash still rested on the bookshelf in the office. A handful of jewelry remained undisturbed in my dresser.

I looked back toward my bed, a heap of unmade sheets bunched on top of it. *Not the right shape for a person,* I told myself. *Even so—*

I pulled back the sheets out of an overabundance of caution. I shrieked before I could stop myself, my knees buckling beneath me. Dozens of paper footballs, a few spilling onto the floor, just like the ones Emily used to pass me. Just like the ones from you.

I picked up one of the notes off the bed and unfolded it carefully. There, in the middle of the page, scratched out in all capital letters, was one sentence: WHY DIDN'T YOU HELP ME MICAH?

I crumpled up the note and threw it into the small trash can in my bedroom. I looked down at it lying there, on top of wadded-up tissues and discarded clothing tags, the blue ink looking back at me, accusing.

Detective Heller's words in that stifling interrogation room. *Why didn't you look for her?* The judgment underlying that question: *I would have looked.*

Call Ryan, I told myself. *He'll be able to think calmly about this. He'll know what to do.* Just like in high school, when he took the notes you had left for me and made them disappear, like they had never existed at all. *We should tell the police,* he'd probably say. *Someone broke into our home. This is serious.*

An image came to mind: the police tearing through our apartment, mud-caked boots on the floor, thick fingers thumbing through papers, snapping pictures of my bed. A female officer sitting with me on the couch, legs crossed, pen poised over a notepad.

"Does the note have any special significance to you?" she'd ask, and I'd explain and watch as her face morphed into uncomprehending judgment.

I would have done something.

Another image: Ryan lying beside me in bed, fingers laced and resting on his stomach, staring up at the ceiling. Silent as I lay on my side next to him, waiting for him to speak.

"Why *didn't* you look for her, Micah?" he'd say, finally, not turning to face me. "She was your best friend."

And what could I say in response? I was too drunk, too caught up in my own thing to notice when an hour had gone by, then two, and I hadn't seen Emily? Too self-absorbed to wonder: *If she's not with us, where is she?*

You don't just abandon someone, he'd be thinking, even if he never broke the silence, even if he never said anything at all.

I had to get rid of them. I went to the kitchen, splashed cold water on my face, and pulled out a large, opaque garbage bag from under the sink. I pulled the paper out of the trash can and threw it in the bag, then grabbed the unopened notes that still covered my bed in handfuls and threw them in, too. I swept a hand under my pillow and beneath my bed to check for any I might have missed.

I was drunk. I was a teenager. And Emily didn't want me to find her.

I brought the bag out to the apartment's garbage chute, opened the small metal door to the stale and overly sweet smell of rot, and chucked it down. It was a relief, watching them drop out of sight, gone. I turned back to the closed door of my apartment.

Someone was in there. I tugged at the hems of my sleeves, taking a small step toward the door. *Was,* I reminded myself. *I checked everywhere. There's no one there now.*

Another step. The hallway completely quiet. My neighbors must have been home by then, settling down for dinner or to watch their evening shows on TV. Had they heard me shout before? It had been so loud, or it had seemed that way to me at the time, and the walls in the apartment were thin, just drywall and cheap insulation. Someone must have heard something.

But there was no movement. I took another few steps toward the door, reached out for the handle. The light weight of the door swung open easily. *Whoever it was, they're gone now.*

I checked the locks on the windows and latched the sliding bedroom door, tugging on the handle to make sure it was closed. Then I sat down uneasily on the couch, pulling my knees in toward me. I checked my phone: eight o'clock. Ryan wouldn't be home for at least another hour. *That's fine,* I told myself. *I'm fine. The notes are gone. There's no one here.*

I pulled the throw blanket up over myself and looped one of its tassels around my index finger, my thoughts a tangled mess, trying to sort out who could have left the notes. *Who other than Joshua?*

I did wonder—just for a fraction of a second—if they might be from you. If you might have come back to Calvary after all this time. If you still held Emily's death against me. But someone would have seen you back in town. I would have known.

I rubbed my legs with my hands, jumping when a neighbor's door slammed shut. *Who other than Joshua?* Ryan knew about the notes you had left me in high school, and Natalie. *Natalie and I talked about the notes at the coffee shop,* I realized, running through that conversation in my mind. I tried to picture who else had been there the day the notes had come up: that long-haired boy, dripping wet, typing furiously on his keyboard. A few other Easton students scattered nearby, listening. Any one of them could have been a Truthseeker. Any one of them could have overheard.

It made sense. *A prank taken too far. That's all. It's just a game to them.*

I pictured how delighted they'd be if I called the police, if I reacted. *We got her,* they'd say, watching the flashing sirens pull into my parking lot.

Eight thirty-five. The muffled sound of a horn blared up from the parking lot. I pulled my legs in closer. *Maybe I should tell Ryan after all,* I thought. Not about the content of the notes—*I didn't open them,* I could tell him if he asked, *I just threw them away*—but about the break-in, at least, the fact that someone had been in our bedroom, left the notes in our bed. *Telling him is the right thing to do,* I told myself. I shouldn't have to shoulder this alone. I stood up from the couch, lit the burner on the stove under the kettle. I felt a little better after making the decision. Ryan would be able to help.

By the time the kettle started to whistle, I was second-guessing myself.

Why didn't you open them? Ryan might ask. *You just threw them away?*

That tone he had started using more and more frequently: *You're being unreasonable, Micah. You're not thinking clearly.*

It was nine twenty-three when I finally heard the rattle of the doorknob and a key being jammed into the lock. I braced myself.

Tell him, I told myself. *You should tell him.*

Ryan swung through the door with a goofy smile across his face.

"Hi," I said, my voice small and cautious. Ryan didn't seem to notice.

"I won!" he announced, hoisting his box of soldiers and carrying them back into the office.

He can help, I told myself. *You need support right now.*

"It was pretty close," Ryan continued, despite my lack of response, volume elevated so I could hear him from the other room. "These new rules don't seem to be calibrated quite right."

Why didn't you save the notes for the police, Micah? What were you thinking?

"They give too much of an advantage to the hussars, which put me at a disadvantage. But I still managed to outmaneuver Robbie—"

It's probably harmless, anyway, I told myself. *A prank gone too far. Just some dumb kids. Nothing to worry about.*

Ryan emerged from his office, still talking about the mistakes Robbie had made as he poured himself a glass of wine, held up the bottle toward me, and returned it to its place on the top of the fridge when I shook my head. He didn't feel it at all—the sense that something was *not right* in our apartment, that it had been disturbed in some way. He didn't notice my agitation, didn't see that I was upset.

"So," he said, as he sat down on the couch beside me, placing his wine down on the coffee table, "how was your night?"

"Fine," I said, taking a sip of tea that had long since gone cold. "Everything here was just fine."

14

pass by a row of antiques shops on a main street stretch, an American flag with thirteen stars displayed in front of one of them, and think of your store. Maybe you've done for yourself what I couldn't. Stonesport Maps & Prints Gallery, a little shop where you can putter around in history, hang up curated maps and antique ship blueprints, lose yourself in a dusty secondhand book while tourists thumb through old sketchings in plastic casings, grouped into different cardboard boxes based on category: the Battle of Falmouth, Photography—Whaling, Shipping Routes. I hope you walk home to your little blue house after work, spend the evening with your family, sleep easily at night.

I hope you've really started over, Joshua. I hope you've done it right. What I worry about is that you lock up your shop early in the afternoon and make your way to the local bar. I worry that your friends are the other regulars and a bartender has to take you home on nights where you've fallen asleep with your forehead resting against the bar. I worry that when it starts getting late and you've found a sympathetic ear, that's when the burden of who you really are comes through. I imagine you leaning in unsteadily from the perch of your barstool, your hand on your new friend's shoulder to steady yourself, your mouth an inch away from his ear. *I am Joshua Winters,* you say, *brother of Emily Winters, and the one thing I've learned is that you can never fucking escape.*

I went back to Stomping Grounds the morning after the break-in as if nothing were wrong. I flipped the chairs over one by one and wiped down the tables, checking to see if each of the small plastic ramekins had enough sugar and Sweet'N Low, trying to run through my mental checklist. *Low on apple cider,* I reminded myself, running a damp cloth over the chalkboard suggestion, scrawling out *Crème Brûlée Latte* in its place. My hand trembled as I gripped the chalk, the *L* in *Latte* awkward and uneven, like something written by a second grader. I willed myself to stop, to get it together, as I wiped the washcloth over the board and tried again.

You can't let them get to you. You can't let them win. I scrubbed at the windows, wiping off a collage of fingerprints the college students had left behind the day before. *Just some stupid kids.*

But when I finally crossed the shop to unlock the dead bolt, I couldn't bring myself to do it. I didn't want them in my space, studying me, watching for a reaction. *A break,* I told myself. *I just need some time to get my thoughts together.*

I turned off the lights in the shop to keep people from looking in and switched on the single light in the storage room. I sat down at the computer and opened the forum, planning to look for any sign of the intruder who had left the paper footballs, a post bragging about his exploits: *Look what I found in Micah's apartment.* I clicked on the search bar and, uneasily, typed in my own name.

There were dozens of threads that mentioned me. I clicked through them, my chest tightening as I read.

helenaa: I was at the trial, and Micah's demeanor was really off. She never seemed upset about what happened—I don't think I saw her cry once—and I remember seeing her and her friend Natalie *giggling* about something on the courthouse steps. Totally inappropriate.

TheMissingKing: That's not really fair. You can't read too much into someone's reaction to trauma. People process grief in a lot of different ways.

helenaa: Yeah, but this was strange. And, now that I think about it, she and Ryan Terrasen seemed uncomfortably close during the trial. I'm just saying, it was kind of suspicious.

MissMaya: I mean, you'd know, wouldn't you? You'd have to notice *something*. Alex and Emily, always sneaking off together . . .

Redhandman: Do we have any Truthseekers in the area who could find out more about what she's up to now? Go to her coffee shop, that kind of thing?

steelrights: Already on it.

I had known it. They were watching.

It was a surreal feeling: strangers pretending to have insight into my life. Baseless gossip and speculation, like high school all over again. But I don't need to tell you that. You'll understand. They were trying to piece you together and pick you apart, too: the strange younger brother, overcome by jealousy and lashing out at your graceful, well-liked sister.

I knew—I've always known—how easy it would be to make you look guilty, if someone was focused on the wrong things. Your family's schedule revolved around Emily: Emily's practices, Emily's recitals, Emily's out-of-state competitions to perform in front of scouts and admissions officers. Which left you thumbing through your encyclopedia of reptiles in the dance studio hallway, and, when you outgrew that, poring over ancient texts in auditorium lobbies. Bored and resentful, the forgotten child.

mrdrfn: The police found out that Emily and Alex were sleeping together and decided it was Alex from day one. There was no real investigation. They never gave any serious consideration to any other suspect. Joshua was amassing swords and God knows what else, and yet somehow the fact that his parents claimed he was at home that night was enough to exonerate him.

The night Emily died: you, in all black. Your boots, heavy and caked with mud.

"What are you doing here?" I asked.

"What?" A nervous smile. "I'm not allowed to play some beer pong?"

Ambivalentaardvark: Why didn't Alex's lawyer bring up Joshua at the trial, then? If there were other possible suspects, wouldn't that have been enough for reasonable doubt?

I had to protect you. I knew what they'd see. So when the police asked me who I saw that night in the woods, I didn't mention you. I didn't lie; I just didn't volunteer that information.

Wellsinceyouasked: Incompetence, maybe? Alex's lawyer decided to run with the theory that *no one* killed Emily—it was all just an unfortunate accident. She toppled out the second-story window all on her own. But there were serious problems with that theory. The bottom of the window was above Emily's center of gravity, so she would have needed to lift herself—or be lifted—to fall out of it. It wasn't a stupid, drunken mistake. Emily didn't drink, and her blood alcohol level showed that night was no exception. It didn't fit with a suicide attempt, either, since the fall just wasn't from that high up. And then, of course, there were the fucking bruises on her arms . . .

I swallowed, a sour taste at the back of my throat. *They were from Alex,* I told myself. They had to be. Any other explanation was fantasy. Speculative, sensationalized bullshit. *The police determined it was him. A jury convicted him.*

I could hear, in the front room, the rattle of the dead bolt against the doorframe, the angry knock of a fist against the window. As if I owed them something. I slid a cigarette out from the pack now resting at the side of the computer and leaned back in my chair. More activity in Julia's thread, more questions and answers.

TheOtherJess: Does Alex have any hobbies in prison? How does he pass his time?

jules: He's become quite the card shark :) He plays a lot of Spades and Cribbage. (Poker isn't allowed.)

The idea of Alex as a card shark was laughable. I remembered making my way down Alex's basement stairs on more than one occasion to find Alex and Ryan at the tail end of a poker game, Ryan with a pile of chips in front of him.

"Just a few more hands," Alex would say, his eyes fixed on his cards, biting his lip hopefully as though this might be the hand that turned everything around. Alex used to watch poker tournaments on ESPN when there was nothing else on and was under the illusion that this made him a card shark. But Ryan actually knew how to count cards.

jules: I wanted to let you all know how much your interest in this case means to me, and to Alex. It's been so hard fighting this battle alone for so long, and now I finally feel like I have a community. We're asking the right questions and we *will* get answers. You are all the answer to my prayers :)

Alex is guilty, I thought to myself, ashing the cigarette. *That's your answer. He's exactly where he deserves to be.* Another rattle at the door. I jumped, collected myself, refocused my attention on the monitor's glare and Julia's saccharine smiley faces. *Julia is the one who contacted Brent Williams. She's the one who riled up a group of strangers and got them to invade my coffee shop, my apartment.* Julia got to enjoy playing the put-upon girlfriend, without any of the loss. Without any of the consequences.

My phone buzzed on the table beside me. A text from Natalie: *Where r u?*

I pushed my phone to the side. *They're wrong about Alex. They have to be.* Julia, too blinded by her fixation to see the truth. The commenters, more interested in drama than reality.

No real investigation. That couldn't have been right. *I was there. I remember the police interviews. The hours in a bleach-filled interrogation room.* I crossed my legs, my right foot bouncing, and tapped a stretched-out paper clip against the plywood desk.

Another buzz from my phone. Natalie again: *Just let me know you're not dead pls!*

Another thread about you. This one a picture: you in front of the hearth in your living room, too old to be dressed for Halloween, in a red cloak with what looked to be a real sword held at your side.

Redhandman: Yikes.

What they didn't show: you, at eight, bouncing excitedly behind me and Emily as we walked down the dirt ridge along Culver Street, a grin stretched out across your face.

I wanted to write back and tell them to leave us alone, that they didn't know what they were talking about. That of course the police had been thorough, of course the trial had been fair. Cindy, my mom's friend, popped into my head. She worked part-time as a receptionist at the police station. I thought about Saturday mornings spent slouched down on her blue-and-white checkered couch with a Baby-Sitters Club book, bored and impatient while she and my mother cackled in the kitchen.

"I shouldn't tell you this," she used to start all of her stories. "But . . ."

Cindy would know what the police did, I realized. I picked up my phone, ignoring the texts from Natalie and scrolling through my contacts. There she was, Cindy Ewing, added at my mother's insistence years ago as an emergency contact. "She's a good person to know, if anything ever happens to you," my mother had said. "Not that I want you going out and getting yourself in trouble. But just in case."

I typed out a quick text: *Hi Cindy, it's Micah Wilkes. I was wondering if you might have some time to talk?*

Progress, I thought to myself. I'd get the information I needed from Cindy: the facts that put Alex away in the first place. In the meantime, I had something else to take care of.

It was easier than I thought it would be to find Julia's address; it only took a quick search online. She owned a small ranch house in an older neighborhood with houses nestled close to one another, porch after porch with peeling paint and old wicker furniture. Julia's house was brick with green shutters, three steps leading up to a screen door on rusted hinges. It reminded me of a grandmother's house, like I'd step inside and find faded orange carpeting and a plaid couch, old dolls and crucifixes scattered around.

I parked my car three houses down, then glanced around to see if anyone was watching. The street was quiet, all of the porches empty. A one-armed snowman sat in the yard by my car, his knobbed carrot nose beginning to sag. I got out of the car and started toward Julia's house, listening for the crunch of snow or the engine of a passing car behind me.

Julia's mailbox was done up to look like a barn, fake red panel-
ing with two white squares with X's crisscrossed over them pasted
on the door. I reached for the metal hook protruding beneath the
black gambrel roof, then drew my hand back, a wave of doubt
flooding over me. *I should go home.* Up Julia's driveway, a closed
garage door, the single row of windows too high to see in. *What if
she's here?* The four windows on the front of the house were closed
off by opaque blinds.

I heard the low rumble of an approaching car and glanced behind me. A minivan rolled down the road, barely moving, and I
stiffened, pulling my shoulders up toward my ears. *Are they watching?* I pictured the long-haired Easton boy and the large-toothed
girl slouching down in their seats and peering out through the
windows. They were, I was sure, part of the No Stone Unturned
crowd.

I couldn't just stand there by the mailbox. I walked with purpose up the driveway and up Julia's brick steps, slick with ice,
pulled open the screen door, and knocked. *If she answers?* I stuffed
my hand into my jacket pocket, fingers brushing the familiar curve
of my lighter. *I'm here to talk about Alex. I want to hear her out.* I
waited. No sign of movement from inside.

The minivan continued rolling past Julia's house, arching slowly
into a driveway two houses down. It idled there, its tinted windows blocking my view, and I shifted my weight, knocked again.
Is it suspicious that I'm still standing here? I wondered. *How long is
normal to wait? One minute? Two?* The driver-side door of the minivan cracked open, then swung out, and a woman in her thirties
stepped down, opening the back door for two small children, who
leaped out of the car and sprinted to their house ahead of her. She
never looked in my direction. She had other things on her mind.

Once the neighbor was out of sight, I tried the door handle. It
didn't turn. *What did I think was going to happen?* Only a small
stretch of land separated the neighboring houses. I imagined hoisting myself into a side window, only to be met by the curious stare

of a neighbor rinsing dishes at the sink just a few yards away in their own kitchen. On Julia's front step were two small pots with the remains of plants in them that hadn't taken well to the cold weather. In front of the door lay a woven mat, WELCOME written out in big letters. I figured it was worth a shot. I lifted the pots, revealing a thin circle of dirt, then the sides of the mat, and there it was, beneath the upper-left corner: a spare key. *Not smart, Julia,* I thought to myself as I grabbed the cold metal and slid it into the lock. The door swung open, and I wiped off my shoes on the welcome mat, replacing the key before stepping inside.

A musky dog odor hung in the air. I froze in the doorway, waiting for the scramble of paws or low, angry barks, but nothing happened. I stepped onto beige tiles streaked with muddy paw prints and called out, just in case: "Julia?" No response. A single navy blue raincoat hung on the hook by the door, no sign of a winter coat. She wasn't home. I took cautious, quiet steps into the claustrophobic kitchen. Cereal boxes crowded the counters; old breadcrumbs and papery garlic skin were scattered around the sink. Two empty dog bowls lay on the floor, ringed by small droplets of water.

I stepped farther in and a stray piece of dog food crunched under my shoe, leaving a crumby residue behind. A casserole dish soaked in the sink, peels of burnt food floating at the top of the water. On the windowsill: a mismatched salt and pepper shaker, the sticky residue of honey, and a small, plastic cow with big, cartoonish eyes and long eyelashes, wearing a pink tutu. I picked up the cow and turned it over in my hands. I wondered if there was a story behind it: an inside joke with a friend, a road trip Julia remembered fondly.

There was something so intimate about it, this little cow in its pink tutu, placed on display where she could see it every morning. My stomach tightened. *I can still leave.* I turned, still holding the tiny cow in my fist, when I saw a pile of mail on her small kitchen table, a letter from the Innocence Project on top. My face burned. Julia, crusading for Alex's release, for attention. I replaced the cow on the windowsill, turned at a slight angle to face the pepper shaker. *She probably just saw the cow in a store selling knickknacks and thought it was funny,* I told myself. *And she wouldn't think twice about doing this to me.* I picked up the stack of mail and shuffled through it, then dropped it back down on the other end of the table, just a little out of place.

I made my way back to the family room, a tiny space in disrepair, small cracks running just below the ceiling where the house had settled, bulges from water damage swelling out on the walls. Papers covered the floors, spilling out from a bookshelf overflowing with heavy-looking legal tomes and true-crime books. I turned toward the couch, small and gray and coated in a thin layer of dog hair. A small space where I assumed Julia must normally sit had been carved out of the notebooks and debris that had otherwise taken over. I sat down and picked up the legal pad on top of one of the stacks. Written across its pages, in small, precise handwriting, were Julia's notes: notes on legal cases she had read, on news outlets she had contacted, on different legal aid organizations that might be able to help. Lists of contact information, careful records noting the time and date of any conversation and the name of the person she had spoken with.

I thumbed through the pages of a binder. Clippings of news articles and printouts from websites on wrongful convictions, the margins filled in with Julia's notes. A list of resources for families of the incarcerated, a few phone numbers highlighted. *Poor, aggrieved Julia,* I thought, throwing the binder off to the side, *who started dating a convicted murderer and then had to deal with the consequences.*

I shuffled through a few of the other stacks until my hand hit on smooth metal. Julia's laptop. I pulled it out from under the pile, cartoon stickers of cows stuck to its lid. *Jesus,* I thought, *I guess that's her thing.* I opened the lid skeptically, expecting to be met by a locked screen. But, instead, the screen flickered on to Julia's desktop, a neat row of folders lined up on the right side, two cows tangoing in the background. I opened Gmail and it went straight into her inbox, no password required. It was so easy it didn't even feel like snooping.

I scrolled through the emails, most of them advertisements. Notifications from "On the Outside," a website for friends and family of inmates, where Julia's username appeared to be jules91. I grabbed Julia's legal pad off of the couch and flipped open to a blank page toward the back, wrote a note to myself. A few messages from an acquaintance at church, mostly about upcoming events: a potluck dinner, a new Bible study. And emails from someone named Rachel Melbourne who mostly sent animal pictures, like a cat wearing oversized sunglasses with its tongue drooping out of the side of its mouth.

I closed the laptop, slipped the legal pad into my messenger bag, and ventured farther into the house. The first door on my left was a small bathroom with tiny white tiles peeling up from the floor, the space between them caked with dirt. *How do you live like this, Julia?* I wondered, eyeing a shadow of mold forming behind the plastic shower curtain, the crusted remains of toothpaste stuck to the sink. I swung open the medicine cabinet to find a large number of pill bottles. I read the unfamiliar names on their labels and returned them to their places after snapping a couple of pictures, turning them at an angle. *This is what it feels like to know that someone has been thumbing through your life,* I thought, but as I eyed the soap scum building up on the ridge of the sink, I realized that Julia probably wouldn't even notice. I needed something bigger.

Across the hall, a small and bare-bones guest room that couldn't have gotten much use. The nightstand by the bed was topped with a thin layer of dust, a small radio clock, and a box of tissues. Its drawer was empty. *Who would visit Julia?* I wondered and felt a pang of pity mixed with irritation. *Julia, who lives exclusively in her fantasy world, where Alex isn't a cold-blooded killer and is coming home to be with her any day.*

I couldn't take the sight of that sad, empty guest room any longer, so I continued down the hall to Julia's room. The dog smell had permeated this room, too, for obvious reasons: a dog bed slumped in the corner of the room, its fabric worn and chewed up, and a damp rope lay at the foot of the bed. Julia had made only a half-hearted effort to make the bed that morning, the sheets pulled up hastily over the pillows. On the nightstand, a hairbrush with a thick bed of blond hair still tangled in its bristles, an old water glass with a ring of ChapStick on its lip. The same photograph of Alex that I had seen at Julia's office, the only photograph, I realized, that I had seen in the house. I tried to pull open the nightstand drawer, which was jammed so full of papers that it resisted, something in the back catching. I started jostling it, hoping the errant paper would break loose. That's when I heard the sound of the front door swinging open and claws skittering across the tile.

I shoved the nightstand door shut again, the caught paper ripping under the force, and scanned the room, considering my options. Two windows led out to the backyard. I crossed the room toward them and pushed up on the glass pane, but their frames were thick with paint, gluing them shut. A sharp scrape echoed from the kitchen as the dog stuck its snout into its food bowl and pushed it across the floor.

I looked down at the space beneath the bed, trying to determine whether I could fit. I pictured the muzzle of an angry dog sniffing me out, teeth bared, right at face level. I looked to the closet instead, packed full of Julia's frumpy sweaters and dresses. *I could hide behind them,* I reasoned, crossing the room again, eyeing the closet floor for space.

The soft carpet in the family room muted the dog's steps, but I could hear the groan of the couch springs as it leaped up, a dull thud as it jumped back down. Short, jagged pants growing louder.

I brushed my hand along the fabric of Julia's sweaters, all grays and muted tones, all a little too large for her tiny frame. If she found me in there, there was no way I could explain.

The door swung open, nudged by the dog's snout, and it looked at me standing there by the closet, more confused than angry. It was a fluffy, squat mutt with tiny legs that didn't look like they should be able to support its weight and yellowed fur around its snout. It let out a few feeble barks and trotted toward me. I held out my hand and it gave me a perfunctory sniff before climbing onto its bed, spinning in circles, and collapsing.

I looked back toward the door. Julia would come back here sooner or later, to find the dog or to change out of work clothes. *Better to get ahead of it,* I reasoned. *It'll be worse if she finds me.* The dog inhaled deeply and let out a snort, its eyes half-closed already. I reminded myself: *I came to talk about Alex. I wanted to help.*

I stepped out of the bedroom's open door and peered out, expecting to see Julia shuffling down the hall, a crumpled tissue in her hand. But instead, the house was completely still, apart from the wheezy grunts of Julia's dog. "Julia?" I called out, waiting for a response: a shout, the sound of footsteps. "Julia, it's okay. It's Micah. I can explain."

I took small, careful steps through the hallway, past the guest room and bathroom, through the family room. Empty and untouched. I rounded the corner to the kitchen and exhaled when it was empty, too. A leash hung by the jacket in the entranceway; the dog bowls had been refilled. *Just someone walking the dog,* I realized. Julia on her lunch break or a dog walker. She wasn't home.

My knees went weak, and I balanced myself on Julia's counter. *Go home,* a part of me urged. *I need to go home.* But I needed her to feel what I had felt. I needed her to know that someone had been here, reading her letters, picking through her things. *What does Julia eat for breakfast? What does she read in the quiet of her own house? Who does she talk to? What has she tucked away in the back of her closet, her dresser drawers?* No information off-limits, everything on display. *That's what she asked for by playing house with Alex. That's what she asked for by inviting the world back in to scrutinize us.* I straightened myself and walked back to Julia's bedroom, moving quickly. I knew that, any second, I might hear the sound of the door swinging open again. The opportunity to escape was slipping by. I dug into the back of Julia's closet until I found what I was looking for: Alex's jacket. The dog's leg twitched, and it opened a lazy eye before closing it again. *An elaborate fantasy,* I thought to myself, slinging the jacket over my arm and walking out the front door toward my car. *I'm doing you a favor, Julia. You need to realize this is all just make-believe.*

15

On the radio, the singer picks at an acoustic guitar, his falsetto floating overtop. I'm alone, finally, no one but me on the road. I could be anyone.

"Mila," I say, trying the name out on my tongue, and it sounds like a new beginning. "Mila Wilson," I say, louder this time, with more confidence. Close enough to Micah that I won't hesitate for too long if someone shouts my name across the room, but without any of the old baggage. Look up Mila Wilson and you'll find nothing. No quotes about the Calvary 4-H fair. No pictures of sixth-grade Mila Wilson in a black-and-pink nylon jacket and braces with color bands to match, posing with the middle school dance team, or ninth-grade Mila Wilson dutifully marching with her clarinet in Calvary's Harvest Parade, after finally dropping dance entirely. No news articles about a dead best friend and unfaithful boyfriend. Mila Wilson is a blank slate. She could be anyone she wants to be.

I look down at the black screen of my phone, which juts out of the cup holder beside me. If I went to the No Stone Unturned forums now, I wonder what they'd say. I wonder if the rumors are starting already, suspicions that something isn't right. Accusations. *We knew she was no good. We were right all along.*

I look away from the phone and tighten my grip on the steering wheel. I need to focus on what's ahead of me now. I need to focus on getting to you.

Ryan wasn't home yet when I returned from Julia's. I rustled through my closet for an old shopping bag, then folded Alex's jacket and slipped it carefully inside. I slid the bag into the back corner of my closet shelf and placed an old shoebox of photographs in front of it.

My phone buzzed on my bed, and I grabbed it. A text from Cindy.

Would love to catch up!!!! :) :) Where and when?!?!

I exhaled, suddenly aware of the tension in my shoulders.

Great! Can I swing by your place tomorrow?

I heard the front door swing open and inhaled sharply. *It's just Ryan,* I told myself, *coming home from work.* I placed my phone on my dresser and peered out the bedroom door. Sure enough, there he was, crouched down to untie his shoes.

"Hey," I said, coming out of the bedroom, and his head shot up toward me.

"Hey," he said back, his surprised expression slowly easing into a smile. "You're home early."

I felt a surge of guilt but tried to press it down. *It's my shop. I can do what I want with it.* The small amount of savings that I had put aside since opening Stomping Grounds was quickly disappearing, but that was my problem, not Ryan's. He didn't need to know.

"Slow afternoon," I said, and he didn't push any further. He gave me a kiss on the forehead, threw a stack of mail onto the counter, and settled down on the couch with his laptop. I flipped through the envelopes but didn't really look at any of them. Instead, I pictured the cow figurine on Julia's windowsill, her notepad in my messenger bag. I threw the letters back down.

"Everything okay?" Ryan asked, and I realized he was looking up at me with concern.

"I'm fine," I said, willing myself to relax. I straightened the mail back into a neat stack and sat down next to him on the couch. He squeezed my leg.

"Looks like there's going to be a big turnout this weekend," he said, and I looked back at him blankly.

"For the reunion," he reminded me. "Chelsea sent out a list. Looks like most of our class is going to be there."

"Oh," I said, picking at the tassels on the throw blanket. I pictured Alex's jacket, folded in my closet.

"I'm sure she could still add you if you changed your mind about going."

"I'm not going to change my mind," I said. It came out sharper than intended. I tried to soften my voice. "They're going to want to talk about her, and I don't think I can handle it."

"I think you'll be surprised—"

"Ryan," I said. "I *can't*."

"Okay," he said, backing off. "Okay."

Over the years, I've had lots of people tell me where they were when they found out about Emily's death. It's a story people love to tell—and the more distant their relationship was with Emily, the more dramatic the reaction, the more profound the experience. Michelle dropped a half-full coffee mug when she saw Emily's face on the news, and it shattered across her kitchen floor, apparently.

She stepped on a shard while cleaning up and almost needed stitches. Helena cried for three days straight and couldn't keep any food down for a week.

"I can't believe she's gone" is what I've always said in response. A slow shake of my head, a long breath in. "It just doesn't feel real."

For me, it was the day after the party when I learned they had found Emily and she wasn't okay. I was sitting at the kitchen table, trying to eat some macaroni and cheese I had pulled out of the back of the cabinet. My chair, missing a furniture pad on one leg, pitched forward as I shifted my weight and then settled back again. Forward and back, forward and back. The small television next to the oven, turned up loud, showed *The View,* sharp laughter, studio applause. My mother was cleaning things that didn't need to be cleaned, scrubbing angrily at the counters. We weren't in a fight, exactly, but the mood was tense. My mother had gotten a call earlier that day from your mother, asking her to send Emily home. They compared notes and realized that we hadn't spent the night at your house or at my house the night before.

My mother hadn't determined my full punishment yet, but she had obviously decided to start by rattling everything around me—her metal mixing bowls, the jar of coins on the counter, various pots and pans. She lifted each item, wiped underneath, slammed it back down onto the laminate countertop. I took small, cautious bites of the macaroni, hoping it would make my nausea go away. It didn't work.

My mother grabbed the phone off the receiver when it rang a second time. She answered sharply, hand on her hip, lips pinched. But then her face turned white, and she said "oh," quietly, like she couldn't quite process what she had just been told. She took her hand off her hip, wrapped her arm around her waist, said: "Are you sure?" She turned away from me and put her head down, as though that would keep me from overhearing.

I leaned forward, my chair tipping, the front right leg clacking against the floor. My mother's voice dropped in volume. "I see," she said. "I see." She rubbed her side with her hand. "Thanks for letting me know."

"Who was it?" I asked, dropping my fork into my bowl, metal clinking against porcelain. She didn't answer. She covered her mouth with her hand, staring blankly at the spot to the right of the phone. Later, I would have the half-formed idea that it had been your mother who called to let us know what had happened. In retrospect, it was probably Cindy, calling from the police station in an unofficial capacity.

"Honey . . ." my mother started. That was a bad sign; my mother always used "honey" when she was about to say something that was going to upset me. "Honey, that was about Emily."

She stopped there and studied my face, watching my reaction. I waited.

"Do you know—did she go off by herself last night? Or with anyone else?"

I tried to raise my eyebrows, to give my mother a look that said I wasn't interested in answering these questions again, but even that small movement made my head ache. Everything was pounding. I needed more water.

"I already told you." I tipped backward with a muted thump. "I don't know where she went. I didn't see her most of last night."

"You won't get in trouble," my mother said gently, and my stomach flipped. "Anything you know."

"Who was on the phone?" I said, louder and more insistent this time.

"It's just that—" Her eyes went glassy, and her hand rose to her mouth again.

"Mom." It came out desperate, almost a shout. "Who was on the phone?"

"I'm so sorry, honey," she said, her voice breaking, and then she collected herself. A short inhale, a look down, then back up at me. "They found Emily."

"What do you mean?" I pulled the sleeves of my sweatshirt over my hands, squeezed my knees into my chest. *The mystery person that Emily had been dressing up for: he was real. Mrs. Winters had found out that Emily had spent the night at his house. She was going to be in so much trouble.* That's what she was supposed to say. That's what she should have said.

"Sweetie, they found her in the woods."

I looked down at the half-eaten bowl of cheesy macaroni in front of me. I looked back up at my mother.

"Her body."

"I don't understand." My head throbbed. It didn't make any sense. *She came home this morning, eyes bloodshot and puffy, obviously hungover. She's going to be grounded for a long time.*

"She's dead, sweetie."

"That's not—" We had just walked through the pillars at the entrance to the campsite together, side by side, Emily's shoulder brushing against mine. "That's not possible." It came out louder than I had expected. My mother collected herself and started toward me, wringing her hands.

"I know this is a lot to process . . ."

I knew, as she started approaching, that she was going to try to give me a hug, and I knew just as certainly that if she touched me the macaroni was going to come back up. I rose to my feet. My legs nearly buckled beneath me, but I caught myself and regained my balance.

"I'm going for a walk," I said, my voice hoarse and distant.

"Honey, I'm not sure that's a good idea."

I stepped back, away from her.

"No," I said. "I just want to go for a walk."

She stopped and rubbed the sides of her arms. A lock of hair fell down into her face, but she didn't seem to notice. Suddenly, she looked tiny and frail, and I realized she didn't know what to do. *How do you tell your daughter that her best friend is dead?* I edged closer to the door. *Not dead. Missing. A boy's house. When she gets home—*

"A walk," I said. "I just need to take a walk."

My mother nodded, small bouncing nods up and down, and I slipped out the front door. Outside, the cold fall air and sharp smell of pine hit me, and I turned and threw up in our azalea bush, little chunks of pasta going everywhere. I wiped off my face and tried to swallow, but the taste of bile stuck in the back of my throat. I turned back toward the front door, recently painted a dark shade of green, and looked through the narrow window that bordered it. Inside, my mother had sunk down onto a kitchen chair and was cradling her forehead in both hands. I kept going.

I reached the end of the driveway and turned right, toward Alex's house. Up the hill and past Calvary Elementary, its large, sprawling parking lot mostly empty. Emily and I had taken that same walk together lots of times before she started driving. Emily had loved driving, loved the old Volkswagen your parents had gotten her for her birthday, loved pulling into my driveway and honking—always three times—when I wasn't already outside waiting. "Tell her not to do that," my mother would say, wincing each time, and I'd remind Emily—"You know my mom hates that"—as I slid into my seat.

I kept going straight, past the new maze of cul-de-sacs on my left. That area had all been woods not too long before, but by then it was a cluster of new homes, half of them for sale. *Where is Emily's car now?* I wondered. I pictured it sitting on Grace Street, abandoned by the side of the road.

The Dawsons' wolfhound barked lazily as I rounded the corner. He lifted his shaggy head and eyed me from the shade of an oak tree, then returned his attention to a gnawed-up piece of bone. My stomach turned.

Where did she go? Bile in the back of my throat. My skin felt oily, the vodka working its way back out through my pores. *She didn't come back to the tarp, and I didn't look for her, did I? I didn't look.*

When I had woken up that morning, my eyelids had felt swollen shut. I had strained to open them to two empty sleeping bags, Ryan asleep on the other side of the tarp.

"Where are they?" I had asked, my tongue thick and sticking to the roof of my mouth. I tried to sort through blurry, fragmented memories of the night before: Michelle staggering into a group of freshman girls, Natalie beside me, Helena leaning against the altar.

Ryan had oriented himself, looked at the sleeping bags. "I don't think they came back," he had said. "I can give you a ride home if you want."

I hadn't waited for her. I hadn't even looked around. *Did the police find the car on Grace Street?* I wondered, as I passed by another Volkswagen, parked securely in an open garage. *Did they take it back to Emily's house, or is it just sitting there, waiting for someone to come get it?*

Alex's street came into view, the street sign bent at a slight angle. Not too far now. Beside me, a row of split-level homes, red brick and beige siding, dated but comfortable.

I thought back to a walk Emily and I had taken a few weeks before, past those same homes, the same row of crabapple trees. She had been tense, I thought, the conversation drifting into long, uneasy lulls.

"My mom's been pushing Easton," I had said, trying to fill the gaps. It wasn't that cold yet, but Emily wore an oversized cardigan, thick gray wool, which hung off her shoulders. She fiddled with the sleeves, pushing them up and then pulling them back down again, distracted.

"What's wrong with Easton?" she asked. A pink hopscotch grid stretched out on the sidewalk in front of us.

"It's literally right here. I'd like to get more than a mile away from home." I stepped over a lopsided drawing of a butterfly. "And everyone goes there. It would be like I was still in high school."

Emily didn't respond, lost in her own thoughts. I tried to fill in the silence.

"I was thinking Penn State, maybe," I continued. "That's where Alex wants to go."

I was expecting that to get a response—*but why do* you *want to go there?*—but instead Emily pulled her cardigan tighter around her, looked up at a bird flitting from tree branch to tree branch beside us.

"Or Villanova. It's close to the city—"

"I'm thinking Columbia," Emily said, almost to herself as much as me.

I nodded, although, I knew, Columbia was a long shot.

"I could go there, and you could go to Juilliard, and we could share an apartment in the city—"

"I meant for me," Emily said. "If nothing pans out."

"That's ridiculous," I said, bristling a little at the idea of Columbia being her backup option. "Something is going to pan out."

Emily had been attending summer intensive programs with serious ballet schools since we started high school and had even received invitations from a few of them to join their full-time programs. She had submitted a prescreening recording of herself to Juilliard and secured an audition; she had done well in competitions with scouts from ballet companies in attendance. She was *someone to watch,* and she was on top of things: contingency plan after contingency plan, all of which involved dance. And the Lionels said—had been saying for years—that Emily had a real shot. The best young dancer they had worked with.

Emily shrugged. "But if it doesn't, though."

"It will," I said. And I believed that. We all believed that. Great things were going to happen for Emily; it was just a matter of time. "And if it doesn't, you can come and live off of ramen and Ben & Jerry's with me and Alex in State College."

"My parents would die."

"They would not."

"You're right. My dad wouldn't notice. My mother would die. She thinks I'm going to be the artist she never was."

"Do you think she knows what ramen is?"

Emily snorted. "That would *really* give her a heart attack."

Now I rounded Alex's driveway alone, the taste of sour maca-roni lingering at the back of my throat. Alex's house looked the same as it always did: white siding, cherry-red shutters. Rhodo-dendron bushes lining the front walk. Cheerful and welcoming, like nothing was wrong, like nothing had changed. I steadied my-self, waited for my stomach to settle, and knocked on the front door.

I didn't wait for an answer. I cracked the door open, leaned in, and shouted "Hello?" I slipped off my shoes and made my way back toward the kitchen. Alex's mother—a petite woman, dwarfed by her husband and sons—was folding polo shirts into a neat pile on the couch in the family room. The end of *The View* played on the television behind her.

"Hi, Micah," she said, her tone polite and friendly. "The boys are downstairs." She didn't know.

I thanked her and opened the door to the basement. Old, un-even wooden stairs stretched down to a concrete floor. They seemed steeper than normal. I took cautious steps down, imagin-ing myself misjudging a step, pitching forward, and tumbling to the ground. I gripped the banister with my left hand.

Alex's basement was unfinished and covered in a layer of dust. Old metal poles rose up into the wooden floor beams, and card-board boxes labeled CHRISTMAS and KITCHEN filled a quarter of the space, almost blocking the path to his father's workbench, a pegboard drilled into the wall behind it. An old Oriental rug cov-ered a portion of the floor, marking Alex's territory. On one side, a boxy television that had been relegated to the basement when Alex's family got their big screen. On the other side, a ratty pullout couch that no longer opened all the way. Alex sprawled out on the rug, controller in hand, playing *Halo*. Ryan lay behind him on the couch, half watching and half dozing off.

I took another cautious step and the wooden stair groaned beneath me. Alex glanced in my direction, just long enough to register my presence, then looked away. His cheeks flared. *Look at me,* I wanted to say. *Please look at me. Make everything normal again.* His fingers twitched rapidly, the rest of his body completely still. "Hey," he said, eyes on the screen.

Ryan groaned, rolled to face the back of the couch, and put a pillow over his head.

"Emily," I said. Alex closed his eyes, bracing himself, and suddenly it all became real. *Gone.* The screen flashed and Alex's avatar collapsed, the camera zooming out. Ryan pulled the pillow away from his face and sat up on the couch, watching as I made my way down the rest of the stairs.

"Emily's dead."

Alex's eyes opened and he blinked, like he didn't know how to react. "What are you talking about?"

I tried to piece together the morning. "My mom got a call— Emily wasn't on the tarp this morning, and I thought—I thought she was okay—with a guy—I didn't know—" I could feel my throat tightening; I knew I wasn't making sense. "On our walk, she—I didn't think she—"

"Hey," Ryan said. He rose off the couch and took a step toward me, his eyebrows arched in concern. "Who called this morning? Who did your mom talk to?" He glanced down toward Alex, whose forehead creased in a frown, his head shaking back and forth in tiny, almost imperceptible movements.

I squeezed my eyes shut. "Mrs. Winters called this morning to say that Emily hadn't come home. To see if we knew where she was." The clang of the coin jar against the counter, my mother's white face.

"So she's missing," Ryan said.

Alex's eyes refocused. He ran his hand through his hair and looked from Ryan to me.

"It sounds like she's just missing," Ryan repeated. "She probably—"

"No," I said, "she's dead. And I didn't—"

"Stop it." Alex threw the controller, which scraped across the concrete floor. "Stop *saying* that. What are you talking about?"

"They found her," I said. I bent back my pinky, far enough that it felt like it might snap. *Why didn't I help her?* "They found her body in the woods."

"No," Alex said, the small shakes of his head growing larger. "No."

"What happened?" Ryan asked, his gray eyes fixed on mine. His voice was gentle but pointed. I shook my head.

Alex's eyes had gone unfocused again, his head bent down toward the rug.

"What happened?" Ryan repeated, louder this time, just as Alex looked up toward him and said: "The police."

Ryan's head shot toward Alex, his jaw pulsing.

"What do you mean, police?" I couldn't keep it all in my head. *Dead. Someone must have—*

"They're going to ask us where we were," Alex said. "What do we say?"

"What are you talking about?" I said, my voice sharp and panicked. Above us, claws skittered across the kitchen tile. Alex's Labrador, Amber, being let back inside.

"When they ask us where we were last night," Alex repeated, still focused on Ryan, waiting for his response. "What do we say?"

"We tell them where we were," Ryan said, his mouth drawn. "We"—he pointed to me and then back to himself, his eyes not leaving Alex's—"were on the tarp we set up. For all four of us." Standing over Alex, his shoulders tight and hands clenched at his sides, he no longer seemed dwarfed. He looked like he was in control. "Where the fuck were you?"

Alex recoiled like he had just been slapped. He scanned the basement, his eyes jumping from cardboard boxes to the spiderweb clinging to the top of a metal pole to the concrete floor, thinking slowly. "I started feeling sick," he said. He was fidgeting, his foot twitching rapidly. "I went and slept in my car. That's where I must have been when—"

"So then that's what you tell them," Ryan said.

Alex shook his head again, blinking back tears. "They're not going to believe me."

"Why wouldn't they believe you?" My voice cut through the basement, sharp and shrill, but Alex seemed not to notice.

"Why wouldn't they believe you?" Ryan repeated, and Alex looked back up at him with his wet eyes. He looked pathetic.

"There was no one else there," he said. "I don't have—I don't have an alibi."

"Why would you need an alibi?" I asked, my stomach turning. *The police wouldn't think—not someone we know—not—*

"They're not going to believe me," Alex repeated. "They're going to think—"

"No one's going to think anything," I said, wanting it to be true. "No one is going to think anyone did anything. This isn't—"

Ryan's shoulders loosened. He rubbed both hands up along his forehead and back down over his eyes.

"Shit," Alex said, rubbing his hands through his hair. "Shit shit shit."

"Why do you need an alibi?" I asked again, my voice rising. "Alex—"

"Stop," Ryan said, and I didn't know if it was directed at me or at Alex. "We'll say you were with us. Okay?"

He looked back at me, and I felt numb. I didn't understand.

"Are you okay with that, Micah?"

I nodded my head, not fully grasping what I was agreeing to. Ryan turned back to Alex, who exhaled in relief.

"See? It's fine. We'll just say you were with us. We were all together." Ryan collapsed back down onto the couch, cradled his forehead in his hands. "Jesus." When he looked back up, his eyes were blurry, the tips of his eyelashes wet. "I don't understand. How—?"

The flickering basement light seemed to dim, black creeping in from the corners of my vision. I steadied myself on a metal pole. *Dead. The police. Why would Alex—*

"I shouldn't have come here," I said, backing toward the stairs. "This was a mistake."

"Micah . . ." Ryan said, but his shoulders sagged and he didn't continue.

"I was with you on the tarp," Alex said, starting to pull himself together again. "Right, Micah? It's important."

I steadied myself on the banister, took one step.

"It's important, Micah," Alex said again, desperation working its way back into his voice. "We were together, right? On the tarp?"

"We were together," I said, the words catching in my throat, and then I climbed the remaining stairs as quickly as I could, ducking my head to avoid Mrs. Swift's confused expression, dodging Amber's snout as I left Alex's house for the last time.

16

hear the rattle of my phone beside me, and I pick it up hopefully, thinking it might be a text from you. But it's Cindy's name, not yours, that I see when I look down.

Sweetie, if you're in trouble, you know you can talk to me. Just call me, please. This is serious.

I set the phone down again, focus on the road straight ahead, try not to think about what that means.

Cindy. I showed up at her house, ready to ask her about Alex, at the exact time we had agreed on. But she still looked surprised to see me when she swung open her front door, its pine-cone-covered wreath tilting slightly to the side. She looked the same as always: the same blond hair that hung long in the front and tapered off to the nape of her neck, a loose floral shirt that reminded me of a nurse's uniform. A streak of flour marked one cheek; a damp washcloth dangled from her hand.

"Micah!" she said, giving me a quick hug with outstretched fingers. A smell I remembered from childhood, citrus and hairspray. "Sorry, you caught me in the middle of baking. Come in, come in."

She ushered me back toward the kitchen, scrubbing her fingers with the washcloth. Back past the blue-and-white checkered couch I used to hide behind while she and my mom drank coffee in the kitchen, gossiping about the other mothers. Past the display of tiny Christmas houses, arranged carefully on white-cotton snow. Magnetic children slid down a tiny replica hill, and my throat tightened. My mother had had one just like it.

"Sorry if I'm a little early," I said, eyes catching on the colorful, fish-shaped plates that hung on the wall, one with teal stripes and a bulbous eye and a small chip on its ceramic tail. I thought about Julia's cow and flushed.

"Oh no, not at all. I'm running late." Cindy didn't notice my embarrassment. She barely looked at me as she buzzed around the kitchen, straightening up in the same distracted way that my mother had always cleaned. She started emptying the dishwasher, returning a mug with JOY scrawled across it to its place in the cabinet, then noticed a spot on the counter that needed to be tended to. A lump of dough sat on the kitchen island, waiting. "Tyler's coming home from college this weekend, so I've just been trying to get things ready."

Pictures of Cindy's son, Tyler, at different stages of life were carefully arranged on the far wall. Tyler at two, holding up a plastic stegosaurus proudly. Tyler at fifteen, standing stiffly in a suit with a baby-pink corsage pinned to his chest. Tyler, face painted and eyes glazed, the Penn State lion on his baseball cap. *What am I doing here?*

"Senior year now, right?" I said, nodding toward the photograph, and Cindy beamed with pride.

"He's doing so well." She looked at the picture and then turned to me, a smile that seemed a little too large across her face. Clumps of mascara made her eyelashes stick together like small spikes. "But how have you been? A coffee shop—how fun!"

"I've been good," I said, trying to sound sincere. *This was a bad idea.* "Stomping Grounds has been keeping me pretty busy."

"Oh, I'm sure," Cindy said, shoving her hands back into the dough. "Anyone special in the picture?" She glanced back toward me, eyeing my left hand.

"A boyfriend." I shifted my weight. "We're living together. His name is Ryan."

"How nice," Cindy said, shoving her weight into the dough. "How did you two meet?"

"He's a friend from high school." I thought I saw her eyes flit up with curiosity. I shifted again, looked down at the hardwood floor. I hoped I wasn't blushing.

"Are you still at the police station?"

"Mm-hm. Twenty-five years. Makes me feel old." Cindy laughed, the same throaty laugh that she's always had, and turned her attention away from the dough again, gravitating toward the sink.

I swallowed and pictured Julia, squeezing Alex's hand in the Frackville visiting room, nodding her head supportively, *I believe you I believe you.* The long-haired Easton student, rummaging through my belongings, rifling through my letters, pulling open my nightstand drawer. "Do you remember Emily's case? Emily and Alex?"

Cindy's shoulders sagged. She turned away from the sink to face me, wiping her hands on her jeans. "Oh, sweetie. Of course I do."

I pulled out one of the island stools and sat down. Cindy was finally still.

"Is this about your mother?" she asked, leaning in toward me. "I miss her, too."

I shook my head, blinking away tears. *Mrs. Klein and the camp-*

site. The texts. Julia and the Easton students. I didn't know how to explain. "There have been—news stories," I said. I didn't want to get into the blog, the Truthseekers. "They've been saying Alex might not have done it."

Cindy clucked disapprovingly. "That's ridiculous."

I felt a wave of relief. "That's what I thought," I said. "Some people are saying that it was a college student who worked close to Emily's dance studio. Or her brother."

"No," Cindy said, confidently, shaking her head. "No. People just like drama. It was clear from the very beginning that it was Alex. He was the last one seen with her that night."

Clear from the beginning. My shoulders tightened. "But did the police have other suspects?" I ran a finger through the dusting of flour in front of me, tracing shapes onto the island counter.

"Well." Cindy pulled a large metal bowl out of the cabinet and dropped the ball of dough into it. She ran a washcloth under the faucet, draped it over top. "That was Joe and Liz's case, and I'm sure they would have checked all their boxes."

I scribbled circles into the flour, then wiped it into the palm of my hand. "What do you mean?"

"Oh, you know. They would have talked to Emily's friends and family members. Made sure there weren't going to be any surprises at trial." I squeezed my hand into a fist around the flour, digging my fingernails into my hand. *No real investigation.*

"But do you remember them looking into anyone else? Specifically, I mean?"

Cindy returned to her cleaning, spraying down the metal sink basin.

"Well," she said, grabbing a paper towel off the rod. "I do remember them looking into Emily's dance instructor."

"Mr. Lionel?" I asked. That caught me off guard. I thought about the reverence in Emily's voice when she talked about him. He had danced professionally in New York until a knee injury ended his career. *Mr. Lionel says I need to focus more. Mr. Lionel says that I have a shot at the real thing. Mr. Lionel says that a relationship, at my age, is the fastest way to shoot a budding dance career in the foot.*

"That's right," Cindy said. "I remember because your mom brought him up. She didn't trust him. But they ruled him out pretty quickly. He was in Philadelphia that weekend, at a dance competition for some of his other students."

"Were there any other leads?"

Cindy wiped imaginary droplets off the counter.

"Not that I remember. It was a pretty straightforward case."

"But did they—I don't know—do all the forensics? Test all the DNA?"

"This isn't *CSI,* sweetie," Cindy said, giving me a smile that was supposed to be comforting. "But I'm sure they tested enough."

Enough. My stomach turned, the smell of dough mixed with Cindy's body spray suddenly nauseating. I must have blanched, because Cindy's eyes widened with concern. *Why did I agree to talk to her today?* I imagined she was thinking. *Tyler will be here any minute.*

"Micah," she said, rounding the corner to squeeze my arm with her damp hand. "You've been through so much. Do you have anyone you're talking to about this?"

Like I was crazy for even wondering, crazy for bringing it up again after all this time.

"I'm fine," I said, sliding off the stool and throwing the handful of flour into the trash. "It's just these news stories. Do you think I could talk to one of the detectives who was involved? Just to . . ." I wiped off the remaining flour, tried to look calm. "Just to put my mind at ease."

Cindy watched me, wringing her hands together.

"I just want to know what happened," I continued. "The whole truth. For closure."

Cindy bit her lip. She glanced back toward the glowing clock on the stove, trying, I imagined, to figure out how to get me out of her house before I had a mental breakdown.

"Sweetie," she said, rubbing the streak of flour off her cheek, "we never get to know the whole truth. That's not the way it works. But I can put you and Joe in touch."

That night, I flipped on the light in the office after Ryan had fallen asleep and eased the door shut behind me. His soldiers were lined up in columns in the center of the desk, bayonets pointed out. I made a mental note—four across, five back—and pushed them to the side.

I opened up Julia's thread on No Stone Unturned, browsed through the new questions. *What's the food like in prison? How does Alex spend his day?* His dog was named Cannoli, a terrier/pit bull mix.

I sucked in my breath and created my own account: *concernedcitizen,* vague and anonymous. Then I returned to Julia's thread and hit reply.

concernedcitizen: What does Alex think about his old girlfriend, the one he was dating when Emily died?

I rocked back in my seat and then leaned in again, adding one last sentence.

concernedcitizen: Has he forgiven her?

I clicked "submit" before I could change my mind. I scrolled through the new threads, waiting for something to catch my eye. I searched the forums again for my name, and then for yours.

TheMissingKing: Does anyone know what happened to Joshua? I just did a little digging around and couldn't find anything on him after the murder.

leezybird: he left calvary a few months after emily's death. to live with his grandparents i think? i don't know anyone who's seen him since.

Wellsinceyouasked: I found public records for 30 Joshua Winters, but only three are the right age (5 unknown) and none have an obvious connection to Emily.

TheMissingKing: Maybe he's dead?

Wellsinceyouasked: If he were dead, there would be an obit. Our guy just disappeared.

Where did you go, Joshua? I asked myself. Wellsinceyouasked linked to the public records for the other Joshua Winters. He was right that none of them looked promising, but I pulled out Julia's notebook anyway and began rummaging through my bag for a pen to take notes. I didn't find one. I pulled on the upper right drawer on Ryan's desk, but it didn't give. I pushed back from the desk, noticing, for the first time, a small keyhole, then tried again. The drawer was locked. I ran my hand along the underside of the desk panel, half-expecting to find a key affixed with tape, but found only a long, narrow scratch running along the edge. I lifted the ceramic mug holding Ryan's paintbrushes and checked under the stack of textbooks on the desk's corner. No key.

It's nothing. Where he keeps his Social Security card, probably. His bank statements. I pulled again, the drawer still catching against the lock.

I'll ask him tomorrow, I told myself, but I knew, even then, that I couldn't. He'd want to know why I was going through his drawers. *There are some things,* I reasoned, *that are better just left alone.*

Julia responded to my question about Alex—what he thought of me—a few hours later.

jules: Micah is dead to us. We don't talk about her.

17

The wind and snow have picked up now, a wall of white out-side my car. Off the side of the road, I see the neon lights of a diner with glowing red and orange trim and a narrow body made out of stainless steel. I need to stop. It will be okay. It has to be okay.

I step inside, and the diner waitress, a woman in her mid-fifties, nods at me in acknowledgment, then nods toward the rows of empty tables.

"Take any seat," she says. I sit down at the booth closest to the door and chew at my nail, which has started to peel. I can smell the tobacco smoke sunk into my skin. I place my phone out on the table, ferret it away into my bag, pull it out again. The screen is blank.

I could search for my name, see what comes up. See what they're saying about me. I drop the phone into my bag again and leave it there this time.

"What can I get you?" The waitress stands beside me, pen poised above her guest check pad. She's looking down at where she's about to start writing, not at me.

I think about the eighty dollars in my wallet. "Just a coffee, please."

She clicks her pen, disappointed, and leaves, and I'm left alone with my thoughts.

Sometimes I still catch a whiff of the cologne Alex used to wear, the spiced, woody smell filling up his car, lingering on his jacket, and I'll be in his basement again, head resting on his lap while Ryan and Emily bicker over what movie we should watch. It's the smell I was expecting as I slipped my arms into his jacket's sleeves for the first time in ten years, not the dank, unwashed smell that rose up instead, sweat sunk deep into the collar from years of use without wash. I only wore it for a few minutes, long enough to feel its familiar weight on my shoulders and take a picture, one that only showed my torso. Just enough. I sent it to Julia using a new email account, with the message: *This is how it feels.* I closed the lid of my laptop, slipped the jacket back off again, and changed into something more professional: black slacks and a gray sweater, polished enough to be taken seriously without looking like I was trying too hard. I looked down at the jacket, crumpled in a heap on my bed, and imagined the panic that Julia would feel when she reached into her closet and realized it was missing, the number of times that she would run a hand through the clothes hanging there, certain it must have been misplaced. The pang she would feel when she realized it was really gone. *She asked for this,* I thought as I lifted the jacket, smoothing and refolding it. I placed it back in the shopping bag and tucked it away again in the corner of my closet shelf.

I called Detective Curtis that morning. I was sitting alone in Stomping Grounds' empty main room, lights down and the legs of chairs sticking up all around me. A group of men in their mid-twenties, all dressed in blue button-downs and khakis, sauntered past. I tensed and glanced toward the dead bolt: still locked. They continued down the street, phones swinging at their sides. *I'll open again tomorrow,* I promised myself. *I just need one more day.*

Detective Curtis answered after one ring, stating his name in a no-nonsense tone: no "hello," no pleasantries, just "Joe Curtis." But there was something warm about his tone at the same time, and I put down the pen I had been chewing on and relaxed into my chair.

"Hi," I said. "This is Micah Wilkes."

A pause.

"I think—I think Cindy told you I might be calling?"

"Micah," he said, with familiarity. "What can I help you with?"

"I think you worked on the Emily Winters case?" I picked up the pen again, rolled it between my fingers. Outside, two teen-agers with backpacks shuffled past Hotel Calvary and turned to cross the street toward me. I shifted in my chair to face away from the windows. "I just had a couple questions."

"Of course. Cindy filled me in yesterday." Another pause.

"Do you have time to meet with me? If I stopped by the police station?"

"You know, I was looking for an excuse to get out of here this afternoon. You own Stomping Grounds, right?"

"I do." I looked at the stacks of papers covering the counter: printouts of articles about Emily, court documents, the indeci-pherable transcript of Emily's autopsy. *Depressed skull fracture. Intra-cranial hemorrhage. Cerebral contusion.*

"Perfect," he said. "How about I stop by there around one?"

I slipped my phone back into my pocket and pulled out a blank piece of paper, trying to think of the right questions to ask. Behind me, a fist pounded on the glass door. I jumped and turned to see Natalie, in knee-high boots over yoga pants, a baby car seat dan-gling from one hand, the other hand on her hip.

"What the fuck, Micah?" she said when I opened the door,

scuffing the snow off her boots before entering. "Where have you been?"

"I've had a lot going on," I said, retreating to the counter and shuffling papers into a neat pile.

"Too busy to respond to a single text?" Natalie followed me to the counter and grabbed the transcript of Alex's interrogation. "What is this?"

I snatched the transcript out of her hand and hid the papers away on the shelves in the storage room, between the antique coffee grinder and a box of coffee stirrers. When I came back out, Natalie had taken off her coat and taken down a chair for herself. She wasn't leaving any time soon.

"What's going on, Micah?" Her no-nonsense voice, the one she used with Ashton. "Are you okay?"

I'm fine, I'm fine, I wanted to say. *Everything is fine.* But instead, I could feel the tears welling up in my eyes, the thick lump in the back of my throat. It felt so good to have someone show real concern. I sat down in the chair next to her.

"I thought I was over this," I said, my voice cracking. "I thought I had finally moved on."

The bells on the front door chimed, and a woman peered in cautiously at the upturned chairs and my red, splotchy face. Her eyes slowly registered that she didn't belong here.

"We're closed today," Natalie said decisively just as the woman opened her mouth to apologize. The woman nodded her head quickly and ducked back out, and Natalie latched the door behind her.

"Is this about the website?" she asked as she turned back toward me, easing back into her chair.

I shook my head, a blur of thoughts struggling for dominance. "Julia started it" was what finally came out. "And now they're breaking into my apartment—"

"Someone broke into your apartment?" Natalie's eyes widened.

The baby stirred in his car seat, and Natalie rocked him gently with her foot, eyes fixed on me.

"The Truthseekers," I said. "The ones from the coffee shop. They left a pile of folded-up notes on my bed."

"Did the police—" Natalie started, and I shook my head, eyes fixed down. EAT ME had been carved into the side of the tabletop with a pen, the blue ink sunk into its grooves.

"You called the police."

I shifted in my seat, and Natalie tilted her head in disbelief.

"First the texts, and then the photograph, and now someone's been in your house? This is escalating behavior." Escalating behavior, like this was one of her crime dramas. I shook my head again.

"They're just kids," I said. "They're just trying to get a rise out of me."

"Just—" Natalie studied me, trying to understand what I was saying. "Just kids? Micah, how do you know?"

Another jumble of thoughts, too many to piece together. *The long-haired boy at the table in the back, his self-satisfied smirk. The large-toothed girl, plotting. Julia, wedged between the stacks of paper on her couch, typing out impassioned defenses of Alex, egging them on.*

"I—" I started, but Natalie cut me off.

"You don't know anything," she said. "This is what police are for. You need to get them involved."

Why didn't you help me?

"Micah," Natalie said, leaning in toward me. "You don't know who it is. What if it's someone unstable?" A pause, but then she decided to plow forward. "What if it's Joshua?"

I knew it wasn't. I promise. I never thought it was you.

"I told you it's not him." I pushed my chair back and stood, wiped a hand over my damp cheeks.

"I know you think of him as a kid," Natalie said. "I get it. But he's *not* a kid anymore. And he's always been—off."

"I just need some time to myself," I said, nodding toward the door. "I just need to figure some things out."

Natalie sat there for a moment longer, lips pressed together, assessing the situation. Then she slid her arms into the sleeves of her jacket and hoisted the car seat up, walking, reluctantly, to the door.

"Fine," she said as she held the door open, looking back toward me. "But talk to the police, Micah. This isn't okay. You can't do this on your own."

I spotted Detective Curtis as he walked past Hotel Calvary through the flakes of snow that had started to fall. He had the unmistakable look of a police officer: hair buzzed short with an angular, prominent chin, barrel-chested under a button-down shirt. He crossed the street toward me, hands in the pockets of his overcoat, and I turned away from the window, focused my attention on the angle of the coffee mugs beneath the counter. I turned each handle so they all faced the same way, jutting out just a little to the right. He rapped at the door with the knuckle of his index finger, and I startled, just a little, even though I knew it was coming.

He glanced down at the CLOSED sign that hung on the door, then back up at me, his eyebrow raised. I abandoned the mugs and rushed to the front door to let him in.

"Officer Curtis," I said, reaching out to shake his hand. I wondered if that was the right thing to do. "I'm Micah. Thanks for talking with me."

He smiled back at me and took my hand, his fingers dry and cold. "It's Joe when I'm not working. And," he said, giving me a fatherly wink, "it's *Detective* Curtis when I am."

"Joe," I repeated. "Can I get you some coffee?"

"That would be great," he said, still smiling. His face was just a little too large for its features, his chin too wide, his forehead too broad. He looked familiar. I tried to picture the police station: the narrow hallway with its speckled panel ceiling and fluorescent lights, Detective Heller walking two steps in front of me, a manila folder tucked under her arm. Had he been with Alex when we passed each other? Had he and Detective Heller exchanged a nod?

"Closed today," he said, choosing a seat for himself.

"We're renovating." I slid a mug in front of him. He scanned the shop, looking, I assume, for hammers or paint cans, some sign of work being done. My face burned. "We haven't started yet."

I sat down in the seat in front of him, cupping a mug between my hands. The warmth stung my palms. I chewed my bottom lip, trying to figure out how to begin.

"So Cindy says you've got some questions about the Winters case," he said, helpfully.

"That's right," I said. "I'm—I was a friend. Of Emily's." My face flushed again; he knew that already. He already knew about all of us. But he didn't react. I set down my coffee, tried to collect myself.

"Have we met before?" I asked after a moment had passed. "I was questioned a few times. Back when it happened."

"Not by me."

"No." I rubbed the sleeve of my sweater between my thumb and index finger and tried to breathe normally.

"I used to teach DARE to middle schoolers," he offered, reclining against the embroidered back of the chair. His large frame made it look like doll furniture.

"Maybe that's it," I said. Our DARE officer was wiry and tall, with arms that hung too far down his legs. Not Joe Curtis.

"I've just been having—not doubts, exactly. More like questions. Cindy thought it might be helpful to talk to you, just to put myself back at ease."

"I'm an open book," he said, his mouth stretching into a playful smile that I imagined he used all the time in interrogations. "Well, not really. But I'll tell you what I can. As a favor to Cindy."

"Okay." I broke eye contact and looked down. "When you were investigating the case, did you have any suspects other than Alex?"

"Let me say this." He took a sip of his coffee. "This was a murder investigation, so we took it very seriously. We spoke with the Winterses, of course, and people who knew them, just to make sure there wasn't anything funny going on at home. That's pretty standard, and we didn't see any red flags there."

"What about Joshua?" I asked, and I felt a pit of guilt in my stomach as soon as the words were out of my mouth.

"Well." A nod, as if he understood why I was asking. "I know that Joshua had a hard time after Emily's death." Another pause as he decided how much to say. "But the Winterses said Joshua was at home with them that night, and we didn't turn up anything to the contrary."

Didn't turn up anything to the contrary. If they didn't even know you were there, what else did they miss?

"Did you do DNA testing?" I asked, the question sounding awkward as it left my mouth. I saw the lift and fall of his shoulders. I knew what he was thinking: *This girl watches too much television.*

"We worked with what we had," he explained, maintaining a patient expression.

"But did you see signs that anyone else had been there that night?"

"Well," he said, his voice measured, "it's difficult to sort out who was there *that night* from who was there *recently.* Emily and Alex weren't the only ones who knew about that building, you know. There were prints all over the place. Not all of them identified, but that's no big surprise."

"But how did you—"

"There's not always a smoking gun, Micah. Not all homicides have eyewitnesses." He took another sip of his coffee, and I wondered if he was masking his irritation. "And, to be honest, not even eyewitnesses are as reliable as we'd like them to be. So we use common sense. Alex and Emily were together at the crime scene that night. We know, from witnesses at the party, that they were fighting. There were obvious signs of a struggle. Bruises on her arms." He leaned forward. "Sometimes that's what we have to work with."

"He was the last one seen with her," I said, my heart sinking. *There has to be more.*

Detective Curtis nodded, looking pleased to be getting through to me. "Exactly."

I sucked in air and looked down at the table.

"Anything else that's been on your mind, Micah?"

I thought about the paper footballs, the photograph on my window. *I'm being followed. Someone is out to get me.* He'd think I was losing my mind.

"No," I said. "No, that's all I wanted to know."

That afternoon, for the second time in ten years, I weaved my way up Culver Street, past the entrance to your neighborhood, past a small deer frozen at the edge of the forest, just off the side of the road. Her black eyes blinked nervously at the sight of my car. *Don't move,* I thought, *don't move.* She didn't. Back up toward Grace Street, back into the thick forest. Back to where it happened.

I have trouble, sometimes, sorting out my own memories from the accounts that followed: the images on poster board in the courtroom, the testimony from my classmates who claimed to have witnessed the fight, the stories that circulated around school in the weeks that followed Emily's death. My memories are soft around the edges, dulled by Keystone and cheap vodka, one sliding into the next. I was hoping that going back might trigger something definitive, concrete, something I could use. I eased my car onto the dirt rut between the road and the woods, not far from where Emily had parked that night. I could still see her twisting the rearview mirror toward herself, the blue sea-glass pendant that hung there jangling from the motion. She angled her chin and fussed with her curls.

"So he *is* going to be here tonight," I had said, and Emily had tensed, catching herself. She readjusted the mirror.

"Who?" A cluster of our classmates passed her car, veering out into the road and then back again, six-packs swinging at their sides. Emily slipped her arms into the sleeves of her jean jacket and looked straight ahead.

"Whoever it is you've been talking to." I smiled and raised an eyebrow at her, hoping to get her to loosen up. She hadn't responded.

The memory of Emily brought a dull ache to the back of my throat. *This is not a good idea.* I reached across my empty passenger seat for the glove compartment and retrieved a near-empty pack of cigarettes. *I shouldn't be back here.* I rolled down my window, hung the lit cigarette out the side. *No real investigation. Prints all over the place.*

I threw the cigarette butt down onto the road, rolled up the window, and stepped out onto the ice. My sneakers, worn flat on the bottom, couldn't find traction. I jerked forward, then grabbed for the car door, balancing myself. Past my car, a shock of red in the forest, a dogwood growing up among the bare oaks.

Alex would have come out of the woods around here, I realized, replaying his version of the night in my head. I could see him fumbling with the keys to his Jeep, struggling to open the door. Flopping down, finally, on the back seat's stained fabric, groping around the mud-caked floor for a sleeping bag that wasn't there. (*It's with Micah and Ryan,* he'd realize, holding his spinning head in his hands. *How did things get so messy?* he'd wonder. *How did they go so wrong?*) He'd have slept that night with his jacket draped over him for warmth, woken up with heavy eyelids and a dry mouth, worried only that Emily would tell me what had been going on, that his parents would figure out he had been drinking. *If he was telling the truth,* I reminded myself. *They fought. They left the party together.*

I straightened myself and shuffled down Grace Street, palms held out flat at my side. *He's a liar.* A gust of wind whistled through the trees, cutting through the thin lining of my jacket. *The last one seen with her.*

The stone pillars that used to mark the entrance to the resort rose up in front of me. Moss crept over them in patches, the rough edges worn down by weather. Next to them, right where Alex had been standing that night, the green shard of a beer bottle jutted out of the leaves and snow. Alex had been waiting there, leaning an elbow against the pillar, pink and blue polo collars spiked beneath his jacket. Ryan had stood beside him in his frayed black hoodie, a brown paper bag at his side.

"What do you have in there?" Emily had asked, pulling at the lip of the bag with her index finger, her nails painted slate blue.

"Rations." Ryan raised an eyebrow at her and slid out the frosted neck of a bottle. From his mom's collection, I assumed.

I tried to remember their demeanor. Had Alex been moody, impatient? I had reached out for him, and he had stepped back.

"Let's go get set up," he had said. He walked five steps ahead of us, gripping a rolled-up sleeping bag and a green plastic tarp.

Had Emily seemed nervous? She had hung back, I thought, walking beside me and Ryan, jacket sleeves rolled up, pulling at her arm hair. Had I noticed it then, chalked it up to nerves, the boy she wouldn't name?

I tried to follow the route we had taken that night. A right to the altar. I guessed at the curves in the path, which was obscured by the snow, and there it stood, four stone slabs.

"For human sacrifices," Ryan had told us once, straight-faced. Emily had swatted at his arm. "No, really—look at the dimensions. Perfect for a small human."

A pile of rocks, Alex had called it in the interrogation.

From the altar to the lodge. There had been a swarm of activity that night: a cluster of underclassmen around a table set up for beer pong, classmates disappearing and reappearing among the trees.

I studied the empty forest and tried to remember who had been there. Michelle had cornered me almost immediately, picking me off from the group. Her dark eyeliner was already smudged, eyes glassy and cheeks bright red.

"He's not here," she had hissed at me in a stage whisper, and I saw, out of the corner of my eye, Ryan make an abrupt about-face, leaving me on my own. Emily and Alex, already gone.

"Who's not here?" I had asked, leaning away from the heat of Michelle's breath.

"Patrick." She kept talking, alternating between tears and anger, the realization that it might not ever be going to happen between her and Patrick Sellers and the conviction that they were supposed to be together.

Behind where Michelle had assaulted me was the concrete slab, now a raised mound in the snow. This was where Caroline Liu had swayed uneasily, balancing herself on Brian Wasserman's shoulder. Or maybe that was another night, an image grafted on after the fact. I tried to make myself focus; I had to remember who was there that night.

I remembered extracting myself from Michelle, who was slurring "I just love him so *much*" for the fifth time. That's when I saw Natalie lingering behind the beer pong table, arms crossed over her chest, a metal thermos dangling from her right hand.

"I'll be back," I had promised Michelle, who rocked unsteadily on her heels, struggling to find her balance.

A dirt-speckled ping-pong ball rounded the lip of a Solo cup. Cheers and groans rose up from the table, a sophomore's fist knocking into my side as I tried to make my way toward Natalie.

"That looked pretty brutal." Natalie nodded her head at Michelle, who had found her way into a group of freshman girls, and lifted her thermos toward me. "My brother's recipe. Courtesy of Sigma Tau."

"Good." Sweet and tangy, with flecks of Kool-Aid that hadn't been fully mixed in. "I'm going to need this to get through tonight."

"New game," Natalie said as Michelle leaned in toward one of the freshmen, whispering in her ear. "Every time Michelle tells someone how much she loves them, we both have to drink."

Natalie mock-staggered toward me, eyes unfocused, and rested her weight on my shoulder. "You're so *pretty*. Has anyone ever told you how *pretty* you are? I just—I just love you *so much*." She refocused her eyes and grinned at me proudly. "Whatever's happening over there counts. Drink up."

I couldn't remember how long Natalie and I had stood there, watching. It felt like no time at all, but the vodka had gone to my head, my vision blurring and face going numb. I tried to remember if I had seen anyone out of place, anyone in the woods who shouldn't have been there, but my mind kept returning to Michelle and that gang of freshman girls and their loud, high-pitched laughter.

The game had ended with another roar from the beer pong table, the reigning champions dethroned. Caroline had staggered backward and bumped into me, causing me to pitch forward. She cackled, wiping unhelpfully at my now-damp shirt with her bare hand. "Whoops!" Another hoarse laugh.

"I'm so over high school parties," Natalie said, her voice nearly drowned out by a chorus of shrieks and giggles. Matt Penna had poured his beer down the front of a freshman's white shirt and was gallantly helping her clean it up. Natalie gave me an exaggerated eye roll. "My brother's home from college, and one of his friends is having some people over. Want to go?"

I shook my head, my temples stinging from the saccharine punch, the world seeming to take a moment to catch up with me.

"I can't." The words seemed to distort in my mouth. "I've got to stay here with Alex."

Another eye roll, an impatient sigh. "Where even *is* Alex?"

I scanned the woods, which kept spinning even when I stopped. "He's here. I just need to find him."

I tried to conjure up an image of what happened next, turning in the empty, snow-covered forest. I had taken clumsy steps away from the crowd. No sign of Alex and Emily, who seemed to have disappeared completely, swallowed up into the woods.

Ryan had shuffled toward me from the direction of the altar, his creased forehead loosening as he smiled.

"Where have you been?" I had asked. Ryan shrugged in response, filled my cup with vodka.

"Come back with me," I slurred at him, and he had complied, looping his arm around my waist for support. "You left me alone with her." I wagged a scolding finger at him, and Ryan laughed, hadn't tried to deny it.

"It's every man for himself when it comes to Michelle," he said, taking a swig of vodka from the bottle. "You know that."

"Want to play a game?" I scanned the crowd for Michelle. It was more dispersed than it had been. Matt Penna lingered with the freshman, who leaned back against the trunk of a tree. He tugged on a strand of her hair, and she batted his hand away playfully. The beer pong crowd had thinned out, a few die-hard participants remaining.

"Where the fuck is she?" I leaned into Ryan for support.

"I don't know," Ryan said.

"Well, fuck." I started staggering away, everything spinning and speeding up and blurring together. You in the forest, flashlight in hand and dirt on your shoes, and then I was keeled over vomiting, Ryan holding back my hair, and then falling asleep, Ryan's hand on my back.

"Where is Alex?" I asked him, and Ryan said softly, "It's okay. It's okay."

The crack of a branch broke through the silence, bringing me back. I jumped, scanned the trees for movement, hoping to see a deer or a rabbit running off into the woods. I realized how alone I was, the trees stretching out in all directions, and a chill shot through me. *It's fine,* I told myself. *There's no one else here.*

The damp slush soaking through my socks stung my ankles. I reached down to brush the snow away, but it was pointless. I tried to orient myself, using the concrete slab as a guide. *The creek bed, a hundred yards back. And down the creek bed . . .*

Down the creek bed, the cinder block house. I pushed through the thorny undergrowth in what I thought to be the direction of the creek, and, sure enough, there it was: the snow sunken in, the rocks jutting out. I followed along the side, sneakers crunching through the unbroken snow until the structure rose up into sight. Still there, after all this time. A new chain looped through its doors, intact.

I ran my hand over the cold chain links and pictured Emily in there. Her head, striking against the stones below. (*Like a pumpkin,* Redhandman had commented on No Stone Unturned. *SPLAT.*)

Left on the forest floor, alone.

I turned to study the surrounding woods, the bare branches of the trees. It had been fall when it happened, the leaves beginning to turn red and orange. Someone could have been hiding in the forest, watching, waiting for Alex to leave. The owner of the flashlight, unhappy to find intruders in his makeshift home. A serial killer, roaming the Calvary woods, as one No Stone Unturned commenter had unhelpfully suggested.

Or, as others had insisted, you.

They were wrong about you: it wasn't possible. I rubbed my hands together for warmth, my eyes catching on the bulky trunk of an old oak. I imagined a flash of movement, the crack of a twig beneath a boot. *Someone watching. Waiting.* There were so many places to hide.

I followed my footprints back, a straight line at first, branching off into loops and zigzags. It wasn't until I reached the stone pillars that I noticed the thin horizontal lines in some of them, the imprint of a heel from a boot. They weren't all mine. They hadn't been there before, I was almost sure of it. Definitely sure of it. How could I not have noticed?

"Hello?" I shouted out, but there was just silence, the forest empty and still. "You need to leave me alone," I shouted. "Just leave me alone."

I shuffled up Culver Street as quickly as I could, peering under my car before getting too close and checking the back seat before getting in. *It's not me,* I thought as I locked the doors and glanced back at the street in the rearview mirror. *It's them. They're everywhere.* Everywhere, Joshua, always watching. So, tell me, how was I supposed to think straight? What was I supposed to do?

18

"Let me know if you need anything else," the diner waitress says as she returns with a pot of coffee and empties it into my mug. Burnt and bitter, probably kept warm on the heater for hours while the diner booths all sat empty.

"Thanks," I say, waiting for her to leave again. Instead, she lingers, glancing back toward the window.

"Not a good idea to be out driving in this," she says.

"No."

"Been dead all morning."

I nod, and she strolls back behind the counter, puts on another pot of coffee.

The wall next to me is covered in memorabilia and photographs. I assumed they were pictures of famous patrons when I sat down, but on closer look they seem to be ordinary people, family and friends of the owners, posing for the camera. Mixed in with the photographs is a framed newspaper clipping, with the headline: *Town Guides Lost Plane to Safe Landing*. I squint at the small, blurry print. A pilot was having engine trouble and needed to land, but there was a heavy fog and he couldn't see the ground. Dozens of people got in their cars and drove to Ellington's airfield. They lit the runway with their headlights.

The newspaper clipping is old, yellowed with age. I can't imagine something like that happening today.

I turn back toward the waitress. She pulls a phone out of her server apron, sits down on one of the swiveling stools, and taps at the screen. I feel my hand tightening around the ceramic mug and remind myself to relax. She's probably texting a friend. No one knows I'm here.

I want to know what they're saying on No Stone Unturned. My hand wraps around my phone in my bag. I start to pull it out. This isn't a good idea. I let go.

The night after I returned to the forest, I couldn't sleep. I'd see the outlines of our curtains in the dark and convince myself I saw movement: a flutter, a rustle. My eyes would catch on a shadowy bulk in the corner, and I'd be sure it was a person crouching, waiting for me to drift off. I'd hear the light footsteps of our neighbors upstairs and squeeze my eyes tight, reach out for Ryan's arm. He slept easily, deeply, completely unaware.

I pushed myself up from bed and, after looking back to make sure Ryan was still sleeping, snuck into the office with my messenger bag. I pulled out the notepad I had taken from Julia's house and flipped through to my notes. The name of the website that Julia liked to visit: On the Outside. Her username: jules91.

The site appeared to be an active forum where friends and families of prisoners could share their experiences or offer advice. Some of the women had signatures with graphics that counted down to the date of a release or a prison wedding or ticked off the number of days that they and their significant others had been together. Others had poems or inspirational quotes: *Anything worth having is worth waiting for.* A thread devoted to pictures of inmates, most taken in front of backdrops that resembled Alex's lopsided bridge. Questions on prison weddings on a state-by-state basis. A poll by one of the users: *Is he just using you?* Fifty-nine percent of the wives and girlfriends were certain that no, he wasn't.

I searched for jules91 and pulled up her posting history. I clicked through post after post offering words of wisdom to other prison wives and girlfriends. There she was, reassuring a woman who hadn't heard from her boyfriend in a month. *Mail and phone access can be delayed after a prison transfer,* Julia wrote. *Don't give up hope* ♡ Encouraging another woman whose husband had ten years to go to take things "one day at a time." Contributing to lists of attorneys who might be willing to help pro bono.

The other wives and girlfriends responded gratefully, enthusiastically. *That's exactly what I needed to hear.* Some treated Julia like she was some kind of expert, asking her follow-up questions: *Can he appeal if he accepted a plea deal? How do we get more DNA testing?* (Julia mentioned, multiple times, that she worked at a law office. She omitted the fact that she was a secretary.) I pictured her responding to each question with a small, self-important smile, feeling needed, wanted. Important.

I clicked on a poll Julia had participated in: *Has jail time made any positive changes in your life?* Fifty-five percent of the women said yes, definitely. Only twenty-one percent said no, definitely not. A post from jules91, supporting her answer: *Alex's imprisonment has given me a strength I didn't know I had before. It allowed us to take our time getting to know each other, and I feel like that brought us to a level of intimacy that might not have been possible otherwise. Plus*—an emoji with its tongue sticking out, I guess she was going for "goofy"—*this way I get him all to myself.* The post had ten upvotes, other women responding with squinty-eyed laughing emojis of their own.

All to myself. The words made me sick. I pushed back from my chair and got myself a glass of water. The ice machine rumbled, prolonged grinding.

"Micah?" I heard Ryan's groggy voice behind me. I turned to see him leaning in the doorway in his threadbare T-shirt, scratching lazily at his shoulder. "Everything okay?"

"Fine," I said. *All to myself.* "I just couldn't sleep."

"Come back to bed soon," he said, retreating into the dark of our room.

I settled back into my seat and pulled up another Julia thread. *My Alex and his puppy* 😍 😍 😍 A picture of Alex and a cluster of other inmates gathered around Cannoli. More than fifty responses, women cooing over the dog, over the program, over "Julia's Alex."

She was enjoying herself on there, playing the knowledgeable girlfriend, the one who had the system figured out. *Here's what to look for in an attorney,* she told one anxious new prison wife, as if that had ever done Alex any good. *So happy to have found my community,* she gushed in another post—"community," the same word she had used for the Truthseekers. Julia finally felt like she belonged, and she was milking the situation for all it was worth.

A thought occurred to me, and my stomach twisted. *Was Julia at the party that night?* She would have gone if she had known Alex was going to be there. I could almost see her: lurking in the background, twisting her braided hair with discomfort, scanning the crowd for Alex. Following as he and Emily slipped away together, always twenty steps behind, unnoticed. Watching from behind the trunk of a giant oak, waiting for them to reemerge, realizing what was happening.

My Alex. All to myself. I logged on to the No Stone Unturned forum and started a new thread: *What if it was Julia Reynolds?*

She had the opportunity.

concernedcitizen: She easily could have been at the party that night. Everyone at school knew it was happening, and Julia used to follow Alex around like a puppy dog. It wouldn't have been the first time she showed up somewhere uninvited.

She had a motive.

concernedcitizen: When she gets to the campsite, she sees Alex disappear into the woods with Emily. She's curious. She follows them down the narrow creek bed. She sees them slip into the cinder block house, out of sight. She realizes what they're doing. It's too much for her to take.

I held my breath, leaned back in my seat. I glanced at the time on the monitor: 3:02 A.M. I was about to close the lid of my laptop when a response came through:

TheMissingKing: I don't know. She knew Alex was seeing Micah, and it didn't push her into any kind of murderous rage. Why now?

I chewed on my lip, picked up an unpainted bayonet and rubbed it between my thumb and forefinger. I didn't get in the way of Julia's fantasies. Emily did.

concernedcitizen: Julia tolerated Micah's relationship with Alex because she saw it as an obstacle that she'd eventually overcome. Alex had gotten involved with Micah before he even knew that Julia existed. She thought that relationship would end, in time, and then Alex would realize that Julia was the one for him. Straight out of the movies. So she's waiting patiently for that to happen, just biding her time.

I paused over the keyboard, rubbed a hand over my face, asked myself why I hadn't realized this before.

concernedcitizen: Then she sees Alex and Emily together, and that puts an end to the delusion that she's somehow next in line, the heir apparent. She's furious at Emily—for jumping ahead, for taking what she perceived to be her place. And so, when Alex comes back out, Julia waits for a moment, then enters, ready for a confrontation.

TheMissingKing: And the petitions for Alex's release? The calls for more DNA testing?

concernedcitizen: Those efforts were going nowhere, and Julia knew it. She loves playing the grieving girlfriend, getting all that sympathy and attention. But I don't think she really wants him out. She wants him in prison. She wants him for herself. And maybe she wants him to suffer a little, too: for picking Emily next, for not seeing her there, waiting.

It all made sense. It all fit together.

Rumblecore: Creepy.

TheMissingKing: Yeah, but is there any proof?

concernedcitizen: She posts in this forum for prison girlfriends, and she's said some truly unnerving things (like her response to this poll).

Rumblecore: How do we know this is her?

TheMissingKing: She's PA-based and the timing seems to add up. It's definitely possible.

Rumblecore: Disturbing.

The next morning, another post.

helenaa: Julia was definitely there that night. I remember thinking how weird it was that she had shown up. She was sort of swaying back and forth by herself like there was music playing. I think she might have even been talking to herself. Real weird.

I pulled out my phone and sent a text to Cindy:

Did the police look into Julia Reynolds?

A few minutes later, a response.

Who?

I was right. She hadn't even been on their radar. I texted back.

Alex's current girlfriend.

Three periods appeared, then disappeared, then appeared again.

Oh, that girl. Poor thing.

I could see it so clearly: Julia following Alex and Emily into the woods, waiting. The beam of Julia's flashlight illuminating the concrete steps, landing on Emily, all alone. Julia reaching out across the visitors' table to hold Alex's hand, his shoulders slumped, defeated. *It's okay,* she tells him. *It's okay. You have me now.*

19

The bells on the diner door jangle, and the bored waitress straightens in her seat, drops her phone back into her server apron. Two uniformed officers enter, both round and stubbled with shiny pink patches on their noses from the cold.

"Pretty wild out there," one of them says to no one in particular.

"Sit wherever you'd like," the waitress tells them. She gestures at the empty rows of tables. Empty, except for me.

I focus down at my placemat and feign interest in the block advertisements for tree maintenance and air duct cleaning. I try to breathe like a normal person: in and out, in and out, no sharp inhales. Swallow. Everything is fine. They're just here for coffee. Just here to get out of the snow.

They could sit anywhere, but they sit down in the booth across from me, just feet away. The shorter one, the one who commented on the weather before, nods at me and remarks on it again: "Pretty bad driving conditions."

I nod in acknowledgment, not trusting my voice. I wrap my hands around my coffee mug, concentrate on the dull warmth against my palms. The simple, square blocks of text on my placemat, the ring of coffee in the upper-left corner. The Northridge Diner has the same placemats: same style, same layout, just different local businesses featured in the little squares. A large picture of the diner storefront in the middle, in case a patron happens to forget where he is. The same chrome table, the same metallic napkin dispenser pushed up against the wall.

When Alex, Ryan, Emily, and I went to the Northridge Diner back in high school, we always sat in the same booth: third from the back windows, a long, jagged scrape across the chrome table.

"Knife fight," Ryan had speculated at one point, and that explanation stuck. More likely, based on my experience in the food-service industry: a bored adolescent, scraping the tine of a fork across the smooth surface just to hear the sound.

I'd sit next to Alex in the booth seat facing the door. Ryan and Emily sat across from us. Without fail, Emily would order coffee and nothing else, and then lean into Ryan when our food orders arrived, stealing his cheese fries.

"I don't even like cheese fries," Ryan admitted once. "It's just that Emily seems to like them so much."

I can feel it: things closing in, collapsing on themselves. I breathe in, steadying myself. I'm in Connecticut now, close to the Rhode Island border. Breathe out. Calvary is hundreds of miles behind me. A new life. I can do this. I can begin again.

"How well do you know Julia?" I asked Ryan the morning after I found her comments on On the Outside. I tried to look casual, focusing on measuring out coffee grounds and pouring water into our coffee maker. I could feel him looking back at me, deciding whether and how to respond.

"Micah."

The coffee dripped slowly into the pot, and I turned to face him.

"What?"

"I'm not sure now is the time." He laced his fingers behind his head and tried not to look at me. He didn't want to start a fight.

"I'm just trying to understand who she is."

Ryan nodded, his cheek puckering as he chewed at the inside of his mouth. This was his weak spot: *If you only understood where they're coming from.* No one was really that bad, once you took the time.

"I don't know her that well." He placed his spoon down on the table. "I know she visits Alex pretty regularly. And writes him." He tented his fingers, thought about what to say next. "I think she's lonely. I'm not sure she has many friends. Only child. Alex says her parents are a little odd. Distant. I don't think they have a good relationship."

For Ryan, that was enough to wipe away all manner of sin.

"I think Alex is just about all she has," he continued. "And she might be just about all Alex has, too."

This way I get him all to myself.

"That's not true," I said, turning toward the coffee maker. "He has you, too." Out of the corner of my eye, I saw Ryan shift uncomfortably in his seat.

I poured the coffee into a thermos and started toward the front door.

"Is Stomping Grounds open today?" Ryan asked, and I stopped. I could feel the blood rushing to my cheeks, like I had been caught doing something wrong.

"Why wouldn't it be?" I asked.

"It's Thanksgiving."

I hoped he couldn't see my relief.

"People still need coffee on holidays."

"We've got dinner at my mom's."

I grabbed my jacket off the hook and turned to give him a smile. "I know," I said, although I had forgotten about it. "I'll be back in time. Don't worry."

In retrospect, I should have kept my routine at Stomping Grounds. Without the ebb and flow of the customers, the checklists, the wiping down and sweeping up, I couldn't stop thinking about Julia. Julia, searching out other lonely women on the Internet who could tell her how *brave* she was, how *strong*. Julia at fifteen, positioning herself ten feet away from Alex's locker, hoping for a nod of recognition. Of course she would have been at the party. Of course she would have followed Alex and Emily into the woods.

I latched the Stomping Grounds door behind me and kept the lights in the main room off. I set myself up in the storage room and lit a cigarette as I waited for the computer to load. There was activity on the Julia thread. Steelrights had posted a link to an old Live-journal page, username lovesickjules91.

I opened the link. Julia must have created the page when we were in high school. On the screen, a baby blue background with a pink border, the first entry a quiz result: *What type of fairy are you?* Julia was a pixie, apparently, a picture of a winged, pink-haired girl displayed proudly on her page. The next few entries were poems—original, by the looks of it. I scanned through them.

> *trembling heart when our eyes meet*
> *a connection so strong it can't be denied*
> *i know the secrets of your heart, my love*
> *i know the truths you hold inside*
> *why do you stay away, my love*
> *what will it take for you to see*
> *i am what you want my love*
> *i am all you'll ever need*

Below that, a drawing, sketched out crudely in pencil, type print from the other side showing through lightly. Julia—I could tell from the braid but not from her other features, which had been rendered generously—locked in what appeared to be a passionate embrace with a bland and muscular figure—Alex, I assumed. *Some day,* she wrote beneath it, with a series of smiley faces. The comments on the Livejournal entries were all encouraging:

Never give up hope, hon!! He'll notice you someday!!!

Ur so good at drawing!! Xoxo

The comments on No Stone Unturned were less so.

steelrights: Lol

forwardslapped: someday i'll lock you away and then you'll be mine 4ever!!! XOXOXOXO

Redhandman: Hawt.

Redhandman had posted a picture of high school Julia, dimly lit and grainy, probably taken from an old webcam. The photograph was angled down, prominently displaying her acne-dotted forehead. With her closemouthed smile and raised eyebrows, she was probably trying to look sultry but instead looked crazed.

forwardslapped: YOU'LL LEARN TO LOVE ME SOMEDAY

I took some small satisfaction in the thought of Julia seeing this broadcast across the Internet, but it was short-lived. This wasn't enough. "So she had a crush," I imagined Detective Curtis saying, hiding his impatience. "Lots of high school girls have crushes."

I closed the forum and texted Natalie.

Do you remember seeing Julia at the campsite the night Emily died?

Silence for a minute before she wrote back.

Don't know. Why?

I set down my phone, but it buzzed again almost immediately. Two texts, one right after the other, from Ryan.

What time are you planning on closing the shop? I'd like to leave for my mom's around 2.

Could you pick up some extra napkins on your way home?

I sighed and put down the phone, intending to respond later. I didn't want to go. The thought of sitting in his mother's cramped apartment, stacks of mail and paper and debris piled up on the floor and the greasy remains of food sticking to the counter, and pretending that everything was *good* was more than I could handle. I turned back to No Stone Unturned.

I looked through comments, news clippings, transcripts of police interviews, anything I could get my hands on for any mention of Julia. I scoured through my classmates' accounts of that night—who was there, what was happening—looking for Julia's name or any descriptions that might match her.

TERASSEN: Brian Wasserman and Matt Penna. Michelle Peterson. Natalie Smith. Um—Lonnie Dunne and Randall Navarro were there for some of it. You know, there were a bunch of juniors crowded around the beer pong table. Lyle Crothers was one of them. He'd probably have a better idea . . .

ABRAMS: Uh . . . and a few freshman girls I don't know. They're friends with Michelle Peterson, I think.

HELLER: Anyone else?

ABRAMS: Maybe. I don't know. There were a lot of people, you know?

PENNA: Oh yeah, Angie Nunez.

HELLER: Is something funny?

PENNA: No, no. Uh, and Morgan Shepherd? That's all I remember right now. I was kind of . . .

No one saw Julia standing at a measured distance, waiting for Alex to turn and notice her. I told myself that didn't mean anything. They didn't mention you, either. I bit into the last half of a week-old croissant and took a swig of coffee, then glanced down at my phone.

I guess I'll meet you there . . . ?

Somehow, it was already four. I swore quietly and typed a message back.

Sorry, lost track of the time. Think I might be coming down with something. Could you give my love to your mom for me?

Those three dots appeared and disappeared, appeared and disappeared.

See you at home.

I studied the text for a minute, trying to discern how upset Ryan actually was. He'd understand, I told myself. This was something I had to do. I set my phone down on the table in front of me and kept reading.

I was in bed by the time Ryan got home, waiting, my eyes fixed on the ceiling. I had checked and double-checked the latch on our sliding glass door, but a part of me still worried I'd hear a gentle tug, the short scrape of the door in its tracks before the lock caught and stopped it. I froze and then breathed with relief when I finally heard the sound of his key in the lock, his footsteps coming down our hall. I closed my eyes as he swung open the door. I could feel him looking me over before climbing into bed next to me, laying his head down on the pillow, and falling almost instantly asleep.

20

"Miss. Miss."

I jolt back to attention. The shorter police officer is leaning toward me, staring. I lower the coffee mug and return his gaze.

"Can we borrow that ketchup?" he asks. "Ours is low." He gives me a smile, one that's supposed to look friendly and benign, but I've seen that smile before. I glance at the ketchup on their table, turned over on its lid, and hand them mine.

"Of course, Officer," I say. Too stiff. Too formal. His smile grows, but it looks artificial, stretched too wide. *Help us understand, Micah. We just want to know what happened that night.*

I pull my phone out of my bag and pretend to check emails, but I'm aware of his eyes, still on me. I need to leave. I need more distance. It's not safe here.

I take a twenty out of my wallet. A quarter of what I have left. I scan the diner for the waitress, who seems to have disappeared into the kitchen to chat with the line cooks or out a side door for a cigarette. I need to go now. I wince and leave the twenty-dollar bill on the table, all of it, nod to the officer, who's still looking at me, still regarding me with that too-friendly look, and try to keep my pace steady as I walk to the front door. I need to get to Stonesport. I need to get to you.

I was already up and getting ready to leave for Stomping Grounds when Ryan came out of our room and sat down at the table. He looked me over, raised an eyebrow.

"You look like you're feeling better."

"Must have been something I ate."

He nodded, his face neutral. I couldn't tell if he believed me.

"How was dinner?" I averted my eyes, pretending to look for my keys on the counter.

"Good. You were missed."

I gave him an apologetic smile. "I'm going to be late."

"Don't let me keep you."

I could hear the tense edge to his voice. I stepped closer to the door.

"I can come home early this evening," I promised, throwing on my jacket. "We can talk then."

"The reunion is tonight."

"Oh, right. Tell everyone I said hi."

"Micah," Ryan said, running his hand along the side of his face, "I don't know what's going on with you. I feel like you've been avoiding me."

"I haven't been—"

"When was the last time we sat down and had an actual conversation? And then you blow off Thanksgiving dinner?"

"I didn't blow it off," I said. "I was sick."

Ryan looked like he was about to argue, but he stopped himself.

"Okay," he said, shaking his head. "I'll see you when I get home tonight." He straightened his shoulders and sighed, then stood to fix himself a coffee. Not angry, just sad.

"I've had a lot on my mind," I said. "That's all. I've been feeling overwhelmed."

He set down the mug and turned toward me.

"I want to help," he said. "Tell me what to do, and I can help."

"I know." I rubbed my eyes. I was exhausted. "Tomorrow. I'll come home early, and we can talk then."

"Tomorrow. Okay."

I grabbed my bag. "Have fun tonight," I said, trying to sound cheery. "Give my love to everyone."

"I will," he said, settling back down at the table, and I slipped out the front door and pretended to go to work.

I went back to reading trial transcripts and police interviews and new threads on No Stone Unturned. The Truthseekers were combing through the background of everyone connected to Emily, and new suspects and theories were popping up, but none that made as much sense to me as Julia.

Redhandman: I did some digging on Emily's dance studio. Looks like the owners got divorced a few years after Emily died, and the husband ended up remarrying one of his students.

MissMaya: 😬 😬 😬

Redhandman: Three months after her eighteenth birthday.

MissMaya: 😬 😬 😬

Wellsinceyouasked: Where is he now?

Redhandman: He moved down to Tennessee after the divorce. Looks like he's working at another dance studio there. Had two kids with the new wife.

Redhandman included a photograph with the description: *New fam.* Mr. Lionel, whose face drooped more than I had remembered, stood next to a much younger woman and two twin boys.

MissMaya: Jesus. She looks exactly like Emily.

That wasn't quite true. They were both slight, and both had dark hair, but this girl receded into the background of the photograph. Emily was always the focal point. I replied.

concernedcitizen: He has a solid alibi. Dance competition in Philadelphia. Gone all weekend.

Only a minute passed before Wellsinceyouasked responded.

Wellsinceyouasked: Source?

My phone buzzed. A text from Ryan.

A lot of people here asking about you!

I bit my lip and texted back:

Can't wait to hear about it.

I opened On the Outside to see if I could find any recent activity from Julia. One new post, with a link to a recent article on wrongful convictions.

jules: Might be some useful information in here for all of you. And I'm in it! :)

At the end of the article, a short quote from Julia. "All we can do is fight," she had told the reporter. "And pray."

I rolled my eyes and turned back to No Stone Unturned, posted a link to her On the Outside post.

concernedcitizen: Maybe she has a form of Munchausen syndrome by proxy. Just look at all the attention she's getting, on here, in the news, on her site for "families of prisoners." She thrives on it.

My phone buzzed again. A message from Natalie, with a photo of breadsticks.

Look what you're missing!

Enjoy, I wrote back. I set down my phone and googled Julia's name. The results were all links I had seen before: articles connected to wrongful convictions, a real-estate site listing the value of her house, a page offering background searches that referenced her age and people she might be related to. It wasn't enough. I felt like I was barely scraping the surface.

I finished off the dregs of my coffee and rose to get a refill. The whir of the coffee grinder didn't calm me the way it once had. I waited, impatiently, for the slow drips to fill the pot. I needed access to someone who knew Julia, someone who Julia confided in. I ticked off questions in my head: *What does Julia say about Alex in private? How does she talk about their relationship? Was she there the night Emily died?*

I flipped open the legal pad from Julia's house. My eyes floated to the email address I had jotted down. Rachel Melbourne. Julia's friend.

I pulled up Gmail, signed out of my account, and opened the page to create a new one. I paused on the prompt for a name. A relative—not so close that Julia's acquaintances might reasonably expect to have heard of her before but close enough that it made sense to be reaching out. A cousin on Julia's dad's side from the next town over.

The email was short and to the point:

I'm reaching out to you because I know you're a friend of Julia's. I'm her cousin, Ellen. She's been acting a little erratically lately, and the family has started to get concerned. I was hoping we might be able to meet up and talk over coffee sometime. I'd appreciate any insight you might have.

Good, I thought when I hit send. *Good, now we're getting somewhere.*

I stood to grab my Parliaments off the shelf. My phone buzzed and I grabbed it, hoping it might be a response from Rachel. Instead, another text from Natalie:

After-party at the Tavern. COME!!

I started to type out another excuse but then stopped, erased what I had written. If I went to the after-party, I could talk to my old classmates and find out what they remembered about that night. Someone might have seen Julia. But then I thought about how it would look: me, still in Calvary, still hung up on Emily and Alex after all this time.

Can't. Working late tonight. Inventory.

She responded immediately.

You're still downtown?? Then you HAVE to come!!!!

I set the phone down and tried to turn back to the computer. The phone buzzed again.

If you're not here in the next fifteen minutes, I'm going to come over there and physically drag you to the Tavern.

Another buzz.

I'll do it. 💪💪

Another buzz.

I'm not going to leave you alone until you get here.

It couldn't hurt to see who was there, I reasoned. I'd just go for ten minutes and see what happened. I took a deep breath and shut down the computer.

You win. I'm on my way.

The outside of the Tavern hasn't changed since we were kids. It still has those Irish-looking stained glass windows and a sign advertising its Yuengling-and-shot-of-Jim-Beam special. It's a bar for locals, with Easton students stopping by on occasion when they get tired of the dueling piano bar and the one-dollar Jell-O shots across the river. I pulled open its heavy wooden door and there they were: my old classmates, faces lit by the Tavern's weak hanging lights and neon beer advertisements. A cluster of our old classmates, Lonnie Dunne and Randall Navarro and Peter Marksman, gestured sloppily at the bartender, a girl in her early twenties who didn't seem used to crowds. Brian Wasserman and Matt Penna, in shiny button-down shirts and dark jeans, played an adult version of photo hunt on the countertop game console at the end of the bar, set up for patrons who didn't want to interact with anyone. They tried to enlist Caroline's help in finding differences in pornographic images as she passed by, but she shook her head firmly and broke away. Someone had put Soulja Boy on the jukebox, and Helena Abrams was dancing, arms in the air and head thrown back. Michelle Peterson joined in, not graceful but game, sloshing her beer on the floor.

I almost turned and left right then. But Lonnie turned away from the bar and our eyes met, and he leaned over to say something to Randall, who stopped leering at the bartender and spun around to stare at me. I squared my shoulders and pushed forward into the crowd.

I felt a hand press down on my shoulder. I jerked away and spun around to see Natalie, holding the necks of two Yuengling bottles in one hand.

"You made it!" she shouted over the music, handing me one of the bottles and nodding toward a table in the back where two shot glasses waited. "Time to catch up!"

"I don't—" I started, but Natalie shook her head, dragging me back toward the table with her.

"You need this," she said.

A pool stick jerked back, narrowly missing my face.

"Hey!" Natalie shouted. "You're not the only ones at this bar, you know."

Isaiah Holland, who used to spend half the school day at the far end of the parking lot, brazenly smoking within eyesight of administrators, shrugged one shoulder and moved to the other side of the table. He leaned down to aim, but then did a double take and looked back up at me, his eyes lingering for too long. I knew Alex and Emily were on his mind. Like no time had passed at all.

I downed my shot and Natalie handed me hers. "I've got a head start," she said. "I'll go get more."

Isaiah stepped back from the table, and, through the crowd behind him, I could see Ryan laughing and nodding, his face shiny from hours of drinking. He turned and saw me, and blinked in surprise before waving me over.

I hesitated, trying to discern his mood. I looked toward the bar but didn't see Natalie. Ryan waved again, more exaggerated this time, and smiled. He looked happy to see me there. I made my way toward him, edging past Michelle, who was lost in the music, loudly imitating Kesha's vocal fry while waving her index finger at Helena.

"Micah!" Ryan said. He put his arm around my waist and

pulled me in. I relaxed into him. *Okay,* I told myself. *This is all going to be okay.*

"So glad you could make it!" Chelsea smiled at me with what looked like a glass of seltzer water in her hand, her name tag from the reunion still affixed to her sweater. She grabbed the arm of the man standing next to her, her smile growing bigger. "This is my husband, Phillip." Phillip looked bored and confused, like he was trying to figure out how he had ended up here next to this person.

"Chelsea was just telling me about the work that she does on literacy," Ryan said.

"Uh-huh."

Someone stepped back from the dart game and elbowed me in the side.

"Micah fucking Wilkes!" It was Daniel Myers, now about fifty pounds heavier than he had been in high school. I nodded my head in acknowledgment. He opened his mouth like he was about to say something, but then just smiled and shook his head, laughing at his own private joke. I wanted to shrink back into the crowd and disappear.

"Excuse me," I said to Chelsea, slipping away from Ryan. "I'll be right back." I started toward the bar, scanning the crowd for Natalie. A cluster of field hockey girls threw back tequila shots and bit into slices of lime. The old a cappella group tried, in vain, to belt out songs over the music playing, then gave in and harmonized to "Bad Romance." And behind them, there was Julia.

She was dressed like she was in mourning. A black sweater over a black dress, gray tights, a stack of paper in one hand and a pen in the other. She had cornered Matt and Brian, who exchanged amused looks. Julia didn't notice.

"Think about everything you've done in the last ten years," she was saying. I stepped closer. I could see her profile now, her red nose twitching. "College. Your first job. Maybe you've gotten married."

Rehearsed lines, carefully recited. Matt and Brian snickered, but she kept going.

"Alex hasn't had any of those opportunities, and it's not fair. You were his friends. His teammates. It's time to make this right. I'm asking for donations to his legal fund. Anything helps—"

Brian caught sight of me approaching and grinned maliciously.

"Look who it is," he said. "Hey, Micah! Want to contribute to Alex's legal fund?"

Julia turned toward me, and I tried to back away. Matt and Brian cackled like hyenas.

"There you are!"

Natalie, behind me, another shot glass in hand. She gave it to me, eyed my bag.

"Cigarette?" she asked.

"Yes, please."

I needed to get out of there. I pushed past Caroline, who stumbled, irritated, out of my way. I could hear people laughing. Bruno Mars came on, to a few cheers and groans. I shoved through the Tavern door and steadied myself. The door swung shut behind us and muted the noise from inside. The street was empty and the air was clean and I felt like I could breathe again. Natalie laughed and shook her head.

"Crazy, right?"

"I don't know if I can go back in there." I passed her a cigarette and my lighter.

"Oh, come on," she said. "It's kind of fun finding out what everyone has been up to. Like, did you know Matt Penna is a high school teacher now? That one caught me off guard."

I snorted. "Poor kids."

"Brian claims to be working at a hedge fund, but it kind of sounds like he's scamming old people in Florida out of their retirement funds. So that—"

"Makes sense." I lit my own cigarette and pulled my jacket tighter around me. *This isn't so bad,* I thought. *I can handle this.*

"And Joy Brennan . . ." Natalie lowered her voice, like someone else might hear. "She's been hitting on Peter Marksman all night, with her husband *right beside her*. They got into a fight about whether or not to come to the Tavern after Rosalina's, and she came and he didn't, so—"

"Oh my god," I heard from behind me. "Micah Wilkes!" It was Helena, a man's coat wrapped around her shoulders, her sheer shirt and bralette still showing underneath. She gave me an exaggerated hug, like we were old friends. "How *are* you? Can I have one of those?"

I slid another cigarette out of the pack, bracing myself. "How have you been, Helena?"

"Oh, you know," she said. "Living the single life in New York. Can't complain." The Tavern door swung open, and Caroline stepped out with someone I assumed was her boyfriend, heading toward Main Street.

Helena wiggled her fingers in Caroline's direction and shouted: "Bye, girl!" She took a drag of the cigarette I had given her, and suddenly Michelle was there, too, behind her, leaning her chin heavily on Helena's shoulder.

"There you are!" she slurred. "I missed my dance partner." Her eyes caught on the cigarette in Helena's hand, and she looked up.

"Hey, can I get one of those?"

Helena nodded her head toward me, and Michelle looked in my direction, finally registering my presence.

"Micah!" she said. "I didn't think you'd be here!"

"Me neither." I slipped another cigarette out of the pack and handed it to her, along with my lighter. She thumbed at the lighter clumsily and I took both back, lit the cigarette for her myself.

"It just doesn't feel right without Emily here," she said, shaking her head slowly from side to side. "I was saying—wasn't I just saying, Helena—that there should have been some sort of, like, tribute to her? Like a slideshow or something?"

"You did say that," Helena agreed.

"I still remember where I was when I found out that she had died." Michelle blinked rapidly, her eyes tearing up a little, and she was about to launch into the story when Natalie mercifully cut her off.

"Hey, Helena," she said, "Peter's in New York now, too, right? Doing some kind of finance thing?"

Helena nodded her head, but she was studying me, curious.

"I hear you and Ryan are together now," she said, tilting her head.

"Sometimes I wish I had spent a few years in the city before having kids," Natalie said, still hoping to change the subject.

"Oh, me too," Michelle said, shifting her weight to her other foot.

"Have you heard anything about Alex recently?" Helena asked. I glared back at her.

"Some people are saying he might not have done it. Isn't that crazy?" Helena continued, either not noticing or not caring. "Although, it does make you think . . ."

"I'm not doing this." I stomped out my cigarette and marched back inside. Natalie followed apologetically.

"I didn't think—"

"I don't care," I said. "Do you see Ryan?" I wanted to go home. I should never have come in the first place.

I pushed into the crowd. More people were dancing now, a crowd forming in front of the bar. Daniel got a bull's-eye and pumped one fist up in the air. Pool balls cracked on the table.

"Micah, wait," Natalie called from behind me.

"Ryan," I shouted. My voice was lost in the music and the hum of talking and cheers from the bar as the field hockey girls ordered another round. The Tavern floor was slick with beer. "Ryan!" I shouted again.

I pushed through the crowd, tried not to make eye contact with anyone. I made my way past the dart board, to the dark hallway that led to the Tavern's bathrooms. That's where I saw him, leaning one shoulder against the hunter-green wall. His back was to me. He was talking to Julia. She saw me and her eyes widened, like they had been caught. Ryan looked over his shoulder and met my eyes, but I didn't wait to hear what he had to say. I spun around and fought my way back through the crowd, alone.

The blood pounded in my ears as I drove home. *Why was he talking to her?* It felt like a betrayal. It felt like he was taking her side. She shouldn't have been there in the first place—it was my reunion, *Alex's* reunion, not hers. She just wanted the attention, the pity, the admiration. *Look what a good person I am,* she was trying to say. *Standing by my man.* If only they knew the truth.

When I got back to the empty apartment, I grabbed Ryan's laptop from the end table and flipped it open. Were Ryan and Julia closer than I had realized? I just wanted to check his emails, see if there were any communications between the two of them. At the prompt for a password, I tried combinations of significant people and things: my name, his mother's name, his first dog's name. His birthday, my birthday, his phone number, my phone number. The date of our anniversary. Waterloo1815. The welcome screen shook each time. *Wrong. Wrong. Wrong.*

I threw the laptop down on the couch in defeat. Ryan probably had a strong password. He probably changed it every month. I went back into his office, opened my own computer, and logged on to No Stone Unturned.

concernedcitizen: Julia showed up at Alex's ten-year reunion, looking for "donations" from his old classmates. She's desperate for attention.

I thought for a second, then posted again.

concernedcitizen: If anyone wants to give her the attention she's after, she still lives in Calvary and works at Harris Law Offices.

I heard the front door open. Ryan's footsteps were heavy. I thought he was just drunk. He walked straight past the office to the bedroom. I heard the rustle of closet hangers, the roll of a dresser drawer sliding along its tracks. I shut my laptop and went to see what he was doing.

"Ryan?" I called out, pushing our bedroom door open. He slammed the drawer of my dresser shut, or tried to, a mustard sweater catching halfway. His cheeks glowed red—embarrassed, I thought at the time. Drunk.

"What are you doing?"

"Julia told me what you did." There was a tight edge to his voice. He wasn't embarrassed. He was angry.

Adrenaline shot through me. Julia, in her funeral attire, leaning forward to speak into Ryan's ear. *She's not the person you think she is.* Ryan listening, in a way he never seemed to listen to me anymore, hearing her out. Taking her at her word before even giving me a chance to explain myself. I stepped in front of my drawer protectively.

"Why are you going through my things?"

"Where is it?" The tendon in his arm pulsed as he squeezed his hand into a fist and released it again, his gray eyes flashing.

"Ryan, stop," I said. "You're drunk."

"Alex's jacket, Micah. Where is it?"

"I don't—"

"Don't play dumb. She showed me the picture."

I looked at the ground, didn't respond.

"Those were our fucking *bedsheets* in the background." Ryan grabbed hold of the crumpled sheets at the foot of our bed and shook them at me. The gray diamonds in the corner of the photograph. I should have been more careful.

I backed up, putting some space between us. "I knew you'd take her side."

"Her *side*?" He turned away from me and stalked across the bedroom. He rubbed at the side of his face, up his cheek and along his jaw. "What does this have to do with *sides*?"

"Did you even think to ask me what happened?" I was shout-ing. I couldn't help it. "She comes to you with some sob story about what a monster I am, and you start going through my things without even talking to me?"

"You're *stealing things,* Micah," Ryan shouted back. "You're *pos-ing* in Alex's old clothes."

"I—"

"No." Ryan shook his head, clenching and unclenching his hands. "No. I can't listen if you're just going to lie to me. I need to take a walk."

"It's two in the morning."

Ryan marched out of our bedroom, and I followed. He swung open the front door.

"Ryan," I shouted after him. "Where are you going? It's *two* in the *morning.*" But he didn't respond.

I sat on the balcony, my knees pulled in toward me, my Parlia-ments at my side. I smoked one after the other. I kept expecting to see headlights below, Ryan's car pulling out of the parking lot, leaving for God knows where, but below me the parking lot was still. *That means he couldn't have gone that far,* I told myself. *That means he'll be back.*

It took him an hour, but he did return. He opened the sliding glass door, and I saw him register the cigarette in my hand, con-sider saying something, decide against it. Instead, he slid down next to me, leaning back against the cold stucco wall.

"We can't do this if you're not going to be honest with me," he said, his eyes fixed forward.

"I can't be honest with you if you're not going to listen."

He rolled his head back, and I shook my head.

"See, that. That is what I'm talking about. I need you to *actually* listen."

Ryan squeezed his eyes shut, then opened them and turned his head toward me.

"Okay," he said. "I'm listening now. Tell me what's going on."

I stubbed out the cigarette in the flowerpot beside me. "I showed you the text I got. About Emily."

Ryan nodded, and a flicker of concern passed over his face.

"It wasn't just the text. Someone taped a photograph of the four of us to the window at Stomping Grounds. It was from Emily's locker." I squeezed my knees in tighter and focused on the balcony railing, bracing myself. "And after that, there was the break-in."

I could feel Ryan tense up again beside me.

"The break-in?"

I bit my lip and tried to avoid his eyes.

"Did someone break into Stomping Grounds?"

I shook my head. "No. Here. There was someone in our apartment."

Ryan twitched. "Someone . . ." He was struggling to stay calm. "Someone broke into our apartment? When?"

"I didn't want to worry you." An engine revved as a car sped past the Lofts, too fast.

"When?" he asked again.

"It was game night. You were at Merlock's."

"But how—did they take something?" He studied my face, trying to understand. "Were you here when it happened? Did they hurt you?"

I rubbed my arms, suddenly feeling the cold. "I wasn't—I didn't see them."

"Then how—?"

"They left something. Notes folded like paper footballs. Like the ones—"

"I remember." Ryan rubbed his hand along the side of his face again, his lips pressed together. He twisted around, looking back toward the sliding glass door as if the notes might still be in the room, in a pile in the corner that he had somehow overlooked. "Where are they now?"

"I got rid of them."

A sharp inhale.

"I didn't know what to do."

"Why didn't you tell me?"

"I told you about the text." I heard the volume of my voice rising and stopped myself, took a breath, tried not to sound accusatory. "But you got so upset—"

"And you didn't call the police."

"No," I said firmly. "I don't want to get the police involved."

I expected pushback, but instead Ryan hooked both hands behind his head and exhaled.

"I think it's someone from that true-crime website," I continued. "No Stone Unturned. They're looking into Emily's death, and Julia's been encouraging them online."

Ryan closed his eyes.

"She's insane," I said. "She's not—" *Not who you think she is,* I was about to say. *It was her.* But I worried I had pushed too far already.

"I know you're going through a lot right now," he said slowly. "Maybe it would make sense to talk to someone."

"I'm talking to *you.*"

He shook his head, looked down. "A professional."

"You think I'm crazy."

"That's not what I said."

"This is why I didn't tell you," I said. "I knew you wouldn't listen."

"Micah." *Be reasonable. Calm down.*

"No," I said. He winced at the tone. "You give everyone else the benefit of the doubt. Alex. Julia. Your mother. But me . . ." Tears welled up in my eyes and I brushed them away with the back of my hand, worried they would undermine me. *Too emotional.*

Calm down. "Someone has been harassing me, and you won't even fucking *listen.*"

Ryan's face crumpled. "Jesus, Micah." He closed his eyes. "I'm sorry. I should have been paying attention."

He took in a ragged breath, and all of the anger I had felt dissipated. I wanted to make this better. I didn't want to disappoint him.

"I want you to be able to trust me," he continued. "If we don't have that . . ."

"I do trust you," I said, my voice starting to break. "I do. I didn't want to worry you. I thought I could handle it by myself."

He pulled me in toward him, and I rested my head against his shoulder.

"I just want it to stop," I said. "I just want it all to go away."

"It will," he said. "We'll figure it out."

Ryan and I both avoided the subject of Julia and No Stone Unturned after that. It was easier to pretend like everything was normal. We sat at the kitchen table together and drank our coffee in the morning. I grabbed my shoes and jacket and told him I'd see him after Stomping Grounds. Then I texted Anna to tell her to take the weekend off, shut myself in the storage room, and started reading.

21

A snowplow has cleared the way in front of me, and the snow has lightened up a little, enough to make out the yellow lines dividing the road, the curves ahead.

I don't see it until I'm almost right on top of it: a blue car that kept going straight when the road turned, its front right corner crushed in against a guardrail. It must have just happened; there's no one else at the scene. The front windshield is a spiderweb of cracks, but I think I see movement inside.

I slow and consider pulling over. They might need help, a phone. They might need me.

I think better of it, press down on the accelerator. The police might already be on their way. And I can't be there, parked on the side of the road, when they show up.

I fumble with my pack of cigarettes, which feels uncomfortably light, and slide one out. I keep driving.

The Truthseekers were brutal. In a matter of days, they dug up all sorts of personal information about Julia. The phone number for Harris Law Offices. Her home address. Her email address. The name of her church: Trinity Bible Fellowship. Redhandman had found pictures of Julia on her church's website and posted them to the forum. They showed Julia and her pastor at a recent potluck dinner, Julia clutching a casserole dish in her hands. Her eyes were watery, her cheeks flushed. The pastor had cropped blond hair and a toothy, wholesome smile. His hand was on her back for the camera.

Redhandman: Looks like Julia has a type.

forwardslapped: that guy better watch out. maybe someone should warn him . . .

She brought this on herself, I reminded myself as I scrolled through the comments in the thread. My phone buzzed, and I checked it. A text from Natalie.

Are you still mad? I was trying to help. I thought the reunion would be a fun break.

I started a response, deleted it, started again.

It's fine. I've just been busy.

A second later, another text from Natalie:

With what? Last I checked, Stomping Grounds is still closed . . .

I set down the phone and turned back to the Julia thread, stopping when I saw my username.

Wellsinceyouasked: concernedcitizen, are you from Calvary? You aren't on our verified locals list.

TheMissingKing: Just checked their history. It's a new account. They've only posted in this case.

Wellsinceyouasked: Seems like they have inside knowledge. Maybe someone in Alex's grade? Who else would have known about Alex's reunion?

TheMissingKing: Could also be a bartender or patron, but yeah, good point.

I should have been more careful. I needed a cup of coffee. I pushed myself up, opened the storage room door, and stepped out into the main room. I jumped when I saw Detective Curtis, looking in through the glass panel on the front door. He waved when he saw me and tapped on the glass. I hesitated, then slipped on my jacket and crossed the room. I opened the front door, just enough that I could slide out, and closed it behind me again.

"Micah," he said, his face unreadable. "How are the renovations coming along?"

I pulled my jacket shut, wrapping my arms around my chest. "You know how it goes," I said. "These things take time."

"So we've had reports of harassment."

My eyes widened. For a moment, I thought he knew about what had been happening to me, and it almost felt like relief. *Ryan is taking this seriously, after all. The concern must have been too much. He filed a report.*

"Did Ryan—" I started, but Detective Curtis tilted his head, confused, and I stopped.

"From Julia Reynolds."

I felt my mouth twist into a scowl before I could stop it. "Julia Reynolds is a disturbed person," I told him.

He nodded, his face still neutral.

"She said you burst into her place of employment and physically threatened her."

"I did not—" I started, then remembered the man with his arm in a sling recording us on his phone. "She came here first. To *my* place of employment." I tried to keep my voice measured, the pitch steady. I knew how it sounded. "I just went over there to ask her to leave me alone. That's all."

"She's claiming someone broke into her apartment, took some things. A jacket."

I shook my head furiously back and forth.

"And she's been getting phone calls."

I waited for Detective Curtis to explain.

"Nasty stuff. Really obscene. Day and night, at work and at home."

The Truthseekers. Behind him, Martin the front desk clerk watched at a safe distance from beneath the Hotel Calvary awning, cigarette in hand. I wanted one, too.

"Look," I said, a wave of exhaustion suddenly hitting me. "Julia's involved with this true-crime blog, No Stone Unturned. She got them interested in Alex's case, and they turned on her. That's not—" *That's not my fault,* I wanted to say, but I worried it would sound too dismissive. "I have nothing to do with this."

Detective Curtis looked down toward his leather shoes, then back up at me.

"Okay, Micah. I hear you. Look." He glanced back over his shoulder at Martin and lowered his voice. "I know you and Julia have your history."

"We don't," I said, shaking my head emphatically. "We have no relationship. I try to avoid her whenever I can."

"She's a sensitive person," he continued, "and this needs to stop. Whoever is responsible. Do you understand?"

"I didn't—"

"I'm serious," he said. He nodded back toward Stomping

Grounds, glancing through the glass door. "Good luck with the rest of your renovations."

He turned and walked away, and Martin kept staring, assessing me from his perch across the street. I lifted my hand to my hair, which was greasy and hanging down in clumps where it had fallen out of my ponytail.

Get it together, I scolded myself. I locked the door behind me and returned to the storage room. New messages had been posted in the Julia thread.

jules: I think concernedcitizen is Micah Wilkes. She won't leave me alone.

TheMissingKing: Alex's ex-girlfriend? Yikes.

helenaa: Totally could be her. I saw her at the reunion and she was look-ing . . . not well.

I pushed back from the computer, my chair bumping up against the wire shelving. Stupid. I should have been more careful, should have watched what I was saying. Now they'd be scrutinizing me, analyzing every word I had said, looking for the hidden meaning in everything I did. Now they wouldn't leave me alone.

22

My tires slip on a patch of ice but regain traction. I catch my breath and slow down. Two short, muffled pulses: a new text. I reach over and shuffle through my bag for the phone, straining to keep my eyes on the road, the windshield wipers struggling against the falling snow. My heart leaps as I see it's a message from you, and then sinks as I read it.

Do not contact me again.

I breathe in, try to recenter myself.

After Detective Curtis came to Stomping Grounds—

My mind is buzzing. I can't think straight. The website, and then all my classmates at the reunion, Julia pulling Ryan aside, whispering in his ear. Detective Curtis, pretending to be neutral, objective, but his mind was already made up. He didn't want to hear my side.

After that—

How do I explain? How do I make you listen?

Do not contact me again. Sharp. Final.

I called you two times this morning, sent multiple texts. *Joshua, this is Micah Wilkes. Please call me.* And: *I need to talk. This is urgent. Please pick up your phone.*

All unanswered, until now. I take another look at your text and throw my phone down onto the pile of trash on the passenger seat, where it lands softly on a bed of wrappers. I keep moving forward. You need to hear me out, Joshua. You need to listen. You need me just as much as I need you.

The same day Detective Curtis came to Stomping Grounds, I found the message carved into my car. That's what happened next. A long, low scratch, dug in with a key, and BITCH written in large, jagged letters. My taillight smashed. My eyes burned. I rubbed at the letters, like that could get rid of them somehow, like I could smudge them away. I half-expected to see the flap of Julia's braid as she ran away in the distance or Easton students peering out from one of the alleys, watching for my reaction, but Church Street was empty, the only movement the rustle of the red bows tied up on the streetlights as the wind swept through.

I felt exposed on my drive home, like everyone on the street was looking, theorizing, speculating about what must have happened. *It's not my fault,* I wanted to explain, but I couldn't. I had to take it, had to keep moving.

I drove cautiously, fingers wrapped tightly around the steering wheel, my eyes darting between the street and the rearview mirror. I watched for any cars following too close or trailing behind me for too long. I watched for Julia's straw-blond hair, for the girl at the coffee shop's toothy smile. I caught a glimpse of a man with long blond hair curling into his eyes in the Toyota behind me and my stomach dropped. But I realized I was mistaken when his features came into better view: broad-nosed with a large chin. *Not him,* I told myself. Not you.

The last time I saw you was the night you showed up at my house, unannounced, demanding to be let in. It was a few days later when Natalie delivered the news.

"Did you hear what happened to Joshua?" she asked me. Her voice, as always, was too loud. That study hall, Mrs. Dowling was hunched over the desk at the front of the classroom, intently focused on a newspaper crossword puzzle, a number 2 pencil in hand. The room was usually used for math classes, and the chalkboard was covered in the faint outline of half-erased equations. Natalie had twisted around in her desk to face me, one hand resting on the hard plastic seat.

"Do I want to hear what happened to Joshua?" I asked. I kept my voice low, hoping Natalie would take the hint. By that time, I had been accepted to the University of Pittsburgh—still Pennsylvania, but far enough across the state that it felt like a whole new world—and my goal was just to keep my head down and graduate.

Natalie scooted her desk around so that it was angled toward me. Mrs. Dowling looked up, and then back down.

"He's in a mental institution."

"What?" My stomach twisted.

Natalie nodded and took a swig of Diet Coke. She tried to look solemn, but I could tell she was enjoying this: the thrill of being close to drama, of knowing something. "He tried to kill himself on Tuesday."

The day after the restraining order was filed. I pictured you again, outside the window. *I need to talk to you.*

"Are you sure?" I asked. It had to be a mistake, I told myself. A misunderstanding, an exaggeration.

"Oh yeah," Natalie said. "I heard it from Caroline. Her mom works at the hospital."

A circle of sophomore girls glanced in our direction, then returned to doodling in their notebooks. The plain, institutional clock hanging above the door ticked forward.

"What happened?" I asked.

Natalie shook her head. "He's always been a little unstable, hasn't he? Emily's death was probably too much for him."

"It would be a lot for anyone," I said. "Is he—okay?"

"It sounds like he's going to be fine," Natalie said, sounding more confident than it seemed like she should be. "And, you know, maybe it's good in a way. This way he gets the help he needs."

"Maybe," I said, but the news left me feeling hollow. I pictured your mother finding you in the bathroom that you and Emily used to share, the shower curtain still bright yellow and blue from when you were children. I pictured you in the hospital wearing a blue plastic armband, on a slew of medications that flattened you into a different person.

You, outside of my house. *Let me in.*

This is Alex's fault, too, I told myself. As if taking Emily weren't enough, he had taken you, too. He had taken everything.

23

turn up the car radio, try not to think about your text. *Do not contact me again.* I try to focus, try to think clearly. I'm not sure how everything got so turned around. I just want to make things right.

The morning after finding my car vandalized, I left my things at Stomping Grounds, locked the door behind me, and started on the now-familiar walk to Harris Law Offices. I rehearsed what I would say to Julia as my feet crunched through the unshoveled snow. *I know what you did. You might have everyone else fooled, but not me.* I shoved through the frosted door and braced myself for a confrontation. But there behind the desk where I had expected Julia was a middle-aged woman with reading glasses on a chain around her neck. She looked up, bored and undisturbed by the sudden interruption.

"Can I help you?" she said, her voice nasally and uninterested.

I scanned the waiting room like Julia might appear in one of its chairs, the snow from my shoes melting into small puddles on the floor.

"Is Julia here?" The question sounded foolish even as I asked it.

"Julia is on a leave of absence." The woman placed her glasses onto her nose and looked back down at a stack of paper on the desk, as if there were nothing unusual about my presence or this information.

A leave of absence. I pictured Julia sitting in the dark of her living room, the walls bulging from water damage, the stacks of paper covering her couch caving in on her. A knot formed in my stomach. *This is what I wanted,* I told myself. *This is what she deserves.*

I pulled at the sleeves of my jacket and glanced back toward the front door. "Do you know when she'll be back?"

"No." She licked her finger to separate the top sheet of paper from the rest of the stack and studied the next page. When I didn't move, she looked up over her reading glasses. "Would you like me to pass on a message?"

I imagined Julia jumping as the phone rang, again, beside her.

"No," I said, backing toward the door. "Thank you."

She brought this on herself, I reminded myself as I turned back onto Main Street, tracing the footprints I had left in the snow. *She opened this up again, brought No Stone Unturned into our lives.* I grabbed the Parliaments out of my bag, slid one out. *She wanted Alex to herself. Whatever it took.* I grabbed my lighter from my pocket and shielded the flame from the wind with my cupped hand. That's when I saw Ryan leaning against Stomping Grounds' Main Street windows, his arms crossed over his chest. He rose up when he noticed me. I dropped the cigarette into the snow, stubbed it out with my toe, and fumbled in my pocket for my keys.

"Where have you been?"

I jammed the key into the lock, swung open the door, switched the sign over to OPEN.

"Just had to run a quick errand," I said. He eyed the upturned chairs. I flipped them over and slid them into place.

"So you just closed up the shop for a few minutes."

"That's right," I said. I adjusted the last chair, rushed to behind the counter, and scooped coffee beans into the grinder.

"Because I talked to the guy over at Hotel Calvary." Ryan leaned over the counter, and I froze, scoop still in hand. "And he said you've been closed for the past two weeks."

I placed the scoop down behind me and wiped my hands off on my jeans.

"*Two weeks,* Micah. What have you been doing?"

"I tried to tell you." I averted my eyes, grabbed a washcloth, and walked back around the counter. I leaned into each tabletop and made large, swooping circles. Ryan spun to face me.

"Stop *lying* to me," he barked. He caught himself, took a breath. He hooked his fingers in his hair and pulled so that a patch on the side of his head stood on end. "You've been doing nothing but lying to me for weeks."

I straightened myself out and threw down my washcloth on the table next to me. "I didn't lie."

Ryan rubbed his eyes with the palms of his hands. "When you got home in the evenings, and I asked you how work was, you said 'good,' or 'okay,' or 'busy,' or 'pretty slow today.' What would you call that?"

"Stomping Grounds is *mine,*" I said, marching around him again and returning to behind the counter. "I started it with my own money, my own labor, my own time. I don't need your permission to close it."

"We live together, Micah." Ryan's tone was slow and measured, his cheeks burning a dark scarlet. "We have expenses. We need to pay rent. And this isn't—this isn't about Stomping Grounds. What have you been *doing*?"

That's when he noticed the stack of papers at the edge of the counter, Julia's notebook underneath the pile. He picked up the first few sheets—transcripts of interviews—and thumbed through them, biting his lip.

"I just want to know what happened," I said, trying to gauge his expression. "If it wasn't Alex . . ."

Ryan's head bobbed as he pulled up the corners of the remaining pages in the stack.

"So," he said, looking back up at me. Those slate-gray eyes, boring into mine. "What have you found?"

My mouth was dry. I ran my tongue over my front teeth and leaned against the back counter, gripping the edge with my hands.

"I think it was Julia."

Ryan blinked and looked away. That wasn't what he had been expecting.

"Julia?" he repeated. He turned to look at the empty sidewalk, then back to face me again, running his hands down his face. "You think *Julia* killed Emily?" That tone: like it was inconceivable that Julia could do such a thing. Like I was the one in the wrong.

"She's obsessed with Alex."

"She's *harmless,*" Ryan said, rubbing at his beard again, trying to regain composure. "She's a good person, Micah."

"And I'm not?" I could feel the corner of the counter digging into my palms.

"I didn't say that." Ryan pulled out one of the chairs and sank into it. He rested his head in his hands and didn't speak.

"She wants him all to herself," I said, but I knew he wouldn't hear me now. "And with him in prison, she has that."

Ryan swayed in his chair, his fingers laced together. "I can't do this," he said, his voice muffled at first so that I almost didn't understand what he was saying.

My eyes stung as I realized what was happening. "Ryan . . ." I said, but I didn't know what was supposed to come next.

"I don't know how I'm supposed to help you." Ryan drew his head up. "I don't know how I can help if you won't talk to me."

"I'm talking to you now," I said. It came out desperate. "We're talking now."

"I don't understand what's going on with you."

I need you to believe me, I wanted to say. *I'm the one who lost my best friend. I'm the one who's being followed and harassed.* But by then, Ryan had pushed up from his chair and started toward the door.

"You need help, Micah," he said, and then he left, the door chimes clanging behind him.

Natalie responded enthusiastically when I told her what had happened with Ryan—or, at least, a very rough approximation of what had happened. *I think Ryan and I are breaking up,* I wrote, and within seconds I got a response: *Come on over!*

I got into my car and turned the corner onto Main Street. An image came to mind: the three of us as children, you, me, and Emily, ambling down the sidewalk, hair sticking to our necks in the humid Pennsylvania summer. Swinging open the door to Mr. Hunt's ice cream shop, pockets heavy with coins. A lump formed in my throat, and I dug the corner of my thumbnail into my index finger, willed myself to think about something else.

But the only other thought that came to mind was Ryan: the hurt that washed over his face when he found out about the break-in, about Stomping Grounds. *You've been lying to me.* He was right. I had shut him out. I thought I could handle this all on my own.

I glanced down at the accumulating garbage on my passenger seat and suddenly my whole body felt leaden. It should have been easy to tell him. *Someone is harassing me.* But something had stopped me every time I got the chance.

I squeezed the cold plastic of the steering wheel and blinked back tears that were starting to well up despite my best efforts.

He had refused to take my side against Julia. He had dismissed No Stone Unturned so quickly, without asking why I was interested, without checking to see if I was okay. He had been so caught up in his own life and his little men and their made-up battles that he hadn't even noticed I needed his support.

I wiped beneath my eyes and pictured Ryan's conversation with

Martin at Hotel Calvary, how his heart must have sunk when Martin told him Stomping Grounds had been closed. I told myself this wasn't Ryan's fault, not really. The problem was my own inability to trust. To have a healthy relationship.

It was, like everything else in my life, about Alex and Emily.

I turned in to Heritage Springs, one of the many neighborhoods that popped up after you left town, and looked for Natalie's home to emerge out of the nearly identical houses. I rolled back my shoulders when I saw the brick arch of her entranceway and pulled into her driveway. In the front yard, a spiral of small footprints and the imprint of a toddler in the snow.

I slung my bag over my shoulder and walked up the path to her front door, past the abandoned base of a snowman. The doorbell echoed through her front hall as I waited awkwardly between two white pillars.

"Micah!" Natalie swung open the door and wrapped her arms around me in a big hug. Behind her, Ashton aimed matchbox cars at our ankles.

"Thanks," I said as we made our way down her tiled hallway. The smell of vanilla and cinnamon rose up from a candle on the counter. "I didn't know where else to go."

"I'm glad you texted. I'm sorry about dragging you to the Tavern—"

"It's fine," I said quickly. In the corner of the kitchen, the baby bounced himself up and down in a small fabric chair, his fist stuffed halfway into his mouth. My eyes rested on an unzipped duffle bag stuffed with burp cloths and bottles.

"We're heading out to Jack's parents' place tomorrow morning," Natalie said, rolling her eyes. "They're ridiculous. This year was *my* family's turn for Thanksgiving, but God forbid Jack's mother is left out of anything, so now we have to have a *second* Thanksgiving this weekend."

I nodded and tried to smile. "I don't want to get in the way . . ."

"Stop." Natalie zipped up the bag and turned back to me. "You know, I always thought you were too good for him."

My shoulders tensed as I thought about Ryan's lopsided smile, his gentle, goofy laugh. *That's not true,* I wanted to say, but instead I scanned the kitchen uncomfortably. On Natalie's fridge hung a white sheet of construction paper crisscrossed with heavy blue paint streaks, Ashton's name written carefully in pen at the bottom. On the counter, an elaborate-looking system of bottles, hanging off plastic pegs.

"This isn't his fault," I said, setting aside a coloring book as I took a seat at the kitchen table. "I fucked up."

"Mom-*meee,*" Ashton whined, pulling at Natalie's leggings.

"Not now," Natalie said, directing him back toward the family room. "Mommy has her friend over."

I watched as she took his hand and led him into the next room, settling him down on the couch and turning on a brightly colored cartoon. The baby watched me, bouncing, his pudgy hand dripping with slobber. I caught a glimpse of my reflection in the over-sized mirror hanging on the wall behind the table. I hadn't realized how run-down I looked. How had Ryan not known something was wrong?

Natalie returned and sat down at the table next to me, running a hand through her hair.

"I fucked up," I said.

"Don't say that." Natalie leaned forward to squeeze my arm. "You can't blame yourself. What happened?"

"I was keeping things from him."

Natalie nodded her head as I explained, only occasionally breaking eye contact to glance back at the baby. I was about to go further, to explain my theory about Julia, when Natalie jumped in.

"Why do you think you couldn't tell him?"

I pulled the coloring book back in front of me, tracing its glossy cover with my index finger.

"I don't know," I said. "I'm worried I'm—" *Going crazy,* I was going to say. *I'm worried I let the Truthseekers get to me.*

"I know why," Natalie interrupted, swooping her hair into a ponytail and pushing up toward the fridge. She reached her hand in and shuffled around until she hit on a tub of guacamole. "It's because he's judgy."

"Ryan?" I asked, uncertain. I thought about our last conversation, the look he gave me when I told him about Julia, then pushed it aside. "Ryan's one of the least judgmental people I know. He's still friends with *Alex.*"

Natalie pursed her lips and took a big scoop of guacamole. "Yeah, I don't think that's an accident. That way he gets to feel superior. Look at what a *good person* I am, so *loyal,* so *forgiving.* It's a load of shit."

"I don't know." All of Ryan's trips out to Frackville. The committed friend: *I'm not just going to abandon him.*

"I mean," Natalie said, holding up her hands, "forget all this if you guys end up getting back together. But I'm just saying. He's kind of an asshole."

I bit into a chip.

"He's never liked me," Natalie continued, scooping up another heap of guacamole. "Am I right?"

I kept my eyes fixed on the table, trying to think of the right response.

"You don't have to say anything. I know I'm right. I'm not blind. I can see him when he rolls his eyes at me."

"He's just . . ." *He doesn't like gossip,* I wanted to say.

"He's a self-righteous prick. And he likes to be in control. Like, why does he care if you shut Stomping Grounds? It's *yours.*"

"That's what I said." And it was mine. I bought it with the money my mother left me; I painted its walls and ripped out the old, refrigerated counter; I picked out roasters and built up my customer base and showed up day after day after day.

"And has he shown any concern for you throughout this whole thing?" Natalie continued between bites. "You're the victim here."

"That's true," I agreed. Ryan had been so quick to respond with anger and frustration when I was the one receiving texts and unwelcome visits from Julia, when I was the one left notes and followed through the woods. When I was the one who had lost my best friend. I felt like I was on my own because I was. I needed to defend myself.

"You're better off without him," Natalie declared. She stood again. "Wine?"

"Yes, please," I said. My phone buzzed on the table in front of me.

"Is that him?" Natalie asked.

My heart leaped when I saw the notification: Julia's animal-obsessed friend, Rachel Melbourne.

Sorry for not getting back to you sooner. Would love to meet up. Have some concerns I'd like to discuss. When works for you?

"No," I said as I typed out a response. "Someone else."

Tomorrow morning?

"Honestly, you deserve better," Natalie continued as she un-corked a bottle of wine. "You deserve someone who gets you."

I sighed, took a scoop of guacamole for myself. "Maybe you're right," I said.

"Of course I'm right." Natalie returned to the table with two generous glasses. "This is his problem. Not yours."

Rachel and I arranged to meet at the Northridge Diner. I left Stomping Grounds in the same careful way I always left the shop now: door locked, street surveyed for any sign of Easton students lingering too close by or a stranger holding his phone up like a camera, a quick shuffle to my car parked a block away.

Once I turned onto Main Street, I glanced up into my rearview mirror. One car, brown, with a layer of salt caked onto the hood and a dented bumper, followed at four car lengths behind me. The driver's hair was short, maybe, or pulled back into a ponytail; I couldn't make out any other details.

When I turned onto Mechanic Street, they followed, maintaining the same space between us. *It's a major street,* I told myself. *A coincidence.* I pushed down on the gas, the needle on the speedometer rising. They kept the same distance. I tapped on the brake and their brake lights flashed, too, the car never close enough for me to make out a face.

When I spotted a break in the oncoming traffic, I swerved left, ducking into a neighborhood entrance just before a school bus rumbled by, blocking the way. The brown car continued straight. I slowed to a crawl and loosened my grip on the steering wheel. They were gone, whoever it was. I tried to relax.

That's when I realized where I was. The entrance to Alex's old neighborhood, the houses just the same as they had always been: split-level homes, sloped driveways with modest cars and well-maintained yards. Two blocks and another left turn would take me to his front door. I reached over, fumbled with the glove compartment door, and grabbed the Parliaments. My car drifted across the street, and I yanked back the wheel and pulled over to the curb.

I pictured Alex opening the door to his house, leaning his weight on the doorframe and pulling me in, and felt a pang of guilt. What did it mean if it hadn't been Alex? I had turned my back on him, handed him over to the police. "He wasn't with us," I had said. "He asked me to lie for him." That was after Detective Heller held up Emily's chain-link heart necklace in the plastic baggie, asked if I knew who had bought it for her, waited for that to sink in.

I rolled down my window and fumbled with my lighter. It wouldn't have made any difference if I had covered for him. There were so many people at the party that night, so many witnesses who would have seen Alex and Emily go off into the woods together.

A thought nagged at me: If I had told them about seeing you, maybe they would have looked harder. Maybe they would have found something else.

I pushed that thought out of my head. I had done the right thing. I had told the truth about Alex. He hadn't been with us on the tarp. And if I had told the police about you, they wouldn't have looked harder, they would have jumped on you, instead.

This was Julia's fault, not mine.

I ashed out my window and ran a hand through my hair, then put the car back in drive. Alex had opened himself up to it, made himself vulnerable. Alex, who got everything he ever wanted, who never had to second-guess intentions or doubt sincerity. Alex, who never had to build up the guarded skepticism the rest of us did. Alex, who everyone loved. *Of course she wants to help me,* he'd think, taking in stride Julia's obsessive devotion, her unwavering commitment. *Of course she has my best interests at heart.*

Alex, curled up in the back of his Jeep, trying to sleep off six Solo cups of beer and a fight with Emily. While Julia climbed up the steps of the cinder block house—

I eased the car back toward Mechanic Street, toward the diner. A new image flashed through my mind: me and Ryan, sleeping obliviously on the tarp while Emily lay bleeding out on the ground.

I turned up the radio, pulsing, synthesized notes taking the place of my thoughts. *I can get justice,* I told myself. *I owe them that much. That's all I can do now.*

I repeated that to myself as I sat at the diner booth, eyes flitting from the clock to the door. *The right thing. I'm doing the right thing.*

. . .

When I saw the door swing open, I knew I had made a mistake.

It had been ten years, but I recognized Rachel Melbourne immediately, and I chided myself for not having made the connection earlier. Her face had cleared up some, but she had that same long, sharp nose and pinched mouth, the same frizzy brown hair. I hadn't known her as Rachel Melbourne back then; I knew her as Rachel Palmer. A classmate of Julia's. Not just classmate—friend. She narrowed her eyes and slid into the booth seat in front of me, and I wanted to slide onto the floor and crawl away.

"Micah," she said, leaning her arms on the table in front of us.

"Rachel." I tried my best to sound surprised. "What are you doing here?"

"I'm supposed to be meeting—someone." She looked me up and down. *Northridge Diner,* I had said. *I'll wear red so you can spot me.* I could feel the red of my sweater pulsing now, drawing all attention toward me. "How about you?"

"The same," I said, weakly.

"Well, we can wait together," she said. She leaned back into the cushioned booth and crossed her arms over her chest.

"Sure." I grabbed one of the creamers from the little bowl at the back of the table and picked at it with my fingernail. "Why not."

Rachel watched me from her side of the table. I placed the creamer back down and glanced toward the waitress, who was chatting with a table across the diner.

"So," I said. "Who are you meeting here?"

"No one," she said. "Not someone you'd know."

"Mm." The waitress made her way to our table and splashed more coffee into my mug. She held up the pot toward Rachel, who pursed her lips and shook her head.

"I didn't realize you were still in town," I said once the waitress had left.

Rachel paused, like she was deciding how to answer, then

sighed. "I'm not," she said. "I'm in Avondale. But my parents are still here, and some friends." She tried to force her frizzy hair into a ponytail. "You remember Julia Reynolds."

I haven't done anything, I reminded myself. *I just asked someone to get coffee. That's not a crime.*

"How is she doing?"

Another exaggerated sigh. "Not well, if you want to know the truth."

"Oh?" I tried to keep my voice calm, noncommittal.

"No," Rachel said, leaning in toward me. "She's being attacked." *Attacked,* as if someone had physically come after her. "Phone calls day and night. Harassing letters to her office. Someone broke into her apartment, so now she never feels safe."

"That's terrible," I said, nursing my coffee.

"It is," Rachel said. "Terrible. She triple-checks the locks on all the doors and windows before she goes to bed, and she still can't sleep."

I nodded, bit my lip. *Now she knows what it's like.* But I felt uneasy. I shifted in my seat, twisted a straw wrapper around my index finger.

"Does she know who—"

"She's got a pretty good idea."

"You know," I said, as the straw wrapper began to split open along its side, "I've had some of the same things happening to me."

"Have you?" Rachel said, her voice flat.

I crumpled the wrapper into a ball, set it down. "Online stuff. Emily and Alex have gotten some attention recently." I waited for some sign of recognition from Rachel, but none was forthcoming. "All these armchair detectives, trying to reconstruct that night, figure out what really happened."

No response.

"It's been happening to me, too. The messages. The attention. Someone broke into my apartment." My voice rose defensively.

Rachel's flat expression didn't change. She looked down at her hands, stretched out her fingers so that she could see her nails. *It's true,* I wanted to shout at her. *Listen to me. I'm a victim here, too.* I leaned in toward Rachel, waited for her to look back up at me.

"Julia started this, you know," I said. "She's the one who opened the door to this, got them all riled up. To them, it's all just make-believe. They didn't live it."

"She doesn't deserve this," Rachel said, punctuating each word. "She's been through enough already."

"She *loves* this. All this attention. Getting to play the loyal girl-friend. This is what she's always wanted."

The couple at the table next to us had begun to sneak glances. They were exchanging looks.

"You don't know anything about Julia." Rachel stood and zipped her coat, then leaned her hands back on the table. "I know what you're doing, and you need to stop. It's not okay. You're caus-ing her a lot of pain."

I grabbed my coffee and avoided her stare. She straightened herself back up and turned to go.

"Rachel," I said. She stopped, looked back toward me. "Were you at the campsite when Emily died?"

She pursed her lips and thought for a moment.

"No," she said. "I was at Julia's."

She could be lying. I sat in the Northridge Diner parking lot, my hands frozen on the steering wheel. *Rachel and Julia are friends,* I reasoned. *Rachel could be covering for Julia, trying to get me to leave her alone. She could have been involved.*

But I realized, even then in the sharp cold of my car, how ri-diculous that sounded. Rachel Melbourne wasn't an accomplice to murder. And I had trouble recalling the reasons I had been so sure Julia was involved in the first place. She was infatuated with Alex, overly possessive. But the only thing placing her at the campsite that night was an unreliable post on an online forum. Helena Abrams, inserting herself into the drama. No one else had seen her there that night. And Helena herself hadn't mentioned Julia when the police interviewed her a few days after Emily's death.

Next to me, an elderly couple lowered themselves out of their car and retrieved canes from the back seat. I worried, for a moment, that they'd see me in there, tap on the window, ask if everything was okay. But they left me alone, pretending not to notice, tottering toward the diner entrance.

I had been wrong about Julia. I pictured the small, tutu-ed cow in her kitchen, with its long feminine eyelashes. I squeezed my eyes shut, trying to shut out the image of Julia returning home to a house that didn't feel quite right, rifling through her closet for a missing letterman jacket, heart racing.

I reached out, instinctively, for my phone to call Ryan, then recoiled when I remembered our last conversation. The cold air pumping out of the heaters slowly took on warmth, and I tried to wrap my head around how I could have gotten things so wrong.

It wasn't my fault, not completely. Julia was the one who couldn't let go of the past. She was the one who invited the Truth-seekers into our lives. And because of her interference, her search for attention, someone had followed me, scraped BITCH into my car, broken into my home. Those paper footballs: WHY DIDN'T YOU HELP ME MICAH? It had clouded my judgment, made me paranoid. What was I supposed to have done?

I reached for my phone again and called Ryan. I had been wrong about Julia, I would say, but I could explain myself if he'd listen. I'd be honest this time. Open.

The call went through to voicemail.

I put the car into reverse, backed out of my spot, and started toward the Calvary Lofts. When I saw him, I decided, I'd tell him he was right. That I should have listened. My stomach turned as I remembered the letterman jacket pushed back into the corner of my closet. A mistake. I had been under so much pressure.

I didn't see Ryan's car in its normal spot when I pulled into our lot. *Good,* I thought. *That's good. I'll surprise him with dinner. I'll tell him how wrong I've been.*

24

grab my phone and type out a response to your text.

I'm sorry. There's no other option. I'm coming to find you.

I hit send before I can change my mind.

When I returned to my apartment, I swung open the door to find cardboard boxes littering the entryway. Most were already sealed shut with duct tape. One box still in progress contained only a handful of items: the lamp from our bedroom, its cord hanging out over the side, a stack of button-down shirts. It struck me, then, the finality of it: Ryan was really leaving. His boots were still lined up by the front door, his throw blanket still draped over the back of the couch, but it was all temporary now. I pictured each item vanishing, one by one, the bare space on the wall where his map of Pennsylvania now hung, two sad mugs left behind in the cabinet. The office—his office—empty.

I collapsed into my seat at our cramped kitchen table, never really big enough for two people. He'd leave me this, probably, a gesture of goodwill. I lifted the table leaf and let it swing back down on its hinges.

Photographs of the two of us stared back at me from the fridge. We looked stupidly happy. I hadn't eaten breakfast that morning, or anything other than guacamole and wine the night before, and I knew there was a package of ravioli pushed to the back of the fridge, behind a week-old container of leftovers and a mystery foil ball. But I couldn't bring myself to heat the pot of water, to wait for it to boil, to sit down to a silent meal by myself. The refrigerator hummed, mockingly. *The new dinner soundtrack from here on out,* I thought to myself. The heater rumbled to a start, and I pushed myself back up and made my way, like a masochist, to his office.

I placed my hand on his dresser, the books stacked neatly on top. They'd be brushed off and packed away carefully into the trunk of his car. The heavy wooden desk, almost too big to fit through our doorway. Hinges unscrewed, doors removed. I sat down at it, studied one of his little army men. So detailed: his pinpoint buttons dabbed on with care, the creases in his jacket shaded with ink. Tiny gray eyes, fixed straight ahead, ready.

I ran a finger along the desk and tugged at the upper-right drawer. To my surprise, it slid open, no longer locked. Ryan must have opened it intending to pack up its contents and gotten distracted. It was still full.

I glanced inside, then felt a twinge of guilt and started to push the drawer shut again. *How would you feel,* I asked myself. It would be an invasion of Ryan's privacy to look: his personal space, his belongings.

But then again. I thought back to Ryan rifling through my dresser drawer, digging through my sweaters for Alex's jacket, and slid the drawer back out on its tracks. This was, I reasoned, my last chance to get a full look at this person who was walking out of my life. I wanted to know what he was keeping in there. I deserved to know.

Our relationship was over. I didn't owe him anything anymore.

The contents of the drawer were, at first glance, unremarkable. A sheet of stamps, five used. Three pens pushed into the corner. Papers that appeared to be work- or gaming-related, covered in lists: search terms for a database, paint colors Ryan needed to buy.

Underneath those, a Post-it note, the sticky strip on the back caked with dust. I turned it over, and it felt like someone had knocked the air out of me.

An email address for Joshua Bishop. Bishop: your mother's maiden name.

A coincidence. I pulled out my phone and googled the name. There it was, a picture of you. Still birdlike: high cheekbones and a sharp, protruding Adam's apple, your T-shirt still too large for your thin arms. But you were smiling, small lines forming around your eyes, your head tilted in an affectionate way toward the photographer. Behind you, a swath of ocean. The first link was a link to Stonesport Maps & Prints Gallery—a shop that sold antiquities, *your* shop. You had made something of yourself. You looked like you might be happy.

I tried to make sense of it. Had Ryan tracked you down? Why? And why hadn't he mentioned it to me?

I set the Post-it note down on the desk and reached back into the drawer. My fingers touched on the smooth gloss of a photograph. A stack of them. Pictures of me and Alex and Ryan and Emily. The four of us getting ready for homecoming in spaghetti strap dresses and suits, lopsided corsages pinned onto Alex and Ryan. One of all of us, posed in front of your fireplace. The next, Emily, in arabesque, one leg extended behind her. Another photograph: me and Alex and Emily on the cold bleachers at a fall football game. A slate-gray coat slung over Emily's shoulders. Ryan's coat.

The sight of the coat made me uneasy, but I tried to push the feeling aside. Ryan lent Emily his coat all the time. I knew that. He was a nice guy. A pushover, maybe. And Emily never dressed warmly enough.

Photographs of us at the campsite, our eyes red from the flash. My stomach tightened. I told myself it was normal for Ryan to have hung on to these. This was a good time in his life. He had friends, he belonged. Alex and Ryan balanced on a log next to each other, Alex's arm slung over Ryan's shoulder, Ryan looking thoughtfully at the camera.

My eyes rose up to the small keyhole on the desk drawer. *But why did he need to keep these locked away?*

Another photograph, one I had taken. Emily and Alex seated beside each other against the lockers in the science wing and Ryan to the side, his eyes fixed on Emily. And another: Emily resting her head on Ryan's shoulder, Ryan's shy grin.

Emily was in almost all of these photographs, I realized. And in all of the photographs where Emily and Ryan appeared close to each other, Ryan looked uncomfortable. Or bashful.

Or interested.

It wasn't possible. I flipped to another photograph: Emily sprawled out on the pullout couch in Alex's basement, her head on a gray fuzzy pillow, her feet resting on Ryan's lap. Emily was looking toward the camera, but Ryan was looking at her.

I needed some air. I went out to the balcony, still gripping the photograph of Ryan and Emily. I took one last look at it, studying the way he was clearly taking her in, the obvious admiration. I folded the picture and stuffed it into my pocket. Then I grabbed my Parliaments from their hiding spot under the ceramic plate, slid out a cigarette, and dropped the pack back into the flowerpot, uncovered. No point in pretending to hide them anymore. I inhaled, waiting for the cigarette to do its work, calm my nerves. It didn't happen. All I could think of were our trips to the diner and the plate of fries that Ryan always shared with Emily, the way Emily would squeeze his arm to get her way. That stupid coat.

Ryan had wanted to be with her.

It seemed so obvious, in retrospect; so unmistakably true. I had even made comments back then, stupid ones. "So," I'd say to Emily as we flew up Culver Street in her old Volkswagen, grinning over at her in the driver's seat. "Ryan . . ." And she'd roll her eyes, turn the music up louder.

I snuffed out the cigarette and threw it over the side of the balcony, letting it fall to the sidewalk below. Ten years, and Ryan was still holding on to those photographs. A little shrine to Emily locked away in his office desk, away from me.

I pictured Ryan late at night, setting aside his miniatures and unlocking that drawer, flipping through those photographs, mourning Emily, the girl he couldn't have. Returning to our room and sliding into bed next to me, the consolation prize. The one he settled for.

I took deep breaths as I walked to the bathroom and splashed cold water on my face. I looked up at my reflection: puffy, swollen eyelids, my dull brown hair hanging limp at the sides of my face. *Never good enough.* I rubbed at my red nose and wiped off my face with a hand towel. I stepped out of the bathroom and saw the piles of cardboard boxes covering the floor.

I wondered what else he was hiding.

I grabbed one of the boxes, ripped off the tape, and dumped out the contents. Old T-shirts, a few ratty pairs of jeans. I left them on the floor and moved on to the next box. CDs and wires, a charger I was pretty sure was mine. The next: every single one of our pint glasses. I guess, technically, those belonged to Ryan, too.

I opened the next box but was losing steam. I was starting to ask myself what I was doing when I came across a lumpy plastic bag, the handles double-knotted. I pulled it out, and it lifted easily, almost no weight to it. I tore into the plastic, and there they were again.

The paper footballs.

My first thought: *It can't be. I threw these away.* But these weren't new, like the notes I had found in our bed. These papers were covered in writing, some smudged pencil, faded with age, others in blue or purple ink.

These were the ones from ten years ago.

These were Emily's diary entries.

I held one in my hand, tried to make sense of it. These had been thrown away, too, years ago.

But no. I had only *assumed* they had been thrown away. I had given them to Ryan, and he had left with them, and I never asked about them again.

It appeared he had held on to them.

My head buzzed. I couldn't think.

It didn't make any sense for him to still have them all this time. He had moved away to college, then to the small apartment above the Tavern, and then here, each time packing them up, taking them with him. Hiding them somewhere in this apartment, in the apartment that we shared, from me. Emily's private thoughts, in Ryan's possession. What possible reason could he have for keeping them?

I ran my finger over the side of one, turned it over in my hand. On the outside of that paper football, I could see five- and six-word phrases, cut off at the fold: . . . *four hours and I'm still not* . . . ; . . . *I need to remember it's* . . . ; . . . *was trying. After that I* . . . The handwriting immediately familiar: the way she switched back and forth between cursive and print *f*'s, the slashed *i*'s. So obviously Emily.

I'd confront him, I decided, my hands shaking. I'd make him explain. I knew exactly where he would be: at his office in the library, hidden away in the basement behind the stacks. I threw on my jacket and boots, stuffed the bag of paper footballs into my messenger bag, and marched out the door, heading for Easton.

.   .   .

Two stone lions sat on the pillars at the base of the library stairs, their faces frozen into permanent growls. A wad of bubble gum was sculpted into a makeshift tongue in one lion's mouth. Students shuffled up and down the steps, eyes fixed on their phones or on the ground. One almost slammed into me with his backpack, slung off the side of one shoulder. I jumped aside and rebalanced myself on the banister, the carved stone cold and rough beneath my palm.

I took each step one at a time, trying to think what I'd say when I saw him. *I found the photographs, the paper footballs. I know.*

He'd try to turn it around, make it about me. *Why were you going through my things?* I needed to be strong. I was entitled to the truth.

I pulled open the heavy wooden door and was met by a row of turnstiles. The woman at the front desk, Miranda, slouched down in her seat, playing a game on her phone that beeped and chimed. I stepped forward, squeezed my numb fingers into fists and straightened them back out again, trying to get feeling back.

"I'm here to see Ryan Terrasen," I said. Behind her, a clock identical to the ones we had in school, plain and institutional. I wondered if the same clocks hung in the visiting room at Frackville. The minute hand lurched forward.

Miranda tapped at her phone and placed it down on the desk in front of her. "School ID?" she asked, just like always.

"No," I said. "I'm not a student, Miranda. I'm Ryan's girlfriend. We've been through this before. I'm just here to see him."

Miranda studied me with her small, deep-set eyes. I ran a hand through my unbrushed hair, wiped a finger under my eyelids.

"Is he expecting you?" she asked, crossing her arms over her chest. She was enjoying this brief moment of power.

"I don't know." I combed my fingers through my hair again, tugging at the knotted ends, and pulled it back with the hairband around my wrist. "Could you please just call him?"

She picked up the phone, her finger hovering over the numbers for a second longer than they needed to, just to let me know she didn't *have* to do this. Her eyes fixed on mine.

"Ryan, there's someone here to see you." Another appraising look, up and down. I pulled the sleeves of my sweatshirt down to cover my hands. "She says she's your girlfriend."

Another pause, a head nod, and she returned the phone to the receiver and eased back into her chair.

"I'll need you to sign in."

She shuffled through a drawer for a binder and dropped it onto the desk. I scribbled my name down and shoved my ID into her hands. She looked at it, looked at my signature, and nodded me in.

Beyond the wooden desk, two yellow, egg-shaped chairs, the kind of futuristic furniture that seems to only exist in libraries, flanked a potted tree. A row of mostly empty wooden tables stretched the length of the first floor. Three students sat around one of them, a stack of textbooks piled up unopened and blank Word documents glowing on their laptops.

"I would never!" said one of the girls, swatting the boy next to her on the arm with an easy, unencumbered laugh.

"That's not what you said last night," he said, shaking his head playfully. Everything a game to the Easton students, all jokes and possibility.

I tried to ignore them and focus straight ahead. I walked past them to the stairs leading down to the basement, gray concrete steps striped with rough black tread to keep the students from slipping. Ryan's office was in a back corner, tucked away behind the stacks, and I could feel my pulse quickening with each step. *I can turn back,* I told myself. But he knew I was there. He was expecting me.

The basement was silent: no giggling students, no clacking keyboards. To my right, shelving unit after shelving unit, pushed up against each other. They were set up on inlaid tracks, so that they could be rolled out or in, creating narrow walkways and then closing up again. An older man in a worn brown jacket with a dramatic cowlick stepped out from one of the temporary walkways, two books in hand. I jumped, surprised to learn I wasn't alone, and apologized. He barely acknowledged my presence, continuing to shuffle down the hall.

Thin fluorescent strips provided the only light, casting an orange glow on the speckled varnished floor. Another identical clock hung from a tile in the ceiling, next to a glowing exit sign. The minute hand quivered and then pushed forward again. I forced myself to keep walking.

I turned when I reached the end of the stacks, and there was Ryan, leaning against the chipped doorframe to his office, waiting. His hair shot out in all different directions, and the heavy circles under his eyes suggested he hadn't slept, either. He ran his hand along the side of his face, just like always: up the cheek, down the cheek, along the jaw. My stomach twisted.

"Micah," he said, and when I heard his voice—gentle, worn out, heavy with sadness—I almost forgot what I had come there to say. I wanted to press my face into his neck, feel the warmth of it.

"Hey." I mirrored his uncertain tone, wondered what would happen if I forgot about the pictures, the paper footballs, about Emily. If I apologized, told him I had been wrong.

"What are you doing here?" He leaned his head back against the doorframe, and all the warmth I thought I had sensed vanished. He didn't want to talk to me. He didn't want to see me. I felt for the photograph in my pocket.

"We need to talk."

"I'm at work." His voice low, cold.

"This can't wait."

He ran a hand through his already-ruffled hair. "Yes, it can. We can talk this evening."

I breathed in, looked down at my scuffed boots, then back up at Ryan.

"Why do you have Joshua's email address?"

The color drained from his face. Behind him, his officemate

perked up and stopped typing. Ryan noticed her listening, placed his hand on my back, and led me out into the hall.

"This way," he said, nodding back toward the stacks. "Let's talk somewhere private."

We walked through one of the temporary walkways, stepping around a short, round stool on wheels.

"What are you doing here?" Ryan glanced to his side, then behind him, trying to gauge whether any of his coworkers might be nearby. It was impossible to tell. The shelves were tall and the rows seemed to go on forever.

"Why do you have Joshua's email address?" I asked again. "I saw it. On a Post-it note. It was your handwriting."

Ryan's hand moved nervously: up the cheek, down the cheek, along the jaw. "You were going through my drawer." It wasn't a question. Or a denial.

"Have you been talking to him?"

"We're in touch."

The dull thud of boots echoed off the floor. It could have been coming from any direction.

"I don't understand," I said. "Did you search him out? Without telling me?"

Ryan shook his head, but it took him a beat too long to respond. *He's trying to figure out what I know,* I realized. *He's trying to figure out what he can get away with saying.*

"We ran into each other," Ryan said. "You remember the rare-books book fair I went to in Boston?"

I did. Was that it, a simple explanation? Ryan was a librarian, and Joshua ran a shop that sold antiquities, so maybe it was possible they'd crossed paths there. But was it *true*? Ryan was looking straight at me. He looked earnest. How often had he looked me in the eye and lied to me?

"You just . . . happened to bump into each other," I said.

"That's right." His gaze still steady. "We exchanged emails, and we've written back and forth a little."

"About what?"

"Just catching up." I thought I saw his jaw twitch. He was holding something back.

More footsteps, growing louder and then softer. On the other side of the basement, a light flickered off.

"Why do you have pictures of Emily?"

Ryan rocked back on his heels, nodded his head slowly. He had known this was coming. He had known as soon as I mentioned your email address, as soon as he realized I had gone through his drawer. He was prepared.

"I have pictures of the four of us. From high school. I wasn't going to just throw them out."

"And the paper footballs?"

A look of concern crossed over his face. A miscalculation: he hadn't realized I had found those, too. His voice softened.

"I couldn't bring myself to throw those out, either."

I felt, again, for the photograph in my pocket.

"You were in love with Emily."

The vulnerability I had seen a second before faded. Ryan rolled his head back and sighed loudly. "Jesus Christ, Micah. What are you talking about?"

I pulled out the picture and shoved it toward him. "Don't act like I'm crazy. I can see it, the way you used to look at her. I'm not stupid."

He took the photograph from me, smoothing out the creases, and pursed his lips. Like he was angry I had damaged it. "You went through my drawer," he said again.

"That's not the *point*." My voice echoed off the wooden ends of the shelves, and Ryan's eyes shot back up toward me—narrowed, angry, *too loud*—then rested, again, on the photograph. I could almost see him thinking: *What move can I make? What can I concede?* He ran his hand through his hair again, took a breath.

"I wasn't in love with her. We were teenagers. I had a thing for her." His words were slow and articulated, the faux-patient tone he used when he thought I was being unreasonable. Like he was explaining something to a child. The photograph swung at his side, young Ryan, those intense gray eyes. "Don't pretend you didn't know that."

I blinked, took a step back. "You never told me that."

"Was I supposed to? It wasn't a secret. Alex used to tease me about it all the time." His face tightened. "And you used to tease Emily."

I braced myself on the smooth wooden side of a shelf. I had been expecting him to deny it, to explain how I had gotten everything wrong. But I had been right: Emily had been his first choice.

"I didn't—"

"I can't do this right now." He was already turning back toward his office. The conversation, he had decided, was over. "I have to get back to work."

His voice was so calm. I thought back to the day Emily's body was discovered, Alex and Ryan in Alex's basement, Alex, panicked, piecing together how it would look to the police, grasping for a way to protect himself. Ryan, in control, directing the situation. *We'll say you were with us.*

"That night at the party," I said, and this time I lowered my voice, too. "You said to tell the police we were all together. But we weren't."

He turned back toward me. "I was just trying to calm Alex down. I didn't think he—I didn't realize what he had done."

This was, I realized, the closest I had ever heard Ryan come to saying that Alex was guilty. My stomach turned over on itself. I shook my head.

"Not Alex. You and me. You said to tell them we were *all* together."

"Micah." A warning. "We were together most of the night. That's what I told them."

The shuffle of shoes. A woman in a knee-length black skirt walked past the end of the row, her hair pulled back tightly into a small knotted bun. She slowed, glanced over at us quickly, trying to discern what was going on without us noticing. Ryan nodded at her, tersely.

"But there were big chunks of the evening . . ." I started. I could see him, staggering toward me at the altar, the near-empty bottle of vodka swinging at his side. How much time had passed from when we had broken off from each other? Minutes stretched and contracted in my mind. Had he been alone in the woods? I hadn't thought anything of it at the time, but now it took on a new, sinister meaning.

"What were you doing?" I asked, lowering my voice to a whisper. "When you were by yourself. What were you doing?"

"What, you want a minute-by-minute account?" I saw Ryan's hand ball up into a fist. "It was a party ten years ago. I don't know what I was doing the whole time. Talking to people."

I shook my head again, blinking back tears. "That's not good enough."

"What were *you* doing all night? Can *you* even answer that question?" The calm façade, gone now. His eyes flared with anger.

I couldn't shake it now, the memory of Ryan in Alex's basement, giving orders. *We'll say you were with us.* As if it could possibly have been that easy. As if there wouldn't be any follow-up questions, any witnesses who said otherwise at a party with dozens of people. Ryan—always planning, always thinking five moves ahead—would have known that.

"I can tell you what you were doing." He stepped closer to me. "You were wandering around, asking anyone who would listen if they knew where Alex was."

I could see it now: Alex, alone with two police officers in the bleach-filled interrogation room, wearing his nicest sweater, the white one with two navy stripes. *Do you want to tell us where you really spent the night, Alex?* they had asked him, poised, by that point, to disbelieve anything he had to say. Ryan's plan hadn't worked. Maybe it was never supposed to.

"Everyone knew he was off with Emily. It was painful to watch."

I forced myself to swallow. "You knew?"

An image of Emily's chain-link heart necklace in its clear plastic bag sprang to mind, the police questioning me. *He wasn't with you on the tarp that night, was he?* Ryan must have known that Emily and Alex's relationship would come out while I was being questioned. He must have known how I would react. Like one of his little men in one of his games, fulfilling its role, I had changed my story. *He asked me to lie for him,* I told the police. *He wasn't there.*

"Of *course* I knew." Ryan rolled his eyes, forgetting to be quiet. "All the sneaking off at parties, the looks they would shoot each other when they thought no one was looking. We were seventeen. No one was any good at keeping secrets."

He smoothed out the photograph again, clearly bothered by the crease. I pictured Ryan in high school, giving Emily his french fries, his coat, waiting for her to notice him in return. Had he been convinced, all that time, that she would come around someday, once she really got to know him? Once she saw what a nice guy he was?

"Why didn't you tell me?"

It was quiet, now, in the basement. I glanced back down the row toward the cinder block wall, the empty hallway, hoping for a flash of movement, the click of heels across the floor, some sign that we weren't alone.

"If you had wanted to know, you would have." Up the cheek, down the cheek, along the jaw. He shook his head disapprovingly, remembering. "I did talk to Alex. Told him I knew what was going on, how stupid I thought he was being. But Alex always did what he wanted."

I remembered Ryan's sullen moods the summer before our senior year, the way he would retreat into himself, shoulders hunched, avoiding eye contact. It made sense now: he had discovered Alex and Emily. Had he been defending me in talking to Alex, playing the role of the good guy? Or was his reaction something more selfish? He had realized it was never going to happen between him and Emily. That Alex was always going to get everything he wanted.

"But that night at the party," Ryan continued, "I found you crying about Alex, 'where is he, where is he,' almost incoherent. I thought you might want some privacy, so I took you back to the tarp."

Ryan could have found Emily and Alex at the cinder block house, I realized. He could have noticed them both missing and figured out where they would be. I took a step backward, down the row, trying to keep my expression neutral. *He knew they were fighting. He could have gone to comfort her.*

"I tried to get you to drink some water, and that's when you started getting sick."

I pictured Ryan climbing those concrete steps, finding Emily in tears, her curls frizzing around her face, her knees pulled in toward her. I could see him trying to reason with her, trying to explain that Alex wasn't right for her. That she deserved better.

"So I stayed there with you, holding back your hair until you fell asleep."

Emily, shaking her head, the tears coming harder. *No no no* over and over again, hiccupping sobs, when Ryan confessed his love for her.

"That's what happened that night. That's all there was to it."

I pictured Ryan grabbing her by the arms. *Listen,* he was saying. *You have to listen to me.*

"I have to go," I said, not taking my eyes off Ryan. He must have seen my fear, because his demeanor changed from frustrated to guarded. He straightened.

"Micah." *You're being ridiculous, Micah.*

"I have to go," I repeated, taking larger steps backward, holding my hands out protectively in front of me.

"Micah, let's talk about this," he said, the forced calmness back. But by then, I had backed all the way up to the cinder block wall and could see the older man I had spotted before, slightly hunched over a book return cart in the corner, studying the small stack of books piled up there with great interest. I turned and walked as quickly as I could, emboldened by the old man's presence, although God knows he probably wouldn't have lifted a finger in my defense. Up the stairs and into the main floor of the library, bustling with bored undergrads, loudly pretending to work on their term papers. I ran down the stone steps of the library and didn't stop until I got to my car, lowered my head onto my steering wheel, and burst into tears.

I couldn't go home; it wasn't safe there. It wasn't my apartment; it was *our* apartment. The space we had built together. He'd find me there, alone, and when he did—

I didn't want to think about that. I needed to focus on the task in front of me: find a place to stay. I turned left instead of right at Mechanic Street, toward Natalie's subdivision. *Natalie will believe me,* I told myself. *She'll help.*

In my cupholder, my phone lit up and then went dark again.

I pulled up to the curb in front of Natalie's house. Her windows were dark, the garage door closed. She was at her in-laws', I remembered. She'd be gone all weekend.

In: *c-a-l-m.*

Out: *d-o-w-n.*

I picked up my phone from the cupholder: one missed call from Ryan. No voicemail. I ignored it. I looked out the window, the phone still clutched in my hand. Across the street, a child waddled out of the front door in a pink puffy snowsuit, almost slipping on a thick sheet of ice. Her mother followed close behind, shooting a look at my parked car.

I thought about Detective Curtis and Cindy. They could help. That was their job, after all. *I could call them, tell them . . .*

That was as far as I got. *Tell them what?* All I had were photo-graphs of Emily, pages from her diary. (*Why do you have those, Micah?* I could hear Detective Curtis asking. *I found them,* I'd try to explain. *Someone gave them to me ten years ago, and Ryan was supposed to throw them away, but he didn't.*) The tone of Ryan's voice when I confronted him in the library basement. (*Cold,* I'd say. *Calculating.* Detective Curtis, raising a skeptical eyebrow. *Uh-huh.*) They didn't know Ryan like I did; they wouldn't see his reaction for what it was, in context. I thought about Detective Curtis waiting outside Stomping Grounds for me, telling me to leave Julia alone. *This needs to stop. Do you understand?*

I was on my own.

The woman across the street was still watching my car, trying to decide, probably, whether to alert the neighborhood watch. I gave her a small wave and dropped my phone back into the cup-holder. There was only one place I had left to go. I put the car into drive and headed for Stomping Grounds.

I paused on the sidewalk in front of Stomping Grounds, taking in the storefront one last time. The wooden sign out front that I had sanded and stained, hanging from a pole that extended out over the sidewalk. The brass doorknob I had affixed myself. The exte-rior I had painted a light shade of green, taking special care with the molding around the windows.

"I can't believe what you've done with this place," Ryan had told me the night before our opening day, hand running along the metallic counter. His eyes flit from picture frame to picture frame on the wall, textured cardboard painted and cut into different shapes, all on consignment from Calvary Art Studio. "I barely even recognize it."

I had beamed, so proud of myself, so sure I was doing the right thing. I had turned this place into something new, made something meaningful out of the past. Started over. That night, Ryan had wrapped his arms around my waist, nuzzled into my hair. "I'm so proud of you."

I thought he loved me. I stepped inside and dead-bolted the door behind me. *All this time, just a second-rate Emily.* I flipped over a chair, the one with the orange-and-red-striped upholstery. Ryan had loaded that chair, along with the others, into the back seat of his car, a jigsaw puzzle of legs and backrests, the helpful boyfriend, always such a good guy. I pulled my phone out onto the table, expecting another call from him, a voicemail this time, at least a text. *I can explain.*

Nothing.

I looked down at my messenger bag, at the bag full of paper footballs. I took one out and opened it gently, the paper weak at the folds.

I'm always so sore in the mornings. My knees, my legs, my arms, my whole body aches. It takes so much goddamned work to appear effortless, like you're floating, weightless, across the floor.

But it's worth it. It has to be worth it. Mr. Lionel always reminds me how many girls would kill to have the talent I have. When you have a gift, he says, it's wrong to waste it. And when I'm performing, and the lights illuminate the stage, blocking out the audience, I can remember that he's right. On the best nights, it's like an out-of-body experience. I don't feel the aching muscles or the bruised toes. I'm Giselle, returned from the grave, Kitri in the Spanish square.

Alex says he experiences something similar on game days. He's on the field and that's all that matters. His movements, the movements of his teammates, the other team's approach. I told him if he wasn't careful I was going to start developing real feelings for him.

"Oh, so there is a real heart beating in there somewhere after all," he said to me, teasing. I think.

.   .   .

I crumpled up that sheet of paper, threw it down onto the ground. *Fuck you, Emily,* I thought, and that familiar wave of guilt followed.

I tried to clear my head, tried to think straight. I thought about you.

I googled your name again—your new name—and scrolled through the results. I tried to piece together your new life in my head, the things you had done and the person you had become since high school. The thought of you running your own antiques shop, somewhere far away from here, was one of the first happy thoughts I had had in a long time. You had figured it out, after all. You had grown into yourself.

The door rattled, and I jumped, my attention pulled away from my phone. It was nothing, though. Just the wind howling down Main Street, the start of a winter storm.

I reached for my pack of cigarettes in my messenger bag, my nerves rattled. My hand brushed against the plastic bag and my heart sank again.

Why does Ryan really have Joshua's email address?

Had Ryan seen you in the woods the night Emily died? Was he worried that you might have seen him, too?

I tried to wrap my mind around this new Ryan: not the always-forgiving Ryan, who refused to abandon even Alex and saw something more in me than just his fuckup friend who couldn't make it out of Calvary. This was a Ryan who kept tabs. Who carefully monitored what Alex was up to, what I was doing.

He was worried about the truth getting out.

He was worried about what you knew.

I glanced down at my phone again. Still no new messages from Ryan, no pleas to talk.

He doesn't want to create a paper trail, I thought, and goosebumps prickled my skin.

I stood up and paced the length of the shop. It had gotten late. *Sleep,* I told myself. *I need to get some sleep. I'll think clearer in the morning.* I set up a makeshift bed for myself behind the counter out of washcloths and rags. The rags had the same dusty odor as the storage room, and the thin cotton did little to cushion against the hardwood floor. But I hadn't slept in days, Joshua. Haven't slept. I haven't slept in days.

I curled up into a ball, uncovered, the cold seeping through the thin rags. Passing cars sent long shadows flitting across the floor, the legs of the tables stretched and distorted. I squeezed my eyes shut, willing myself to sleep.

I pictured Ryan stretched out in my bed, our bed, next to me, the rise and fall of his chest, the warmth of his skin. Draping an arm around me, pulling me in. *Who is this person who is this person who is this person?* A car outside screeched to a stop at the intersection, its motor revving, and I jerked my legs in closer, wrapped my arms around them. I thought about Ryan making the hour-and-a-half drive out to Frackville, greeting Alex with a quick hug, sitting across from him at a visitors' table. Did he feel guilty? Was he taking pleasure in seeing Alex behind bars?

The heating rattled as it started up. I pictured Ryan in his office, carefully dabbing paint onto his plastic soldiers. His advice to Alex: *It's fine. We'll just say you were with us.* Ryan, pretending not to react when I mentioned No Stone Unturned. Looking it up, realizing there was renewed interest in the case. Searching you out.

I slept fitfully, waking at any noise: the click of the heater shutting off again and the sudden silence that followed, another whistle of air gusting down the street. The rattle of the dead bolt in the doorjamb.

I sat upright, my senses heightened. *Just the storm,* I told myself. But then there it was again, the front door shaking, refusing to give. I peered over the counter and saw Ryan, his mouth set in a grim line, trying to get in.

He saw me just as I saw him and started shaking the door harder. He leaned forward, cheeks blazing red from the cold.

"Micah," he said, his voice muffled through the glass door. "Micah, let me in. We need to talk."

I shook my head forcefully.

"Micah, it's cold out here." For an instant, I saw you again, on my front steps, your slender fingers clenched into fists, demanding to be let in.

"Go home," I said, backing toward the storage room. Ryan turned away, retreating down Church Street, and I gasped with relief. But a moment later, he was back.

A spare key, I realized. *He has a spare key.*

"Don't come in here," I warned, but he was already inserting the key into the lock, opening the door. The chimes jingled, and he stepped forward onto the wooden floor. I couldn't stop him. I didn't know how to stop him.

"We need to talk about what happened." That calm, measured tone.

"There's nothing to talk about." A step back. The floorboard groaned under my heel. Ryan rubbed his hand along the side of his face, then raked his hands through his hair, already standing on end.

"You were right," I said. "It was silly to bring it up. It was so long ago." Another step. "Just a crush."

Ryan stepped toward me. He wasn't tall, but he was larger than me. His arms, lean but muscular. When our hands pressed together, the tips of my fingers barely reached his knuckles.

"Back at the library, I got the impression you thought I had misled you," he said. "And I didn't—that was never my intent."

I looked out the windows at the still sidewalks, the empty streets.

"I couldn't sleep," he continued, "knowing that you—" He took another step forward, reaching into his coat. I thought he was reaching for something: a knife, the weighty body of a flashlight. I turned and bolted for the storage room, slamming the door behind me. I pressed the tiny push-button lock. It wouldn't keep him for long. I kept a key, just a straight stick of metal, on top of the doorframe. Ryan knew that. He knew everything.

"Jesus Christ, Micah." His calm tone had given way to anger. "Come on."

"You need to leave," I shouted through the door. I scanned the boxes scattered across the floor, the wire shelving, looking for some way to protect myself, something heavy enough to push up against the door. Nothing was big enough to keep him out. If I could move it, so could he. That's when my eyes caught on the copper coffee grinder, Ryan's opening-day present, sitting between the boxes of napkins and sweeteners, heavy and sharp-cornered. I grabbed it, felt the engraved vines winding under my fingers.

"Now," I said. "You need to leave now."

But he didn't move away from the door. I could hear him shuffling just on the other side, imagined his hand reaching up, scraping the top of the doorframe. I needed to act first.

I threw the door open and swung, made contact with a dull thud. He staggered backward, lifting his hand to his forehead. Between his fingers, dark red blood.

"Fuck, Micah." He pulled his hand away, looked down at it and then up at me, sank into the orange-and-red striped chair. We had found that chair, together, at an estate sale off of Quail Run. Wooden and sturdy, not like those chairs Mr. Hunt used to have when this was an ice cream shop, white plastic, the edges sharp and blunt, digging into my back, easy to clean, probably. I thought about Emily, hair hanging down over the plastic as she burst into a genuine fit of giggles, loud and unencumbered, back when we were ten and you were eight and there wasn't anything to worry about yet, nothing but possibility ahead of us. You, wiggling in your seat, ice cream dripping down your hand.

"Fuck," Ryan said again. His forehead was bleeding heavily. A swipe of red across the chair, splatters on the floor. On the grinder, on my hands. It was everywhere.

"I told you to leave," I said. My voice wobbled. I dropped the coffee grinder onto the floor.

Ryan tried to stand, but then dropped back down, unsteadily. He grimaced.

"I told you—" I started again, backing toward the front door.

Behind me, the door chimes jingled. I turned to see Anna, frozen in the doorway, round eyes staring at Ryan, covered in blood. Saturday morning. I hadn't called her to cancel her shift. And, for once, she was on time.

I opened my mouth. *I can explain,* I wanted to say, but I couldn't explain, could I? What could I have said that would make her listen?

"Anna," I said, her name catching in my throat, and her eyes rose to meet mine, questioning.

Ryan, at the same time, called out: "Go get help."

A click of recognition, like all the pieces had finally come together for her. Anna turned and ran.

25

Ahead of me is the Bourne Bridge, its crisscrossing metal beams rising up into an arch. A sign for would-be jumpers: DESPERATE? CALL US. Twelve-foot-high curved barriers between me and the canal, a hundred feet below. Then snow-covered hedges carved out into letters welcome me to Cape Cod. I exhale a sigh of relief, and, for the first time, allow myself to feel a flicker of hope. *This is where I'm supposed to be,* I tell myself. *I'm doing the right thing.*

You need to hear the truth about what happened to Emily. You need to hear the truth about Ryan. He knows where you are, and he's worried about what you know.

I start the drive up the Cape.

I burst into my apartment, which was just as I had left it. Boxes still scattered across the floor, *Napoleon and His Marshals* on the end table, the sliver of a bookmark poking out. A mug painted with pastel seashells, half-full of old coffee, sat out on the kitchen table.

The pictures from the fridge lay in a pile on the counter. I had taken them down but hadn't had the heart to throw them out.

I scrubbed at my hands in the kitchen sink, rubbing between my fingers, my nail beds. I pictured Detective Curtis at Stomping Grounds, helping Ryan to his feet, listening to what he had to say.

"Micah," Ryan would tell him. "Micah did this to me."

But he wouldn't stop there, would he? I could hear it—a practiced pause, like he was deliberating, and then: "I confronted her about what happened ten years ago. She lost it. I don't think it was Alex. I think it was her."

He'd turn it around on me, twist what had happened to his benefit. They'd be coming for me. I needed to move fast.

I stripped off my old clothes, which were splattered with blood. I threw them down on the floor and then thought better of it, balled them up, placed them in a pile to take with me. I pulled a black sweater and jeans out of my closet.

I'd need more than just that. I wasn't coming back here.

I grabbed a garbage bag from under the kitchen sink and returned to my bedroom. I tore shirts down off their hangers, stuffed them in. I hesitated, then pulled Alex's jacket out of the back corner of the closet shelf and stuffed it in, too. I couldn't leave it for the police to find if they tore my apartment apart, digging through each box and drawer for clues, the story of what happened.

"Whatever you need," Ryan would say to the officers, showing them around. "I just want to help."

I scanned the room, frantic. I needed money, something valuable. The jewelry from my dresser drawer. The wad of money folded up on the nightstand. It wasn't much, but it was what I had.

A framed picture of Ryan and his mother, taken last year, sat on the dresser. His arm rested protectively around her shoulder. Ryan, always so loyal. A flicker of doubt: *Was he capable?* I shook my head and blinked back tears. It was him. It made sense. His gray eyes looked back at me from the photograph—unreadable, like a stranger's.

My head ached. The room seemed foreign, hostile. Any minute, there would be pounding at the front door, a crowd of neighbors looking on, curious. I grabbed my garbage bag full of clothes and made my way down the hall, eyes casting around for anything else I should bring. The door to Ryan's office was open. I took one last look inside. The big oak desk loomed in the middle of the room, Ryan's little men lined up on top. My mind raced, the same thought over and over: *Who is this person who is this person who is this person?*

The Cape looks so quiet in the snow, so serene. I pass a church with blue siding and large, arched windows, a giant clock mounted on its bell tower. An old-fashioned brick library with a flag swinging out front. An inn with a decorative wooden sign announcing vacancies, its empty parking lot recently plowed.

I didn't know, when I left my apartment, that this is where I would end up. I got in my car and drove without any destination in mind, just to get away. I followed the grown-over railroad tracks that used to transport steel, their metal beams now rusted. Over an old stone bridge, stretching across the river that used to power the manufacturing plant. Into the woods, the trees bare and branches twisting upward. Away from Calvary.

I stopped at the near-empty parking lot for a store called Frank's Bait & Tackle. I parked away from the store, on the other side of the gravel lot, and turned the key. My heart was pounding, my fingers sore from clutching the steering wheel too tightly.

I needed a plan. I closed my eyes and willed myself to think.

I had nowhere to go.

I pulled the wad of money out of my pocket and counted it out. One hundred twenty. Enough for a tank of gas, a room for a night. Maybe two.

I pulled out my phone and opened its browser. The last page I had been looking at—an article on local businesses in Stonesport that mentioned you by name—appeared on the screen.

. . . a welcome addition to our Main Street stretch. Joshua Bishop curates the shop collection with a keen eye toward local history . . .

Ten years ago, you had done what I couldn't. You left Calvary behind; you started over. Stonesport, Massachusetts: a quiet town, tucked away from the rest of the world. A place where people can forget. *After so many shipwrecks, a safe harbor.*

I thought about your email address in Ryan's drawer. "A book fair." I didn't buy it. He was keeping tabs on you. He was worried you knew something. I had to find you first.

It only took a White Pages search and a few dollars to find your address. I pulled out of the Bait & Tackle parking lot and set off to find you.

26

pull up to a gray-shingled house tucked into a compact neighborhood. It's surrounded by a low white fence, bare vines wrapping around a narrow arbor. A teal plastic sled leans up against the front steps, the right size for a small child. Bare bushes, branches spiking up out of the ground, lead up the path to the front door. This is not what I was expecting. You were supposed to live by the sea. A small blue house, brightly colored against the ocean in the background. I squeeze my eyes shut, blink them open again, check the numbers on the circular plaque on the front of the house.

This is the right place. This is where you live.

I pull my car over to the curb across the street and catch my breath. This is where you've been, all this time. I picture you returning home from Stonesport Maps & Prints Gallery, walking up that stone path with the same loping gait you had in high school, opening that front door to your family.

The windows are dark and the driveway is empty. I look down at the clock, then check the Stonesport Maps & Prints Gallery website on my phone. Still open. You won't be home for another hour. I roll my head back against the headrest, and tears well up in my eyes. I rub the worn fabric brim of Ryan's hat between my fingers, slip it off my head, and throw it into the back seat.

It lands beside the plastic bag of paper footballs, their corners sticking up out of the hole ripped in its side. I think about you, reading through Emily's diaries and tearing out the pages, folding each one with care, leaving them in my backpack. To remind me of your sister. As if I could forget.

I reach back and grab the bag, set it down in the passenger seat beside me. I pull out one of the notes and unfold it, begin to read. An entry dated September 5.

I don't know how I let myself get caught up in this.

I've been telling myself that Alex was the instigator, that he was the one who pursued me, that I resisted, resisted, resisted and finally gave in in a moment of weakness. Then, once I gave in, the damage was done. If once, why not twice?

But maybe that's not entirely true. He sensed my interest, after all. And, sure, I told him no the first few times he tried to make a move, but a part of me knew he liked the pursuit. And I'd be lying if I said I didn't like being pursued.

The really sick thing is, I'm not even sure I would have liked Alex if he hadn't already been seeing Micah. He's good-looking, obviously, but lots of guys are, and he's talented enough, but he's not exactly brilliant. There was something about him being off-limits that made him interesting. I always do what I'm supposed to. I didn't want to do the right thing anymore.

Mr. Lionel saw us together. He said I'm being selfish, that I'm throwing away years of our hard work. Any dumb slut can open her legs, he said, but only a handful of girls ever get the chances I'm going to have. Which kind of person did I want to be, he kept asking. I need to be willing to make sacrifices. If I'm not focused, I'm nothing.

Another entry, from September 7.

I keep waking up frozen, unable to move. My arms and legs feel leaden. My chest feels like it's being pinned down to my mattress. The first time it happened, I thought I was dying. I thought: This is it. This is the end. You've been a selfish, terrible person and now you won't even have anything to show for it.

But then it subsides, leaving behind just the familiar aches and pains, and I stretch, sneak downstairs to the basement without waking anyone, and start my morning routine: stretches, lunges, and planks, arabesque lifts, pliés and relevés and tendus. It's just me, and the movements, and Don Quixote piped in over my speakers. I can focus on counting. I can pretend I don't have a decision to make.

I glance back toward your house. The driveway still empty, the lights still off. I reach into the bag and pull out another entry.

October. Two weeks before Emily died.

I can't stop thinking about it.

I brace myself for more musings about Alex: the first time they overcame the guilt that had been holding them back, the first time they slept together. Details I've never known, and never wanted to know. It shouldn't sting this much after ten years, but it still does. Mostly, it's shame. How could I have been so stupid? Why didn't I see it? And how could the two people who were supposed to care about me the most be so completely callous toward me?

The dream I keep having: Otto at the quarry, hair dripping, hands rough and fingernails caked with dirt. He reaches the top. He turns to look at me. He smiles.

I read the entry a second time, then a third.

Who is Otto?

My phone lights up again, and it's Ryan's picture I see, and I feel like the air is being squeezed out of the car.

Who is Otto?

I catch my breath, look back out to the street in front of me. I need to make sense of this, need to clear my head. I need some air. I fumble with the car door, push it open. Feet on the ground, and the cold wraps around me. I grab the notes and shove them into my messenger bag. I start walking.

There aren't many cars in the driveways I pass. To my right, a house with blue siding and a small plaque listing the original owner and year the house was built: 1843. It looks empty, boarded up for the winter. I pull out a cigarette, try to think.

I can think of exactly one Otto I've known: a leather-and-fedora-wearing German who lived next door to me in Chicago. No one from high school or Calvary, no one who would have known Emily.

Was he someone she knew through ballet? Another dancer, maybe, someone she met at one of her competitions?

It was possible. But then, anything was possible. There was so much about Emily that I didn't know.

I think about Ryan, blood between his fingers. Alex, the way his face froze when the jury read its verdict. My head throbs.

A boat sits in the next driveway, wrapped up in a green tarp. A metallic fish swings from the wood fence. A heavyset man with a beard emerges from the garage and lumbers toward the front door. He gives me a small head nod. I nod back, look down toward the ground, keep going.

I wrack my brain for any references that Emily made in the weeks leading up to her death to anyone new. But she was always so cagey about her feelings—and for good reason, it turned out. I would have noticed if she had mentioned a relationship or a crush. She hadn't. I'm sure of that.

A white house with green shutters, a cheerful-looking red door. This one is from 1845, its owner, at the time, William Baker. I can see the raised plot that will be a vegetable garden in the spring.

If there was someone else—

I push the thought down, keep walking. I turn up a tree-lined road, follow it past an old shed, its windows missing. I picture the cinder block house, the hollowed-out stone. That's behind me now. I've left that behind.

I keep expecting the sounds of the water. I listen for seagulls cawing, waves crashing up against the shore, but I only hear the occasional gust of wind, a truck rumbling in the background. A sign for the boardwalk directs me to a dirt path leading through tall grass. Another sign posted nearby: AREA CLOSED. NO SHELL-FISHING. I can smell something now: the briny, pungent air. My shoes sink into wet mud.

When the tall grass comes to a stop, there's nothing but marsh-land in front of me. A short, rickety pier hangs out into a pool of murky, stagnant water, which stretches out in pockets in the dead grass. I squeeze my eyes shut.

Emily wanted to end things with Alex but didn't know how. Then she met someone new—Otto—and Alex found out.

Could Ryan have been telling the truth?

I don't know what to think anymore.

I lift my foot and the mud beneath it slurps back into place. I backtrack, away from the marsh and toward the street. I follow the street down to a main stretch. A row of stores side by side, with names that sound like gift shops and women's clothing stores. The Glass House, Purls of Wisdom, The Village Boutique. The windows are all dark. I spot a chalkboard sign in one of them: SEE YOU NEXT SPRING!

Light shines through the big glass windows of one of the storefronts: Lola's Diner. I see a handful of occupied booths inside. An unhurried waitress makes her way from table to table, pot of coffee in hand, stopping to shout something back to the kitchen. I realize, suddenly, just how cold my hands are, my fingers numb and red. I push through the swinging door and stop by the PLEASE WAIT TO BE SEATED sign.

"Right this way, hon," the waitress says. She has an easy familiarity that I never quite got down as a server. I was professional, competent, knowledgeable. Not warm.

I sit down at a booth and ask for a coffee. The waitress flips over my mug and fills it. I pull out my phone and open the No Stone Unturned forum.

I search for any threads mentioning an Otto. Nothing. I set down my phone and cradle my head in my hands. Breathe in and out.

"You okay?" the waitress asks, passing by my booth.

"Fine," I say, looking back up. "Just a long day."

"I hear that," she says, and then she drifts off again. I pick up my phone. "Secret boyfriend," I try in the forum search function. Nothing I haven't seen before.

A new screen pops up: Detective Curtis is calling. I can feel the hot prickle of tears forming.

The image of Ryan, stunned, falling back onto the orange-and-red striped chair. It could still have been him, I tell myself. He held on to those pictures and notes for ten years. He must have been obsessed with her. He was there at the party that night.

Helping me, I think to myself. His hand on my back, rubbing in circles.

"Happens to everyone, Miks," he said. Miks, just like Alex used to call me. Ryan stopped using that, after. "You're okay. You're going to be okay."

He had the time to do it. But was he capable? I squeeze my eyes shut, my head pounding.

I pull the notes out onto the table, open one and flatten it with my palm. More about ballet class, Emily's struggle to improve her fouetté. Another about the searing pain in her calves. No other mention of Otto, no clues as to his identity, no hints about Ryan's creepy obsession or Alex's jealous fits. I unfold a last note and lay it down on the table in front of me.

We drove 14 hours out to Mississippi for the competition. The a/c wasn't working in the car, and Dad didn't notice, of course, and Mom didn't bother to get it fixed. "Details," she calls all the things she doesn't do, like they're unimportant, when the house is literally falling apart around her. And Joshua, of course, hadn't showered, so the whole car stank, and with all the suitcases we had to bring with us there was barely any room to move. Truly hell, but I wasn't even allowed to complain because, as my mom likes to point out, "we're doing this for you." Which, I guess, is true, except I'm doing this for her, too. She conveniently forgets that part.

I like to visualize my performance before a competition, so I was trying to listen to Kitri's variation in Act III on my headphones. Joshua, beside me, had his textbook on his lap and was drilling declensions. "Luso, luseis, lusei," he kept saying, at full volume.

I closed my eyes and tried to picture the series of hops and flutters that Kitri performs with her fan. But instead, I kept hearing the thwack thwack thwack of Joshua's pencil against his textbook, "lusomen, lusete, lusousi."

"Did you know," he said to us all, "that Doric Greek—"

I snapped. I was sore and anxious and the car stank, and I could barely even move my knees back and forth. I said: "Could you just stop for two fucking seconds and try to be normal?" And I regretted it as soon as I said it. Joshua started moping and my mom closed her eyes and rubbed her temples, and my dad's eyes flicked up toward the rearview mirror and then back toward the street and then back up again, surprised, like he had just realized that, hello, he has kids back there.

"Emily," my mom said. "We're doing this—"

"For me," I said. "I know, I know." I looked out the window at the highway, the noise barriers rising and falling, blocking my view of anything that might distinguish one place from another.

It came out all wrong, but I did mean it. Dad doesn't notice any-thing we do, and Mom pretends that it's fine that Joshua doesn't shower regularly, isn't it great that Joshua has his own interests, we need to just let Joshua be Joshua. And I keep trying to tell her that it's not okay, that kids are savage and cruel, that he's going to end up isolated and alone and picked on. She says I'm being melodramatic, but I'm just trying to look out for him. I want him to have friends. I want him to have a life. And it doesn't always "work out" when you just "let things run their course." Sometimes you end up baking in a rancid, run-down car where everyone hates each other because you couldn't be bothered with "details." Sometimes I wish we could all just be fucking normal. Would that really be so bad?

The entry cuts off there, the end of the page. I fold the note into a square, place it back into the plastic bag. I rub a hand over my face and wave at the server to get her attention. It's your clos-ing time now. You'll be pulling into your driveway soon, the ga-rage door creeping open. It's time to talk to you.

27

walk through your arbor and run a finger along its latticed side, feeling the splintering wood. The cracks between the stone on your front path are caked with snow. I take a careful look behind me from your front porch. The street is empty. I knock on the door and wait.

There's movement inside, a dog leaping into action, scrambling toward the front door. The squeal of a toddler. Slow, heavy footsteps approach, then stop. A long pause, as whoever stands on the other side peers out of the peephole, looks me up and down. I shift my weight and pull at the sleeves of my sweater. The door creaks open.

It's you standing in the doorway, unmistakably you, but so foreign at the same time. Joshua. Your hair—his hair—is cut short now, but still curls up above the right eyebrow. Your eyes—his eyes—colder than I remembered, squinting back at me with skepticism. He's wearing a fleece pullover, pushed up to his elbows. Clean. No dragons. One of his hands rests toward the top of the doorframe, the other on his hip. I'm not welcome in.

"Micah." A deeper voice than I remember, filled out with age.

"It's been a while." He looks over his shoulder, positions his left leg to hold back a terrier that is trying to nuzzle its way out the door, then steps out to join me on the front porch. He closes the door, his hand lingering on the doorknob as if holding it shut.

"Joshua," I say. My voice hoarse. Everything I thought I knew is unraveling. I need a cigarette.

"What are you doing here?" He tugs the sleeves of his pullover down, covering the scarred skin on his forearms, and suddenly I wonder the same thing.

"How—how have you been?" I ask. Joshua crosses his arms over his chest.

"What are you doing here?" he asks again. Mrs. Klein and the campsite and the texts and Julia, it all blurs together in my mind. Ryan and the email—why did he have Joshua's email? I don't know how to piece it all together anymore, how to begin.

"Emily's death," I say, and Joshua's mouth tightens. "It's been getting attention lately. This website—"

He smirks. I worry I might be sick. "Which one?"

"No Stone Unturned," I stammer. Were there others? Had there been other strangers, too, poking and prodding and examining? "It's—"

"I know what it is." A pickup truck rolls down the street, and Joshua's eyes jump up. His shoulders tighten.

"I just need to talk to you," I say, glancing toward the door. Inside, the dog whines and scrapes a paw down the wood. "Can I come in?"

He doesn't move. "My family lives here."

"Please," I say, my voice breaking. "It's important."

Joshua surveys the now-empty street. He cracks the door and calls to someone inside: "I'm taking a drive."

He glances back at me, then nods toward his car.

"Great," I say, bobbing my head up and down. "Great. Thank you." But he doesn't respond. He's already walking ahead, his head bent down, and reaching out for the driver-side door.

.   .   .

Joshua doesn't turn on the car radio as we back out of the drive-way. A long strip of masking tape holds the fabric of my seat to-gether, crumbs ground into the seams. A sour, milky smell rises up from the thermos in the cup holder. I try to look straight ahead. I can hear Joshua breathing beside me and the soft, electric buzz from the auxiliary cord when it hits up against the plastic wall of the driver's console.

We pass the houses I walked past before and turn onto the main drag. The Glass House and Purls of Wisdom flash by. The pastel sign for Andie's Cupcakes, the darkened windows of the Book Nook. An empty restaurant. Long stretches of unclaimed parking spots. It's winter. There's no one here.

I twist around and see the car seat buckled in behind Joshua, a well-worn rabbit flopped over on its side.

"You have a kid."

He nods, eyes still fixed forward.

"Boy or girl?"

I try to keep my voice light, but it's not working. Joshua doesn't answer. At my feet, a discarded sheet of paper, scuffed with shoe prints. I pick it up and examine the doodle on one side. A sketch of a lighthouse, the top half shaded, its lantern room caged in by a balcony. On the other side, an advertisement: CELLPHONE RE-PAIRS, TWENTY PERCENT OFF THROUGH THE END OF THE WEEK.

"Did you draw this?" I ask, holding the sheet toward him. "It's good."

He looks toward me but still doesn't answer. I let the drawing flutter back down to the floor, onto a bed of crunched leaves. We pass a mini-golf course on our right, with a red-and-white wind-mill and a large replica pirate ship floating in the middle of a fake lagoon. The blades of the windmill are still and the spotlights strung up to the ship's mast are off.

"Where are we going?"

"We're just driving," he says. "You said you needed to talk."

The locked drawer. The email address. The paper footballs. I nod, my mouth dry.

"I don't think Alex killed Emily."

Joshua squeezes his eyes shut, then blinks them open again. "That's what you came up here to tell me."

I can't tell if he's surprised.

"That, and I'm worried about you."

He smirks and gives a short laugh. "Since when have you ever cared about anyone other than yourself?"

"That's not true," I say. I'm unsure of how to defend myself. Unsure of what, even, I'm supposed to be defending myself against. *That's not fair,* I want to tell him. *Don't you remember all the times I defended you? The secrets I've kept for you?*

"Don't worry," he says, and there's an edge to his voice. "It's not like I'm any better."

Dark houses rush past. Next to the thermos in the cup holder, a half-drunk bottle of passionfruit-flavored water.

"Bishop," I say, watching for a reaction. "Does your wife know your real name?"

His cheek twitches. "That is my real name now."

I breathe in, trace a looping line on the fogged window.

"I never told anyone I saw you at the campsite that night," I say, my voice softer. "The police asked me who was there, and I left your name out. I didn't want—I didn't want them to get the wrong idea."

"I know." His voice has lowered, too.

"But I think Ryan might have seen you, too. I think he's been keeping tabs on you. On both of us."

Joshua's forehead creases.

"He wants to know what we know."

His eyes dart toward me, with a flicker of—surprise? guilt? concern? I'm not sure. I keep talking.

"I found your email address in his desk drawer—"

Joshua shakes his head and cuts me off.

"I gave him that," he says. "We bumped into each other in Boston last year. Ryan recognized me."

Boston. My heart sinks. "At a book fair?" I ask.

"Yeah."

So Ryan wasn't lying about that. But there were still the photographs he had hidden, the paper footballs he had kept after all this time.

"What do we know, Micah?"

Is he mocking me? There's something so bitter in his tone.

"I think Ryan—" I start, and Joshua glances over at me again, his eyebrows rising when he realizes what I'm struggling to say.

"Ryan?" he says. He's smirking again, and I hate it. "You think *Ryan* killed Emily?"

My throat throbs and I fight to keep myself from crying.

"He wanted to be with her," I say. Why was I so sure? "I saw him, alone, in the woods that night. He was the one who convinced Alex to lie to the police."

"Ryan didn't do it," he says with a certainty that makes my stomach churn. I feel it, too: of course it wasn't Ryan. I see Ryan at Stomping Grounds again, blood in streaks across the white-washed floor, and my heart aches.

Another turn. The houses and shops are gone now. All around us, stubby trees with branches low to the ground.

"How do you know?"

"How do you think I know?"

I don't respond, and Joshua sighs, impatient.

"I was there."

He takes a sharp right and my stomach lurches. The houses that line the street now are dark and boarded up for the winter. The static seems to be getting louder. I turn to study his expression, but I can't read it.

"I want you to stop the car," I say.

"Here?" Joshua asks. "We're in the middle of nowhere."

I suck on my bottom lip. "What do you mean you were there?"

A side glance toward me. "You *saw* me, Micah. You know this already."

"I don't remember," I say.

"Bullshit," Joshua says.

I try to picture that night. I see Joshua, in the woods, dressed in all black. A flashlight in his hand. We were close to the cinder block house. I had followed the creek bed into the woods, was almost there.

I squeeze my eyes tight, try to think of how I got there. I remember Helena, leaning against the altar. She was smoking, or pretending to, a red Solo cup balanced precariously on the uneven stone behind her.

"Have you seen Alex?" I had asked her, and I remember, now, the look she gave me in response: pity mixed with the pleasure of knowing a secret, of having the upper hand.

"Not recently," she said, taking another short puff on her cigarette.

Joshua tightens his grip on the steering wheel.

"I knew you and Emily were going to that party," he says. "I could hear the two of you talking. The walls in that house were so thin. And I heard you teasing Emily about some guy, and I knew. I had suspected for a while—I had heard Emily on the phone with someone, talking in a low, secretive voice, and I had noticed a change in the way she and Alex behaved when you were around. They were nervous. They kept their distance. But, until that day, I hadn't *known*.

"So I decided I was going to go to the party, too. I almost changed my mind a dozen times, but, in the end, I stuck with it. I climbed out my window when my parents thought I was sleeping and biked over to the campsite. Everyone was already a mess by the time I got there, and those people weren't—I wasn't *friends* with anyone there. It's not like I had anyone there to talk to. So I stayed on the periphery, watching, until I saw Emily and Alex disappear into the woods together. I followed them back to the cinder block house, just to confirm for myself, and sure enough, there was Alex, placing a hand on Emily's back, and the two of them disappearing inside together."

I try to keep my breath steady, try not to think about what this means.

"I went back to the party to find you. You had been drinking. You were alone."

I remember the glow of the campsite, lit by a bonfire and the headlights of Brian's Land Rover, which he had pulled up close to the pillars. Outside that circle of light, the woods were dark. Helena behind me, smirking. I pushed ahead, back into the forest. I remember the feel of my flashlight, heavy in my hand, my fingers numb and clumsy. The scrape of branches across my face.

I jumped back, held my hand up defensively, then pushed ahead. My foot slipped on an uneven rock and I lunged forward but caught myself before sprawling out onto the forest floor. The forest was spinning, and it was so dark.

I took smaller, more cautious steps, the beam of my flashlight bouncing from the forest floor to the path ahead. Then: the crack of a branch behind me. I turned, sucked in my breath. Joshua winced as the light hit him and held up one hand to shield his eyes. He wore a black fleece jacket, black denim and boots, a black knit cap pulled down over his ears, his hair curling out from beneath. His pale face stood out in stark contrast.

"Joshua?"

"Hey," he said, like this was a chance meeting, like we were bumping into each other in the hallway at school. He held a flashlight in his right hand, but it was off.

"What are you doing here?"

Fear, but I couldn't place it. *It's just Joshua,* I told myself.

"What do you mean?" he asked.

"What are you doing here?" I repeated, and this time he gave me a nervous smile.

"I'm not allowed to play some beer pong?"

"You saw me," Joshua says now, not looking at me anymore, "and I thought to myself: This is it. This is my moment. It felt big, important." He laughs, but not like what he said was funny. "I guess I was right, after all, but not in the way I imagined."

I realized, when he smiled, why I felt so uneasy. It was the flashlight. Why was the flashlight off?

"Are you following me?"

"No," he said, shaking his head quickly. "I mean, yes, but . . ."

The woods felt cold and damp. I wrapped my arms around myself, realizing just how vulnerable I was. How far I had drifted from the group. Back at the campsite, the echo of laughter. No one there would be looking for me.

"They're together, you know." Joshua straightened himself. He had gotten tall. I pulled my arms in tighter, trying to process what he meant.

"Emily and Alex," he continued, gesturing with his flashlight— *off, why was it off?*—toward the cinder block house. The forest spun, taking a moment to steady itself, when I looked in that direction.

"You're following me," I said again.

"Micah." Joshua sounded impatient now. He stepped toward me. "You're not listening. They're together. Alex is *cheating* on you. With Emily."

"I don't understand." I lost my balance, stepped back to steady myself.

"It's been going on for months. He doesn't love you, Micah." Another step forward, and I knew, could feel it in my gut, what Joshua was about to say next: "*I* love you."

"Stop," I said, but he took another step closer.

"I've always loved you." He had obviously planned this out in advance, rehearsed what he would say. "Since we were kids. You're not like other people. You care about things other people don't."

I thought about my first walk with Alex. The first time he had pulled me in, his rough palm against my cheek. The first time we had slept together, on the ratty pullout in his basement on an evening we knew his parents wouldn't be home until late. A seven-dollar bottle of prosecco poured into two of his mom's stemless wineglasses.

"—I can talk to you," Joshua was saying. "I feel comfortable when I'm around you."

I thought about Emily, our faces six inches away from each other under an ivory duvet, a flashlight turned on under the sheets after her mother stuck her head in—*lights out, ladies*—and then shouted a warning down the hall five minutes later—*I still hear giggling*.

"Alex doesn't appreciate you. He never did."

I thought of Emily, at seventeen, Alex's hand against the small of her back, his mouth against her ear: *It's different with you.* And: *You're not like Micah.* And: *She doesn't have to know.* Emily, pretending to resist but leaning into his touch.

Emily, who always outdid me.

Another shout from the campsite, the beer pong crew. I wondered how many of them knew. How many of them had watched as Emily and Alex had snuck back into the woods together. Joshua was oblivious, his eyes fixed on me, unblinking. "You deserve someone who sees you for who you really are."

Emily and Alex, seated next to me at a football game, pretending I *mattered* to them. Had she pressed her knee into his when I looked the other direction? Had he been thinking about her when I leaned my head against his shoulder? How could I not have known?

"I don't believe you," I said, interrupting Joshua's monologue, and he blinked, confused. "They wouldn't do that to me."

"They don't give a shit about you," he said. His eyes flashed excitedly. "*I* care about you."

An offer from Alex: *I can drive you home,* and Emily accepting, *sure, thanks,* and me thinking—like an idiot—so *nice* that they get along so well, that we all just click, that it's all so easy. Emily, pretending like she had chosen an ascetic existence, devoted to dance, but, really, she got to have everything she ever wanted.

Joshua took another step forward. "Micah," he said, and I jumped back, my feet slipping into the creek. The water was cold, soaking its way through the canvas of my shoes.

"Stop," I said, holding my hands up in front of me.

"It's the truth, Micah." He blinked, surprised by my reaction, his eyes searching out mine.

"I thought I *loved* you," Joshua says now. "I was fifteen and you meant the world to me. I used to hang around the kitchen or the family room when you were over, just to be close to you—it drove Emily crazy. I thought you felt something, too. I thought you cared about me, at least."

I remember him stepping forward. "He doesn't love you like I do." He reached out toward my face, maybe to tuck a lock of hair behind my ear. It was an awkward gesture, something swiped from a movie, and I slapped his hand away.

"Get *away* from me, you freak."

It was meaner than I had intended. His face changed, shocked and hurt and disappointed. I felt nauseous.

"I have to go," I said, not able to look at him.

"Micah," he said, sounding confused.

"I just have to go," I said again, starting back toward the campsite. It wasn't right, what I had said, and if I had gotten another day I would have apologized. I would have explained that he had caught me off guard, that I was hurt and confused, that I hadn't been thinking. But our lives changed that night, and I never got the chance.

"After that," Joshua says, "I went back to the cinder block house."

A refrain in the back of my head, growing louder: *Please no please no*. I try to keep my face neutral, keep my voice calm.

"Why?" I ask.

"Because what they were doing was wrong," he says. "Or that's what I told myself, anyway. I was hurt. I wanted someone else to hurt, too. I wanted *Alex* to hurt. It wasn't fair. That's what it really came down to. It wasn't fair."

Joshua's eyes are so much colder than I remembered. All the softness is gone, replaced by jagged cheekbones, a hard scowl. A stranger.

"So I went to the cinder block house. I stepped inside and listened for them, but it was silent. I thought, at first, that maybe I had been wrong. Maybe they weren't there after all. But then I heard this noise, like a gasp, from upstairs."

His eyes dart back and forth, remembering.

"I climbed up the steps and saw Emily, sitting in the windowsill. Her shoulders were shaking like she was crying, but she wasn't making any noise. Her feet were dangling out the window. I remember she lifted one leg, then the other, pointed and flexed her toes. She must have heard me step toward her, because she twisted around to look at me over her shoulder. 'Oh, Joshua,' she said to me. 'It's you.'"

Joshua's eyes tear up as he says this. Is it the memory of Emily? Is it guilt?

"She smiled at me, but it wasn't a real smile. Her cheeks were wet and she was having trouble catching her breath. 'I'm not a robot,' she said. 'I'm not heartless.' I told her of course she wasn't. I took another step toward her, and she started teetering, back and forth, and I stopped."

I shook my head, squeezed the door handle in my right hand. I can see where this story is heading, but I don't understand it. It doesn't make any sense.

"Emily wouldn't have done that," I say. "She wouldn't have killed herself."

"No," Joshua says. "I know. That's not what I'm saying."

My stomach flips over. *Please no please no please no.*

"You need to let me out of the car now."

"I thought you finally wanted to talk."

"Now."

He doesn't slow. What would happen if I threw myself out? I can almost feel the impact, skin scraping against the gravel, the screech of brakes. I don't move.

"Emily kept on shaking her head, saying she didn't want to do it anymore. 'Do what?' I asked her, and she just kept repeating herself. I was worried she was going to lose her balance. I thought maybe she had been drinking. I thought—I didn't know what to think."

I study Joshua, try to anticipate what he's going to say. He looks back over at me.

"They wanted her. Did she tell you?"

I frown, not sure what he's talking about.

"Pennsylvania Ballet. She got in. As part of their company of younger dancers, like a training program, but still. That's how you start. She got a letter from them a few weeks before."

"That's . . ." I don't know how to respond. I shake my head. I don't understand what he's telling me. That was Emily's dream, for as long as I could remember. She would have said something. I would have known.

"She didn't tell me, either. She didn't tell anyone. I found the letter underneath a stack of other papers in our study. I thought of it when I saw her on that windowsill. I told her I saw it. I thought it would help. I said how *exciting* that was. And then she started shaking her head even harder, her eyes squeezed shut, saying 'no no no no' and I didn't understand."

Joshua's voice breaks off. He rubs at his eyes with the back of his hand. His mouth tightens into a grimace as he tries to regain control. An old train track stretches out beside us.

"I have a daughter," he says, and I squint back at him, confused. He looks at me and his eyes are red. "She's two now."

I nod, glance at the road in front of us. Tiny beads of ice strike the windshield, slowly at first, then picking up momentum.

"She takes after Emily, I think," he says. "She's a perfectionist— you can see it already. She has this little bike we got her for her last birthday, and she loves it. She's dead-set on learning how to ride it, getting it right. A lot of kids cry when they fall over, scrape their knee, but not—" He almost says her name but thinks better of it and swallows instead.

"She's passionate," I say. "Like both of you."

Joshua's mouth loosens into a small smile.

"Like both of us."

We fall into silence again, and I wonder if he can hear the way my heart is pounding against my chest. He presses his lips together, drums his long fingers against the steering wheel. I picture Emily, balanced on the edge of the window. Joshua, edging closer, that same hand wrapping around her arms. *Who is this person who is this person?*

"I think she felt trapped," he says, finally. "Her whole life, for as long as I can remember, everyone made this huge deal out of what a great dancer she was. What a *gift* she had. And the Lionels—"

I can see his face twist into something like disgust.

"You know, my mom had them over for dinner one time, and they spent the whole evening talking about what a *rare talent* Emily was. Mr. Lionel was going on and on about how *this* is what makes the hard work of running a studio—all those Wiggle Worm classes and delusional parents and dramatic teenagers—worth it. She was *fourteen*. And after dinner, my mom, who had probably drunk too much wine at that point, turns to Emily and says '*this* is your calling.' She kept saying how lucky Emily was to know what she was meant to do at such a young age. That if she had only started early on her own music career, if she had had the kind of opportunities that Emily had, the kind of discipline, her own trajectory could have looked very different. How fortunate Emily was to have been tapped by someone like Mr. Lionel, who knew what needed to be done to make it. 'You are going to be *somebody*,' she kept saying."

Joshua readjusts his hands on the steering wheel, twitches his head.

"But she wasn't enjoying it. She was doing it because she felt like she had to, like that's what she had to do to *matter* to someone. She was worn out, and she wasn't taking care of herself." He looks at me, and I can feel the judgment in his expression. "You must have seen it."

Emily's comments about being sore, or exhausted, or left out, just brushed aside.

"She could have just quit," I say.

"I don't think she knew how to tell the Lionels no," Joshua says. "She was a *child*. And my mom thought she was this brilliant virtuoso, and my dad had no idea what was going on at all."

"Emily wouldn't have killed herself," I say again, and Joshua looks at me, angry this time.

"You need to listen, Micah," he says sharply. "You never *listen*."

We're both quiet again. The static hum of the auxiliary cord fills the car.

"I think part of her was hoping that it would work itself out. You know, Juilliard had gotten her audition tape. They had liked it. She was supposed to have an in-person audition a month before she died. She ended up getting sick the day before. She had this throbbing pain in her abdomen—she was doubled over, howling with pain. My mom took her to the hospital, thought it might be her appendix, or something more serious. It turned out to be nothing. Just, nothing."

"You think she was faking?" I ask.

"Maybe," Joshua says. "But it seemed so real at the time. I think it might have been her body doing what she couldn't. It was saying no."

Had Emily been that unhappy? Why hadn't she said more to me? She must have known that she could talk to me. She must have known that I would listen.

"So she missed the audition, couldn't go. But then she heard from Pennsylvania Ballet. They had seen her perform. They liked her. They offered her that spot."

"And she didn't feel like she could turn them down."

Joshua shakes his head. His eyes are too wide.

"The Lionels—they acted like Emily *owed* them. Like it was their hard work, not hers, that had gotten her to where she was. And I think she believed it. She didn't think there was a way out."

We're going too fast for the bends in this road.

"So you wanted to help her," I say, trying to give him an out. "You were just helping her."

Joshua turns to me, his eyes narrowed. I try my best not to move. My hand, frozen on the armrest. My eyes fixed straight ahead. I wait for his confession. Instead, he asks me: "Do you remember Otto Palgrave?"

My stomach seizes up. *Otto.* The name from Emily's diary. I shake my head.

"He was in my class. He was crazy. He and his older brother and a few of their friends used to do a ton of stupid shit, like slamming each other in the head with folding chairs and car surfing down Mechanic Street."

Did Otto somehow hurt Emily? It doesn't make sense.

"The summer before I started high school, he tried to do a backflip while swinging off the highest ledge at the quarry. Where that rope swing used to be. But he didn't jump out far enough and ended up landing in shallow, rocky water. He broke both his legs. He was still using a cane when I left Calvary."

I remember a boy being injured. The rope swing was cut down immediately after, and stayed down the rest of my time in high school. Eventually, people must have forgotten. When I returned to Calvary, there were always cars parked off the side of the road by the quarry, teenagers in bathing suits with towels slung over their shoulders climbing over the guardrail and slipping into the woods.

"I talked to Emily about it once, and she asked me: 'How much do you think it would hurt?' I told her it would probably hurt a lot, and she shook her head, totally serious, told me she thought the shock would set in pretty quickly. I thought she was just being weird. I didn't do anything about it. I didn't—"

Joshua breaks off, catches his breath. "Everyone always thought *I* was the one they needed to worry about." He gives me a wry smile. "Emily always seemed so in control, like she had it all together, like she knew what she was doing.

"She looked back at me that night, and said: 'You weren't supposed to be here.' I told her I knew that, but I *was* there. I was there, and I could help her down if she—" Joshua's voice catches again, and suddenly I see it: the hair down to his shoulders, the dragon tail wrapped around his arm. The same Joshua I knew. We're in this together. A shared history. "She said she was done dancing, and I said okay, fine, just come down. And then I took another step toward her. It was too much, too fast. I saw her steeling herself, her arms tensing up, her eyes determined. The last thing she said to me was: 'You won't tell anyone it was on purpose.' It wasn't a question. And then she pitched forward."

Joshua's jaw twitches.

"She didn't want to kill herself. She wanted to break her legs. I tried to stop her. I grabbed her arms, but it was too late. I couldn't hold on. She must have turned in the air, because she didn't land right. She hit her head. She made this sound, almost like a yelp, and then she was quiet. I looked down out the window, and she was so still, and then I ran down the steps and she was—"

Joshua puts one hand over his mouth, closes his eyes, opens them again. "I thought she was dead. There was so much blood, and she was so still."

"She probably—"

"She wasn't." Joshua cuts me off, his voice cold again. "I saw the autopsy report. She didn't die for hours. *Hours.*"

"You just left her there," I say, my voice soft.

"No." Joshua shakes his head. "No, I didn't just leave her there. I shouted for you. You couldn't have been that far. It was all so fast. But you didn't come."

I remember unsteady steps toward the glow of the campsite. A noise behind me—a bird, I told myself, an owl—and then my name, quiet at first, so that I thought my mind was playing tricks on me. Then louder, more panicked.

Micah. Help.

I didn't turn around. I heard it again, Joshua's voice: *Micah.* I ignored him. Tried to push his voice out of my head. I couldn't face him again. All I could see was Emily and Alex, together in the cinder block house, laughing at me. *Of course she doesn't know.* The whole school knowing, *Joshua* knowing, everyone but me.

"You didn't come, and I couldn't—I thought she was dead. And I asked myself, how is this going to look? The jealous younger brother, who everyone already thinks is a freak, who followed her into the woods. Who just so happens to come across her body. They'd think I—"

"So this whole time," I say, trying to piece together what this means, "this whole time you knew it wasn't Alex."

Joshua shakes his head. He's blinking back tears.

"No," he says. "It wasn't him."

"And you never said anything." I try to keep the judgment out of my voice, but I can hear it come through. Joshua winces; he hears it, too.

"I thought the truth would come out on its own. It wasn't him. I thought that would be enough. Someone else must have seen him back at the party, I told myself. Something about the fall would tell the police she hadn't been pushed, that the timing didn't add up, *something*. But then there were those bruises on her arms, and . . ."

"No one else came forward. But you still didn't say anything."

"He's a prick, Micah. You know that. He only cared about himself. If the tables had been turned—"

"He spent the last ten years in *prison*."

Ten years of his life, gone. Ten years when he should have been at Penn State, meeting his future wife at a happy hour with his rec league soccer buddies, buying a place out in the country, raising a pack of blind, unwanted shelter dogs. Julia had been right all along. It hadn't been him.

"What was I supposed to do, Micah?" Joshua asks. "Go to the police, months later, and say 'Oh, actually, I *was* in the woods that night. And I know for a fact that Alex wasn't the last one with Emily, because *I* was the last one with her. I'd be the one in Frackville right now if I did that."

"So you did nothing."

"I didn't do *nothing*," Joshua says. "I tried to talk to *you*. I thought you could help. We'd tell the police we found her together, or that you *were* with Alex when it happened, or—I don't know. I thought we could come up with a way out together."

Phone calls after Emily died. My mother, leaning in my doorway, *it's for you.*

"Tell Alex I don't want to talk to him," I had said, pulling a pillow over my face.

"It's not Alex. It's Joshua."

"Tell him not to call me," I had told her.

"You wouldn't talk to me," Joshua says now. "And Emily was gone. I was all alone. I didn't know what to do."

I see him again at fifteen, pounding on the pane of glass with his bare fist. *Micah, let me in.*

"Every day, I told myself tomorrow will be the day I come clean. Tomorrow will be the day I tell the police what happened. I even made a deal with myself early on. I told myself, okay, at some point the police are going to figure out I was in the woods that night. Someone is going to mention seeing me—*you* were going to mention seeing me. They'll question me again, and that's when I'll tell them. If they question me, I have to tell them."

"But they never figured it out."

"They never did." Joshua straightens himself. "Why didn't you tell them you saw me that night?"

"I was worried what they'd think." My voice is low, mumbled. "I was worried how it might look to them if they knew you were—"

"That's such *bullshit*." He shakes his head violently. "You were worried how it might look if they knew *you* were in the woods, away from the rest of the party. You stumble across your best friend and your boyfriend, and . . ."

"I was looking out for you," I say again.

"You were looking out for yourself," he says. "You're always looking out for yourself."

He inhales, a staggered breath. "After a few days had gone by, it was way too late. It was too much. I couldn't handle it. I didn't know what to do. I needed to talk to you. I tried calling you, but you wouldn't take my calls. And then I saw you at school just continuing on with your life, all buddy-buddy with Natalie like Emily had never even existed, like none of it had ever happened."

I remember the crushing weight of returning to school, being overwhelmed by the crowds of students between classes, by the laughter and shouting and slamming lockers. In English class, while Michelle struggled over lines from *A Midsummer Night's Dream,* an image of Emily's body on the forest floor flashed before my eyes. I pushed up out of my desk—*excuse me*—and rushed to the closest bathroom, threw up in the sink affixed to the tile wall.

"I went through her diary and tore out those pages. I thought maybe you'd read them and realize you couldn't just pretend everything was okay. That you needed to help me. I went to your house."

Joshua taps his finger against the steering wheel. "When I found out about the restraining order, I knew that was it. Now I really couldn't say anything. No one would ever believe me. I tried to . . ." He trails off and glances down at his wrists. "But I couldn't do that right, either. My parents found me, shipped me off to live with my grandparents in Minnesota. And I tried to put it behind me. I ignored the news about Alex's trial, pretended it wasn't happening. I refused to go back to Calvary. I pretended it didn't exist anymore, that that was all a separate lifetime, someone else's problem. But I could never stop thinking about Emily, about Alex. I think about them every day."

Saliva builds in my mouth. I swallow.

"And then," he says, "I ran into Ryan in Boston. I tried to ignore him, at first, but he recognized me. He came over to see how I had been. And then he starts telling me about *you.* About how you had come back to Calvary and were doing *so well,* how the two of you were moving in together and were *so happy,* and it made me furious. I didn't understand why you got to move on, when we both let her die."

"I didn't know," I say, shaking my head. "I didn't know what had happened."

"You must have heard it," he says.

"No. If I had known, I would have—"

"You were *right there,* Micah."

That awful sound, and then my name, behind me in the woods. I hadn't understood. If I had known, I would have turned back. I would have helped.

"It wasn't fair. I've spent a decade carrying around this guilt, and you've moved on."

"You don't know anything about me," I say.

"I know a *lot* about you," Joshua says. "I know you were in Chicago. I've seen the pictures of you out with your new friends, drunk and sloppy. I know you were able to go back to Calvary, to pick up where you left off. I know about Stomping Grounds."

He had searched for me, too. He had found my social media accounts, the small news item in the *Calvary Gazette* when Stomping Grounds opened its doors.

"I know you drink your coffee black with three Splenda."

My shoulders tense.

"I know your bedsheets have gray diamonds on them and Ryan reads way too many books about the Napoleonic wars."

He had been in my apartment. The paper footballs.

"I didn't think you had been back to Calvary," I say, trying to keep my voice calm.

"Not personally. It's pretty amazing what you can talk kids into online as a prank."

I swallow, try to find my voice. He had orchestrated the break-in. I wonder if it was that long-haired boy, after all, watching me, reporting back.

"Why would you do that?"

"It wasn't fair," Joshua says. "It wasn't fair that I had to suffer alone."

"We've all suffered," I say, my voice muffled under my hand. And it's true, but what he said is true, too. I think about Emily, lit up by the beam of Joshua's flashlight in the window of the cinder block house, squinting back at him. Turning back toward the forest, tipping forward.

"Why didn't she say something about what she was going through?" I ask. "Why didn't she talk to us?"

"Because we're selfish people," Joshua says. "And she knew we wouldn't listen."

A wall of trees, approaching fast.

"Slow down," I say, but he doesn't listen. I hear the engine straining, his foot on the accelerator.

"Joshua!" I shout. "Stop!"

The tires screech against the pavement, and we jerk to a stop, my body lurching forward. I suck in air, my hands trembling.

"I thought you were going to—"

"What?" He reverses, slowly, and turns the car around. "You thought I was going to, what, kill us both?" The sleet slows, and Joshua eases the car back in the direction we came from, eyes fixed ahead. "I've got a family, Micah. I've got responsibilities now."

Another turn, back to the main stretch.

"Where are we going?" I ask, my voice hoarse.

"Home," he says. "I'm going home."

We roll up the slope of Joshua's driveway. Light outlines the upstairs window, sneaking around the drawn curtains. His wife is up there, probably, awake and waiting for our return.

"Does she know?" I ask, nodding toward the house.

"No."

He turns the key in the ignition but doesn't move. He returns his hand to the steering wheel, and I see that he's steadying him-self. He chews on the inside of his cheek.

I think of Alex again, that sad photograph that Julia keeps on her desk, the lopsided bridge in the background.

"You need to tell someone."

Joshua shakes his head forcefully. "It's too late."

"We could—"

"It's too late, Micah." He looks at me again, his eyes hard. "We've made our choices."

He swings open the driver-side door and ducks his head to exit. I climb out of my seat, and he starts toward his garage door, his neck craned forward.

"That's it?" I call after him.

He shrugs. "I don't know what you want from me."

"You're a coward."

"I know." He's looking down. Behind him, a workbench with a stack of sawed-off wood beams, a pegboard for hanging tools. A pink motorized car parked beside a small blue trampoline propped on its side. Shelves stacked with terra-cotta pots, spray bottles of weed killer, gray gloves caked with dirt. He opens the door leading in from the garage. He steps inside.

"Joshua," I say again, trying to sound forceful.

He closes the door behind him.

I stand, for a moment, beside his car, unsure of what to do. I could bang on the door, make him come back. Threaten to tell his wife, to blow his whole life up myself. He'd tell her I was crazy. *Just look at her,* he'd say. *Does she look like she's in her right mind to you?* I go back to my car and rest my head against the steering wheel.

28

've checked in to a motel on the outskirts of Boston. The room is clean and sparse: a framed picture of a harbor hanging over my bed, a reading light with a nautical lampshade mounted to the wall. The navy blue curtains are drawn. The walls are thin, and I can hear the couple in the room next to mine fighting.

"Oh, come *on*," the man shouts. I turn on the television and turn up the volume to block them out. The effect isn't better. On-screen, a middle-aged woman hawks a leather purse with adjustable straps that comes in five colors.

"Unbelievable," she says. "Dress up, dress down, it goes with everything."

There's a small table by the window. It's covered in Emily's diary entries. I've unfolded them all, pressed them flat, and arranged them in chronological order. I sit down in front of them now. My chair tips forward on the uneven floor.

I have a decision to make.

The diary entries tell a story: Emily's uncertainty about her future, how trapped she felt. Maybe even her relationship with

Alex was a way of testing the waters, showing herself she wasn't hemmed in by expectations, after all. Expectations that the Lionels and her mother placed on her. Adults in her life who she trusted, who were supposed to have her best interests at heart.

The diary entries support Joshua's story, but they don't tell what happened that night at the cinder block house. Only Joshua knows that.

And now, me.

I look over toward Alex's old jacket, bulging out of my bag of clothes in the corner. I think of him sitting at that wooden table in the courtroom, nervous but trusting that everything would work out in the end. I think of him in prison, still, after all this time, *a model prisoner,* Julia said. Making the best of it. Refusing to give up hope.

It's not right.

I could go back to Calvary. I could tell the police, now, about seeing Joshua in the woods that night, about what he told me. I could show them the diary entries, recount my own memories of Emily in the weeks leading up to her death.

In the next room: "You always do this!" On the television, "*Five* compartments, one for your wallet, one for your keys, one for your lipstick. Sunglasses, hand sanitizer, you name it. Lots of options here." Heavy footsteps in the room above me, crossing from the windows to the bathroom and then back again.

My hand flits to my phone. Out of habit or fear or morbid curiosity, I give in and pull up No Stone Unturned and look for Ryan's name. Anna had called the police that morning, after all, and a couple of officers had showed up at Stomping Grounds soon after. Their presence, and Ryan's injury, had attracted attention and inspired a flurry of comments about what might have happened:

MissMaya: It must have been Micah, yeah?

forwardslapped: that guy is a fkn pussy lol

jules: Definitely Micah. This is what I've been trying to tell everyone. She's totally unstable.

Micah Wilkes, the crazy ex who wouldn't leave poor Julia alone. Micah Wilkes, who violently attacked her boyfriend. Micah Wilkes, who was at the party in the woods that night and did have a motive . . .

It was a mistake to look. My eyes sting as I think about what Ryan must be going through. I think about calling him, but can't shake the image of him at Stomping Grounds, looking at me in disbelief, like he didn't even recognize me.

If you just apologize, I tell myself. *If you just explain what Joshua put you through.* But I know, if I'm being honest with myself, that it wouldn't be enough. The trust between us is gone.

I look back at the diary entries and try again to wrap my mind around what Joshua told me. Emily hadn't been murdered. She had fallen and died alone in the woods, so close that I could have heard her. Did hear her.

Micah Wilkes, who only ever looked out for herself.

My mind drifts back to Joshua. He's probably in bed now, asleep next to his wife who doesn't have any clue about the secrets he's keeping. He'll wake up tomorrow, kiss his daughter on the forehead, go to his shop like it's just a normal weekend, run through his daily routine. He'll keep on living the life that Emily and Alex never got to live.

We've all lost so much, and all because Joshua couldn't bring himself to tell the truth.

Headlights illuminate my window and then blink off, an engine shuddering to a stop. I pick up the diary entries and straighten them into a neat stack.

I think about stepping into Detective Curtis's office, these papers in hand. *I saw Joshua out by the cinder block house,* I'd say. *We had a confrontation and I left, but he stayed. He went back to find Emily. He knows it wasn't Alex. He's been lying this whole time.*

I imagine the flicker of Detective Curtis's eyebrow, his skepticism as he leans forward over his desk. *You knew that Emily and Alex were sleeping together? You were there, in the woods, where she was found? You kept quiet about this for ten years?*

My stomach turns. I stand up, cross the room to a bare-bones bathroom with white tiles and bright ceiling lights. A porcelain sink juts off the wall.

Why didn't you say something, Micah?

I pull back my hair with the hairband around my wrist, lather soap into my hands.

Why didn't you help her, Micah?

Going back to Calvary wouldn't do any good. It would just be my word, and everyone is already poised to disbelieve me. It's Joshua who needs to come forward. He's the one who can set this straight. He's the one who saw Emily fall. The truth has to come from him.

I rub at my face and rinse the soap off with hot water. If I go to the police now, he'll deny the whole thing. Or, worse, point the finger at me.

I pull out my phone again, type out a text to Ryan.

I'm sorry. I'm not coming home.

I can't convince Joshua to do the right thing, but maybe someone else can. Tomorrow morning, I'll drive to the closest post office and mail Emily's diary pages to Julia, along with a note: *Joshua Winters is Joshua Bishop now. He knows what happened. Make him help you.* She'll persuade him. She'll never let go until Alex is free.

I pull my hair down again and study it in the mirror: dull brown and flat, unremarkable. After the post office, a trip to the drug-store. Scissors and hair dye can't cost much. I'll start over. Here, in Boston. Why not? I'll pawn my mother's jewelry, get a job wait-ressing, get back on my feet.

I've been living in the shadow of Emily's death since I was seventeen. I can't do this any longer.

It's best for everyone this way.

I look down at my phone again. There's a new response on No Stone Unturned to Julia's comment.

TheMissingKing: I'm starting to think you're right. Micah Wilkes is not a good person.

Just a stranger. He has no idea what he's talking about.

I close out of the forum, then think better of it. I open No Stone Unturned again and delete my account entirely. It feels like a step in the right direction, like progress. I open Facebook and do the same. My Twitter and Instagram accounts, gone. *Are you sure? Yes.*

My phone lights up with an incoming call. Ryan. I look at his picture, that lopsided smile. The call goes through to voicemail, and, a second later, a new text pops up.

Micah. We should talk.

I pull out my SIM card and toss it in the trash.
I love you, I think, *but there's nothing to discuss.*
A new beginning. A slate wiped clean.
There is no Micah anymore.

ACKNOWLEDGMENTS

Thank you to my agent, Julia Kenny, for your enthusiasm and your invaluable insight and guidance, and to Arielle Datz and the entire Dunow, Carlson & Lerner team. I am so lucky to be working with all of you.

Thank you to my editor, Andrea Walker. Your thoughtful comments and vision made this book so much better, and working with you has been an incredible experience. Thanks also to Emma Caruso and the rest of the team at Random House for all of your work in bringing this book into existence.

Thank you to my friends and family who read early drafts: Nathan Boon, Iris Chamberlain, Suz Cornell, Madeleine Helmer, Jenny Kraft, Ali Lawler, K. J. Lawler, Marsha McClain, Emma Wujek, and my parents. Your insightful suggestions shaped this book into what it is, and I can't say how much I appreciate your love and support.

Thanks to the Rittenhouse Writers' Group for your helpful comments and feedback.

Thank you to Jon Tavares for taking the time to answer my questions about ballet.

And, finally, thank you to Vince: for your love, enthusiasm, and encouragement, and for reading each new draft and talking over each new idea. This book would not exist without you.

ABOUT THE AUTHOR

ALLISON BUCCOLA is an attorney with a JD from the University of Chicago. She lives outside Philadelphia with her husband and two young children. *Catch Her When She Falls* is her first novel.

allisonbuccola.com
Twitter: @allisonbuccola
Instagram: @allisonbuccola